MOUNTAIN OF
MARS

BOOK EIGHT
OF THE STARSHIP'S MAGE SERIES

Mountain of Mars © 2020 Glynn Stewart

This edition published in 2020 by:
Faolan's Pen Publishing Inc.
22 King St. S, Suite 300
Waterloo, Ontario
N2J 1N8 Canada

ISBN-13: 978-1-988035-98-7 (print)

A record of this book is available from Library and Archives Canada.

Printed in the United States of America
1 2 3 4 5 6 7 8 9 10
First edition
First printing: March 2020

Illustration © 2020 Jeff Brown Graphics

Faolan's Pen Publishing logo is a trademark of Faolan's Pen Publishing Inc.

Read more books from Glynn Stewart at faolanspen.com

STARSHIP'S
MAGE

MOUNTAIN OF
MARS

BOOK EIGHT
OF THE STARSHIP'S MAGE SERIES

GLYNN STEWART

FAOLAN'S PEN
PUBLISHING
faolanspen.com

CHAPTER 1

DESMOND MICHAEL Alexander the Third, Mage-King of Mars, took a certain degree of satisfaction in the awareness of both his power and his limits. He was the third person to ever sit the throne in Olympus Mons that controlled the most powerful magical amplifier known to mankind. He was the oldest living Rune Wright, the eldest of that strange breed of Mage who could not only wield magic but *see* it.

A century of life had taught him that knowledge of his limits was more important than knowledge of his power. The Protectorate of the Mage-King of Mars—*his* Protectorate—was embroiled in an ugly war against a breakaway state, which limited the reach of his word and his power. He could not command the Republic of Faith and Reason to lay down their arms. He could not simply order the Councilors who represented his worlds to fall into line and support him.

The Republic's atrocities were being met with a newly forged fleet. The Council's support was being bought with a newly written Constitution.

There were days, though, that he thought all of the tasks that came with the Crown and the Mountain paled in comparison to negotiations with his teenage daughter.

"Yes, Kiera, I will pass your regards on to Damien," he said patiently, glancing around the shuttle and *daring* the Royal Guards around him to say anything. Each of those Mage soldiers was clad in a two-meter-tall combat exosuit. If they were laughing at their monarch in *beleaguered father* mode, they didn't show it.

His son was less concealed. Desmond Michael Alexander the Fourth, the Crown Prince of Mars, was *grinning* at his father. But the young man—who was arguably closer to a clone than a biological son, sharing over eighty percent of his father's DNA—was at least *silent*.

"I don't understand why I couldn't come up with you," Kiera's image told him grumpily. "You took Des with you!"

"And that's why you couldn't come," Desmond said calmly, checking his wrist-comp. The shuttle was leaving Olympus Mons' defense perimeter as they spoke. The destroyers *Glorious Shield of Freedom* and *Virtuous Beacon of Liberty* were already in position along his route.

This was Mars, but even here, the Mage-King's safety could never be taken for granted.

"There are half a dozen reporters on this shuttle," he continued. "Another hundred waiting for us at the research station. Activating the first Link on the Protectorate network is a *big deal*, a big enough deal to require the Crown Prince as well as me.

"But an Alexander must sit the throne of Olympus Mons," Desmond reminded his daughter. "If two of us are going to be somewhere, that means the other must be at home."

"So, I get to be the spare, as usual?" the sixteen-year-old demanded.

Negotiating with the Council was *much* less fraught. That was only going to shape the next two hundred years of the Protectorate's future. Talking with his daughter could shape her happiness for months...which was of at least equal weight, to a father's mind.

"I pray to all that is sacred that you are never 'the spare,'" he told her. "For that to ever matter, both Des and I would be gone. But we are the Royal Family of Mars, Kiera. A hundred and ten worlds look to us, even if ten of them are currently glaring."

And, hopefully, one of those hostile worlds was occupied. The Republic had developed the Link to provide themselves with a relatively portable instantaneous interstellar communicator. Without the same technology, the Protectorate had relied on Runic Transceiver Arrays, massive artifacts of rune magic that took years to build and could only transfer a Mage's voice.

There were three RTAs in Sol, an achievement of magic and science that boggled the mind since it was almost impossible to build *two*. One of the Core Worlds had managed to build two, but only Sol, the home system of the Rune Wrights, had managed to build three.

But the RTAs were magic...so there was no RTA at Legatus, the besieged capital of the Republic of Faith and Reason. There were Links, however, and one had been sanitized and reset to connect only to the one here in Martian orbit.

The connection would allow Desmond to have a live conversation with his First Hand and Desmond's sister, the Admiral, for the first time since the Royal Martian Navy had sortied from Ardennes.

"But I want to see Damien. And Aunt Jane," Kiera told him. "Couldn't we have brought the Link here?"

"We could have," Desmond agreed. "But I don't trust a Republic-built device in my Mountain, Kiera. Once we have built our own versions, we'll have one in the Mountain. Probably several.

"For now, though, we can only use sanitized versions of their equipment. I am confident in our encryption and security to make certain that we are not overheard. I am *not* confident that the Republic can't use any of our commandeered Links as targeting beacons."

That silenced Kiera for a moment.

"I'm not afraid for your safety in the Mountain," he told her. "I'm not even really afraid for my safety or Des's in orbit of Mars, or we wouldn't be here."

A blip on the wrist-mounted computer told him that the two destroyers had handed off security for the shuttle to one of the orbital battle stations. The final leg of their journey would be under the guns of the battleship *Gauntlet of Honor*.

At no point in the journey was the shuttle in range of less than several hundred antimissile turrets and multiple trained RMN Mages with their hands on military-grade amplifiers. No external threat could approach the shuttle.

Something still niggled at Desmond's senses and he shook his head roughly.

"Duty requires many things that are far from pleasant," he reminded his daughter. "That we can only safely gather in the Mountain itself is one of those things. An Alexander must sit the throne, which means an Alexander must always survive."

"I've seen the maintenance schedule for that shuttle, Dad," Kiera pointed out. "You'll be fine. You need to get off the planet more."

He snorted. It wasn't even for *his* safety, really. So long as an Alexander sat the throne in Olympus Mons, Sol was invulnerable. But no other Mage could use the Olympus Amplifier. There was something *wrong* with it...but it was also far more powerful than any amplifier humanity had built since.

The Eugenicists, the mad conspiracy that had given birth to modern Mages, had used the Olympus Amplifier as a test site to make certain they were making progress. In the hands of the first Alexander, it had destroyed them.

"An Alexander must sit the throne at Olympus Mons," he repeated.

"We both know that's not the exact truth," Kiera replied, a sign that the teenager had more discretion than he gave her credit for. A *Rune Wright* had to sit the throne.

But they'd only ever identified two Rune Wrights who weren't Alexanders. One was dead...and the man who'd killed him was the other non-Alexander Rune Wright. And also one of the two people Desmond was flying out to speak to.

Damien Montgomery. The First Hand of Mars and the most powerful *non*-Alexander Mage Desmond knew about.

He was also the friend of the family that Kiera was upset she wasn't going to get to talk to.

In a world that relied on Mages for interstellar travel above all else, it was certainly possible for Desmond to have teleported himself and Des to the research station trailing Deimos's orbit. Unfortunately, few Mages could have teleported *themselves* that far, let alone brought friends.

Desmond could have moved the entire shuttle, but without an amplifier, it would have wiped him out for hours—and he made a point of not doing magic most Mages couldn't. It wasn't exactly secret that the Mage-King of Mars and his family and Hands were far beyond ordinary Mages, but it was in *everyone*'s interests for the full scale of the advantage to remain secret.

So, he was aboard a shuttle, passing from security zone to security zone, surrounded by armed bodyguards. He should have been as safe there as on Olympus Mons itself, but the itch at the back of his neck wasn't going away.

Leaning back in his chair, he sighed and reached for his power.

There was more to being a Rune Wright than the ability to carve Runes of Power on oneself and become the most powerful Mage alive. It came with the ability to *see* magic in play, to intuitively understand it in a way no regular Mage ever could.

A Mage could be taught spells and iterate on what they already knew, but it was difficult to create something *new* without that ability to study the flow of power.

And the spell Desmond was weaving now required that ability to see it. The King saw his son register what his father was doing and tense in his chair, the prince wide-eyed as he watched threads of magic flow through the air to the beat of an invisible conductor.

A hundred threads of magic took shape around the Mage-King of Mars, flickering out across the shuttle as they scanned for threats. The future couldn't be predicted with magic, not really, but probabilities could be assessed by a complicated enough spell.

And this spell was as complicated as it came. Desmond Michael Alexander had been trained as a Rune Wright decades before. He'd trained with his Sight for longer than most of his subjects had been alive.

Even as he was sending tendrils of magic through the shuttle, other tendrils were forming runes in the air, invisibly writing the complex magical code that underpinned greater magic.

His Guards were clear. He'd expected that. There were fewer than three hundred Royal Guards, each of them an experienced Combat Mage from the Marines or Navy chosen for their skill and loyalty.

Next, his magic wove through the reporters in the second section of the shuttle. Nothing. None of them were armed and only two were Mages. No threat there.

The shuttle's crew were busy preparing for landing. They were coming up on the research station quickly, at which point they were presumably safe.

He was about to pull the spell back and write off everything to nerves when *something* flashed a warning. Desmond yanked on that tendril, hauling his awareness to the warning, and paused, studying the shuttle's fuel tanks through the magic.

Security should have prevented any explosive being sneaked aboard the ship, and the armored and shielded antimatter tanks would keep them safe from anything short of a nuclear weapon.

Wait. There were access valves, pulling antimatter out of the tanks to feed it to the engines. They were safed and quiet while the engines were offline, but the thrusters would come online in moments to bring them into the station safely.

It wasn't a bomb. It was a power tool, a cutting arc designed to open up these very conduits for maintenance.

He found it *as* the engines came online and some sensor activated. Even as Desmond tried to unleash his power through the remote viewing spell, it was already too late.

There was a sensor in the tool to stop it cutting an active conduit. That sensor had been disabled with every other safety feature, and a beam of plasma sliced the piping open, disrupting the magnetic fields for a critical fraction of a second. A flash of antimatter exploded from the pipe with enough force to shake the shuttle—and there was nothing to stop the reaction reaching the main fuel tank.

Desmond didn't even have time to pull his attention back to his son before the matter-antimatter explosion obliterated the shuttle.

CHAPTER 2

THE ROYAL Martian Navy *Mjolnir*-class dreadnought *Durendal* wasn't home by any stretch of the imagination, but Damien Montgomery was getting used to it. His own operations were mostly based out of the battlecruiser *Duke of Magnificence*, but Her Highness Mage-Admiral Jane Alexander had moved her flag over to the dreadnought when the Siege of Legatus had finally ended two weeks earlier.

Those two weeks had tested Damien's diplomatic acumen to its limits, and he missed Dr. Robert Christoffsen, his political advisor, fiercely.

There'd been no reason to take the man on a deep-penetration covert investigation into Republic space, and Damien had gone right from that investigation to the final battle for Legatus—and then from there into intensive negotiations with what was left of the Legatan planetary government.

"We're going to be late," Special Agent Denis Romanov noted calmly. The Marine Mage-Captain and Protectorate Secret Service detail commander had the same slim dark-haired build as his charge.

Of course, Damien had that build at a hundred and fifty centimeters and Romanov had it at a hundred and *ninety*, which usually worked out to people being more intimidated by the bodyguard.

"His Majesty will forgive me," Damien pointed out. "We *did* just end a two-week impasse most of us were expecting to resolve with orbital bombardment."

The third person in the room grunted in exhaustion.

"And thank you for that," James Niska told him. The Legatan Augment had once served in its intelligence operations. He'd been a sworn, if covert, enemy of the Protectorate for his entire life.

Damien wasn't quite sure just what the broad-shouldered and graying cyborg qualified as now, but he seemed to have become attached to Damien's team.

"I think it helped that I had a Legatan standing with me the entire time," he told the old spy. "So, thank *you*. I didn't want to have to start bombing military bases, let alone cities."

"You'd have done it," Niska said grimly. "I know you."

"The military bases? Probably," Damien conceded. "The cities?"

He shivered.

"I'd have needed a far clearer and more present threat," he finally admitted. He'd ordered it *once*, as a contingency if his primary plan failed. That time, though, a billion lives had been on the line. Forcing Legatus's surrender hadn't been *that* important.

"My Lord," the pilot called back on the intercom. "We're entering the shuttle bay now. Admiral Alexander sends her regards and requests that you hurry. I believe she may have been left alone with reporters."

Damien concealed a smile. There was no way Alexander was *entirely* alone with the reporters—like him, she had both Royal Martian Marine and Protectorate Secret Service security details—but she was a career military officer in her nineties.

So far as he could tell, soldiers and the media weren't the natural enemies they often pretended to be, but the game stuck enough that the Mage-Admiral wasn't going to enjoy being in a room with an entire press conference without civilian coverage.

And while Damien held what Romans had called *imperium*—the right to command Martian troops—he was most definitely the senior Protectorate civilian in Legatus.

Or anywhere else short of Mars.

The most notable thing about the new dreadnoughts was that they were *big*. Twice the mass of the battleships that had been king of the Navy when Damien had entered the service of the Mage-King, they were a full kilometer from bow to stern.

Without using magic, which the situation hardly called for, it took Damien a full five minutes to get from the shuttle bay to the heavily armored missile magazine that had been turned into the Link communication center.

If the Republic had some ability to use the sanitized communicator as a weapon, he wished them luck with damaging the dreadnought through armor designed to control containment failure on antimatter warheads.

The entrance was secured, but a wordless exchange between the Marines on both sides got Damien through without slowing down. Normally, he'd complain about that—security procedures helped everyone, even if he was probably the most recognizable person on the ship—but he was already late.

The room he entered was surprisingly quiet for that. The crew had set up seating for the press gallery through the room, but the focus was on the big video-call screen that had been set up just for this.

An interstellar videoconference was new for the Protectorate. They'd probably find better and more useful ways to communicate with the Link over time, but right now they had *two* fully sanitized units.

One aboard the most powerful warship in the fleet and the other at Mars...and the call had been supposed to start several minutes earlier.

He could feel the reporters' gazes following him as he walked up the aisle to Admiral Alexander. His bodyguards spread out behind him, joining Alexander's bodyguards along the walls.

Just their personal details alone left the room feeling like it was lined with soldiers. It was only a dozen or so people, but Damien was considering the look and vibe of the guardians' presence. It...wasn't good.

On the other hand, the Republic had managed to infiltrate assassins aboard Martian warships before. The Navy *thought* they'd cleaned up the leftovers of that, but they couldn't be sure.

"They're late," Alexander said softly. "There's no reason for them to be late."

"*I'm* late," he told her. "The talks ran long—but I have the news we were hoping to give His Majesty on this call."

"They're surrendering?" she asked.

"They made it very clear that they only spoke for Legatus itself," Damien said. "The local Republic officers have signed off as well, but this is functionally only a surrender of the planetary government.

"But I have them in contact with the Marines, and plans are being drafted as we speak." He shook his head. "Occupying a planet isn't an easy task, but we can at least get *started*."

"Good." Alexander looked at the video screen, currently showing the stylized rocket-and-red-planet seal of the Royal Martian Navy. The reporters were starting to get restless, though they'd so far respected the quiet conversation of the two people at the front of the room.

"I thought the call was supposed to start by now," one of them finally called. "What's going on?"

"We don't know," Damien replied, turning to face the audience. "Remember that this was scheduled by a courier ship that left Mars almost five days ago. Things change in five days, people. Some delays are to be expected."

It was going to be irritating if the big event they'd scheduled fell through. A non-event here would be lost beneath the news already going out from the reporters who'd accompanied him to the surface.

"Legatus Surrenders!" made for better headlines than "Interstellar Phone Call a Bust." He hoped, anyway.

"They're ten minutes late," Alexander muttered. "Desmond is *never* late."

"Not without being delayed, anyway," Damien agreed. "Something's happening. Is the system working?"

"We've been running data pings back and forth for twelve hours," she told him. "We weren't going to let the big video call be the *actual* first use of the Link without making sure it worked. It's just connection pings, but we know the system is online."

"I think we need to call home, Admiral," he said. "I know it was supposed to come from Mars for the best effect, but—"

The screen dissolved into a moment of black, then the image of a single man appeared on the other side.

That wasn't right. There'd been supposed to be a crowd of reporters, with the Mage-King and the Crown Prince standing in front—much like the setup here in Legatus. Instead, there was just one man—a man Damien Montgomery knew.

Malcolm Gregory was the Chancellor of the Protectorate, the man who stood at the Mage-King's right hand and managed much of the day-to-day operation of running an interstellar state.

"Damien, Jane," he greeted them. He was a large man, usually jovially smiling in a way that led some to underestimate his intelligence or competence. Today, Gregory looked haggard and exhausted.

"There's not much point in sending the reporters away," he continued. "They'll know soon enough and the news will spread fast enough. I almost forgot this was scheduled in the chaos, and my message is being relayed from the Mountain."

Damien wished he were sitting as he reached out and grabbed the edge of the lectern. Somehow, he knew what was coming—but it was impossible!

"There was a shuttle accident en route to Research Station Deimos-Three. Mars One was destroyed with both His Majesty and His Highness aboard," Gregory said, the words flowing in a rush like a broken dam.

"Desmond Michael Alexander the Third and Crown Prince Desmond Michael Alexander are both dead."

He paused, frozen for several long seconds before he shook his head.

"First Hand Montgomery, Admiral Alexander. We need to talk in private," he told them. "I'm sure that's scoop enough to appease the press gallery, but we *must* speak to the future."

Damien turned to face the reporters again, many of whom had the same glassy-eyed expression he could feel his own face trying to assume.

"Please, everyone," he told them. "If you could vacate the conference room quickly. This has now become a matter of national security.

Admiral Alexander and I will be relocating, but we will be locking down the Link center."

He should probably have checked with Alexander, but he had a pretty solid idea of where the Admiral was. *Damien* was nearly in shock, but Desmond the Third had "merely" been his King and his mentor.

He'd been Jane Alexander's older brother. Damien didn't even need to look at her to know that she *was* in shock.

CHAPTER 3

BY THE TIME they were in the smaller meeting room that had been put aside for the planned follow-up call with the Mage-King, everything was starting to sink in on Damien. He focused on supporting Alexander, who hadn't said a word since Gregory's statement.

He guided her to a seat, then put a coffee in front of her.

"Are you okay?" he asked.

She shook her head mutely, then slowly exhaled a long sigh.

"No," she finally said. "Desmond... Des... *FUCK.*"

Damien looked back at the door to meet Romanov's eyes. The Marine gave him a crisp salute—and then sealed the room, leaving the two Rune Wrights alone.

The First Hand of Mars knew a lot now about how the Mage-King's family had made sure they didn't lose the Rune Wright gift. Jane Alexander, like her brother, was an eighty-percent clone of their father... who'd been a *full* clone of *his* father.

She'd been born ten years later as the spare heir in case Desmond died before having kids. Damien doubted anyone had been expecting the hard-edged Admiral to have kids of her own at any point, but given the cloning and genetic engineering involved, well.

Damien suspected that the next generation of the Alexanders was going to have a significant chunk of *his* DNA in them. The doctors responsible for the process were working off a limited certainty of just *what* made a Rune Wright versus an ordinary Mage.

"That makes Kiera Queen, doesn't it?" he asked softly.

"It does," Gregory's voice answered, the Chancellor linked in once again. "She's...gods, she's handling it better than I feared, but I'm not sure it's real for her yet. It's only been an hour."

"That poor child," Alexander murmured.

"She's stronger than you think, but this is a lot to dump on her," Gregory replied. "She can't take this alone." He exhaled. "She also only has one Rune of Power yet, and I stand by the doctors' and Desmond's insistence she not get the rest until she's nineteen.

"We say an Alexander must sit the throne at Olympus Mons, but the three of us know it needs to be a Rune Wright. With Kiera so young, we need a second Wright." Gregory swallowed. "I need one of you to come home."

"We just finished negotiating the surrender of *one* world," Damien pointed out. "Ten systems seceded with the Republic and we only scattered their fleet; we didn't destroy it. I don't expect all of the deserters to return to the fold, but they still *have* a fleet even if no one rejoins them."

"That's why I can't go," Alexander agreed. "This is war, Damien. You exposed their atrocities, opened a massive crack in their armor, but you're not a soldier. Not an Admiral. The Sword of Mars isn't needed here.

"But I am," she continued. "I command the fleet, and with Legatus secured, we'll be moving out against Nueva Bolivia within the next few weeks. We're just waiting on a new load of missiles to refill our magazines."

They'd expended most of their new-generation Phoenix IX and Samurai I missiles in the battle for Legatus. The missiles currently in their magazines were the only new missiles they had left.

Freighters were hauling tens of thousands of missiles to Legatus to fill the Navy's colliers with the new weapons, but right now, the only reloads available to Alexander were the older weapons they'd started the war with.

"I'm not an Alexander," Damien countered. He was torn. He wanted to go back to Mars, to hold his friend's daughter while she grieved and support her as the new Mage-Queen, but he also had to think about the

Protectorate. One of them had to lead the fleet as they finished off the Republic.

And one of them had to go home.

"That's an argument for sending you, not me," Alexander replied. "Since Des turned ten, we've been doing everything in our power to convince everyone to forget I was ever the Crown Princess."

"You are the heir again now," Gregory pointed out.

"Which is, again, why it has to be Damien," she snapped. "We don't want people looking at the teenage girl and then looking at her aunt the Admiral and going, 'Wouldn't the aunt make a better Queen?' We can't risk it, Gregory. I agree we need an adult Rune Wright on Mars to back Kiera up.

"But it can't be me. There are too many risks—and I'd do a shitty job at what you need, anyway. You need a politician, not a soldier."

"I'm not a politician either," Damien countered. "You're family."

"So are you," Jane Alexander barked. "You are not that *fucking* blind, Damien Montgomery. Blood be damned, you're an Alexander in our hearts and the entire damn *Protectorate* knows it."

It was a good thing he was sitting. Because, apparently, he was just that blind.

It didn't help. He'd already lost two people he regarded as dear friends. To lose family he hadn't, quite, realized he had...that was worse. That hurt more.

"I'm not a politician," he repeated.

"But you are a diplomat in a way I'm not," Alexander told him. "You've been in the middle of the negotiations with the Council for a while now. Hell, Damien, you've brokered peace treaties and mutual-usage agreements over entire star systems.

"I'm barely aware that there *is* a Constitution being drafted right now. How much do *you* know about it?"

Damien sighed.

"His Majesty was sending me updates on the process," he admitted. "It's a mess. The first Mage-King really should have done a better job of setting this up."

"He had the Charter and the Compact, and they laid out what he needed," Gregory replied. "Everyone knelt to Mars and no one fucked with the Mages. Everything else was irrelevant to him."

"And *our* Desmond was trying to lay a foundation for the next two hundred years," Damien said, blinking back hot tears. "Damn it. What happened, Malcolm?"

"No one's sure yet. Everyone's going over sensor data in detail, but we're pretty sure no one shot at them. Best guess is a maintenance failure."

"Or a bomb," Damien said grimly.

"We're pretty sure we've cleaned up the RID's cells on Mars," Gregory replied. "I don't know who else would try to kill Desmond. It may just have been an accident."

All three of them choked up, and Damien sighed and bowed his head.

"I know it has to be one of us," he said softly. "I just..."

"Desmond wanted you to come home if something happened to him," Gregory said softly. "For Des or Kiera, he knew you'd be the best to back them up. They both trusted Jane—but they both *knew* you."

"One of us has to fight the war and one of us has to hold the Protectorate together," Jane concluded. "Do you really think that the Protectorate will do better the other way around?"

"No," he conceded, choking back tears as he stared down at his gloved hands. "No. Very well, Chancellor. *Duke of Magnificence* and I will be back in Mars in five days."

Once, he could have gone faster. But that had been before he wrecked his hands. The elbow-length thin black leather gloves he wore covered skin and bone reduced to a scarred mess by the molten metal that *had* been his jump runes and two of his Runes of Power.

Now he had to rely on others to bring him home.

CHAPTER 4

DAMIEN MADE it most of the way back to his shuttle in a state of shock, with Romanov and Niska trailing in his wake with the rest of his escort. Neither his bodyguard commander or the Legatan spy who'd been acting as his "local guide" for the last few months said anything.

What was there *to* say? Desmond the Third had been the Mage-King of Mars for over *seventy years*. His father had ruled longer, but only by a few years—and given Desmond's health, the government had already been quietly planning the celebration of him becoming the longest-reigned Mage-King.

The bedrock that had underlain Martian and *human* politics for decades was gone. They'd recover and the Protectorate would survive and go on, but to lose both the Mage-King and the Crown Prince in a single day was a shock to the system that it would take time to process.

Time Damien was grimly aware they might not get. The Republic was bloodied, its capital in Martian hands, but they were far from beaten. The Lord Protector and key Members of the Republican Assembly had fled.

What was left of the Assembly hadn't even been involved in the surrender negotiations. Everybody appeared to regard them as irrelevant now—including the remaining MRAs themselves.

And Damien was left with his own suspicions around what had happened to his King. He'd clashed with the Royal Order of the Keepers of Secrets and Oaths, a secret organization set up by the first Mage-King before, but he had a *great* many questions about what had happened to them.

They'd vanished into the darkness in an unexpected spasm of violence on Mars that had ended in an attack on the Council and Mage-King alike. That attack had left Damien without the use of his hands—and with the grim certainty that *someone* had moved against both the Keepers and the Protectorate.

"My lord!"

Damien's mental enumeration of their potential enemies had brought him all the way into the shuttle bay, where a familiar young red-headed woman was waiting for him.

There was little of the teenager he'd originally met, in jail for vandalism and assault at the time, left in the image that Mage-Lieutenant Roslyn Chambers projected now. She saluted crisply once he met her gaze.

"I heard the news," she said. "The Admiral says you're heading back to Mars?"

"I am," he confirmed. "I'm sorry I didn't get a chance to catch up, Lieutenant. We've both been busy."

"I know," Chambers replied. "I want to say thank you before you left. Without your help, I'm not sure I'd have ever made it into the Navy at all."

"We'd all be worse off if that had been the case, wouldn't we?" Damien asked. "You and Captain Kulkarni have been instrumental in getting us this far, and every report I've seen from Nia Kriti says we wouldn't have either of you if you hadn't been on that sensor console."

"Thank you, my lord. That means a lot, coming from you," she admitted.

"Even if I could be here to watch over you, Lieutenant, I suspect I'd be wasting both our time," he told her. "I have every faith in your ability to support Admiral Alexander in the days to come."

"This war is far from over," she told him grimly. "We need to know the Protectorate is okay behind us."

"Leave that to me," he promised. "You and Admiral Alexander just need to deal with the Republic and Legatus."

He paused, considering the shuttle in front of them. Then he gestured for Roslyn to step out of the way of traffic while he turned to James Niska.

"Speaking of which, James," he addressed the old cyborg, "I need you to stay here. Not necessarily on *Durendal*, but in Legatus and supporting the Admiral."

"I'm...not sure how much good I can do here anymore," Niska admitted. "I'm a traitor by any reasonable standard."

"You know Legatus better than any of us," Damien replied. "You know the Republic and the UnArcana Worlds in a way no one who wasn't on the inside ever could. You helped *build* the Republic."

"And now you want me to help destroy it," the Legatan said sadly.

"The Republic's leaders already destroyed it," Damien said. "They buried any truth or honor in blood and lies. We both know this. But there was a *reason* they convinced ten star systems to follow them into war.

"Someone has to speak for the UnArcana Worlds as we fight this war," he continued. "Someone has to stand at Admiral Alexander's side and speak for the *people* behind the face of the enemy.

"It has always been the duty of the Mage-King's Hands to deal with the underlying problems as well as the overt conflicts," Damien concluded. "I have to leave, which means someone else must speak for those who might be forgotten. It has to be you, James. It can *only* be you."

Niska snorted.

"You know how to dance on all of my buttons, don't you?"

"Consider it a fair return for you dancing on mine," Damien replied. "You talked me into giving the Republic's people a chance. Now I'm making it your job to make them take it."

"All right," he said, shaking his head. The graying cyborg turned his attention to Chambers. "I know it's not your job, Lieutenant, but you think you can help me get in touch with the ship's crew and get my things transferred over?"

"I think that falls under the Admiral's staff, personally," Chambers replied. "I'll talk to my team. Will you need to go back to *Duke*?"

Niska glanced around, then shrugged.

"I don't *need* to say goodbye to Persephone, I suppose," he allowed. "I travel light; I'm sure Lord Montgomery's people can get it packed up and over?"

"My cat *might* forgive you for leaving without saying goodbye eventually," Damien said, letting the moment of humor ease some of the tension. "I'll have Commodore Jakab's people package your things and send them over." He paused, shaking his head. "I guess that's Mage-Captain Denuiad's people. The Commodore won't be bothered with that."

Mage-Captain Milena Denuiad had taken over as Captain of *Duke of Magnificence* after Damien had promoted Kole Jakab to avoid confusion. That meant she'd inherited Jakab's role as Damien's "driver," though she seemed okay with that so far.

He carefully clasped forearms with both Niska and Chambers, forcing a smile for them both.

"We'll be on our way within twelve hours," he warned them. "Alexander's people should be arranging the transfer of a few Mages—which I suspect I'm trading Mage-Commodore Jakab for."

No one was going to argue with his taking a cruiser, but he figured he should probably leave the cruiser squadron *commander* with the squadron. He'd miss Jakab, but there were a *lot* of people with the fleet he was going to miss.

"I'll tell Persephone you both said hi and give her some pets from you," he told them. "The sooner everything is moving, the sooner we're on our way and the sooner I'm at the Mage-Queen's side."

And much as he disliked leaving a job half-done, he had to admit that was the place for him. He was the First Hand of the Mage-King of Mars. When the Mage-Queen needed a sword and a strong right hand, well, that was his job.

CHAPTER 5

PERSEPHONE'S OPINION of Damien's being back aboard *Duke of Magnificence* was very clear. The moment he entered the observation deck that had been converted to his office, the cat was *running* through the specially installed tunnel from his quarters to the office. He heard claws on metal for a good fifteen seconds before she came barrelling across the floor and leapt onto his chest.

Magic held her in place while the First Hand of Mars, inarguably one of the two or three most powerful human beings alive, carefully slid an arm into place to hold the purring ball of black fur up.

"Good to see you, too," he told the cat as he delicately lowered himself into his chair.

"I swear the cat misses you more than any person has ever missed me," Denis Romanov said dryly, the Special Agent leaning against the heavily armored window looking out over the fleet. "You'd think she'd be more attached to Jeff. He *feeds* her."

"Jeff feeds everyone who comes into his orbit," Damien pointed out. Jeff Schenck—properly, Chief Steward Jeff Schenck—was the Royal Martian Navy NCO tasked with keeping one Damien Montgomery organized and alive.

He was also only a few moments behind the cat in stepping into the office to check in.

"From her reaction, I'd think you'd been gone for days instead of hours," Schenck noted. "Can I get you anything, sir? You're still scheduled for dinner with Captain Denuiad in four hours."

"We'll cancel that dinner, Jeff," Damien told the older man. "I'll eat here. Captain Denuiad is going to be busy: we'll be moving out in about ten hours."

"Of course, sir," Schenck said. "Anything in particular you need?"

Damien manfully refrained both from sinking his face into Persephone's and from asking his steward to bring him alcohol.

"Coffee, please," he finally ordered. Schenck would know what to bring. Damien's supply of small-batch coffee from the best coffee growers in the Protectorate was one of his few luxuries.

"For both myself and Agent Romanov," he continued. "Have you been briefed on what happened back home?"

There was a long pause, then Schenck bowed his head.

"I was, my lord. I didn't know His Majesty, but it's still terrible news. You have my condolences."

"In a perfect world, we'd all live forever," Damien murmured. "We're going home, Jeff. I'm not sure how long I'll be on Mars, but Mage-Captain Denuiad may end up reclaiming this space. You'll probably need to at least plan packing as we travel."

"Of course, my lord."

Even magic couldn't have made the coffee appear faster, and Damien took a slow sip as he considered the situation in front of him.

"Is there anything you still need to take care of here, Agent?" he asked Romanov.

"I go where you go," the Marine-turned-bodyguard replied. "So do my people. *You* may want to touch base with LaMonte and her crew and give Alexander your files on the Republic. Just in case."

"Both of those were on my list," Damien confirmed, "but thank you. Any concerns with the detail?"

"Mostly for the future," Denis said. "How much security do you really need in the Mountain, after all?"

"The last time I spent significant time in the Mountain, I acquired a girlfriend who tried to kill me and then nuked herself." He shook his head. Hand Charlotte Ndosi had been in the same kind of "recuperate in safety" status as him when they'd met on Mars.

She'd also been a Keeper and had fought him to protect their secrets. She'd been vaporized in the nuclear explosion that had destroyed their archive—but she'd already been dead at that point. One of her own Mages had killed her.

Someday, Damien would find that Mage. Today, he wondered if that betrayal had anything to do with the Mage-King's death.

"I'm seconded to the Secret Service and to your detail until you don't need or want me anymore," the Marine finally said. "I hope we don't need to worry about Hands turning on you again. Or girlfriends, for that matter."

"My girlfriend has a battle fleet," Damien said quietly. "I prefer not to upset her."

"You certainly know how to pick them," Romanov confirmed brightly. "Like I said, I suggest you talk to LaMonte before we leave. God alone knows when you'll see each other again."

"We both entered the service of Mars in the end," he murmured. "We knew what we were getting into."

"Did you?" the Marine asked. "Because I signed on 'cause the girl I was crushing on thought the uniform was hot, and now I'm in the Secret Service, guarding the First Hand."

He shook his head.

"I *definitely* didn't know what I was getting into."

There was more involved in getting ready to leave the fleet behind than just passing his files over to Alexander, and it took Damien several hours just to get the data transfers handled. Between his files on *Duke of Magnificence* and the copies on the stealth ship *Rhapsody in Purple*, Damien probably knew as much about the Republic as some of the people who'd been running it.

He certainly knew more about the Daedalus Project and the Promethean Interface it had created. That sickening merger of magic and technology was the key to the Republic war fleet, using the extracted brains of Mages to jump ships.

Most of the Republic's first wave of those brains had come from them kidnapping and murdering the Mages born in the UnArcana Worlds. Several thousand children had been murdered to fuel the Republic's war machine, a revelation that had shattered the fleet attempting to defend Legatus.

A revelation that had broken a lot of Damien's faith in humanity. The Mage-King's death didn't help. Everywhere he turned right now, he was looking at reminders of just how low his species could sink.

But, well, humanity was the only game he had, and he'd made a few promises along the way.

With the data handled, he followed Romanov's suggestion and pinged Kelly LaMonte. *Rhapsody in Purple*'s Captain was an old friend and an ex-girlfriend. She was married to her Ship's Mage and her First Pilot now, the three of them running what he figured was the most efficient covert-ops ship he knew about.

"Damien," she greeted him within moments of the connection being made. "Are you okay?"

"You heard," he replied. It shouldn't be a surprise, he supposed. The Mage-King's death was *the* news of the day. Hell, of the *year*.

"Of course I heard," LaMonte snapped. "Both Desmonds gone. I know you were friends with both of them, too. Rumor has it you're going back to Mars, so I repeat my question. Are you okay?"

"No," he admitted, a word that was getting more familiar than usual. "I'm not okay. I don't even know what... I don't know what to think or what to do."

There weren't many people he'd admit that to, but *Rhapsody* wasn't a large ship. Everyone aboard had spent the last few months living in each others' back pockets, and he'd known Kelly LaMonte well before that, too.

"Head back to Mars?" she asked. "That seems to be the next step."

"I haven't heard from Kiera yet, but that was what Gregory asked. We've got two extra Mages reporting aboard, which makes it a two-day trip if we push it," he told her. "I...want to be home, I think. I lost two good friends today and I was too far away to do anything."

"If it wasn't for the Link, we wouldn't have known for at *least* two days," she pointed out. "I see the advantage of the thing, even if I want to curse it right now."

"You'll have one on *Rhapsody* soon enough." Damien sighed, then smiled as Persephone jumped on his desk to be in the camera.

"You're not supposed to be up here," he scolded her. She ignored him, nosing at the image of the currently blue-haired covert-ops captain before settling down on the desk.

"You spoil her," LaMonte told him.

"It's true," he admitted. "She also knows I can't pick her up, so..."

He made a vague gesture with his left hand and Persephone vanished from the desk with a *pop*, reappearing on the floor with a disgruntled meow.

"I have no idea what's next on your agenda," he said to LaMonte. "I'm heading back to Mars to deal with everything there. I have my suspicions about what needs to be done there."

"It's been seventy years since the last succession. It's going to be messy—and it's a mess centered on a kid who just lost her father and brother," she agreed. "Kiera's going to need you. As a friend and as her First Hand."

"I know. And I'll be there," he told her. "Which means I need to get moving, which means I leave everything here in the lurch."

"Don't worry; if there's a secret Republic accelerator ring, we'll find it," she told him. That was the *second* biggest fear they had: both Republic and Protectorate warships needed antimatter for power, engines and weapons.

The Protectorate produced it with the services of transmuter Mages. Legatus had built a particle accelerator ring that had encompassed an entire gas giant. The sheer scale of the installation meant that its construction had never been repeated, and its capture *should* have cut the Republic Interstellar Navy's fuel supply.

Should. But if there were a second accelerator ring...it would fall to the scout ships to find it.

"I'm more worried about a second Prometheus facility," he admitted. "We know of at least one extraction facility that had been shut down to move operations here. Something like that could be reactivated if we don't do something about it."

LaMonte shivered. She hadn't boarded the Prometheus Station in Nueva Bolivia with Damien, but she'd been the one hacking its systems.

They'd all seen the footage of the first place the Republic had murdered children to steal their magic.

"If there's another one of those hells, we'll find it, too," she said coldly. "Finley died too easily. The next fucker who follows his research is going to *beg*."

"I *want* to agree with you," Damien admitted. "But we can't become them, Kelly. If we get down into the mud and the shit with the monsters, we become monsters. Anyone senior from the Prometheus Project is going to get a *very* clean, very transparent trial."

And they'd get a clean death. But there was no question at all in his mind of how that trial would end. The Protectorate didn't have the death penalty on the books for very many crimes.

Mass murder was one of them.

CHAPTER 6

IT WAS still reassuring to Damien to be back in the Royal Martian Marine Corps assault shuttles he'd done most of his flying in since becoming a Hand. He'd had to give up the blatant and heavily armed spacecraft when he'd made his journey into Republic space to find the Prometheus Project.

He returned to Olympus Mons in the style to which he'd become accustomed...and then some. His own shuttle was at the center of a formation of other spacecraft, half-escort and half-decoys, and their course kept them in full line of fire from *Duke of Magnificence* for the entire descent.

Mars Defense Command was taking no chances. They'd lost their *King*. They weren't going to lose the First Hand.

"Olympus Control has just changed our landing pad," the pilot reported. "Agent Romanov?"

Talking to Damien and Romanov was easy enough for the woman. Damien had taken over the copilot seat, and Romanov was strapped into the back of the cockpit. The shuttle behind them was empty, but Damien wanted to see where he was going.

"Part of the plan, Lieutenant," Romanov said calmly, the Marine Secret Service officer clearly having been briefed. "No one outside Olympus Mons had the real landing pad until this moment. Even I only knew it was going to change."

"All right, following the ball," the pilot confirmed.

Damien shook his head.

"Everyone's on edge," he said quietly, watching the immense mountain grow in the distance as they dropped through Mars's atmosphere and the "red planet" came into clear view.

Not that twenty-fifth century Mars was red. The First Mage-King's magic had finished what a century-plus of terraforming efforts had begun. The planetary rotation had been accelerated to match Earth's day. The last of the ice caps had been melted and the channels had been controlled. The small sample forests had expanded explosively over Desmond the First's reign, his magic allowing the works of centuries to be done in years.

Mars was a green world now, but there was an ever-so-slight ruddy tinge to most of the plant life. Damien suspected that tinge was intentional, inserted by the geneticists and biologists assembling an artificial ecosystem to keep the planet red.

Olympus Mons rose from those green plains like the solitary god it was. The tallest mountain in the Solar System and still among the ten largest mountains known to humanity. Olympus City encircled its roots, a metropolis of the tens of millions of souls required to run even the loose nation of the Protectorate.

"I have atmospheric interceptors rising from the Mountain," the pilot told her passengers. "IFFs make them Royal Guard Air Squadron Three. Formation in sixty seconds, shuttle escort breaks off in seventy-five."

"Understood," Damien confirmed. Long practice allowed him to make out the moving sparks above the city that were the next wave of their escort. He shivered at the name, though.

The Royal Guard were nothing to be trifled with, even for a Hand. Less than three hundred strong, every one of them was either a Marine or a Navy Combat Mage and a proven veteran. Trained in a dozen different roles, they were given armor, weapons and magic that the Protectorate couldn't justify for any larger or less critical force.

Nine had died with the Mage-King of Mars.

The Protectorate Secret Service guarded the Mountain, the secondary heirs, the Hands and the Voices of the Mage-King. But the Mage-King—the Mage-Queen now—was guarded by warriors without peer. Only the Mage-Queen and her immediate heir would have Royal Guards.

Which meant, Damien realized, that a team had to be on their way to Legatus to resume their watch over Jane Alexander. Unless Kiera opted to do something unusual, Jane was going to be her niece's heir for a while.

The interceptors weren't that different from those used by planetary defense forces around the Protectorate. They flashed into view in a blur of red, flipping and falling into formation perhaps a bit faster than another squadron might have.

Once the dozen aircraft were in position, the shuttles flashed their running lights and brought their engines up to full power, blazing back to orbit on individual pillars of flame.

"We're two minutes from landing," the pilot announced. "We are inside the Mountain's defensive perimeter in sixty seconds. Lord Montgomery, can you do the copilot list?"

Damien grinned and switches started flicking around him without his moving an injured finger.

"I know the list," he told the pilot. "So long as you don't mind that I won't actually be *touching* anything."

The technological and magical artifice of the Protectorate didn't stretch to making it safe for human beings to stand on a landing pad as a shuttle came down. There were *ways* for a human to survive that— Damien had once, memorably, stopped an orbital bombardment—but they tended to send the Mage doing it to the hospital.

Instead, there were safety barriers and blast doors that slid aside and opened once the shuttle was settled, allowing the greeting party to approach the shuttle once it had cooled. Since that took about the same amount of time as it took Damien to get from the cockpit to the shuttle ramp, he didn't see the party emerge from Olympus Mons.

When the ramp finally extended onto the still-cooling concrete, his bodyguards went first. The pad was not yet cool enough for an unarmored human, but that was part of what exosuit battle armor was meant for. Two fully armored Marines went through the door ahead of everyone else to interface with the welcome and make sure everything was secure and safe.

He waited another minute and then followed them down, flanked by Secret Service Agents in subtler body armor under traditional black suits.

The advantage to moving with a group, he supposed, was it made it easier to keep going when surprise might otherwise have stopped him in his tracks.

He'd expected the neat files of Royal Guards lining his path and guarding the back of the party. He'd expected Malcolm Gregory and Kiera Alexander, both looking exhausted despite being dressed in full formal suits.

Fortunately, Damien had expected to end up in front of cameras at some point today and had dressed in his usual suit and black gloves. The outfit had become an almost-uniform for him over the years, though the purpose of the gloves had changed.

He'd spent most of his adult life wearing simple wrist-length gloves to cover the jump runes inlaid into his palms. Most Jump Mages did. After the Council Station incident, though, he'd switched to elbow-length thin leather gloves that were mildly painful to put on.

The new gloves didn't cover runes, because he didn't have any left on his forearms or hands. They covered the scarred and ruined claws that the melting runes had left of his limbs. He was slowly regaining the *use* of his hands, but they were far from pretty.

The uniform had been a good call because *behind* Gregory and Kiera Alexander were at least a dozen dignitaries of various assortments. He spotted four Councilors he knew, the Mayor of Olympus City, Admiral Amanda Caliver—the woman in charge of Mars Defense Command—and he figured he *should* know the other half-dozen.

The twenty-plus reporters behind *them* suggested as much, anyway. Something more was going on here than simply the return of the deceased Mage-King's favored Hand.

With Secret Service Agents flanking him and Marines laying out the path forward, there was no way he could go anywhere else even if anxiety fluttered in his chest. At least the two waiting for him were old friends.

The Chancellor of Mars bowed slightly as Damien approached. The First Hand returned the gesture, a sign of respect between the two men that political analysts figured were tied for second-most powerful individual in the Protectorate.

"It's good to have you home, Damien," Gregory told him. "You made good time."

"I borrowed more Mages from the Navy than I should have," Damien admitted. "It seemed urgent."

"It was," Kiera interjected, the girl sounding tired.

Damien turned to face her, and for a moment, the mask cracked. She looked at him with all of the fear and grief and exhaustion of a sixteen-year-old girl who'd just lost her entire immediate family.

"Kiera." He pulled her into his arms and held her tightly. "I am so sorry."

"I know. Thank you."

The moment faded and he let her go, both of them allowing the masks of their roles to take over their faces again as Kiera stepped backward to clear some space. To his surprise, she then gestured the reporters and audience forward.

"These people are here as witnesses," she told him. "Welcome home, Damien. You return to Our Mountain in the darkest of hours, carried on the wings of magic as only Our Hands can be. You served Our father well, and now We must ask: are you prepared to serve Us as you served him?"

"I am," Damien said levelly. "My life—my service—belong to Mars and the Protectorate. That oath did not die with your father."

"Good," the young woman told him, her words almost lost as a cold wind whipped around the mountain and distracted everyone. Kiera smoothed her jacket and adjusted the plain gold circlet she was wearing before she nodded again and gestured to Damien.

"Kneel," she ordered.

Damien knelt. He'd been through the drill before, but there *wasn't* anything heavier the Mage-Queen could lay on him than the platinum Hand he already wore.

"Damien Montgomery," she said formally, "by Our father's will and Our own, We name you Lord Regent of Mars."

Nothing had changed on the side of the mountain. It was chilly that high up on Olympus Mons, and the cold wind was picking at jackets and hair across the landing pad. Three dozen reporters, officers and dignitaries stood there, all of them stunned to silence by Kiera Alexander's soft-spoken words.

"Will you accept this charge?" she asked, holding out her hand to him with a golden chain hanging from it.

That hand was small. So very small. Kiera was a delicately built young woman, barely ten centimeters taller than Damien and only slightly more heavily boned. The gold chain didn't carry any symbol but had far heavier links than the fine chain that had held his old platinum Hand.

The chain itself was the symbol, a length that would need to be doubled up to hang up comfortably. Damien had never seen it before—but there'd never *been* a Regent before. Desmond the Third had been thirty when his father died. His father had taken the throne at twenty-four.

And Kiera was sixteen. *Barely* sixteen, by only a few weeks. He didn't know what the charter rules on her regency were, but it made sense she needed one.

He didn't know if he could do the job, but looking up at Kiera's tired gaze, he knew one thing: he couldn't let her down. Not today.

"My life and my service belong to Mars," he echoed. "If you would have me serve as your regent, then I am yours to command."

Both of them knew he wasn't able to take the chain himself. He could use magic, but that seemed...inappropriate.

Kiera laid the chain over his shoulders herself, resting it above the platinum hand that he was charged to carry to his deathbed.

"Thank you," she murmured, softly enough that no one else could hear her. "I don't think I can do this alone."

"You won't have to," Damien promised. "Malcolm and I will be with you every step of the way. No matter what, we'll have your back."

She blinked away tears and gestured for him to rise. Taking his arm, she guided him to face the array of cameras.

"We ask you all to stand as witness that Damien Montgomery has accepted the burden laid upon him," she said loudly. It sounded like the words had been written before and she'd been practicing them.

That was *more* than fair in his books.

"Lord Montgomery has borne first Our father's Voice and then Our father's Hand for three years. He has been on the front lines of the war against the Republic and was instrumental in discovering the truth behind George Solace's atrocities.

"He has been a hero of the Protectorate as Hand and First Hand, and he will now stand as *Our* Voice, *Our* Hand and *Our* Sword as we move forward through this dark time.

"People of the Protectorate, We give you your Lord Regent."

Thankfully, Damien was quite sure the cameras weren't picking up his shivering under his jacket. Far from all of *that* was from the cold.

CHAPTER 7

DAMIEN DIDN'T even make it back to his quarters. He and Romanov found themselves surrounded by Royal Guards and swept off with Kiera and Malcolm to the Chancellor's office.

Gregory's space was...sumptuous. The chairs were overstuffed, with active machinery in them to adjust to the form of whoever sat in them. In both Kiera and Damien's case, the system lifted them up several centimeters to make it easier for them to see everything as well as making them more comfortable.

There were bookshelves in the room, Damien knew, but they were hidden behind three-meter-tall tapestries woven by artists from cultures he'd barely even *heard* of. Malcolm Gregory had made a hobby of finding obscure artists from half-forgotten peoples and making them famous.

His "hobby" was probably directly responsible for the careers of half of the Protectorate's top textile artists, especially, but it also resulted in a spectacularly gorgeous and baroque personal office.

Food was already waiting for them, a tray tailored to each of their individual tastes...and including a French press of coffee on Damien's versus insulated carafes on the other two trays.

Taking advantage of the distraction, he carefully sniffed at the steaming brew before pressing the lever down. He didn't recognize it but it smelled good.

He poured himself a cup and took a sandwich from the tray before studying Gregory.

"You trapped me," he told the Chancellor. "You *knew* when you got me to come home."

"I knew that Kiera would prefer you as Lord Regent over just about anyone else," Gregory said calmly. "I knew Desmond wanted you home to back up Kiera or Des after he passed. I didn't know what was in his will, but I suspected."

"There was more in the will about you, too," Kiera told Damien quietly. "You're a millionaire now. Dad sliced off a portion of the Alexander fortune for you. I'll admit I don't remember the number—I wasn't paying that much attention during the reading."

"I never served Desmond for the money," he said grumpily. He *knew* his anger was as much at the loss of his mentor and friend as anything else, but that didn't make it any less real. "He knew that."

"And he wanted to be sure you were taken care of, no matter what," Kiera replied. If she was bothered by—or even *noticed*—his anger, she showed no sign of it. "As do I. I...I never expected this, Damien. I wasn't trained for this."

She grimaced.

"We were studying *research universities* for Her Majesty two weeks ago," Malcolm Gregory said. "It will be impossible, unfortunately, for the Mage-Queen of Mars to become a research biologist."

"I'll admit that's not really my biggest problem right now," Kiera snapped. Then she closed her eyes and took a long breath. "Apologies, Malcolm. This is hard."

"For all of us, but most of all for you," Gregory told her, taking the sudden anger in stride. "Damien, right now you and I are the entire Regency Council. We'll probably want Kiera to select some more Councilors as we go forward."

"Why? I trust you both," she told them.

"Because right now, for all intents and purposes, Damien Montgomery is the Mage-King of Mars," the Chancellor said calmly. "The Charter says you must be nineteen to be Queen in your own right. Until then, *he* wields your authority."

"And I trust him," Kiera repeated.

"I know. But there is nothing currently stopping Damien and I spending the next three years using every scrap of that power to line our pockets. Hell, given that we're writing a new *Constitution* right now, there's nothing stopping us from running off with the *Protectorate*."

"Neither of which you're going to do," the Mage-Queen of Mars said levelly.

"But appearances are everything," Gregory told her. "You trust us. I trust Damien and I'm reasonably sure Damien trusts me...but the entire Protectorate is watching us. The more honorable voices we have on the Regency Council, the better we look from the outside and the safer Damien and I are from accusations of abuse of power.

"You need to select additional Councilors to protect *us*. Please."

"I see," Kiera conceded with a long sigh. She rubbed her face with her hands. "I...I don't know what I'm doing, Malcolm. I just..."

"You just lost everyone," Damien said quietly. "And duty demands we keep going anyway. But you don't have to do it alone." He forced a smile. "Malcolm and I won't *let* you."

She nodded, blinking back tears.

"I miss them so much," she admitted. "This wasn't...at all what I expected."

"It's a nightmare for us all," Gregory said. "We're with you." He leveled his gaze on Damien.

"And we have a lot of work to do," he continued. "We need to brief Damien pretty heavily in the next few days, which I want you to sit in on as much of as possible, Kiera. All of us know large chunks of what Desmond was up to, but I don't think any of us were fully briefed on everything.

"Only Des was," he admitted grimly.

"What do we know about their deaths?" Damien asked.

"Not much," Gregory said. "It looked like a containment failure. Could have been a once-in-a-century unpredicted failure, incomplete or incompetent maintenance...a lot of things. But it does look like an accident."

Damien was about to argue with that, but he saw Kiera's expression out of the corner of his eye. This was going to be hard enough for her without going over her father's and brother's deaths in detail.

"What do we need to worry about first, then?"

"We're currently arguing out whether the formal coronation will be delayed until she takes the throne in her own right or not," Gregory admitted. "Part of that is the mess with the planned transition from the old Charter to the new Constitution."

That had been the outgrowth of the agreement between Desmond and his Council that had followed the attack on Council Station. The first Mage-King's Charter was a *very* loose set of rules, and the Protectorate had filled the gap with bilateral funding agreements with the member worlds and informal tradition.

Combined with the Charter and the Compact that defined Mages' relationship with mundane humanity, those informal traditions and bilateral agreements had built a functional interstellar state.

But the Charter called for an advisory Council, not a true legislature. While it mostly stayed out of any given star system's affairs, it left all interstellar law and regulation entirely in the Mage-King's hands.

A new Constitution was being drafted. Desmond's death would delay that, but it would also inform it in many ways.

"What does the Charter say?" he asked.

"It doesn't," Gregory admitted. "It says she needs a Regent until she's nineteen. You're Lord Regent for three years, Damien."

"Or until I die or she finds someone better," he replied. His Queen's full-body wince suggested that wasn't the right joke for today.

"Sorry," he apologized. "It's hard for all of us."

"First big ugly on my list is that, Coronation or no, the Mage-Queen has to be presented to the Protectorate," Gregory noted. "In this case, the Lord Regent needs to be presented as well. I've scheduled a proper news conference for the two of you to meet with the reporters together.

"But Damien has to give the speech, sorry."

Damien hesitated, then sighed.

"I hope you wrote it already," he told Gregory. "My speeches are usually very short and in the style of 'you know who I am; move or die.'"

"I'm not sure that's invalid for this situation," Kiera observed. "But yes, Gregory had my father's team write the speech. They're used to Dad being involved in the process, but I think what they've given us is good."

"I agree. We only have two hours before that conference," Gregory warned. "The Mountain's PR team is going to need to swarm over both of you for clothes and makeup for at least an hour before that and you can read the speech then."

"At some point, I need to reach out to Sherwood," Damien said. Grace McLaughlin was the Admiral commanding their system defense force as well as his girlfriend. She needed to know he was stuck on Mars for a long time.

"Personal isn't the same as important, but I'll need RTA time for that," he noted.

"Of course," Gregory agreed. "But if you'll allow a suggestion? As soon as you're done with the conference, the two of you need to get to the throne room. I sealed it when Desmond died.

"I don't *think* the Olympus Amplifier is going to lash out because of his death, but all *I* really know is that it's a bloody weird piece of magic that requires a Rune Wright."

"It doesn't require Runes of Power," Kiera told the Chancellor. "I should be able to handle it myself, but I agree with waiting for Damien. We'll go together and see what we can make of it."

She glanced at Damien.

"Did Dad go through it with you at any point?" she asked.

"I've seen the simulacrum in the throne room," Damien admitted. "I've never interfaced with it myself. I..." He shook his head. "I didn't get the impression from Desmond that using the Olympus Amplifier was something that could be taught. Like putting an extra Rune of Power on yourself, it's something that only a Rune Wright can do and it's done entirely on instinct."

"Speaking of Runes of Power..." Kiera noted.

"No," Damien told her, surprised at the fierceness in his voice. "Yes, we could use you having five Runes instead of one, but there's a reason your father wanted you to wait until you were nineteen.

"Even one Rune of Power is influencing how your magical strength and your *body* grows," he continued. "He went through the research with me at one point, and I'm sure you have a copy of it."

"The research is a bunch of Mages and geneticists with no damn clue going over the records of six kids growing into adulthood," Kiera pointed out. "That's hardly scientifically valid."

"But it's all we have. And the last thing you can afford is to risk limiting your magical power or damaging yourself," Damien told her. "For now, you have me if we need multiple Runes."

"Fine." Her tone told him the argument wasn't over...and that was probably for the best.

The last thing *he* wanted to do was get used to giving orders to his Queen.

Red-armored and anonymous Royal Guards fell in around Damien and the Mage-Queen as they headed to the audience chamber. His security detail was tagging along as well, looking small and underequipped—if unintimidated—compared to the Guards.

He met Romanov's gaze across the seeming crowd of escorts and gave the other man a firm nod. Until the Secret Service detail was officially dissolved in favor of a Guard detachment—something Damien hadn't realized would have to happen until that moment—Romanov and his people needed to be there.

Some of those Marines and Agents had been with Damien for three years and two detail commanders. Security, protocol and tradition said he replaced them now, but he needed to be sure they knew he appreciated all they'd done.

There were very few of his original detail left, and only two had ever managed to resign. It felt like he'd left bodyguards and Marines buried on every world he'd visited since accepting Desmond's charge.

"Smile, Damien," Kiera Alexander muttered, pitching her voice as they cut through one of the major arterial corridors of Olympus Mons. "You're more visible than you think."

She might have only been second in line to the Throne, but Alexander had been raised a royal scion in the public eye. She was more aware of what was going on around them in terms of the political veneer than Damien was.

He was more aware of threats and had been registering the crowd on the other side of the bodyguard detail from that perspective. He hadn't been considering how he appeared to them.

The Mage-Queen was right, of course. Lost in unpleasant thoughts, he wasn't smiling and he doubted his expression had been at all reassuring to the crowd looking to their new Lord Regent.

"Thank you," he murmured, forcing himself to smile. He had a practiced "I am a friendly negotiator" face at this point, and it would serve the purpose.

He was going to need to learn some new masks.

"This is so strange," he told her. "I was a diplomat and a cop, not a politician. I'm not used to having every eye on me at all times."

"Get used to it," Alexander replied. "This is your life for the next three years, Damien."

"Yours forever, I suppose," he agreed. "How did your father handle all of this?"

"I don't know," she admitted. "I thought I understood, but now it's all focused on me instead of him. You think you know what the goldfish bowl is like...but this is something else."

"I think we got transplanted to the lobby's display tank," Damien told her, continuing the metaphor as they slipped into quieter corridors.

The massive complex inside Olympus Mons was many things. Among them, it was still a fully functional geothermal power plant supplying a significant portion of Olympus City's power needs. It was also a vast office building, a library, a museum...there was a city inside the mountain as well as outside, and the corridors only lacked vehicles to be streets.

The Royal Family and the Hands lived in a smaller, more private section near the top of the mountain. Even *Damien* knew they could reach the audience chamber they were headed to without traveling through public corridors.

Gregory had picked the path with intent. Damien could only hope that "being seen" wasn't going to lead to "being shot at."

It wouldn't be the first time someone had tried to assassinate him on Mars, after all.

CHAPTER 8

IT WASN'T the first time Damien had been stuck in a chair while makeup artists worked him over. Even with all of the technology at the Protectorate's disposal, cameras still needed help to make the people in front of them look good.

He'd never been as thoroughly worked over as the Mountain's PR experts managed. At one point, one of the young women had turned up with a manicure tray and reached for his gloves before he'd warned her off.

If nothing else, removing the gloves would hurt and the Protectorate didn't need to see the scarred mess that was his hands. There was transparency and there was rubbing salt in wounds.

Once the experts were done, Damien and the young Queen found themselves on a stage he'd seen a thousand times. He'd never been the center of attention in the grand audience hall before, but he'd been there before and even stood on the stage—and he'd seen uncounted recordings of briefings and speeches given from this space.

The stylized crowned-red-planet-on-blue flag of the Kingdom of Mars—a distinctly and importantly separate entity from the *Protectorate* of Mars— hung to his and Kiera's left. The flag of the Protectorate itself—a white mountain in front of a red planet on a black flag—was hanging to his right.

The lectern had the seal of the Protectorate on it. While Kiera Alexander was the ruler of the Protectorate by virtue of being the Mage-Queen of Mars, no one was going to pretend the Protectorate *wasn't* the more important entity.

"With me," he told her as she started to slow down to join Gregory at the back of the stage. "This is about you as well as me."

He saw her swallow, but she kept going as everyone except the two of them split off. Six red-armored Royal Guard were positioned around the edge of the stage, almost entirely out of view of the camera.

Gregory and four other key members of the Protectorate administration were visibly in the camera view behind Damien and Kiera as they reached the lectern and he looked out at the crowd of reporters.

There were at least a thousand people in the room, packing it to capacity, and they almost didn't matter. What *mattered* was that everything was being recorded. It was being transmitted live across the Solar System, only delayed by the speed of light. Summaries of his speech would be sent to every world with an RTA within hours, and copies of the recording would go out on every ship leaving Sol.

Specialized courier ships would see the video playing in every system in the Core within a few days, but it would be as much as three or four weeks before some of the Fringe Worlds saw it. There were worlds of the Protectorate that didn't even know Desmond was dead yet.

The Link would change all that, and it was almost *better* for humanity as a whole that the Republic had kept it hidden. A private enterprise would have rolled it out in the most profitable way—but the *Protectorate* controlled the technology now.

Like the prefab clinics manufactured in Olympus City and spread across the Protectorate to enable the Charter's demand for state-funded healthcare, the Link's presence would be underwritten by the Mountain. Damien wasn't sure how long it would take to connect the entire Protectorate into a single real-time communication network—but it was going to be done as quickly as humanly possible.

A soft *click* in his ear told him that the cameras were recording, and the contact lens the Mountain's expert had helped him put in started scrolling his prepared remarks.

"Good afternoon, everyone," he told them. "I suspect you all know who I am, but on days like today, introductions are paramount.

"My name is Damien Montgomery. Until very recently, I was the First Hand of the Mage-King of Mars."

He paused, glancing over at Kiera. She was smiling, but it was very forced.

"But Desmond the Third's will called for me to take on a new role," he continued. "As Her Majesty, Mage-Queen Kiera the First, has confirmed. She has called on me to take on the role of Lord Regent of Mars.

"I'm sure every reporter in the room already knew that," Damien added, "but not everyone watching the feed did. Until Her Majesty turns nineteen, I will act in her stead and speak with her voice."

He *had* read the speech in advance. He wasn't sticking entirely to the script, but the point he was making was important as well.

"I am your Lord Regent," he repeated softly. "But she is your Mage-Queen. I promise to you, the people of the Protectorate, the same thing I promised her: to never forget that. I am a caretaker and it is my duty to watch over the Protectorate as Desmond Alexander would have.

"But I am *only* a caretaker, and all I do is in the name of Mage-Queen Kiera Alexander."

That was why he'd brought her up to the stage. He suspected it would be far too easy to fall into the trap of acting as Lord Regent without considering that his authority was borrowed.

Whoever was controlling the text in his contacts was paying attention. They'd paused when he'd gone off script, and the next lines of the speech were waiting.

"I take up this role in a dark time for the Protectorate," he read. "With the Mage-King's death, we are weakened even as we face challenges on multiple sides. It is our task, as a nation, to come through this time and rise stronger.

"His Majesty had many projects and plans underway. It is my intent and Her Majesty's to go through these plans and make certain that nothing is lost or abandoned. We will continue the process of drafting the new Constitution that has been promised.

"But above all else, our joint focus must be on the war. My own investigations revealed the depths of the atrocities committed against the people of the UnArcana Worlds to create the Republic. I do not—we *cannot*—hold the people of the Republic responsible for the sins committed in their name.

"But we also cannot abandon them to the Lord Protector and his allies," Damien noted. "The Protectorate will do everything in our power to bring George Solace to justice for the murders involved in the Prometheus Project. We will do everything in our power to end this war in an expeditious and humane manner.

"But we will not forget that the Protectorate was betrayed. The Republic *will* fall. The Protectorate *will* endure. We *will* stand together."

He smiled thinly as the speech ended, and gestured Kiera forward.

"People of the Protectorate, I am your Lord Regent," he repeated. "And I present to you Kiera Michelle Alexander, the Mage-Queen of Mars!"

CHAPTER 9

DENIS ROMANOV slung his kit in a different room that evening than he'd started in that morning. He was used to that. After the chaotic shitstorm that had been Damien Montgomery's "investigation" inside Republic space, the Marine was still a little surprised they'd managed to deliver the Hand back to the Protectorate alive.

Bouncing from planet to ship to planet to ship to ship to planet...that was part of the job of guarding one of the more active troubleshooters the Protectorate and the Mage-King had.

The tall Marine shook his head as he took a seat on the bed. Right now, he had two Secret Service Agents standing guard outside Montgomery's quarters, but he was only spinning his wheels. There were *also* two Royal Guards standing guard outside the suite of rooms the Regent had occasionally visited as a Hand—Denis, more than anyone, knew how inaccurate "lived in" was as a descriptor for the suite.

Each of those Guards was a fully trained Combat Mage in armor that somehow—Denis wasn't entirely clear, but he suspected it involved runes for some reason—augmented their magical power.

It wasn't to the level of a Hand with a Rune of Power, let alone the handful of Rune Wrights kicking around with multiple Runes of Power, but it elevated top-tier Mages above their already-impressive abilities.

If the Royal Guard were watching over Damien Montgomery, Denis Romanov was about to be out of a job. He'd been seconded to the Secret Service for long enough, he wasn't even entirely sure what the Marine

Corps was going to *do* with him, even if he was *reasonably* sure two years wasn't long enough to break his career.

The chime at the door was unexpected, and reflex had him on his feet with a gun concealed behind his back before it finished echoing through the apartment.

"Overreacting much, Denis?" he muttered to himself and then crossed to the door.

"Who is it?"

"General Spader," a calm voice told him. "May I impose for a moment, Mage-Captain?"

Denis had the door open before his brain had truly registered any word except *General*. The woman standing outside the new apartment was only vaguely familiar to him, but he knew her *name*.

General Bethany Spader was a tall woman with silver-streaked red hair that offset brilliantly the dark burgundy uniform worn by the commanding officer of the Royal Guard. Formerly a Marine, she'd risen to Mage-Colonel in the Corps before taking a demotion to transfer to the Royal Guard and command Crown Prince Desmond's personal guard...when Des was *born*.

"Sir!" Denis saluted crisply. "How may I help you, General?"

"Walk with me, Mage-Captain," Spader ordered. "You're familiar with this part of the Mountain, I understand?"

"Yes, sir," Denis confirmed in confusion. He fell in beside Spader as she walked down the hallway of rooms provided for visiting Secret Service Agents. As the Senior Agent for a Hand's detail, Denis got one of the larger suites—but unlike the Hands themselves, he didn't have permanently assigned rooms.

"My people are in these rooms, even the Marines," he said aloud. He knew Spader knew that, but he felt like he had to say *something*.

"Do you know who is responsible for the security of these rooms, then?" Spader asked calmly. "The Agents and Marines staying here are responsible for watching the backs of some of the most powerful individuals in the Protectorate. Who watches them while they rest?"

"OMDC," Denis responded immediately. The Olympus Mons Defense Command had a lot of moving parts, but the last time he'd coordinated security around Montgomery's quarters, a Marine security team had been watching this section. "They report to you, don't they?"

Spader chuckled.

"Yes," she confirmed as she gestured a secured door open. "Security posts around this block of apartments are watched by a full company of Marines at all times...and a four-man fireteam of Royal Guards.

"What the Secret Service does for the Protectorate is often undervalued and underappreciated, but the Royal Guard has always made a point of making clear to our people that your job is as critical as ours," she told him. "I hold ultimate responsibility for OMDC and the security of Olympus Mons, but even on the rest of Mars, my reach is limited. Beyond Sol?

"The Royal Guards have almost never left Sol."

Denis had no idea where Spader was leading to, physically or conversationally. She was clearly waiting for him to say something though.

"The Guard protects the Mage-King. He doesn't leave Mars," he noted. "Why would the Guard leave?"

"In theory, we also protect the Lord Regent and the Heir," Spader told him. Her security badge opened another secure door as they continued their way out of regions of the Mountain Denis knew.

"Shortly after I joined the Guard, a team of twenty returned to Mars from guarding then-Mage-Commodore Jane Alexander," she continued. "None of us were Mars-bound before we became Guards, but all of us have remained here with the Mage-King since.

"Do you know why the Mage-King rarely leaves Olympus Mons, Mage-Captain?"

Spader had timed it perfectly. She dropped the question just as she led him through the last set of doors into an empty observation deck. Like the ones designed for tourists, it looked out over the sweeping hills and plains around Olympus Mons and the city at its foot. Unlike the tourist decks, there were no telescopes. Just a wall of armored glass and a breathtaking view.

"An Alexander must sit the throne at Olympus Mons," Denis quoted. "I've never been briefed on why, but I'm guessing it has something do with the amplifier and the Rune Wrights."

"*Well* done," Spader said. "What do you know about the Olympus Amplifier, Romanov?"

"That it was the first amplifier ever made by humans and was used by Project Olympus to measure Mage Gifts that couldn't necessarily be activated," Denis reeled off. "It was a critical component of the Eugenicists' plan to recreate mages."

"And we have no idea where it came from," Spader told him. "None, Mage-Captain. From the way the Eugenicists reacted when Desmond the First used the amplifier against them, they didn't know it could be used like that.

"The Olympus Amplifier is unlike any other amplifier we've built in terms of both scale and complexity," she continued. "*Only* a Rune Wright can use it. And until recently, we thought the only Rune Wrights were Alexanders."

"There's only been two others," Denis said quietly. "And one of *them* is dead."

Shot by a Republic Intelligence Directorate operative, of all people. The Republic had drastically underestimated how badly discovering Project Prometheus would shake their people's loyalty.

Even many fanatics blinked at discovering their government was knowingly murdering children, after all.

"And the other is now the Lord Regent. Your charge."

"A duty I expect to give up but will miss," Denis admitted. "Desmond chose well in that one."

"I have nothing but his record to judge that from," Spader pointed out. "Montgomery and I have met three times, and I don't think we had an actual conversation any of those times. Yet he is now one of the three people I am charged to protect above all others.

"Do you see my dilemma, Mage-Captain?"

"Not entirely," Denis admitted. "Damien will...be as cooperative as he ever is with the Guard. He knows the change is coming. You can work with him."

"I could work with Desmond, and Desmond handpicked Montgomery as his Sword and his daughter's Regent," Spader agreed. "But I'd rather smooth the process as much as I can."

She gestured out the window at the city and farms that stretched into the distance.

"Two billion souls on Mars. About thirteen billion in the Solar System. So long as a Rune Wright sits the throne of Olympus Mons, those people are safe. Crime and small problems will continue, yes, but a real threat? A fleet? An army? An invasion?

"So long as a Rune Wright sits the throne of Olympus Mons, *Sol is invulnerable.*"

The night outside suddenly seemed even quieter.

"Which makes the Rune Wrights—the Alexanders, Montgomery— critical. They are both our greatest defense and the only vulnerability this star system has. I cannot afford to conflict with the Lord Regent, nor can I afford for his life to be in danger."

"You want me to keep guarding him."

It wasn't a question. It wasn't really an answer, either. Denis Romanov wasn't sure what guarding Montgomery would entail now.

"I do," Spader told him. "It can't be a secondment, Romanov. There's no moving on from the Guard. If you join us, you are no longer a Marine. You are no longer Secret Service. You are a Royal Guard."

"You can't make a Marine not a Marine," Denis replied.

"I can if I call him to a higher cause," she snapped. "There can be no divided loyalties or questions of command, Denis Romanov. The Guard can have only one commander: me. Only one master: Kiera Alexander.

"You are a fully trained Combat Mage with more direct battle experience than ninety percent of the Corps. You are a perfect candidate for the Guard, and given the circumstances, we would bring you across as a Lieutenant—the same rank *I* received when I joined."

Denis didn't need her to clarify that a Royal Guard Lieutenant was paid—and treated, for authority purposes—at the same level as an RMMC Colonel. She was effectively offering him a promotion, but the price...

"We spent a lot of time indoctrinating Marines with the claim that you never stop being a Marine," he told her softly.

"It serves a purpose. But now I call you to serve a larger one, Denis Romanov. You were a Marine before. You've been Secret Service for two years. You've stood at Montgomery's side through more battles and crises than I suspect even I know about.

"Will you follow him into this challenge and stand at his side when he faces the highest duty the Protectorate can demand? Or will you cling to the legends of the Marines?"

"I'm sure there are better ways to phrase that," Denis said drily, looking out at the plains of Mars. "To be a Marine...is central to who I am."

"And it was central to who I was," Spader replied gently. "But what is more important, in the end, Romanov? The name or the oath? An identity or the service you took up?"

"What happens when Damien is no longer Regent?"

"We have three years to sort that out," she said with a snort. "But I'm leaning towards we never let a Rune Wright wander around without Royal Guards again. I'm starting to feel like they're more vulnerable than they think they are."

Denis shivered at a memory from one of his first missions with Damien. The Hand had halted an orbital bombardment with his magic, saving thousands of lives—including Denis's own—but had fallen into a coma and needed to be carried to safety.

"Far more vulnerable," he admitted. "No such thing as an ex-Marine, though, sir."

"No. Only Marines who transcended that to become something more," she agreed. "Are you with me?"

"For Mars," Denis said quietly. "I'm with you."

CHAPTER 10

EXHAUSTION HAD claimed Damien before he could take on Gregory's second "big ugly." The morning saw him something resembling fresh and refreshed, so he and Kiera met at the throne room before they'd even eaten.

There were no Secret Service Agents in his detail this morning. Two armored Royal Guards trailed in his wake as he and Kiera approached a space that was rarely open to the public. The audience hall he'd given his speech from was probably closer to the usual connotations of *throne room* than the *actual* throne room of Olympus Mons.

Heavy blast doors sealed the entrance. Even if an attacker somehow managed to penetrate this deep into the Mountain, past every other layer of security, those doors would resist nuclear weapons and Rune-empowered Mages. To Damien's Sight, the runes that covered them spoke of near-invulnerability, of drawing the power of the roots of the stone to stand against any threat.

Thankfully, they had the access codes.

"Wait here," he ordered the Guards. "We have an hour before we're scheduled to be anywhere. We'll probably need all of that time."

"Of course, Lord Regent."

The title still left Damien shivering—and that was before he thought about what it meant. Who had died for him to *be* Lord Regent.

That reminder carried him into the throne room with unshed tears burning his eyes.

"Damien?" Kiera asked as the blast doors slid shut behind them.

"Every time someone uses the title, I am reminded of what happened," he admitted. "I'm sorry. I know it's worse for you."

She exhaled a long sigh as her own eyes glistened in the dim light. Shaking herself, she looked around the cavern.

"I was expecting more," she noted. "More *lights*, if nothing else."

Damien chuckled and gestured to the PC on her wrist.

"We both have the access codes for the room's systems," he told her. "But you have an easier time with a computer right now than me."

Between magic and an operating system specially designed for accessibility, Damien *could* use his wrist computer. It was just a slower process than he'd like, and there was no point in pretending he wasn't injured when they were alone.

The lights slowly came up around them and the two of them moved forward, studying every line and curve of the room as they did.

"It's an exact duplicate of the Mountain at one-thousandth scale, isn't it?" Kiera asked.

"I hadn't realized, but I think you're right," Damien confirmed. The circular room rose to an inverse-domed ceiling twenty-some meters above them. He couldn't be certain without a comparison, but Kiera was probably right.

It would make sense.

"Look, is that it?" she was pointing.

Damien had missed the web of silver strands tracing through the smooth stone walls and into the air, but he didn't miss the silver orb that the young Queen was pointing at. It was at least three meters across, suspended in the middle of the room and out of reach of either of them.

Directly beneath it was the throne. It wasn't anything impressive. Even the Rune Wrights had been hesitant to change anything in this space, so the throne remained the same plain stone seat it had always been.

As they approached, Damien could see where the chair had once mounted metal buckles and leather straps. The children strapped into the seat hadn't been there voluntarily. Much of the non-power-generating aspects of Olympus Mons had been built for Project Olympus.

It might be a palace now, but it had been built as a prison and a slaughterhouse. Thousands of children had been born there, raised until they were thirteen, and then tested in this room. If they didn't show enough magic to meet the standard the Eugenicists had been looking for, well...the slopes of Olympus Mons had entire sections marked off as memorials, full of unmarked graves for children only ever given numbers.

"You can feel it, can't you?" Kiera said softly. "The weight of blood and death in here."

"I think that's just that we know what was done here, what Project Olympus was about," Damien countered. "I don't think that's the amplifier."

"Where *is* the amplifier?" she asked. "I was expecting runes like a simulacrum—probably on the chair."

He hadn't even thought of that—or of the obvious problem if the amplifier *did* need a Jump Mage's interface runes.

"Desmond the First used it without runes of any kind," Damien pointed out. "I don't think it's an interface thing. I'm not sure we'll even see runes as we understand them. If a Rune Wright can use this amplifier, then..."

He took a seat on the stone chair and reached into his Sight.

He always had some awareness of the magic around him, in a way he'd assumed most Mages shared until he'd learned otherwise. He could feel the eddies of power and energy that flowed through the Mountain, of the magic and runes carved into and drawing on the living stone, but to truly *read* magic, he needed to focus.

Opening his Sight fully inside that space was stunning. He had to close his eyes after less than a second, exhaling heavily.

"Be careful with your Sight," he murmured to Kiera, keeping his eyes closed. "Your general feel for magic is underestimating the power in here."

"That's so weird," the Mage-Queen said. "Normally, I *know* how much magic is around me. I thought it felt...weak here."

"This is different."

Damien opened his eyes again and looked into chaos. Every strand of silver wire supporting the globe glittered with power. Every line of silver inlay in the walls, natural or artificial, gleamed at him.

There was more than just the physical present. Studying the trails of power, he could see that many of them weren't even connected to a rune. Damien had *never* seen a permanent construct without an anchor before, but there it was. At least a third of the flow of power in the room ran through the air.

"The runes on the walls are Martian Runic," Kiera noted. "Don't worry," she continued after a moment, "I'm keeping my Sight under control. I need you to link in and show me how, just in case the Runes are more important than we thought."

He followed her pointing hand and nodded. He'd been so stunned by the awe-inspiring display of power he was sitting amidst that he hadn't been looking for patterns yet.

The key part of what Kiera was observing was that most of the amplifier wasn't Martian Runic, the categorized and formalized language of magical constructs. That language was complicated enough, with seventy-six characters and fourteen different connectors.

The outer shell of the room was carved in those runes, the same ones found in any human spaceship and, memorably, in one alien ruin. In fact...

"The runes on the walls are the standard amplifier matrix," Damien told Kiera. "Everything inside is...the simulacrum? Except not."

The first Mage-King had copied the runes from the outer wall to create humanity's amplifier matrix, the key to the stars and the most powerful weapon of the Royal Martian Navy. But none of the Mage-Kings had ever attempted to copy the construct *inside* the room, and as Damien studied it, he knew why.

"It's a Rune of Power," he said softly. "Except not for a human. Not for a living being at all."

"I don't understand, Damien," Kiera told him.

His fingers didn't bend well yet, but he could still gesture with his hands. Channeling power through them, he drew a pattern in the air.

Kiera could see the glowing runes as they linked his flesh into the magic around them.

"The amplifier is immense," he said distractedly as he continued to weave the growing construct of pure magic around himself. He was only vaguely sure what he was doing, operating entirely on instinct.

"The sheer scale of Olympus Mons means that the amplifier we see here is layered inside two more." He wasn't even sure how he knew that from there, but he did. Even *that* wasn't supposed to be possible. "That alone would give someone wielding it nine times the power of a regular amplifier.

"But this...this chamber is what makes it something more. What allowed children with no magical gift to be tested. Just sitting here and focusing on the silver would be enough to get *some* result...but a Rune Wright could feel the truth of it."

"Which is?" Kiera asked. "I can see what you're doing, but even I'm only following half of it."

"I'm making an interface rune," he said softly. "To link into the main runes here." He shook his head, even that gesture part of the forging of the rune.

"From here, we are linked to the molten heart of Mars," he continued. "Everything around us is an amplifier, Kiera, but this room is both an interface and a Rune of Power for *Mars itself.*"

He took a moment to study the construct he'd been building, assessing its flow of magic compared to the structure around him. Then he made the final adjustment, slipping the entire artifice of magic up a dozen centimeters and slotting it into the runes above him.

There was a mental *click* and the universe changed.

The first visible sign of something changing was that the silver sphere exploded. One moment, a solid sphere of silver three meters across was suspended above their heads. The next it was gone, a flash of magic turning the sphere into untold billions of liquid silver drops.

Hundreds of tons of silver were liquefied in an instant, but there was no heat in the space. Just an overwhelming sense of power as the Olympus Amplifier woke up.

Damien was linked, bound to the power of the construct he'd just activated. His own interface runes were bound to his power instead of his flesh, resulting in a bond even more intimate than a Jump Mage's link with a starship.

A moment's focus brought up the "default view" of the simulacrum, the one Desmond the Third had usually shown him. The liquid silver coalesced into a scale model of the inner solar system, even the planets only a few centimeters across on a scale that filled a room several hundred meters across.

"Whoa."

This version of the simulacrum wasn't visually useful except...

"Kiera, there's supposed to be a computer program that links to this," he said aloud. "Can you—"

"Got it."

Concealed hologram projectors around the room lit up, and icons materialized across the simulacrum. Presumably, cameras and scanners were feeding the current state of the simulacrum to the computer, allowing it to match the icons to the right locations.

"Lightspeed delay on the computer system data but not the simulacrum itself," Damien said softly. He stood and walked over to a set of icons. A gesture changed the simulacrum, zooming it in on a task group of RMN cruisers patrolling the asteroid belt.

The holograms happily told him the names of both cruisers and all four destroyer escorts. Older ships, as expected. Most of the new ships in the Royal Martian Navy were with Jane Alexander.

"What can you do from here?" Kiera asked, fascinated.

"Anything," Damien said softly. "And the amplification factor...my god. I could bring that entire task group back to Mars with the effort it takes to teleport my cat down from my desk."

There was a long pause.

"Testing that would really screw with them, wouldn't it?" Kiera asked in a disappointed voice.

"Yes," Damien agreed. "But...I can see how Desmond the First managed to accelerate the terraforming of Mars. I'm not sure what *isn't* possible with this."

"My dad spent at least an hour every day in here," she said, her voice suddenly very quiet and sad. "He said even that hour meant he needed to spend at least twice that dealing with paperwork and similar crap to remind himself that he was mortal.

"It was too easy to forget that in here."

"I could see that." Damien pulled the simulacrum view back out from the squadron, watching as the computer system followed his control of the artifact. "But I also see why only a Rune Wright can use this. You need to be able to *see* the magic of the interface and build your own key.

"My key wouldn't work for you, and Desmond's wouldn't have worked for me. Much like a Rune of Power but even *more* unique."

He exhaled a long sigh and released the interface. It took the silver a few seconds longer to re-form into the ball than it had taken to explode out, but it was still impossibly fast. He could see tears in Kiera's eyes in the reflection from the sphere and stepped over to her.

"All of this and he died to a *fucking accident*," she snapped, the last two words a scream that echoed around the chamber. "He could have remade *worlds*, but he couldn't keep himself alive."

"That's where we all fall down in the end," Damien said softly. "For all the power we might wield, we are only human. We are mortal."

"*I don't want him to be!*"

Power flashed through the room, uncontrolled force as Kiera unthinkingly lashed out. The amplifier was basically immune to human tantrums. Damien was more vulnerable, but he'd been half-expecting this since he arrived.

"Neither do I," he told her calmly, his power wrapping around hers to safely contain her. He fed his own grief into that shield, keeping both of them—and everything *else* nearby—safe.

"What do you fucking know?" she snapped, a spike of force trying to fling him away. "I just lost *everybody*."

"I was a year younger than you are now," Damien said coldly, trying not to be angry at her. He doubted she'd ever read his formal file, and it wasn't like he *talked* about his family.

"A car accident. Drunk driver who'd hot-wired the security systems. My siblings were two and four, both in safety seats in the back of my parents' car. My parents were in front.

"I was at a boarding school for Mages. I didn't find out about the accident for seven hours, not that it mattered. My entire family died before emergency services were even on the scene."

The tsunami of power died down as multiple forms of grief warred across Kiera's face.

"I didn't know," she whispered.

"You weren't supposed to," he told her, stepping into her personal space and opening his arms. She curled into him like the lost child she was and started sobbing into his shoulder. "It hurts to talk about it, even now. But I know what you're feeling, Kiera, even more than just because I lost them both too.

"What you're feeling is *right*," he said softly. "You're not just *allowed* to feel like this; you *should*."

He chuckled.

"Throwing magic at people because of it is a *little* less okay," he reminded her, "but I understand where you are and what you're dealing with. Not everyone will. Some might if you weren't the Mage-Queen of Mars. Others will think that duty must subsume all."

"But duty *must* overcome," she replied through her tears. "We can't—"

"We *can* grieve," Damien interrupted her. "We *must* grieve. And then we put on the uniform, be it a business suit or a vac-suit, and we go to work. Because duty must overcome," he echoed back, "but that doesn't mean we aren't human behind the uniform."

"I just want my dad back," she whispered. "And Des and...Roger and Han and Xi and..."

She disintegrated into tears before she finished naming the Royal Guards who'd died on the shuttle.

"No power in the universe can undo death. Not even this amplifier, or there would be far fewer graves on the slopes of Olympus Mons. So we grieve, because we have to. And then what do we do?"

Kiera Alexander sniffed, dabbing at her eyes with a sleeve as she looked down at him.

"We put on the uniform and we go to work?" she echoed back at him.

"Exactly. Today, 'work' for you is school," he told her. "You may be the Mage-Queen of Mars now, which means your classroom days are unfortunately done, but your tutors are still scheduled to meet with you in an hour."

She snorted a pathetic attempt at a laugh, but her smile was genuine. Washed and weak, but genuine.

"Thank you."

"I am your Regent, Kiera," he reminded her. "That makes me your guardian, your sword, your shoulder to cry on. I'm not your father, but you've asked me to stand in his place. That means I'm here for you, both to listen and to tell you when you're wrong.

"And these tears?" He produced a pack of tissue from inside his jacket. He'd have to replace them—Kiera wasn't the only one grieving—but this was definitely a use for them.

"These tears aren't wrong. Lashing out with magic *is*, my Queen. Mostly because I'm the only person in the Mountain who can take it. Understand me?"

"Yes, Damien." She blew her nose and looked back up at the silver orb above them.

"Should I be leaving the amplifier to you for the next few years?" she asked.

"No," he told her after a few seconds' thought. "The next few *days*, perhaps, but you'll need to build your key. We can't be dependent on one person to defend Mars."

CHAPTER 11

"THE BIGGEST THING on our plate after the war is the Constitution," Gregory told Damien an hour later. "There are probably a few hundred million minor things I'll only remember to bring you up to speed on as we hit them, just because there's so much going on."

"Desmond was keeping me briefed on those negotiations, mostly because I was in the middle of the disaster that started it," Damien noted. He even managed *not* to look at his hands as he mentioned that, too.

The Belt Liberation Front had been nobodies, a spacegoing angry supremacist militia. An unknown player—they had two names for them, "Kay" and "Nemesis," but neither had proven useful in tracking them down—had provided the BLF with a stockpile of weapons enabling them to attack the neutral and mostly unarmed Council Station.

Saving the Station and its seventeen thousand inhabitants and guests had cost Damien his hands and two Runes of Power. Even after two years of living with the handicap, Damien wouldn't have made a different choice.

"That's good. Saves me some time," Gregory replied with a chuckle while carefully *not* looking at the Regent's hands.

"It's been two years, Malcolm," Damien said dryly. "I'm okay with people looking at my hands."

The Chancellor snorted.

"Fair, sorry. It's easy to be overly conscious of it."

"I'm fine with what happened, Malcolm, and the price I paid for it," Damien noted. "Today, we need to get work done. Hell, I'm not even sure where I'm supposed to be working out of. My old office, I guess, at least to start."

It wasn't much of a space, but it would give him somewhere to send people.

"You know where you're supposed to be working out of," Malcolm Gregory replied. "But nobody, especially me, is expecting you to take over Desmond's office right away."

Damien winced.

"No, that's going to take a bit," he admitted. "Day at a time, I guess. What's on today's agenda?"

"Well, first you and I have about an hour to go over things together," the Chancellor told him. "Then we have a meeting with the funeral organizer, which is going to be uncomfortable for everyone. Your lunch engagement is with Councilors Granger and Ayodele at noon and runs for ninety minutes."

"Alone?" Damien asked.

"You'll have the Guard," Gregory said drily. "I have my own meetings."

"I'll deal. I also need some time to sort out something for my old detail," Damien said as that reminded him. "Feels weird to abandon them for the Royal Guard so casually. I need to do *something* to recognize their service."

"Food, drinks, money, words," Gregory recited. "That's in increasing order of value, in my experience. *Tell* them you appreciate them and that's worth the most, but money and paid meals always go down smoothly as well."

"I'll talk to Romanov," Damien decided. "Do I have time for that?"

"You've got about an hour after lunch allocated for you getting familiar with the information and messaging systems of the Mountain and a first glance at your new inbox," the Chancellor told him. "I can tell you right now, you need an aide *and* a secretary."

"I *need* Christoffsen," the Regent said. "The Professor managed most of the political side for me for a year. He's on his way, I hope, though I have no idea when he'll make it."

He'd sent a message when he left Legatus, but only Legatus and Mars had Links so far. If there was an answer or an update, it was probably in that inbox Gregory had mentioned.

"I stand by the secretary suggestion," Gregory told him. "Unfortunately, Zheng Yaling was on the shuttle with Desmond or I'd suggest her."

Damien sighed.

"Have your people put together a list and I'll try and take a look in that window," he told the other man. "I'm guessing we're busy after that?"

"We're booked for the rest of the day with the Councilor from Alpha Centauri," Gregory agreed. "It's a friendly horse-trading session, but Newton isn't a loyalist the way Granger is. With a Constitution finally in play, he's more on our side than I would have expected back when he was kangaroo-trialing you, but we *are* trying to get the Core to come up with the cash for another sixty warships, six of them dreadnoughts."

The cherry the Protectorate was going to get out of formalizing the Council into an interstellar assembly was money. With the member worlds formally recognizing the Mountain's rights to certain taxes and tariffs, Mars would be able to fund the newly expanded Navy *without* requiring the special funding arrangements that supported the Protectorate's operations now.

"And we're having dinner with him, too?" Damien asked. "I assume we'll include Kiera in that?"

"I hadn't planned for it, but we can," Gregory allowed. "I'm...unsure how much to involve her in everything."

"As much as we practically can," the Regent replied. "Three years, Malcolm. In three years, I want to go retire on a beach on Sherwood and trust that the Mage-Queen I shepherded can run the Protectorate."

Because he certainly wasn't sure *he* could run the Protectorate for those three years!

"I'll make sure she's on the list and that her Guards know," Gregory agreed. "It's going to be a transition. None of it's going to be fun."

"No. But it's all necessary." Damien sighed. "Speaking of necessary, where are we on the investigation?"

He didn't specify *which* investigation. He didn't need to.

"All evidence is still pointing to accident, with some hints of potential lack of due diligence on the part of the maintenance staff," Gregory told him. He didn't even look at any notes. "We have the staff currently in protective custody."

"I want to be looped in," Damien said grimly. "We've already impaneled an inquiry, yes?"

"Yes, we were fortunate enough to have a special prosecutor from Tau Ceti arrive the day after the accident," the Chancellor told him. "Mylene Vemulakonda was supposed to be here for a conference on forensic data analysis and she's one of Tau Ceti's top cops. We snatched her up and put her in charge of the inquiry to make sure we had a fully neutral party heading it up."

"Then I want her to loop me in," Damien repeated. "I have my own suspicions about this, and I don't want to let it slide as an accident without going over every scrap of data."

"Damien, the shuttle's pieces were scattered across several hundred square kilometers," Gregory said. "There's only so much that can be done. No one shot at them and the security system doesn't show anyone unexpected in the maintenance bay. There's no sign of foul play. Accidents happen sometimes. Even if we hate it."

Damien forced a thin smile.

"I know," he conceded. "But I want full access. I wasn't on Mars any more than Vemulakonda was."

"But you do have a conflict of interest," the Chancellor pointed out. "So do I. I can't see any rational person seeing the loss of a friend and a King as worth the slight advancement we got out of his death, but it's something we have to consider. The inquiry must be handled by a neutral party."

"I don't want to handle the inquiry, Malcolm. I just want to be in the loop."

"I'll make sure she knows," Gregory said with a sigh. "Right now, though, we have a laundry list of mid-sized crises to go through.

"Shall we get started?"

CHAPTER 12

THE FUNERAL planning meeting was just as bad as Damien had feared—and he'd been expecting it to be bad. He managed to get through the as-clinical-as-possible discussions of ceremonies, memorials, seating priority and choreography without breaking down into tears.

He didn't make it much past that, dodging out of the meeting room and finding a corner to sob for a few moments in privacy. By the time he had managed to clear his eyes with an awkward combination of magic and tissue, three armored Royal Guard had formed a solid wall barring anyone from seeing their boss cry.

"Thank you," he told them once he'd regained some more composure. "I haven't caught your names yet; I apologize."

"We just swapped off while you were in the meeting, anyway," a familiar voice emerged from the center set of armor as Romanov turned around and opened his helmet. "My armor wasn't ready before that."

Damien was silent for a second, completely surprised by the presence of his old bodyguard. Unless he was mistaken, though...

"It still isn't, most likely," he told Romanov carefully, playing for mental balance and checking to see there was no one else around. "The runes have to be tailored to you as well, and there's only two people on the planet who can do that."

"Other than that, the armor is ready," Romanov conceded. "General Spader wanted me transferred over and taking command of your detail as quickly as possible."

Damien was silent for a moment, considering the three Guards escorting him.

"I owe the General a vote of thanks, then," he admitted. "I hadn't even thought of asking to have you transferred over, but it's reassuring to have you at my back, Romanov. I *did* ask all of your names, though."

"Christine Holgersen," the Guard on the left introduced herself.

"Misaki Suzuki," the other Mage added. "We're your Team Bravo."

"You have four teams," Romanov clarified. "Including me, nine Royal Guards assigned to your safety. I *know* how hard keeping you safe is, my Lord, but it'll take me time to find enough Guards to watch your back."

"Are there enough?" Damien demurred. "I assume you have my schedule as well."

"We're heading to a private dining room on level ninety-three," Romanov replied. "That's in the Family section of the Mountain and only about five minutes from here with your elevator priority."

"Well, then, we should get going, shouldn't we?" Damien asked. "Thank you, Denis. I appreciate you sticking with me."

"The rest of the detail is heading back to the Service and the Corps," Romanov told him. "They'll be fine."

"That's true enough," the Regent allowed as he followed the Guards into the elevator. "I'm supposed to pick a secretary shortly. Not sure how long that will take, but I'll need you to organize a thank-you dinner or something before they get scattered."

He snorted.

"And I'll need to find out who organizes payroll around here. A cash bonus is the least I can do after the time you lot spent dodging bullets with me."

"It was our job, my lord, but I'll set it up," Romanov promised. He checked a system on his arm. "There is one thing you need to know, off the record," he said quietly.

"Romanov?"

"General Spader runs Olympus Mons Defense Command. All of it," the new-fledged Royal Guard told him. "Including the people who maintain the Mage-King's shuttles. A message percolated its way up to her from Chief Sasithorn Wattana. She's the team head for that maintenance department."

"She's under house arrest, right? What does she want?" Damien asked. He didn't ask why it was relevant to him. He assumed Spader and Romanov had a reason.

"Someone to hear her out, Spader thinks," Romanov told him. "The inquiry interviewed her and now she's sitting in her quarters stewing. Spader was *here* when it happened. She's under the inquiry's eye and pretty limited in what she can do that comes anywhere near the investigation.

"You weren't here and you're the *Lord Regent*." The armored shoulders shrugged.

"I don't know if it's worth it, sir, but you're about the only person who could talk to Wattana without being at risk of damaging the investigation."

A chime noted that they were approaching the elevator stop and Damien nodded slowly.

"You have my schedule," he told the Guard. "I'll see her tonight. No matter what that does to my sleep allowance, all right?"

"I am yours to command, my Lord Regent."

The dining room Damien finally arrived at was guarded by a pair of Secret Service Agents. They didn't have the armor or magic of the Royal Guards, but the decorative-seeming carbines they held at port arms were insanely expensive overpowered weapons capable of penetrating exosuit combat armor.

If anyone *other* than the Secret Service paid the price tag that came with those guns, Damien had never heard of it. Both of the Councilors he was meeting would have their own bodyguards, but in the Mountain, only the Royal Guard and OMDC were allowed serious weaponry.

Romanov held up a hand and one of the Guard stepped through the door ahead of them. A moment later, the officer lowered his hand.

"Room is clear. The Councilors' bodyguards are in a waiting room next door." Romanov looked down at Damien. "Everything should be safe and we should be aware if anything goes wrong, but you have a panic button on your PC."

"I know," Damien told him. "This is overkill, you know that, right?"

"You're the Lord Regent of Mars," his bodyguard said levelly. "There is no overkill protecting you. It's our job."

He exhaled a long sigh.

"Then I guess I should go do mine. Thank you, Denis."

With a final nod to the Royal Guard and the Secret Service, Damien stepped into the space. It was larger than he expected for a meal for three people. It wasn't immense, but it was large enough that there could have been half a dozen tables.

Instead, there was one round table, covered in a plain black tablecloth and laid out for three people. Both of his guests were already waiting for him, rising to greet him with small formal bows.

It was the bows that really drove it home. They were signs of respect, yes...but they were also formalities that were *required*. The two men in the room were known to him and had been allies, if not exactly friends, in the past.

But today they were his guests and his *subordinates*. The Councilors, men who spoke for entire star systems, were there as guests and subjects greeting their temporary monarch.

Damien Montgomery the Hand had been ranked higher in the Protectorate's chain of authority, but his area of responsibility had been very different.

Damien Montgomery the Lord Regent was the man they were there to negotiate with, the ally they needed to shape the future of the Protectorate.

He swallowed down his nerves and returned the bows with a firm nod.

"Councilor Ayodele, Councilor Granger," he greeted them. "I'd shake your hands, but you both know how mine are."

"And how they were injured," Farai Ayodele responded. Ayodele was a shaven-headed black man from North Africa who spoke for Earth. He was also the Mage who'd saved Damien's life after he'd nearly killed himself saving Council Station.

"Believe me, my Lord Regent, none of us who were in that room that day will ever forget," Suresh Granger told him. The Councilor for Tau Ceti spoke with a faintly French-sounding accent. The old man's hair was more white than brown now, and his skin was only pale in comparison to Ayodele's pitch-black skin.

"I did my duty, nothing more," Damien told them. "Please, sit down. I have no idea what the menu is, but I have faith in the Mountain's culinary staff."

That got him chuckles from both men. Someone was paying attention, too, as two young men in traditional waiters' suits emerged from a side door with trays the moment they were seated.

"My understanding from Chancellor Gregory is that Councilor Ayodele requested this meeting," Damien told them. "I'm at your disposal for roughly the next ninety minutes, but I presume you realize that I won't commit to anything without taking it away to think about and probably discuss with Gregory and others.

"My first day on the job is not the time to sell planets for magic beans, I don't think."

"It's fortunate I left my magic beans in England, then," Ayodele replied. "Councilor Granger and I represent what's usually referred to as the Loyalist faction in the Council, the group that was working with His Majesty to fulfill his objectives, first for the Council and now for the Constitution.

"With His Majesty's death, we are at something of loose ends," the Councilor concluded. "To be frank, Lord Montgomery, we don't know what your objectives are. We only know you as the man who saved our lives.

"That gives you a large amount of influence in the Council, but you are also now Lord Regent, which makes you the voice for Desmond's successor. We need to know what you are planning and, well, who you are, before we decide if we will continue supporting you as we supported His Majesty."

Damien considered Ayodele's words as he took a mouthful of soup.

"I am not Desmond Michael Alexander," he finally said. "I am also not Kiera Michelle Alexander. I am Kiera's Regent, but I have every intention of consulting her on major decisions.

"I was Desmond's top troubleshooter and he was my mentor," he continued. "While I tend to presume I will support what he supported, that is not entirely guaranteed.

"Certainly, His Majesty and I shared a fundamental view of the purpose of the Protectorate of Mars: that the name defined what we are and what we must do," Damien told them. "What purpose is our Protectorate if we do not protect people? That above all else defines us."

He smiled and took another spoonful of soup.

"I don't know if that's what you're looking for, Councilor, but it's my starting point as it was Desmond's. Beyond that, well, I guess the point of this meal is for the three of us to get to know each other better. I'll admit, Councilor, that I've never been to Africa. Tell me about it."

Ayodele laughed.

"I can hear him in your words, do you know that?" he asked. "I suspected Desmond had picked carefully. I now begin to suspect he may also have picked well.

"As for Africa, Lord Regent, I am from Nigeria, specifically the city of Lagos. Do you know it?"

CHAPTER 13

BY THE TIME his first full day as Lord Regent came to a close, Damien was ready to do nothing but fall over. But he'd told Denis Romanov to arrange the meeting with the maintenance chief for Desmond Alexander's shuttle, so he returned to his office for the second time that day instead of heading to his apartment.

The space set aside for him in the Mountain had been permanently his, but it would have taken a visitor under ten seconds to guess that it wasn't an office the owner used much. There was a framed, hand-painted portrait of Admiral Grace McLaughlin of the Sherwood Interstellar Patrol on the wall, an addition Damien wasn't even sure of the *source* of, and that was it for personal decoration.

The portrait of his girlfriend had probably been intended as a surprise gift, and the answer to who had sent it was probably buried in his messages somewhere. He was reasonably sure it wasn't from Grace herself, which meant it was either from Desmond or the McLaughlin himself, the Governor of Sherwood and Grace's grandfather.

It struck him as Governor Miles McLaughlin's idea of an encouraging joke.

He'd been busy enough earlier in the day that he hadn't paid much attention to it. Now he took the time to study the painting and couldn't help but smile. The painter had caught her personality and force of will perfectly.

Plus, the frame was Sherwood oak, the vaguely viridian-tinged hardwood that was one of his homeworld's main exports. The portrait had almost certainly come from Sherwood itself and, unless he missed his guess, had been painted from life.

He was tired enough that he almost missed the admittance chime on his door. Even *one* day was enough to sell him on Gregory's insistence that he get a secretary.

"Enter," he ordered.

Romanov had passed the close detail command to someone else and shed the heavy red exosuit battle armor in favor of the simple burgundy uniform of the Royal Guard. The woman he was escorting was in a black RMMC undress uniform and looked more than a little confused and concerned.

"Chief Sasithorn Wattana?" Damien asked.

Something in his tone triggered a clearly instinctive salute from the Thai woman. He returned the salute, studying her as she recognized him.

"Yes, my lord," she finally responded. "I'm Chief Wattana, Royal Martian Marines, Olympus Mons Defense Command."

"I'm Damien Montgomery," he said gently and probably unnecessarily. "Lord Regent of Mars. You kept trying to reach General Spader, but with the inquiry ongoing, there's a limit to how involved the General can get without getting herself—and you—in further trouble."

He shrugged.

"*I*, on the other hand, wasn't here when the accident happened and don't answer to anybody except a grieving sixteen-year-old child. So, Chief Wattana, you get your audience somewhat higher up than you were expecting, but someone is listening. What were you so desperate to say?"

She looked like she was in shock. From the pliant way she reacted when Romanov pulled a seat over to her and helped her sit, she *was* in shock.

"I..." She swallowed and started again. "I wasn't sure what was going on," she admitted. "With the way the inquiry treated me, I was half-expecting to get marched in front of a firing squad."

"That won't happen," Damien said flatly. "There is a lot of anger and grief tied up in the inquiry over Desmond's death, but I will *not* permit the abrogation of due process or your rights. Do you understand me, Chief?"

"They seemed convinced the maintenance was negligent before even speaking to me," Wattana told him. "I don't feel like I'm getting much of a fair trial."

That was a problem and Damien grimaced.

"I'm not involved in the inquiry, Chief," he warned her. "I can't be, for reasons that should be obvious."

"I don't expect any special treatment, sir," she said. "I've been on the investigation team for this kind of inquiry, though with less...weight, I guess. But I've been cut off from everything, sir. That shuttle was one of my babies, I know it inside and out, and they won't even give me the sensor data."

That seemed wrong to Damien. Chief Wattana was being investigated, yes, but giving her a copy of the data to see what she could turn out made sense to him.

"Romanov?" he glanced over to his head bodyguard.

"Prosecutor Vemulakonda had the security clearances of everyone involved revoked," the Guard told him. "Security precaution as our experts went over the footage and sensor data."

"And those experts are coming back with it being an accident, Chief," Damien said gently.

"Vemulakonda's people are clearly thinking negligence," Wattana replied. "I swear to you, sir...my lord...my..."

"*Sir* works, Chief," Damien told her.

"Thank you, sir," she half-whispered. "But sir...we go over those shuttles with ultrasound and every other scanner before they're cleared to fly. I could almost rebuild it *exactly* the way it was twelve hours before the flight.

"You can say accident or negligence all you want, but I *know* that craft. *It shouldn't have failed.*"

"There were no missiles, no weapons fire, no unusual explosions, nothing, Chief," Damien told her. "No one shot down His Majesty's shuttle. Everything I am hearing and seeing says it was an accident."

"Sir...my lord...*he was my King.*"

Wattana's sad words hung in the room for a long time as Damien looked at her. She dropped her face into her hands, and he suspected the woman was crying.

He'd checked her file earlier. She hadn't been picked out of a hat to run the maintenance team for the Mage-King's own shuttle. Like she'd said, she'd done a tour as an accident investigator and had served as a shuttle tech through a number of combat engagements.

She was probably the best shuttle tech in the Royal Martian Marine Corps.

"He was mine, too," Damien reminded her. "Everyone's. He was also my friend, my mentor...and I don't believe in accidents that kill the Mage-King of Mars and the Crown Prince in one neat little explosion."

"It's possible...but we do *everything* to the royal shuttles," she told him. "Most of your once-in-a-century seemingly-random failures are material failures. The deep scans we did would have caught those.

"There is no way I can think of for the shuttle to have had that catastrophic a failure."

"The security on the shuttle is similarly complete," Romanov noted. "The rest of OMDC is just as sure they let nothing through as you are. Somewhere, something failed. Isn't an accident more likely?"

"I don't know," she confessed. "But so long as I don't have the data, I *can't* know...and I know the people doing the forensic analysis of the data and the shuttle, sir, by reputation if nothing else."

"And?" Damien asked.

"They're good. I'm better," she told him. "I don't want to undermine the inquiry, sir, but Desmond was my King. Please. I have to do *something.*"

"Romanov?" the Lord Regent asked calmly. "You were the Marine."

"I don't know the analysts Prosecutor Vemulakonda has acquired," Romanov said carefully, looking down at the seated woman. "I know *of* Chief Wattana, though. The Corps say she's one of the best shuttle techs in the business and a *better* crash analyst.

"You've crossed paths before, too. She handled shuttle turnaround during the capture of Darkport, my lord."

Damien snorted softly. Darkport had been a pirate station, deeply involved in the Protectorate's never-to-be-sufficiently-damned sex-slave trade, along with less-grotesque-if-still-evil-criminal commerce. He'd visited it, back before he became a Hand.

His visit hadn't been *directly* responsible for the asteroid market being bombarded by a rival criminal syndicate and half-stormed/half-rescued by a Marine landing force...but the indirect causality chain was very clear and very short.

"I can't interfere with the inquiry," he told Wattana. "Perhaps more accurately, I shouldn't. I might have been a long damn way away, but most people would qualify ending up as Lord Regent as *benefiting from Desmond's death.*"

Most people was not a list that included Damien Montgomery. He wasn't even sure where they got the idea that this kind of responsibility was a positive at all.

"But." He raised a finger. "I can do a lot of other things. Romanov—I don't have an aide or a secretary yet, and I think we want to keep this black-on-black, so I'm going to dump it on you."

"Black-on-black works best with as few people as necessary, my lord," the Guard agreed.

"Get her a copy of that data. I'll authorize whatever you need, but Chief Wattana gets a copy of every piece of data we have on the accident. But I want as few people to know she has it as possible, even once we've seen her conclusions.

"Does that work for you, Chief?"

"I'm not sure of the secrecy, sir, but I'll do whatever it takes to be *certain* of what happened," she told him.

"Welcome to black investigations under the direct authority of the Mountain," Damien told her. "They're exactly as much fun as they sound. Find me some answers, Chief. If it's an accident, I want both you and the inquiry to come back with that answer.

"If it's not an accident..." He trailed off as he realized that his own ability to run the investigation was going to be badly curtailed, then smiled thinly.

"If it's not an accident, well, I'm going to need to work out whether *I* can issue a Voice's Warrant or if I need Kiera to sign it. Because if it wasn't an accident, I'm going to tear Mars apart until I find the son of a bitch who killed my King."

CHAPTER 14

DAMIEN WAS halfway through his third interview of the morning with a prospective secretary when Kiera barged into his office. He almost welcomed the interruption—Gregory's staff had selected three spectacularly qualified individuals, and he had *no* idea how he was going to choose between them.

"Sorry, Damien," Kiera said, without sounding very apologetic. She glanced over at the woman he was interviewing. "Sorry, Moxi," she added.

"I need to talk to you," she continued to Damien.

"I have this thing called a calendar," he pointed out gently. "Which you have access to and says what I'm doing for the rest of the day in thirty-minute chunks."

And he suspected that even those thirty-minute chunks were Gregory's staff being nice to him for the first few weeks. He wasn't entirely sure how Desmond had handled all of this.

"I know, but you're seeing Moxi and I can always lean on Moxi," Kiera replied dismissively. "And I need you."

"I understand the concept of priorities, my lord," Moxi Waller said calmly. The tall blonde had turned in her chair to study Kiera. "And I'm familiar with Her Majesty's idea of decorum. If she needs your time, I can give way to that."

Damien managed to not glare at his young monarch, but it took effort. Selecting his new secretary was *important*, much as he was already hating the process.

"Thanks, Moxi," Kiera told the older woman. "It *is* important, I promise."

"I presumed," Waller said dryly, and Damien managed not to *smirk* as Kiera melted under the other woman's gaze. She clearly *knew* Kiera and had a pretty good sense of how much bullshit the new Queen was capable of.

That alone was a high recommendation, he figured, and he made his decision on the spot.

"Well, if nothing else, this little encounter has made my job a bit easier," he told Waller. "Thank you for your patience, Ms. Waller. I'll have Chancellor Gregory's people reach out to all of the candidates...but I suggest you start thinking about who you'll want for your support staff."

He offered his arm to the woman he'd just decided to hire.

"We'll see each other again shortly," he promised as they clasped forearms, the woman clearly registering that he couldn't shake hands traditionally. "But it is important that I remember who my monarch is."

Waller gave the Queen a small bow before stepping out of the room. Damien returned to his seat and regarded Kiera Alexander levelly.

"Did you *actually* need to see me or were you just stress-testing my secretary candidates?" he asked.

"Letting Moxi show off under stress crossed my mind when I saw what you were booked for," Kiera told him. "But I did need to see you. Two things, really."

"Okay," he allowed. "Which are?"

"First, I need you to tell Dr. Gunther that I am *not* having kids anytime this decade," she said flatly. "I *understand* why she's worried, but the genome can survive needing Aunt Jane to produce the next generation of Alexanders.

"Hell, it's not like they *need* me to find a partner for the process—*or even be alive.*"

Damien winced at Kiera's rant. He'd only had passing encounters with Dr. Ulrike Gunther, the head geneticist responsible for making sure the Mage-King's line remained Rune Wrights. The woman probably knew more about cloning and test tube babies than anyone else alive, but her focus was on the propagation of the Royal line and the maintenance of its power.

Such points as "the sixteen-year-old child should not be worrying about babies" could slip her mind. And Kiera wasn't wrong about the level of effort the Mage-Queen needed to put into the process. They could easily produce a perfect clone of her or Des—or even their father, for that matter—to be the next generation of Mage-King.

The Royal Family just preferred not to draw attention to the level of genetic engineering going on with the Alexanders, and having Kiera pop up with a baby that explicitly had no father would be a problem.

"I'll talk to Dr. Gunther," he promised. He wasn't sure he'd get out of that conversation without being harassed to get on producing little Rune Wrights himself, but that was a less problematic demand in many ways.

If one he wasn't likely to concede on anytime soon.

"We do need to keep the inheritance in mind," he warned her. "Admiral Alexander is almost a hundred. I don't think you're going to get more than that decade before you'll *need* to be knee-deep in toddlers."

Kiera snorted at the image and shook her head.

"I like kids," she pointed out. "I just would like to decide to have them on my own schedule, please and *fucking* thank you."

"I am *your* Lord Regent," Damien said, her relieved smile showing that she picked up his emphasis.

"What else did you need to see me about?"

"I need to be in the Constitution discussions," the Mage-Queen of Mars told her Lord Regent, her tone suddenly edging to formal and harsh. "That document will define the rest of my life and the life of every Alexander to come after me.

"I'll keep my mouth shut and run my comments and concerns through you if that'll keep people happy, but I need to be in the room where it happens."

Damien nodded, thinking for a moment as he turned his attention to his desk.

"Computer, load my calendar and show me the next meeting with Councilor Granger and the Constitution Committee," he ordered aloud. The voice commands were good, if not perfect...and they were faster than trying to poke around the data with his injured hands.

The appointment details filled the screen above his desk and he nodded.

"Gregory and I are meeting with the Committee aboard *Storm of Unrelenting Fury*," he told her. "It's a compromise gesture, not imposing the Royal presence onto Council Station itself. Of course, *Storm* has been Council Station's watchdog since the attack, so it's *only* a gesture."

"And that we're having the meeting on a battleship sends another message, doesn't it?" Kiera asked.

"Of course. I'm not sure your father did much without intention when dealing with the Council," Damien agreed. "I'm not up to that level of game yet, but Gregory is."

And thank God for that. Three days in and he was already feeling overwhelmed.

"So that's a day each way for, what, a four-hour meeting?" Kiera asked.

"I'm almost looking forward to the flight," Damien admitted. "Less meetings on a shuttle, even if I suspect I will forever be in catchup mode on my messages."

"Give Moxi a week," the young Queen said drily. "Her son was one of the 'let's please try and get the Royal Brats some regular-people friends' students inserted into our classes when I was younger."

Her description made Damien want to wince again, but she probably wasn't wrong. Moxi Waller had been a senior bureaucrat in the Mountain for thirty years, but she'd never been in the immediate circle around the Royal Family.

Damien hadn't even known her son had been in those courses.

"You know her, then?"

"Yeah, Brad and Des used to date way back when," she said with a wave of her hand. "She used to organize birthday parties for us all. That may not sound like much, but when you're trying to organize two royal brats who are seven years apart in age and a functionally randomly selected group of six age-mates for each of us, *while* serving as the admin assistant and organizer-in-chief for the head of Olympus Power..."

Damien half-whistled.

"Okay, I saw that role and assumed it ate her life," he admitted. "I'm impressed. I hired her based on her handling *you*, though."

The Queen laughed.

"Fair enough." She looked around the room. "If you're bringing in staff, you realize you need to get out of this office, yes? We *can* move Grace's picture."

"I know," he allowed. "But I know where I'm supposed to move to and I'm dreading it."

"Haven't been in there myself since." Kiera looked at Damien's calendar. "Look, your next appointment is with Malcolm and Jess Karling. She's...actually the current boss of Olympus Power, replaced Moxi's old boss a few years back.

"Check with Malcolm if you can leave him to handle that, but I think you and I need to go to Dad's office...*your* office...together."

Damien exhaled slowly, then nodded.

"Fair," he agreed. "I'll check with the Chancellor."

CHAPTER 15

THE OFFICE of the Mage-King of Mars was at the absolute top of the Royal Family's section of the construction inside Olympus Mons, which meant it was one of the highest excavations inside the mountain.

The air on the other side of the transparent transmuted titanium window wasn't even breathable. They were above the breathable atmosphere that magic and artifice had given Mars—and the window, Damien knew, was rated to withstand a direct hit from at least a small nuke.

It was his office now, he supposed, but he still half-expected to see Desmond standing by the window, waiting for him. The bookshelves were sparser now, at least, the books removed by the Mountain's librarians to be re-cataloged and stored with the rest of the Alexander Family's massive collection.

The empty bookshelves lined one wall. The opposite wall had a selection of small paintings, about twenty centimeters high, of every member of the Alexander Family from the first Desmond to Kiera herself.

The back wall, behind the desk from the perspective of the door and the floor-to-ceiling window, held four meter-wide seals: the mountain and red planet of the Protectorate, the rocket and red planet of the Royal Martian Navy, the crowned red planet of the Kingdom of Mars, and the rocket and rifle imposed on a red planet of the Royal Martian Marine Corps.

There were a *lot* of red circles on the wall, but the four emblems were well spaced on the stone wall and it managed to avoid being overwhelming.

The big wooden desk was plain. Built solidly from heavy wood and reinforced at key points with metal, it was that distinctive type of simplicity born from being built to last forever. Most of the furniture that belonged to the Alexanders shared the style.

Concealed technology in the desk and the walls would act as monitors, computers, hologram projectors...whatever Damien needed. His wrist-comp was already interfacing with the system using the codes Gregory had given him.

The chair was in the same vein as the desk, though the concealed technology in that case was ergonomic. The chair in his office was of the same plain-but-expensive style, and he knew it would automatically adjust to hold his back in the right position to avoid discomfort.

The magic in the room buzzed against his skin and now, standing there with the Royal Guard outside and only Kiera in the room with him, Damien leaned into his Sight, *looking* at just what Desmond and his predecessors had done to the room with magic.

The runes carved into the window had been done *spectacularly* well. Silver was traced through the titanium, but in thin-enough lines that the human eye couldn't pick it out. To Damien's Sight, the magic flowing through them glowed gently.

He'd need to recharge those runes with power every so often, just like the artificial gravity runes on a spaceship. So long as they were charged, an attacker would have better luck trying to blast through the starship-grade armor on either side of the "glass" than getting through the window itself.

The defensive runes on the windows were far from the only magic in the room. Much of it was linked to subtle runes hidden in corners or in the paintings. Anyone who decided to try and assassinate a Rune Wright in this room was in for a *world* of hurt.

Others were more informational, the magical equivalent of software alerts for people approaching the door. Even if the Mountain's security system was somehow overridden or disabled, magic would still warn Damien when someone approached the room.

He could see and understand *most* of the magic in the room. But there was still magic, in runes forged entirely of magic that hung in the air like the interface he'd forged with the Olympus Amplifier, that he didn't begin to understand.

"What is this?" he breathed, stepping up to a glowing orb of magic that hung in the air above the desk. He could trace the interlacing lines of magic, but this was magic that had never been anywhere near Martian Runic or any other codified language.

This was the power of the Rune Wrights at its most basic, reality bent to a will that didn't *need* language to impose itself on rules of reality. He could follow the traces, study its purpose, but he couldn't see its nature at a glance.

Any script in Martian Runic was simple enough that Damien could understand it instantly. This kind of magic was at the limits of his understanding...or potentially even beyond.

"I'm not sure," Kiera admitted. "It's a Rune Wright working—I can even tell you that it's my father's—but beyond that?"

"I think it's something to do with health," Damien finally concluded, stepping away as he blinked the brightness from his eyes. "I *think*—but I'd have to study it for hours to be certain—that it is pushing the bodies of everyone in the room to heal just a bit better.

"I might have to be more familiar with Mage-healing to be certain," he noted, "but I suspect that this helps explain the health and long lives of the Mage-Kings if this is within their power."

The spell was, at least theoretically, inside Damien's power. He could certainly *maintain* it without much difficulty, but he'd need to learn far more about magical medicine than he'd ever known to create something similar.

That was knowledge Desmond had had and Damien didn't. He sighed and shook his head.

"I've known I was a Rune Wright for six years and spent most of that learning," he told Kiera. "Things like this remind me that your father was over a century old and knew he was a Rune Wright from the moment he was old enough to wield power. Six years of study and experimentation pale against *nine decades*."

Kiera was studying the room with an odd look to her eyes.

"I barely managed to think of him as the Mage-King some days," she admitted. "Let alone as the godlike being of amazing power the people around him thought he was. He was just...Dad. Dad contained all of that, but it wasn't important when he dealt with me.

"The politics were more so." She sighed. "I miss him."

"You should," Damien told her. "We all should."

The funeral was still three days away—they were heading out to meet with the Council beforehand and would be back with about twelve hours to spare. He wasn't sure if that was going to help him lay his friends to rest or just drag everything back up again.

With a sigh, he stepped around the desk and lowered himself into the chair. It whirred softly, adjusting to his form...and then stabbed him.

"Ow!" Damien was on his feet, staring down at the chair looking for the needle or whatever had bitten him.

"Damien?" Kiera demanded.

"It poked me with something," he told her. "I'm guessing it was set to do it to anyone who required the chair to reset, but I don't know wh—"

A hologram of Desmond Michael Alexander the Third appeared in the middle of the room and Damien suddenly knew *exactly* what the chair had needed a DNA sample for.

The hologram was facing the desk, but from the way the image jerked, Alexander had just been pacing before the recording started.

"This recording is for Damien Montgomery," he said calmly. "Think of it as...worst-case-scenario insurance. For it to activate, Damien, you sat in my chair after the system was informed of my death. There're a few other criteria the program is using, but it's pretty brute-force.

"If you're seeing this, you're expected to be using my office and I am dead." Desmond shrugged. "Forgive me, Damien, for what I have done—and I pray to the holiest of holies that you are seeing this message as Kiera's Lord Regent and not as Mage-King of Mars in your own right."

Damien sat back down hard. That hadn't even been a *possibility*, had it? Except...he could see the logic. It took a Rune Wright to wield the Olympus Amplifier. A Rune Wright had to sit the throne of Olympus Mons.

If the entire Alexander family had somehow died, he would have been the only one left. Desmond had prepared for all contingencies, it seemed.

"These messages are refreshed every few months and they are a morbid and fascinating exercise," the hologram continued as if he hadn't just yanked the ground out from under Damien. "There is a similar note for Des, as you can imagine, but if you are seeing this...well, Des is also dead. I can't imagine what would bring us to that point, but these are for disaster planning, not optimistic scenarios."

"I am recording this message in early July of twenty-four sixty," the hologram told them. Damien glanced at Kiera, realizing that she probably wasn't taking it well.

She apparently knew how to summon the chair from the concealed closets in the walls and had taken a shaky-looking seat.

"As I record this, I am aware of my sister's victory at Legatus and your role in it. You have once again served my Protectorate beyond all rational hope, even if what you uncovered is a horror beyond all rational nightmares."

Alexander paused, marshaling his thoughts.

"I see a small number of key problems that I want to warn you about. There are more detailed files in my computers that the system should pass on to you, but I want this message to give you a baseline for the state of the nation.

"Unless the war has ended, in which case I'll probably record a new one of these messages, the Republic of Faith and Reason remains our greatest threat. We won a major battle but we have not won the war.

"You must be prepared to fight a long war still, my young friend," the dead man told them. "The Republic prepared for this for longer than even my worst nightmares projected. The expansion of the Navy must continue, which will be a fight for you.

"The Council will be your challenge now, and the Constitutional nego-tiations are only the tip of the iceberg. Until the Constitution is approved by the governments of the member worlds—*every* government, Damien—the individual funding agreements with the Core Worlds remain critical.

"But the Core World governments know that gives them power, and they will use it. Worse, I fear they are beginning to realize that the Constitution and the new tax structures that come with it will undermine that power. I believe I have already short-stopped the worst attempts to unbalance the new governing structure in their favor, but you must re-main vigilant for changes to the text that I did not approve.

"My death will cause chaos and confusion. I hope Gregory remains with you, as between the two of you, I think the Councilors and polit-icians who seek to take advantage of Kiera's inexperience and the inevit-able weakness of Mars will find themselves badly bruised.

"You are here because I believe you are the best man for the job, be-cause the job for the next few years is to hold the course, and I've met few men less likely to be deterred from their path," Desmond told Damien with a chuckle.

"We must rebuild and reform the Protectorate. I knew that even be-fore the Secession. A dozen stars could be treated as effectively independ-ent under the semi-formal auspices of the Charter, but a hundred stars and a hundred billion people? We need a structure, a guide...a nation. We're halfway there, but I hoped to pass a reformed humanity on to my children."

Desmond's smile quirked sadly.

"If you're seeing this, I failed. I hope that this message will go the way of the others like it I've recorded before. They're a useful way to focus my thoughts on what are the key components of my current affairs.

"If I have failed, then I leave my Protectorate in your hands, Damien Montgomery. I hope I leave my daughter in your hands," he added softly. "She is vulnerable. This will not be an easy time for her, but I fear the events that might lead to my true worst-case scenario.

"I leave you Mars and all mankind, my Hand. My Sword. My friend. I bind you to this duty as I could chain no other. I know you, Damien. I know you won't fail me."

Desmond shook his head.

"But I also know I pray that these messages never get played," he admitted. "But prayers or no, I record them, nonetheless. Tell my daughter that I love her. There is no world in which I ever said that enough."

The hologram fizzled out and Damien stared out the window at the weak sunlight streaming down over Olympus Mons.

He hadn't truly needed any *more* reminder of how critical a time this was for the Protectorate. A sniffle reminded him that he wasn't alone, and with a swallowed sigh, he rose again and crossed to Kiera to give her a hug.

"I'm with you," he told her gently. "Side to side and back to back. The Council is never going to know what hit them."

CHAPTER 16

MOST OF THE Royal Martian Navy's battleships had been designed in an enduring peace that no one had *really* expected to end. They'd been built to be warships first and foremost, intended to outfight their own mass of lesser warships, but they'd *also* been designed as flagships and mobile headquarters for the Protectorate government.

Damien was sure there'd been *more* thought put into the arrangement of *Storm of Unrelenting Fury*'s missile batteries than into the battleship's conferencing facilities—but the fact that the warship *had* a dedicated section that was basically a conference center said everything.

Storm's conference rooms had seen a heavy workout since she'd taken up her current position as the Council's watchdog. According to the notes Damien had received from the Mage-King, Desmond the Third had been out here at least twice a month.

Re-formalizing the relationship between a hundred stars wasn't an easy process. The woman responsible for the Protectorate's contribution bowed as Damien and Kiera left their individual shuttles.

This time, at least, it was absolutely necessary to bring the Mage-Queen to the Council. Damien wasn't sure they could justify it in the future, but today...today they needed to remind everyone that Kiera was in charge and Damien merely spoke for her.

And in case anyone forgot the first part of that, they'd travelled aboard the only *dreadnought* left in Sol. The meetings would take place aboard *Storm*, but *Masamune* loomed large in the back of everyone's thoughts.

"Welcome aboard *Storm of Unrelenting Fury*, Your Majesty, Your Highness."

"Please don't call me that," Damien told her with a chuckle. "I can live with 'my lord,' I had to learn that one, but, well...I look for someone else in response to 'Your Highness.'"

His humor faded. The *someone else* in question was Des now, and Des was gone.

"I understand, my lord," Martita Velasquez told him. "Your Majesty, my deepest condolences on the loss of your father," the tall Spanish woman continued as she turned to Kiera. "He and I were working closely together on this file."

"We're talking about the future of the Protectorate and the shape it will take," Kiera told the older woman. "There are few more important tasks on my plate or my father's. He selected you from the entirety of the Martian diplomatic service, Envoy Velasquez. I hope that together, we won't disappoint him."

Damien concealed a smile. Kiera might have been the "spare," but she'd had a lot of the same training as her brother—and a teenage girl's desire to manipulate her father and brother. She was *far* better at manipulating people than Damien himself.

"I hope not," Velasquez murmured. "I hope you have access to his files, though. While I'm tackling most of the negotiation, there are certain aspects of the Constitution that the Councilors only wanted to talk to him about."

"Which aspects?" Damien asked as the diplomat gestured for them to follow her. "My understanding is that the negotiations are mostly complete and we're approaching the point of creating full drafts of the document?"

"Soon, I hope," the diplomat demurred. "But the ground seems to shift a lot around here. I spend most of my time on Council Station, surrounded by Lictors."

She glanced back at the red-armored Royal Guards following in Damien and Kiera's wake.

"It's somewhat reassuring to be surrounded by *Martians* with guns."

"Let's get to a secure conference room before we follow that thought further," Damien suggested. If the woman responsible for the Protectorate's voice in the Constitutional Convention going on didn't feel she was safe on Council Station...

They might have a *real* problem.

One of the Royal Guards swept the room before the trio entered, and Damien hung back outside a moment to check in with Romanov.

"If Velasquez is feeling twitchy, I'm prepared to humor her," he murmured to the commander of his bodyguard. "Do me a favor?"

"I'm pretty sure that's included in my job description, yes," Romanov deadpanned. "What do you need?"

"Mingle with the Marines," Damien told him. "*Storm* has been on station for almost two years. We've been cycling the crew and the Marine contingent for leave and regular promotions, but the units have been here.

"I want your assessment of..." He tried to find the best way to phrase it. "Where their loyalties lie, Denis. I don't think things are that rough with the Council, but if our envoy is feeling threatened, I'm not prepared to write it off as nerves yet, either."

"And you want to know that the Marines on hand will back her up," the Guard commander summarized. "I can do that, my lord."

"I trust your judgment, Denis," Damien told his bodyguard. "But I need that assessment."

"First job is keeping you safe," Romanov reminded him. "Second job is helping you do yours. We'll poke around, but most of us are staying right here."

"You know your job better than I do," the Lord Regent said. "But I don't expect to be stormed by a company of rogue Marines today. I'm concerned about what those Marines might do—or *not* do—if the Council were to kidnap our envoy."

"Ears to the ground, sir," Romanov promised. "Now go do the diplomatting. Somebody's got to—and better you than me!"

The conversation hadn't been long enough to cause any noticeable delay. Kiera and Velasquez had just acquired drinks from an automated side bar and took seats at the small table set up for this meeting.

"My schedule says we're meeting with the Committee on Constitutional Balances in a little under two hours," Damien noted as he took a coffee for himself. It smelled acceptable, at least, if far from the standard he preferred.

"That's the group that generally refuses to talk to me," Velasquez said grimly. "The rules defining the balance of power between Mage-King and Council."

"Wait, you're our representative in the drafting of the Constitution, and you're not even talking about what powers rest with the Mage-King versus the legislatures?" Damien asked.

Not least, the last set of notes he had from Desmond suggested that the *Council*, in its current form, was going to be dissolved and replaced by a dual-house system of elected representatives.

"My focus has been on the financing structures and the inter-member relationships sections of the document," she admitted. "I have a staff of four, Lord Regent, and I'm negotiating with over a hundred Councilors. They've split things up into committees on various components to make it easier, but the truth is that this was an intentional division of labor between His Majesty and myself.

"The Council just doubled down by scheduling the meetings of the Committee on Constitutional Balances at times I could not attend initially, and then declaring that they'd only discuss their proposals with Desmond."

"Which means that we have no input on those proposals, only a veto," Damien concluded.

"Unfortunately, yes," she confirmed.

Damien glanced over at Kiera, who subtly nodded to him. She was thinking what he was thinking.

"That won't be acceptable going forward," he told her. "We'll expand your staff as rapidly as we can, but you need to be sitting in on those meetings. We'll start with the one this afternoon," he concluded with a smile.

"Of course, my lord," Velasquez allowed. "That may be convenient, as I understand today's meeting is mostly to bring the two of you up to speed on where the proposals for the legislature and judiciary currently are."

"Good." Damien paused thoughtfully. "Now, to your comment earlier. You implied that you don't feel safe on Council Station."

"The only armed personnel on the Station are Council Lictors," Velasquez told him. "That's fine in theory, but recently I swear I'm being followed...*by* Lictors. They're theoretically just cops, but..."

Damien exchanged a glance with Kiera.

The Lictors were more than cops, really. They were responsible for the security of the Council and Council Station. They'd staffed the defenses before those defenses had proven obsolete. While the attack had cost them lives and reputation alike, they were still granted a monopoly on weapons on the station by long tradition.

"I'll see what I can arrange," Damien promised. "Now is not the time to toss aside more of the Council's privileges." He took a sip of his coffee while he thought things through, then smiled.

"An *unarmed* Marine Corps Combat Mage, however, should more than suffice to guarantee your safety," he concluded. The rules said nothing about Mages, after all, and that was the usual compromise with the Royal Guard when the Mage-King had come aboard.

Not to mention that any Hand present on the station could dismantle the entire strength of the Lictors if given a few minutes' warning. The ban on armed Martian personnel was a gesture, not an actual guarantee of safety.

Not least right now, when a fifty-megaton battleship orbited barely fifty thousand kilometers from the station.

"That should help," Velasquez agreed. "Thank you, my lord, Your Majesty."

"More to the point of today, though, I'd like you to brief us on where we're at with the parts of the Constitution you have been handling," Damien told her. "What's most critical?"

"The most important part to all of this is the funding arrangement," she answered instantly. "We're pretty much locked in on that. All of the prior bilateral funding agreements will be phased out over five years and replaced by a new, Protectorate-wide income tax levied as a percentage of the system's gross domestic product.

"The Constitution leaves the exact final form of the tax up to the local government, but the expectation is..."

CHAPTER 17

"COUNCILOR GRANGER, it's good to see you again," Damien greeted the Tau Cetan Councilor again. Granger was the head of the Committee on Constitutional Balances. Eight other Councilors made up the rest of the Committee, each taking their seats around Granger on their side of a wide table.

On the other side, there was Kiera, Damien, Velasquez and two of Velasquez's staffers taking minutes.

"Lord Regent." Granger gestured at Velasquez. "I believe there has been a mistake here. The Envoy is not part of these particular discussions."

"That has now changed," Damien said calmly. "Envoy Velasquez has our full confidence and will now be attending *all* major Committee meetings of the Constitutional Convention."

"We can't arrange the entire Convention around the schedule of one woman," Granger objected.

"Then you will not have the Mountain's assent on the document you produce and will have to start again," Damien told the Councilor calmly. "This isn't negotiable, Suresh."

"We are not here to be bullied," another Councilor interjected. Damien recognized the redheaded woman with the pale skin as Gol Abbasi, the representative for the Eridani System—technically the Epsilon Eridani System, but the first word was usually dropped. Another Core System, which brought an interesting point to mind.

There were eleven Core World Systems represented in the Council. Eleven among one hundred Councilors—and four of those eleven Councilors were on this committee.

"It is not practical for Kiera Alexander or myself to be here as often as Desmond the Third was," Damien replied. "I must also remind you that we are *not* Desmond, either. While we will honor his agreements and discussions around the document we are attempting to draft, we are not necessarily going to approach that drafting the same way.

"Velasquez speaks for Mars. I can make that more formal, if you wish," he told them. Velasquez was a diplomat, not a Voice. She did not formally and metaphorically speak with the voice of the Mage-Queen in the same way someone carrying a Warrant or a Hand did.

"That will not be necessary," the Councilor for Sherwood interjected, Angus Neil turning a concerned glance on his compatriots. "We would rather this not become a combative process."

"Of course, of course," Granger conceded. "We are all familiar with each other here, I believe? Do you have any concerns you or Her Majesty wish raised before we begin, my lord?"

Damien smiled.

"I think we've already addressed my one request and concern," he told them. "Otherwise, perhaps you could explain just what the 'Committee on Constitutional Balances' is responsible for?"

"It is a meaningless mouthful, isn't it?" Granger conceded. "From our perspective, Lord Regent, this committee is probably doing the most important work involved in drafting the Constitution.

"That Desmond the Third was working directly with us showed that he shared that opinion," the Tau Ceti Councilor continued.

"This Committee is responsible for laying out the proposals of the division of power between the legislative, executive and judicial branches of the government of the reformed Protectorate—and for establishing the framework for the legislative and judicial branches."

Granger's smile seemed unusually fake to Damien at that.

"We are forced to presume that the structure of the *executive* branch, the Mage-King—Mage-Queen now—and their Hands and Voices, will not change."

"I see," Damien noted noncommittally. That lined up with the notes he had from Desmond, though those notes had also included several complete and agreed-on proposals to cover most of that structure.

"We are currently drafting the final proposals on judicial appointment as well as the structure of the legislature," Angus Neil interjected. "There are several competing discussions around that point, which we hope to have resolved before we present a proposal for Her Majesty's review and assent."

Damien had to almost physically bite his tongue to stay silent. Something wasn't right here.

The legislative structure *had* been approved by Desmond. Damien had seen the summary files himself. It was *possible* that he'd misread what Desmond had sent him or misjudged where they were in the process.

So, he remained silent and noncommittal.

"The current proposals around the legislature revolve around a similar structure to the current council, with senior representatives appointed by the planetary governors and a body of junior legislators elected by the general populace," Granger told Damien.

"We're still sorting out the exact structure of power between the senior and junior legislators, of course, which ties into the process around judicial appointments.

"To date, the interstellar judiciary has been very much the province of the Mage-King with no restriction or limitation," he noted. "It behooves us to recognize that the Mage-Queen's predecessors have leaned heavily on the planetary judiciaries as a source of both candidates and recommendations and that this informal advice-and-appointment structure has *worked* for over two hundred years.

"Most of the proposals we are currently going through call for the Mage-Queen to retain her current position of choosing the Star Court judges and the Supreme Court judges. It seems reasonable, however, for the new legislature to have approval of the justices who will speak to interstellar law. Currently, we are leaning towards that being primarily or entirely in the hands of the elected junior representatives."

Damien was still remaining silent. All of that was mostly in line with what he knew Desmond had agreed to, but the proposal *Desmond* had agreed to put the power of assent in the hands of the senior legislature—a legislature that most definitely did *not* have anyone appointed by their Governors but also a legislature that was assigned one representative per planet as a shield against the Core Worlds' greater population.

One of Desmond's key concerns had been making sure that the MidWorlds and Fringe didn't get squeezed out by the fact that half the Protectorate's population was in the Core Worlds. The structure Granger was describing failed to meet that standard...and the proposals Damien thought his King had agreed to *did.*

As Granger passed the floor to the Councilor for Eridani to start talking about the power of the purse, the Lord Regent realized he needed to go over Desmond's notes in detail. It was *possible* he'd missed something and the proposals hadn't been agreed to.

But it was looking like the Council was using Desmond's death to try to reset entire swathes of the negotiations.

CHAPTER 18

"OKAY, DAMIEN, spill," Kiera ordered once they were back in the secured conference center. "Your poker face isn't bad, but you learned it from my father. I *know* that mask."

Damien bowed his head to her as he crossed to the autobar. "Give me a moment," he asked.

The machine poured a coffee. Damien then studied the side bar for several moments before using magic to lift the bottles and add a hefty dollop of first cream and then rum to the drink. He wouldn't do that to *good* coffee, but while the Navy's coffee was *drinkable*, it wasn't *good* by the standards of the coffee he preferred.

Normally, he at least pretended to hold a cup in his hand, using magic to provide the grip his barely moving digits couldn't. At that moment, he didn't bother. He used magic to lift the cup to his lips, the focus of using power helping to clear his mind and stabilize his thoughts.

"My lord?" Velasquez finally asked.

"You weren't being briefed on Desmond's negotiations with that Committee," Damien replied after another sip of the doctored coffee. "I'm not certain why he agreed to that, but that was his choice to make.

"Fascinatingly, I *was* being briefed," he continued. "Or, at least, copied on the updates he was giving Des. My own absence from Mars meant my true briefings were few and far between, so I'm restricted to recordings and diary entries."

"But you knew what he was talking with them about?" the envoy asked.

"Exactly. I *thought* I knew what proposals had been agreed to between him and the Committee on a number of items." He shook his head. "Most notably, I am *certain* that a proposal had been written by the Committee and both reviewed and approved by Desmond the Third with regards to the structure of the new legislature."

"Oh." Velasquez sounded more *tired* than surprised.

"I'm guessing one that doesn't involve the Governors continuing to handpick their reps," Kiera said calmly. "That was one of the things Dad wanted to throw in the trash can of history. We can't force the *Governors* to stand for election, but we can tell them they need to send *us* elected officials."

"The only thing that was really left for discussion around the structure of the legislature was who held final responsibility for the new agency we'd have to build to support the elections," Damien told her.

"The proposal I saw was for a bicameral legislature: a Martian Parliament of one thousand elected Members, allocated at a minimum of one per planet, and then one per hundred million citizens after that, combined with a Senate of one Senator per system."

He grimaced. He was remembering it better as he thought about it, and the more he thought about it, the more he was certain Desmond had signed off on that proposal as final.

"Election terms—two years and ten years—and term limits had been included, the judicial appointment review was with the Senate and the power of purse was with the Parliament.

"I don't know if it's a perfect system, but its one that makes sense and tries to balance the Core Worlds against the rest of the Protectorate, as well as balancing an *entirely* elected legislature against the power of the Mage-Queen of Mars."

"And that balance is necessary," the Mage-Queen in question stated firmly. "We cannot continue to rely on our ability to produce moral and upstanding monarchs worthy of the trust the Charter placed in them."

"The intent wasn't for them to be worthy of that trust," Damien pointed out. "The intent was for Desmond the First to get the rest of humanity to sit down and listen to him and his descendants.

"We're past that point now, and the system needs some refining to avoid it becoming the unilateral dictatorship that Desmond the First ran it as. His was a mostly benevolent dictatorship, but let's not be blind to the fact that your father and grandfather both softened the structure of power they inherited.

"The Charter sets up a constitutional monarchy, yes, but inside those limits the Mage-Kings were absolute rulers," he concluded. "Everything else was by *choice*. And your father *chose* to formalize that."

"We have to," she repeated. "What purpose is our Protectorate if we do not protect people? Even from ourselves."

"Thank you," he murmured. "We need to go back over all of Desmond's notes and briefings. I think we can safely assume that anything where Velasquez has been actively involved won't have changed, but I think the Committees might be assuming that our side will have lost continuity where Desmond was in charge."

"That raises some very uncomfortable questions, my lord, Your Majesty," Velasquez said quietly. "If they're taking advantage of his death...did they present proposals they knew he'd accept that they didn't expect to have to honor?"

The room was silent for a long time, and Damien took several long gulps of his rum and coffee before using magic to set the cup aside.

"You think they knew he was going to die?" he asked.

"It doesn't make sense, though," she replied. "It was an accident, yes? I haven't heard anything else!"

"Neither have I, yet," Damien allowed. "But this isn't helping the paranoid itch between my shoulder blades. I want to say that I can trust Granger, that I can trust Neil or Ayodele or the others. At the least, I want to say I can trust the damn *Loyalists* not to have murdered the King they aimed to support."

"If they were hoping to take advantage of the confusion of my father's death, they must fail," Kiera said grimly. "Were we supposed to see any proposals today?"

"A couple of freshly finalized ones are supposed to be presented this evening," Velasquez told her. "I sat on the committees for them. I mean, we're talking tariff rights and the role of the Hands in interstellar disputes. Most of this was pretty cut and dried from the beginning—the Council wanted to transfer certain powers from the Hands to the courts, and His Majesty was never going to let that happen."

Damien snorted.

"We're writing a Constitution to limit the powers of the monarchy, but that doesn't mean we're giving away the entire Mountain," he agreed. "We'll take those proposals back to Mars with us for Kiera and me to review with our staff in support.

"That seems like a good excuse for us not to do anything substantive just yet, but we need to go over *everything*. Envoy? I need you to get me the current drafts of every proposal at every committee."

"I can do that, but...that's a lot of paper to go through," Velasquez told him.

"An old friend is due back in Sol in the next couple of days," Damien replied. "He was going to be bored without reading material."

Christoffsen might resign when he saw his opening project, but he'd also recognize that Damien *needed* him.

"I'll see what I can do, but if people are playing games, that may draw more ire than we're expecting," she warned.

"We'll deal with it," Damien told her grimly. "You'll return to Council with Combat Mages from *Storm*'s Marine contingent and a panic buzzer. It's considered rude to fire boarding torpedoes into friendly space stations, but I'll rank it below kidnapping our ambassador.

"Am I clear?"

"You are, my lord," Velasquez replied, with a faintly stunned look he'd grown familiar with.

"This is *our* fight, Envoy, but you are the scout on the front lines," he warned her. "That makes you critical and vulnerable, but you have my and Her Majesty's backing."

"One hundred percent," Kiera agreed, backing him without hesitation. He hadn't really worried about that.

"I understand, my lord, Your Majesty," Velasquez promised after a hard swallow. "What purpose is *Her* protectorate if we don't protect people?"

He smiled. It seemed that Martita Velasquez understood the driving principles of the Protectorate of Mars.

"Romanov," Damien greeted his bodyguard as the Royal Guard fell in around the Mage-Queen and her Regent.

"My lord," the Guard murmured through his red armor. "I've had my people and the Secret Service exterior detail making friends. The Marines here might be even twitchier than the Envoy. They *don't* like the Lictors, and it sounds like there's been some ugly arguments between *Storm*'s crew and the senior Lictors. Not Constable Lucas, she still has her head screwed on straight, but her subordinates are causing friction."

"And much as the Marines and the Navy play up their little feud, the Marines know their side in *that* kind of fight," Damien whispered back.

"Exactly, my lord. I'm not saying that *Storm*'s crew is one bad day from opening fire on Council Station...but I *am* saying that no one here is going to cry crocodile tears if you sent the Marines in to *convince* some uncooperative Councilors to write the Constitution your way."

"We can't do that," Kiera said softly from Damien's other side. "That's nearly the *opposite* of what we want to be doing here. Are we going to have a problem?"

"I don't think so," the Guard replied. "No one's going to go off without orders; they're just hoping for those extremely unlikely orders more than is really appropriate."

Damien snorted.

"I need you to coordinate with the Marine CO," he told Romanov. "Envoy Velasquez needs a security detail. Our agreements say we don't send armed personnel aboard the station, so I want at least two Combat Mages detached to her personal security."

That would be a third of the Combat Mages available to the Colonel in charge of *Storm*'s short battalion of Marines. As a Hand, Damien would have expected pushback.

As Lord Regent, he suspected he'd only get prompt obedience.

"They're also to give her an emergency locator beacon to link into her wrist-comp," he continued. "Panic buzzer. If she triggers, the Marines go get her, Council Station neutrality be damned."

Damien smiled thinly.

"We'll have those orders for the Colonel in writing before we leave."

"She'll want them in writing," Romanov agreed. "Especially the ones authorizing her to storm Council Station."

"Even in my worst-case scenarios, I don't expect that to be needed," Damien admitted. "But if it is, there can be no hesitation, no question of authority."

Romanov glanced over at Kiera.

"You two are the final word," he noted. "I'll pass the word, but those written orders would be handy."

"She'll get them."

CHAPTER 19

MASAMUNE **WAS** settling into Mars orbit when Damien received a message from Moxi Waller. He opened it on his wrist-comp as the two of them boarded the shuttle back to Olympus Mons, surrounded by red-armored bodyguards.

The largest item on it was his schedule for the next two days, broken out into half-hour segments. Even his meals were specified as to timing and who he was having them with.

The Lord Regent of Mars did not have casual lunches as a rule. Damien hoped that would change in time, once they had everything running more smoothly, but he recognized that the transition period demanded that he meet a *lot* of people.

The final piece of the message was probably the most important:

Chief Sasithorn Wattana has requested to speak with you. Since her schedule is wide open due to house arrest, I believe I can squeeze her in immediately after you land. Should I include Her Majesty in this meeting?

Damien glanced over at Kiera. Part of him did want to include her. She deserved to know about his suspicions and investigations into her father and brother's deaths, but he wasn't sure how well she'd take it.

It was hard enough for *him.*

On the other hand...

He took his seat on the shuttle almost absently, the Guard stowing the bag he couldn't easily carry himself anymore.

"Kiera," he called her attention to him. "We need to talk about something."

"We usually do, Damien," she replied. "What did Moxi have to say?"

"You're not supposed to read other people's mail over their shoulders," he told her. "Or at least you shouldn't *admit* it."

"I wouldn't if it wasn't *your* email, my Lord Regent," Kiera said. There was humor to her tone, but also sadness and a sharp edge.

And a point that Damien had to concede.

"*Touché.*" He carefully tapped a command on one of the overlarge buttons.

"Miz Waller, set up the appointment with Chief Wattana," he dictated. "We will include Kiera in the meeting, I'll brief her on what we're guessing so far. Thank you. End recording, send."

The computer on his arm chirped confirmation at him, and he turned his attention back to Kiera as the shuttle's thrusters gently pushed him back into his seat.

The shuttle was a Marine Corps assault shuttle. It would have to be accelerating at a dozen gravities before it would do more than gently push him unless the cruiser's Mages had failed to keep its magical gravity runes up to date.

"What's going on, Damien?" Kiera asked after glancing around the shuttle to make sure they were alone.

There were Royal Guards in the room, but Damien trusted Denis Romanov explicitly and completely—which meant he *also* trusted the Guards Romanov selected to guard him and the other man's opinion of the *rest* of the Guard.

"Do you know Chief Wattana?" he asked.

"The name sounds familiar, but I don't recognize them, no," Kiera admitted.

"She's the RMMC NCO who was in charge of maintaining your father's shuttles," Damien explained. "The inquiry has her under house arrest, since Vemulakonda seems to have decided we're looking at either random chance or negligence."

"If someone's lack of care killed—"

"Peace, Kiera," he cut her off. "Even the inquiry seems to be moving towards random chance. But we have the entirety of the maintenance staff who touched that shuttle in temporary house arrest—protective custody, really.

"But they also had their clearances revoked, so Wattana couldn't access the scans and flight data we have of Desmond's last flight."

"So? That seems right to me," Kiera admitted.

"And most people," Damien agreed. "But I'm told by people I trust that Sasithorn Wattana is one of the, if not *the*, best shuttle techs in the Marine Corps and has worked on forensic crash analysis before.

"And she knows that shuttle inside and out. She had every reason to try to prove it wasn't her negligence, so I agree she shouldn't have been part of the inquiry...but I still feel like we ignored an asset by not having her even *look* at the data."

"So, you gave it to her," his Queen said levelly.

"I gave it to her," he confirmed. "Black on black, Kiera. Even Waller only knows that I told her to squeeze Wattana in if she asked for a meeting. Romanov"—he gestured toward the Marine with his chin— "is the only other person fully read in on what I'm doing here."

"We already have an investigation into my father's death," Kiera said, and her tone was cold and slow now. "Are you *undermining* that? Because I need those damn answers, Damien."

"You do," he agreed. "So do I. But Kiera...I don't believe in accidents that kill the Mage-King of Mars and his heir. It's too neat."

"You think someone killed my family."

Her tone was still cold, but it wasn't directed at him now.

"Yes," he told her. "I *suspect* we're looking at the same group that manipulated us into conflict with the Keepers and then wiped out the Keepers...and there's data to suggest that they were behind the BLF's attack on Council Station."

"That's a lot to hang on one asshole," Kiera told him.

"It is. I think we're looking at a rogue Keeper, a man named Winton. He tried to recruit me to *something* on Tau Ceti. At the time, I thought it was the Keepers. In hindsight, I have to wonder."

"And he's still breathing?"

"He had a hostage, a young woman I'd pulled into matters at the time without realizing the danger." Damien shrugged. "She's a Lieutenant in the Navy now, so it worked out for her, but at the time, I owed her protection.

"There's another individual we encountered named either Kay or Nemesis. I believe the two are working together and I believe they acted against your father and brother. They wanted to put you on the throne because you are young and, I'm guessing, they believe you are weak."

"Or they wanted you on the throne," Kiera suggested. "How many people knew what was in my father's will?"

"I don't know," Damien admitted. "But it can't be many. Even *Gregory* didn't know for sure."

"This all seems very vague and conspiracy theory-esque, Damien. I..." She sighed. "I almost want to think someone killed my family. Then I could have revenge, closure, some logic to the whole affair.

"But it might have just been an accident, a fluke failure."

"It might have been," he agreed. "And if both Wattana and Vemulakonda's inquiry come back with that as the answer, I'll even try to believe it.

"But Wattana asked for a meeting, and I suspect that means she found something."

Kiera looked thoughtful for a few long seconds, then looked at him grimly.

"I want in that meeting, Damien," she told him.

"Good. That's why I was filling you in."

CHAPTER 20

DAMIEN STILL wasn't comfortable taking over Desmond's office, but he was forcing himself to use it anyway. He and Kiera were waiting behind the big desk when an armored Royal Guard escorted Chief Wattana in.

The door closed behind them and Romanov removed his helmet.

"Chief Wattana, my lord, Your Majesty," he said calmly as he took up a statue-like position near the door.

Wattana looked back at him in confusion and Damien chuckled.

"Guard-Lieutenant Romanov has been my bodyguard since he was a mere Mage-Lieutenant in the Royal Martian Marine Corps, Chief. There's a reason he was the one who delivered the data to you. He is one of the half-dozen people I trust most in the Sol System.

"Her Majesty, of course, has one of the closest and immediate interests in this as well. The four of us in this room are the only people who know I gave you that data."

Wattana sighed, taking a seat in the chair in front of the desk.

"Okay. I, um..." She paused.

"Take your time, Chief; I did ambush you with the Mage-Queen of Mars," Damien told her.

"Chief Wattana, if you've learned anything about why my father died, I need to know," Kiera added. "Not just for Mars. For myself."

"Right." Wattana nodded. "May I show you something? I presume you've all seen the footage of the flight?"

"Kiera?" Damien asked, glancing at the Queen. *He'd* watched it, but he wasn't sure if the young woman went in for that kind of self-flagellation.

"I have," she confirmed.

"All right. My lord?"

"Computer, give Chief Wattana access to the holodisplays," Damien ordered aloud.

A chirp on Wattana's wrist-comp confirmed the temporary transfer. A moment later, a familiar set of scan data appeared in the middle of the room. The representation of the shuttle itself was a digital construct, but the data codes around it were from the scanners of the battleship *Gauntlet of Honor.*

"This is starting about fifteen seconds before the explosion," Wattana told them, her voice firming as she started what he suspected was a prepared presentation. "I'll run it in real time first."

Damien had seen—and flown himself—a lot of surface-to-orbit transfer flights. Every change in aspect, every maneuver, was entirely familiar. The shuttle started the clip in ballistic flight, moving on inertia from its earlier maneuvers as it headed toward the research station.

The flip-and-burn to shed velocity and rendezvous with the station was textbook. Even with an antimatter rocket to play with and magic reducing the impact of thrust on the passengers, the shuttle was still bound by the laws of physics.

Everything was textbook...right up to the moment the shuttle exploded. Damien was intimately acquainted with the stark white explosion of matter-antimatter annihilation. The data froze and he checked in on Kiera.

She might have seen it before, but that didn't seem to have reduced the impact. It was a very clinical way to watch your family—and seventeen other people—die.

"Is there something we should be looking for?" Damien asked as the recording reset. "It all looks, well, standard."

"It does, doesn't it?" Wattana agreed. "Now I'm going to play from minus point five seconds at one-hundredth speed. Watch carefully."

This time, it started in the middle of the flip and burn. Everything continued to go perfectly normally except...

"Wait, what was that vector change?" Damien asked.

"What are you talking about?" Kiera demanded.

"You were a pilot, right, my lord?" Wattana replied. "*And* you're looking for something weird. *And* we're going through it frame by frame, metaphorically. What did you see?"

"I'm not sure," he admitted. "Something jarred the shuttle?"

The scan data reset to a specific moment.

"*Jarred* isn't necessarily the word I'd use," Wattana told him, then glanced at Kiera. "But yes. Point one one seconds before the explosions, we have this vector change."

The velocity lines around the image of the shuttle adjusted as the image played out.

"It wouldn't have been noticeable aboard the ship, not with the gravity runes. Plus, well, human reaction times aren't actually fast enough to register that kind of bump in one hundred and seven milliseconds," she continued.

"The shuttle was accelerating and had a vector change," Kiera said. "What's the problem?"

Wattana tapped a few commands and the model of the shuttle expanded to a roughly meter-across image.

"This is a modified and upgraded Model Twenty-Four-Forty-Five Assault Shuttle. The model is mass-produced in Tau Ceti and Sol, primarily for the RMMC. Seventy-two Twenty-Four-Forty-Five-Zulu Shuttles have been built as speciality VIP transports, almost entirely limited to the Solar System.

"Sixteen of the Zulus were purchased by the Mountain and underwent a second layer of upgrades and augmentations to bring them up to the standard required to act as Mars One. All sixteen, including the one His Majesty and His Highness were in, have been kept updated to a functionally identical standard."

Green arrows appeared all around the spacecraft.

"With all of those upgrades, these are the vectors on which one of the

Royal shuttles can accelerate."

There were a lot of them. The primary engines could be adjusted to fire at up to sixty degrees away from the center line, and there were two sets of maneuvering thrusters at the front of the ship.

"And *this* is the line that vector change was along."

A red line cut through the diagram and it was suddenly *very* clear.

"What are we looking at, Chief?" Kiera asked.

"A sudden and unexpected velocity change like this is indicative of some kind of traumatic event. If the velocity change was higher, I'd be looking for debris or a weapon. At this level, I'm almost tempted to write it off as a data artifact."

"Except that this was the Mage-King's shuttle a tenth of a second before it exploded," Damien said dryly. "So, we're looking at..."

"Shaped-charge bomb. Not on the actual antimatter fuel tanks itself—there's no *way* someone could have got a bomb powerful enough to penetrate *that* armor—but somewhere on the fuel lines. The shielding is still tough there, we need specialty tools to cut it, but you could potentially have sneaked something aboard to damage it.

"I don't see *how*, but it's the closest match I can think of."

The room was silent as Damien stared at the red vector line.

"Is there any possible other explanation?" he asked gently.

"If one of the conduits detached without engaging the safety measures," Wattana told him instantly. "There are *seventeen* layers of safety against that, my lord. You need an instantaneous catastrophic severing of the fuel line within one point two meters of the fuel tank. Any farther along the lines and even that catastrophic breach won't have a reaction that reaches the main tank before the final safeties engage.

"The shuttle would be a wreck, but the passengers and crew would be protected. This was very deliberately done, sir, by someone who knew these shuttles and who knew our forensic analysis procedures."

"And knew what they could get through the Mountain's security," Damien concluded. "Which raises questions of *how* they got whatever it was onto the shuttle. My understanding is that not only do we not have any unauthorized people in the shuttle bay after the maintenance crew went through six hours before the flight, but the security systems don't show *anyone* in there."

"I expected as much, my lord, but take a look at this."

The shuttle disappeared, replaced by an image of a collection of piping and conduits. Years of study and practice didn't fade much, and Damien could recognize them all.

"We record *everything* when we do that maintenance check and review," Wattana told them. "This is our most likely culprit. There is a thirty-six-centimeter zone between the armoring and safeties around the fuel tank and the point where the fuel-tank safeties will engage in time if the conduit safeties have a catastrophic failure.

"It...barely even qualifies as a weak point, my lord," she noted. "The conduit safeties themselves are five layers deep. This is *antimatter.*"

"But it's the weakest point on the shuttle where a single bomb could take out the entire craft," Damien concluded.

"Yes. And it lines up with our vector change," Wattana agreed. "But this is that section when we did that maintenance check. There's nothing out of the ordinary here. *Nothing.* I can give you deep ultrasound checks of the materials present, too. We took no chances with His Majesty's ship."

"So, in a six-hour period when the security systems say no one entered or left the shuttle, someone *did* enter the shuttle and left behind some kind of charge or device that didn't trigger the Guard security systems but was sufficient to sever those conduits," Damien said. "It's a stretch, Chief."

"I..." She inhaled and nodded. "I agree. I don't want to question the Mountain's security, but...my lord, that shuttle shouldn't have blown up."

"And the Mountain's security is not impenetrable," Romanov reminded them from the door. "The Keepers undermined it repeatedly, enabled by having at least two Hands in their ranks that we know of."

The room was silent and Damien stared at the image of the clean and undamaged conduit that had probably killed his mentor.

"Computer," he said slowly. "show me all uses of one-time override codes generated from Charlotte Ndosi's or Lawrence Octavian's Hand."

The platinum icon sitting on his chest was identical to the old gold icon in one way: it contained a tiny computer that could interface with and override almost any electronic device in the Protectorate. It could also generate a list of one-use codes that could achieve the same effect without needing the Hand present.

Hand Charlotte Ndosi had been a Keeper. She'd been the one leading the defense when Damien had raided the Keeper's archives—and the nuke that had destroyed the archives had been a deadman switch tied to her vitals.

Hand Lawrence Octavian had also been a Keeper, though Damien now suspected the man had been deeply involved in the attempt to *destroy* the Keepers. He'd died at Damien's hands well before Ndosi had killed herself.

And from the list that appeared in the air in front of him, both of their one-time codes had been used against the Mountain a *lot*. A cold sensation settled into his chest.

"Computer, filter to uses after Charlotte Ndosi's death," he instructed. There were still almost two dozen. Two were the night before the Mage-King's death.

"If an override code was used on our security systems, that data is probably gone forever," he finally said grimly. "But we'll need to take a look."

"Do we loop in the inquiry?" Kiera asked. "It seems...right."

"We need to know more, I think," Damien told her. "If you tell me to, I will, but I want to keep this black for a while longer. Bring in an investigator, someone we can trust beyond reason."

"Someone killed my father," she said. "What's more likely to find them?"

"If they have the penetration to get this close to pulling it off without getting caught, I don't know who we can trust," he admitted. "A black investigation with as few people involved as possible increases our chance of catching them."

"You'll need a Hand," Romanov warned. "You can't do it yourself, Damien. You need someone with Kiera's Voice and the investigative chops for this job."

"I know someone I can trust with the skills," Damien said slowly. "She is—was, I guess—a Voice of the Mage-King. We haven't renewed any of those Warrants, so I guess she isn't right now."

"Then we fix that," Kiera said flatly. "You're thinking Inspector Samara?"

"I am," Damien agreed. The Martian Investigation Service detective had been critical in unraveling the BLF and its attack on Council Station. Her Warrant had been to complete that investigation, but he hadn't heard of any progress over the last two years.

The people behind the BLF had been both thorough and homicidal in covering their tracks.

"I'll bring her in," he said aloud. "Wattana, I'll want you to put together a briefing package. Everything you've learned, everything you remember or have records for from the night before that flight.

"I don't think I can cleanly get you and Samara in the same room, so you'll need to transfer as much as you can to her by text."

He smiled as a thought struck him.

"And, Denis?"

"My lord?"

"How's your second-in-command?" Damien asked.

"Olufemi Afolabi is a solid Guard, Spader swears by him and everything he's done has me agreeing with her. Why?" the Guard asked slowly.

"Because I'm detaching you to Samara to provide her with muscle and the authority to access a lot of the Mountain's systems without using the Warrant. Less attention is better until we have some proof.

"There's no way someone planted a bomb on Desmond's shuttle on a whim. They were working for someone else and I want to follow the chain all the way back. I don't want the trigger-puller. I want the brain."

"Agreed," Kiera said. "I'll want to meet with Samara, Damien. I've only met her once before. I trust your judgment, but..."

"I refuse to hand out Warrants and Hands without you making the final call," he told her bluntly. "I'll have Waller make an appointment. I even know where I want to meet her."

"Damien?" Kiera asked carefully.

"You and I need to check into the Amplifier again," he said. "You need to be able to use it."

Because a Rune Wright had to sit the throne at Olympus Mons—and if Damien was chained to the throne, he couldn't go after whoever had killed his King himself.

CHAPTER 21

THE INTRICATE and stunning complexity of the Olympus Amplifier was no less overwhelming or intimidating to Damien when he wasn't the person sitting at the center, trying to build an interface that couldn't be codified or defined.

He couldn't even be certain if what Kiera was doing was right. There were parts of the runic structure she'd forged around herself that were almost directly contrary to the interface *he'd* built, but he could *see* that they were working for her.

The one thing that was different from the outside was the awareness of time. He hadn't realized that building his interface had taken twenty minutes until well after he'd done it. Watching Kiera Alexander do it, he was aware of time passing and how intricate the construct she was building was.

Once built, the construct could be set up in less than five seconds. Building it in the first place was a slow process. And that, he reflected, was with them knowing what the Olympus Amplifier was and how it worked.

The first Desmond—and he'd been DMA-651 at the time, a nineteen-year-old number with an active question mark of how much longer the value of a powerful Mage as breeding stock would outweigh the *threat* of a powerful Mage prisoner—had built that construct *without* knowing any of that.

The Eugenicists had calculated wrong and all of humanity had to be grateful for that. It was from this room that the Eugenicist War had been ended, with Desmond the First teleporting the Martian invasion fleet from Earth orbit to the Martian desert.

Most historians agreed that if Desmond hadn't activated the Amplifier and turned on his creators, the Eugenicists would have won the war. This room had changed the course of history again and again.

A muffled chime on his wrist-comp told him that Romanov had arrived with their guest. He studied Kiera's interface for a few seconds, then stepped away. She needed more time and she didn't need him, not yet.

"Bring her in," he ordered softly.

Inspector Munira Samara had been a senior inspector at Curiosity City when Damien's investigation of the Keepers had gone weird. She'd ended up first attached to the roving party of experts most Hands carried with them, and then promoted to Voice in her own right after his injuries.

She was a small woman with dark skin and brilliant blue eyes. Today those eyes gleamed in the dim light, highlighted by a very pale blue headscarf tucked into her conservative black suit.

"Damien Montgomery," she greeted him. "I knew we would meet again sooner or later. Inshallah."

"God works in mysterious ways," he responded. "In this case, though, I needed someone I could trust. How fares your investigation into Nemesis?"

"Poorly," she said crisply. "The trail was lost somewhere after the ship we tracked 'Kay' to left Sol. That ship wasn't seen again for over a year, and *that* was in a salvage auction in Amber."

She shook her head.

"They'd bought it from a scavenger and hadn't asked questions, because it was Amber," she concluded.

Amber was the Protectorate's perennial problem child, a colony founded by libertarians who ran the closest thing to true anarcho-capitalism the Protectorate had. Problem child they might be, though, when Damien had sent out a call for ships to help hold back the Republic's first attacks, Amber's militia had answered.

Amber's government and people were *loyal*. They were just a pain in the ass.

"I don't think I left you many leads other than that," Damien admitted.

"We were chasing them as we could, but the investigation was basically cold," Samara admitted. "His Majesty and Chancellor Gregory found it convenient to have an investigator as a Voice, but most of the cases they looped me in on were far more straightforward."

"I have a new one for you," Damien told her. "If you accept it, we'll renew your Voice and you'll work directly for me and Her Majesty."

It was that exact moment that Kiera's interface finally completed and the amplifier came alive. The silver orb exploded outward, forming the simulacrum of the entire star system as Kiera linked into the magical artifact with an audible squeak.

"What..."

"Welcome to the true throne room of Olympus Mons, Munira Samara," Damien told her. "The Olympus Amplifier."

She looked around in awe.

"This is incredible. What do you even need anyone else *for*?" she asked.

"From here, Kiera can carry out grand miracles, but *precision* is hard," he admitted. "And it's not a tool for investigation and discovery. We have a question we need answered, and the ability to move worlds does not open doors."

The Amplifier could teleport ships, move space stations, even adjust entire planets. But it couldn't zoom in far enough to affect individual people. That level of precision was impossible with a tool of this scale.

"I am yours to command, Lord Regent, Your Majesty."

The simulacrum shifted slightly as Kiera rose from the chair and crossed to join them.

"This is a black investigation, Inspector Samara," the young Queen told the woman. "Even the existence of your Warrant will be classified, restricted to as few people as we can manage. You'll work with Guard-Lieutenant Romanov and through Lord Regent Montgomery's staff as much as possible."

"That's...non-optimal, but I can probably make it work," Samara agreed. "But...I should probably ask what I'm investigating, if we're going that black."

"Someone murdered Desmond Michael Alexander the Third and Desmond the Fourth," Damien said flatly. "And seventeen other people on that shuttle. We have grounds to believe that the Mountain's security systems were compromised, potentially with a one-time security code generated from Charlotte Ndosi or Lawrence Octavian's Hands."

Damien had never met Hand Octavian...but he had *killed* the other Hand, destroying the man and his Keeper-designed warship in self-defense. Like Ndosi, Octavian had been a member of the Keepers—and unlike Ndosi, Damien believed he'd been a member of whatever cancerous organization had metastasized *out* of the Keepers and manipulated Damien into destroying them.

Munira Samara was silent for at least ten seconds. Twenty.

"You're certain," she finally said. "Why isn't the inquiry acting on this?"

"That, Inspector Samara, is why this investigation will be black," Damien told her, finally admitting aloud what he'd been trying not to accept all along. "The investigation has focused on negligence or accident from the beginning. While we believe a lot of effort went into making the murders hard to detect, the inquiry's focus worries me.

"I'm not certain I trust Vemulakonda. I'm not sure I trust Olympus Mons Defense Command. I *do* know I trust you."

"That's quite the vote of confidence, my lord," Samara replied. She looked up at the silver model of the solar system above their head and shivered.

"Why would anyone kill the Mage-King?" she asked.

"I can think of several hundred reasons," Damien admitted. "I need you to find out which one. And who did it. Someone got into the Mountain's security systems, which should barely be possible with a Hand's codes.

"They appear to have *used* a Hand's codes, since we know we had at least two renegade Hands in play, but the security system should still have stopped them wiping the data. But we know roughly how the shuttle was destroyed, and it couldn't have been done without physically installing something in the shuttle."

"So, we need to identify an intruder that isn't on the security systems, trace them back and find out who hired or recruited them," Samara summarized. "What kind of backup am I going to have here beyond Romanov?"

"A team of the Royal Guard will be on standby," Damien promised. "If you need a door kicked down, we've got some damn big boots on hand."

"That's not really the Guards' role, Damien," Kiera pointed out.

"I know. That's why no one will be expecting it," he told her. "Let's consider it *proactive* bodyguarding."

He met Samara's gaze.

"I'm not sure who to trust, Munira," he repeated. "But I won't force you to take this on. If I'm right, we're sending you after some extremely dangerous, extremely capable people."

"Just like Nemesis," she pointed out.

"I suspect it might well *be* Nemesis," he told her. "And I wonder if that's one man or something bigger."

"I'll just have to find out, won't I?" she asked. "I'm in, my lord, Your Majesty. I'll need everything you've got and a secure office here in the Mountain. I've been working out of Olympus City's MIS offices, but it sounds like we need this locked down."

"I'll talk to my staff and get it sorted," Damien agreed.

Kiera was already taking the archaic parchment of the Warrant out of her suit jacket and holding it out to the investigator.

"These *people*, whoever they are, killed my father and my brother," she told Samara. "I want them, Voice Samara. I want them nailed to a wall with enough evidence that there is no question before anyone that they are guilty as sin.

"I want to know who killed my family and I want to know *why*. I'll settle for revenge, Samara, but I *want* justice and I want to know they won't hurt anyone else. Understood?"

Samara dropped to one knee and held out her hand for the parchment.

"I understand completely, my Queen," she told Kiera. "I can't guarantee fast results, but if we can follow this trail, we will. To the end."

"Then We name you Our Voice in this matter, Munira Samara," Kiera said formally. "We grant you Our Warrant and send you forth in Our name. Know you speak for Us. Do not abuse this privilege. Do not fail in your charge."

"You have my word. Bi-smi llāhi r-ra māni r-ra īm."

In the name of God, the Most Gracious, the Most Merciful.

That was a promise Damien could accept in any language.

CHAPTER 22

THE FIRST WEEK had passed in a blur before Damien even managed to find time to "borrow" the Mars RTA for a personal discussion.

Sol was one of only two systems with multiple Runic Transceiver Arrays. Even one was an immense undertaking to build, and adding a second required incredibly careful balancing of energy and magic.

Even for the Rune Wright Mage-Kings, Damien suspected that building a *third* had been a nightmare. He wasn't even entirely sure how Tau Ceti had built their second one—but he did know it had taken twelve years.

Today the extra two in Sol meant that he could take over the Martian RTA for a personal call without worrying about disrupting communication for the entire system. The solutions that would allow that on a regular RTA didn't work *quite* as well with the sheer volume of communication coming into Sol.

Those protocols would be in place on the Sherwood end of the call, with unconnected messages being directed to side chambers in the RTA and recorded. The Transceiver Mages who ran the RTAs knew more of everyone's secrets than they were ever supposed to admit, but outside of them, even a recorded message was secure.

Claiming the primary chambers in two RTAs would be an expensive proposition for most people, but the Arrays were government property. Rank had its privileges—and since the *responsibilities* of that rank were why Damien had taken this long to make this call, he didn't even feel guilty about leaning on them.

Much.

"We have a connection," an unfamiliar voice echoed in the room. "Passing over to you, Admiral."

"Thank you," a *very* familiar female voice said. "Damien?"

"Grace, it's me," he replied. "How...how are things?"

He chuckled at the inanity of his own question. Grace McLaughlin was the commanding officer of an entire star system's militia. Some of her "things" were in the reports that were hitting his inbox. The rest were often buried under her work.

"The star system is still here and my fleet is mostly repaired from our little excursion to Ardennes to save your cute butt," Grace told him. "My folks and Granddad say hello. It was buried in a slew of other concerned questions, but that's really the only important bit that won't make it by formal channels."

Grace's "Granddad" was Miles James McLaughlin, the elected Governor of Sherwood. Her parents were major figures in the planetary government, positions earned on the back of competence and dedication to service as well as their family's position as one of Sherwood's major Mage families.

Like most Protectorate worlds, Sherwood's Mages held to their privileges carefully. In Damien's experience, at least, most of Sherwood's Mages did so by making sure they *earned* those privileges with service.

That part wasn't as universal.

"I'm glad to hear the planet is still there," he told his lover. "I might not get back there much, but it's still home."

There was a pause. The only thing the RTA was transmitting was the voice of a Mage—tests suggested that it wasn't even the *sound* of the Mage speaking so much as the *intent*, too. The Link and its ability to send digital information and video was going to be a game-changer for the Protectorate's interstellar coms.

"Obviously, I know the news from Mars," Grace finally said. "It seems you've been *literally* chained to the job, from what my research says about symbols of the job. How are you doing?"

"Desmond was a mentor. Des was a friend," Damien said, then sighed. "I've buried enough of both, but I'm not looking forward to tomorrow."

"The funeral?"

"Yeah. The funeral of a Mage-King is a grand affair these days, in a way I don't think any of them would actually *want*."

"A funeral is for the living, not the dead," Grace reminded him gently. "I guess it was pushed out to let people make it to Sol in time?"

"I get to meet at least six Governors tomorrow, yeah," Damien confirmed. "I hope no one expects me to remember their names. Burying the Desmonds is going to be more than enough to remember for one day."

"You have staff to remember names now, I hope," she told him. "Has the Professor caught up yet?"

"His ship just jumped into Sol," he replied. "Christoffsen will be joining me this evening, and I have missed his sage advice. God knows I didn't ask for this."

"But He knows you don't have it in you to say no," his girlfriend reminded him. "I'm guessing the Lord Regent doesn't get many vacations?"

"I can't leave Sol until I give this chain back," Damien confessed. "I..." He sighed. "I'm sorry, Grace; we knew this would be hard, but I expected to at least be able to swing through Sherwood once or twice a year."

They were far from the first people whose careers had dragged them apart.

"Then it falls to me to make sure *I* make it to Sol once or twice a year," Grace said firmly. "The reason we were mostly counting on you to come to me was that you were never going to be in one place as a Hand. If you can't leave Sol, well, I know where to find you, don't I?"

Damien chuckled.

"I hadn't thought of it that way," he admitted. "I'm sorry, my love."

"Mmm," she purred. "Say that last bit again?"

"I'm sorry?" he repeated, confused.

"No, the very last bit," she told him.

"My love," Damien echoed, smiling. "Right, sorry, I'm an idiot."

"I've known that for a long time, Damien Montgomery," Grace said. "But you're *my* idiot. Kiera can borrow you to be her Lord Regent, but you're *my* Damien. My idiot. My love."

He bowed his head, knowing she couldn't see him.

"I can live with that," he said.

"You'd better. Last time I checked, I had a battle fleet."

The entire Sherwood Interstellar Patrol would barely blip as a threat against Mars's defenses, even *without* the Olympus Amplifier—but that wasn't the point.

"Thank you," he murmured. "I've had the job for a week and it's probably been the busiest and most overwhelming week of my life."

"I seem to recall one week spent swinging back and forth between Sherwood and Mínglià ng to stave off a civil war," Grace pointed out. "There's at least no assassins and massive space battles?"

"Yet," Damien said. "I'm actually flying out to the research station with the Link after this. That's a mirror of the flight where Desmond died, so you would not *believe* the security in play."

"It better be *more* than I would expect," she told him. "I'm not losing you, Damien. We've come too close a time or two already."

"I don't think being Lord Regent has the same threat level," he admitted. "I'll be here when you can make it out."

"Good. I want to *see* you, and not just in a recording."

"That's one of the other things I'll be talking to people about at the research station," he told her. "We need the Link *everywhere*. Live interstellar data transmission in a device the size of a refrigerator? Yes, *please*."

"I look forward to it. I'll try and let you know when I can make it out to Sol—and I'll try and do it soon. We're about to have the final tranche of the frigates come online, and I think we're better off if I'm here for that."

Damien doubted that the fourth tranche of Sherwood's homebuilt warships was going to be the final one they built. If the McLaughlin hadn't already had potential buyers knocking on his door, the Flotilla's performance at the Battle of Ardennes would have brought them out of the woodwork.

"Bringing six new ships into service does rather need the Admiral, doesn't it?" he asked. "I'll be here when you come," he repeated. "I look forward to seeing you, but I had to talk to you."

"I figured." There was a pause. "Are you okay?" she finally asked.

"No," he admitted. "I'm not even sure I will be. But I'm upright and functional and doing the job, and that's enough to keep me going most days. I won't fail Desmond. I took the chain to stand in for Kiera until she's nineteen. I won't fail *her*, either."

"I know. I just hope it doesn't kill you. A lot of people would have their eye on that throne, that chain."

"I don't know why," Damien told her. "Too much responsibility for me. I just didn't have it in me to say no."

"And all of that is why you're going to be a good Lord Regent," his girlfriend replied. "I wish I could support you more, but I have my own responsibilities here. I can't leave them."

"And I wouldn't want you to," he said. "Sherwood needs you."

"The *Protectorate* needs you," Grace replied. "I knew what I was getting into when I said I wanted to make this work, Damien Montgomery, and in some ways, this makes it easier. Like I said, I know where to find you now!"

He chuckled.

"That's an improvement, I guess. I'll keep that perk in mind as I keep going."

"I know you will," she said. "I love you, Damien Montgomery. But I always knew that part of what I loved you for was going to drag you away from me. We work around that. We have to."

"Thank you," he repeated softly. "I love you too, Grace."

CHAPTER 23

DAMIEN SPENT the entire flight up from Olympus Mons to the Research Station Deimos-Three tensed, half-expecting trouble and with an escape teleport spell ready and fluttering around him and his companions.

It was all unnecessary in the end, but he was still glad Kiera hadn't even argued against her remaining on the surface.

"Welcome aboard Deimos Station," a white-suited woman greeted him as he stepped off the shuttle. Two armored Royal Guard flanked her, having already checked the landing bay for dangers.

"Dr. Yu," Damien greeted her with a nod. Yu Yaling was the administrative head of the Research Station, responsible for organizing a somewhat eclectic array of projects for the Protectorate.

Deimos wasn't a military research station, though research from there had ended up in warships from time to time. It was explicitly a *non*-magical research facility, which occasionally ended up with it getting deprioritized.

"The Link has been set up and is waiting for you in the conference room," Yu told him. "Is there anything else you need while you're here?"

"I don't have a lot of time, but if you can pull the team leads working on duplicating the Link into a meeting before I leave, I'd appreciate it," Damien asked.

He suspected his softly spoken request would be taken as an ironclad order, which was fine by him.

"I'll see what I can arrange," the tall woman in the white suit told him. "This way, my lord."

Legatus was over a dozen light-years from Mars. Damien wasn't even entirely certain that Second Fleet was still *at* Legatus, for that matter. Alexander had full authority to wage the war as she saw fit, and if she'd moved the bulk of her fleet or her flagship from the occupied Republic capital, that was within her authority.

Damien would probably know about it, but he wouldn't have argued it.

Despite the distance, the image of the friend and ally he'd left behind a few weeks earlier was crisp and clear. Legatus was closer than Sherwood, but that was irrelevant for either system so far as Damien could tell.

"Admiral Alexander," he greeted her after confirming he was in the camera's field of view and his image was being transmitted back. "I just spent a chunk of my afternoon in an RTA. This is very different."

She smiled and nodded.

"Agreed. How's Mars, my Lord Regent?"

"Heavy with responsibility," Damien admitted, then tapped the gold links of the chain around his neck. "The chain is heavier than it looks, and it doesn't even *look* light."

"I was the heir for most of my life, Damien," she reminded him. "I understand completely. I'm glad to have escaped the responsibility for now, even if I'm the heir again until Kiera finds a partner."

Damien blinked as that jarred a memory loose.

"Right, I need to talk to Dr. Gunther," he admitted. "She apparently was already poking Kiera on that, which means I need to remind her that Kiera is sixteen."

"You know Dr. Gunther will then point out that having a *second* family line of Rune Wrights to hand would be *very* useful," Alexander warned him. "It would be to everyone's advantage to have some little Damiens running around."

"Desmond never harassed me about that, and I'm not going to rush that on anyone's account," Damien countered.

"My brother valued the autonomy of the people around him more highly than was perhaps wise," Jane Alexander said quietly. "Bodily and otherwise. No, it's *not* morally right to push you and Grace to have children. But the Protectorate needs you to."

"There are a lot of things I'll do for the Protectorate, but that's not on the list," he said calmly. "If and when Grace wants to discuss that, we will. Until then, getting on my back is pointless—and getting on *Kiera's* is actively dangerous."

"Fair enough," the Admiral allowed, but her tone suggested that the conversation wasn't done. "This was supposed to be a military briefing, anyway. Will Kiera be seeing this?"

"A recording of it, yes," Damien confirmed. "And Gregory and whoever else we get on the Regency Council that I'm supposed to have assembled in, oh, three days."

Fortunately, it was actively unwise for Damien to be picking the rest of the Regency Council. Gregory was making the selections and running them by Kiera. The Chancellor had given Damien a veto on the candidates—none of the three of them were pretending they *didn't* want a Regency Council that was going to follow where Gregory and Damien led—but Damien had declined to do more than glance at the names.

He didn't recognize any of them from his mental list of enemies. That was enough.

"I see we're keeping you busy," Alexander replied.

"A hundred star systems, five of them still UnArcana Stars despite the Republic's secession," Damien replied. "They've, ah, a *few* questions that need to be answered."

The humor faded as both of them considered why Damien was answering those questions. The death of the two Desmonds was a black cloud hanging over every conversation Damien had.

"Right." Alexander considered the situation, then shrugged.

"Thanks to you convincing the Legatan government to surrender, we have several intelligence windfalls over the last week," she noted. "The biggest is we now know how many warships were built in Legatus *and* how many warships were in commission in the RIN."

"If that number is different, I'm concerned," Damien admitted. Legatus had the only site the Protectorate was aware of that had produced and installed the Promethean Interfaces with their murdered Mage brains.

If the Republican Interstellar Navy had more ships than had been built in Legatus, Damien didn't like what that suggested—and that Alexander was drawing the distinction meant...

"It's different," Alexander confirmed. "The RIN had thirteen carrier groups in commission prior to the final battle of the Siege of Legatus. That was eight *Courageous*-class ships and five smaller *Bravado*-class ships.

"Supporting them were twenty-nine battleships and a hundred cruisers. Almost all of that was at the Battle of Legatus, which means I'm not sure *anyone* knows how many hulls the RIN currently has in play."

That was a hundred and forty-two capital ships...each of which had required *six* murdered Mages to fuel their "jump drives." Damien had been conscious of how many *children* had been kidnapped and killed to build the Republic's fleet, but that was still a stark figure.

"Eight hundred and fifty murders," he said quietly.

"I know," Alexander agreed. "The scary part is that the records here show that Legatus only built six of the *Courageous* ships and twenty-five battleships. The *Bravado*s and cruisers were all built here, but that's still six heavy capital ships I can't source."

"So, they have a second shipyard and a second Prometheus facility," Damien concluded.

"Any record of that yard is gone," the Admiral told him. "I can tell you the name of every carrier in the Republic fleet, but I can't tell you where they were built. The shipbuilding records we have are from the yards themselves where the commissioning lists were retrieved on Legatus."

"So, they might have been hoping that we wouldn't realize there was a second yard," he said. "We'd have realized soon enough when they kept reinforcing."

"Agreed. That means my priority is finding that yard," Alexander told him. "There's hints through the documents and interrogations of a secondary command-and-control center, but no one knows where.

"What I *am* certain of is that we're looking at a second accelerator ring."

Damien nodded slowly.

The Centurion Accelerator Ring had been a forty-year, incomprehensibly expensive project, wrapping a particle accelerator around the full circumference of the gas giant it was named for. Fueled by cloudscoops pulling hydrogen from Centurion and feeding it right into fusion power plants, the accelerator had provided a technological solution to mass production of antimatter.

"That was our biggest fear," he noted.

"And now I know it exists," Alexander told him. "I just don't know where."

"Their fleet came apart pretty badly at Legatus," Damien noted. He'd challenged the RIN on the source of their jump drives, forcing them to take a good look at themselves and their ships.

That probably wouldn't have been enough on its own, but it had turned out that the Promethean Interfaces were wired to nuclear safeties to make sure they weren't tampered with. That had turned fear and confusion into hesitance—and a hard overreaction from the fleet commanders had turned hesitance into active desertion.

"I have to assume they're going to reassemble all of it," Alexander told him. "We're beginning to scout Nueva Bolivia. If they're still scattered and weak, we need to take advantage as fast as we can."

"And we need to find that accelerator ring."

"If you've got any more of those MISS stealth ships, I'll take all of them I can get," the Admiral replied. "*Rhapsody in Purple* is worth her weight in antimatter, but we've only got one of them. I've got Chambers and Kulkarni drafting up a pattern to use destroyers as best as we can, but the destroyers have to go through fast and distant to be safe.

"The stealth ships can get in closer."

Stealth in space required a massive investment of magic and technology and even then was only so reliable. Damien had used *Rhapsody in*

Purple to get him around Republic space safely, but the kind of scouting Alexander was talking about was one of the ship's main purposes.

"I'll ask and see if we can break free more," he told her. "My understanding is there's only three."

"That's fair. Who do I get to build me fifty more?" the Admiral demanded.

"That would be me," Damien told her. "We'll see what we can do. A lot of stuff is in flux for RMN funding still, but it does look like we've got the next round of capital ships locked in. That's another twelve battleships and six dreadnoughts."

"I'd kill for them," Alexander said bluntly. "But I *need* stealth ships yesterday and they should build faster."

"Don't count on that," he warned. "But I'll see what I can do. You're authorized to do whatever you can with what you've got. If you locate the accelerator ring, that opens up a chance to end this war."

"It does," she confirmed. "If I'm pissed at anything, Damien, it's that I thought I already *had* ended this war."

"Solace was a step ahead of us. Again." Damien shook his head. "I'm getting sick of enemies being a step ahead of me, but we're digging for some answers of our own here."

"That sounds dangerous," she said slowly, clearly picking up on some of what he *wasn't* saying. Parts of this briefing would be handed over to a lot of people who didn't need to know Damien was running a black side investigation into the Mage-King's death.

"That's the job. Is there anything else critical? I have another meeting here before I head back to the surface—my secretary just about hurt me when I told her I needed four hours off-world."

"Your meetings move on your convenience, Damien, not theirs. That's not just ego or power talking, either. You *need* to realize and rely on it," she told him. "You're the Lord Regent of Mars. Stuff *will* come up.

"As for the war, things are quiet right now. Your apprentice is turning into quite the useful set of hands. I'm glad to have her, but I can't promise to keep her safe."

"Roslyn Chambers isn't my 'apprentice'," Damien countered. "I might call her a protégée, but she's more *your* protégée now. But I'm glad she's useful. We've put a lot of pressure on that young woman."

"She's at the heart of the war now. Shit place for anyone, trust me, but her contributions will save lives. Your job is to make it all worth it."

"Admin, admin, negotiation, and admin," Damien told her. "How did your brother handle this?"

"Dad had him involved in everything from the moment he turned twenty, almost ten years before Dad's death," the Princess of Mars told him. "I don't think he ever really knew anything different. Does a goldfish know there's water in the bowl?"

Damien snorted.

"Probably not. We'll keep this channel mostly open to enable reports from Legatus, but I hope to have more of these things sooner rather than later. The team responsible for letting us *build* them is my next meeting."

"Good luck. The RMN needs the Link. Mass-produced, secured, reliable—and on every ship."

"The Protectorate needs it in much the same state," Damien told her. "We'll need to consider phase-out for the RTAs and retraining and transition for the Transceiver Mages, but we need a Link *everywhere*."

"That's your job, Lord Regent," Alexander said with a chuckle. "Mine is running Second Fleet and poking you and Kiera to make sure I *stop* being Heir sometime sooner rather than later!"

CHAPTER 24

THE MEETING with the Link mass-production team took longer than Damien had hoped but had also been more positive than he expected. In the end, he left Deimos Station half an hour later than planned.

"Dr. Christoffsen is in the Mountain and has been advised of the delay," Waller told him when he let her know. "He doesn't have any *other* plans, he tells me, so he's fine with waiting for dinner."

"I appreciate his patience and your flexibility, Moxi," Damien replied. "Not every meeting can go as scheduled; not every task can be completed on time."

"I'll make it work," she said serenely. "I was always entertained by how much flexibility I could convince people to find when I told them who I worked for before. Now, well." She chuckled. "It's *amazing* how many things that were impossible suddenly become 'let me check' when I tell them I'm booking for the *Lord Reg—*"

"Moxi?" Damien said into the sudden dead air. "Moxi Waller?" he demanded sharply.

Silence.

"Afolabi, what's our status?" he asked, turning to check on the red-armored Guard next to him.

"Shuttle coms are down," the bodyguard replied. "Checking with the pilot."

"We just took a micrometeorite hit to the com array," that worthy told them over the intercom. "External coms are down until we install a bunch of new antennas."

"That's possible," Damien agreed, "but damn suspicious. Pilot, bring up the defensive suite, if you please."

The man coughed.

"Our defensive radar and systems have been online since thirty seconds after we cleared the station, sir," he reported. "I've still got *Gauntlet* on the screens and we're still under their guns. I think it's a fluke, but I'm keeping my eyes very wide open, sir."

"And nothing so far?" Damien asked.

"Nothing so far," the man confirmed. "We hit atmosphere in twenty minutes and we're on the ground in thirty-five. I'm scanning for potential threats, but I'll admit I wouldn't mind if everyone strapped in and prepared for things to get messy."

"When do we leave *Gauntlet of Honor*'s security zone?" Damien asked.

"They're with us the whole way. Once we're in atmosphere, there's a limit to what they can do, but we're inside Olympus Mons's defense perimeter from there. There's a thirty-second overlap; we made sure of it this time."

"I wonder if someone doesn't know that and thinks we're vulnerable then," he murmured. "Afolabi, get on the scanners. Is there anything close to our descent path? I know the flight path was cleared, but what's *close*?"

"Understood." The Guard removed his gauntlets and started typing on a keyboard Damien couldn't see. It was presumably projected on the inside of his helmet and the suit system was reading his fingers' movement.

"Nothing looks like it's violating the security zone, but I've got a surface-to-orbit heavy shuttle that's supposed to pass by at about ten thousand kilometers," he noted. "Their flight path has them on the other side of the horizon, though."

"Show me," Damien ordered. Something was crawling up the back of his spine, and he glanced at the velocity measure for the shuttle.

He could teleport himself and the two Royal Guards with him to the surface safely, but there was a mass component to how much velocity he could shed in a personal teleport. He could *take* the shuttle...but they'd collide with the ground at several kilometers per second.

It was an option, but not a good one. Not without a better idea of what was going on.

"Watch that shuttle," he ordered. "It and the next four closest vehicles to our descent. I don't buy coincidences anymore."

The engine failure on the heavy-lift shuttle barely qualified as a surprise when it finally happened. The holographic projection the Guard were running showed the adjusted course as gravity started to take control of the spacecraft—and swung it right into the middle of the restricted space around Damien's flight path.

"Do we shoot it down?" Afolabi asked.

"With what?" Damien asked. "They've calculated it well. We're already too close in to the planet for the shuttle's long-range weapons, and we're not in range of her air-breathing missiles yet.

"If we had coms, we could call for fire from *Gauntlet*, but we don't." He studied the chart and sighed.

"Quite possibly, there's someone on that shuttle right now in contact with *Gauntlet*. They're saying they had an accident; they're begging for a rescue." He shook his head. "Quite possibly, the crew of that shuttle is innocent. It depends on the plan."

"You're the Lord Regent! *Gauntlet* should shoot them down regardless!"

"No," Damien told his bodyguard. "They won't shoot down civilians on suspicion—and they shouldn't, either. We can handle ourselves, Guard Afolabi."

The two shuttles were now barely two thousand kilometers apart, well within range of any weapon designed for deep space. They were also clearly under the guns of the battleship, and anything that went wrong would see rapid intervention.

"How long until we're in range of the Olympus Mons defenses?" he asked calmly.

"Seventy seconds. We're in *Gauntlet's* range for one hundred."

"Watch for the attack fifteen seconds before we enter the range of OMDC," Damien ordered. "Keep the scanner data up as cleanly as you can and I'll protect us."

The Royal Guard knew exactly what kind of person of mass destruction they were escorting. Any of the three red-armored Guards in the room could probably do what Damien was going to, but the Lord Regent was uninclined to go with *probably.*

He watched the data, watching his ship continuing its descent. They *could* change course, open the range—if the pilot hammered on the emergency thrusters, they could reverse their entire descent and head for *Gauntlet of Honor.*

"We'll see how this plays out," he murmured.

"You do realize you are *allowing* them to take a shot at the Lord Regent of Mars, yes?" Afolabi asked, his voice sounding slightly strained.

"I know," Damien told his guard. "But this is amateur hour, Guard Afolabi, compared to some of what we've already seen on Mars. So, let's remove the amateurs from the board, shall we?"

The heavy-lift shuttle was carrying four of the Protectorate's ten-thousand-cubic-meter shipping containers. From the thrust it had been throwing out before the engine had failed, they were full. Fully loaded like that, the "shuttle" was a fifty-thousand-ton cargo hauler that dwarfed the Model 2445-Z assault shuttle.

And as Damien studied them, two of the cargo containers *exploded,* sending the shuttle spinning off course again, helplessly out of control now.

That was for Mars Orbital Control and the ships in orbit to deal with. Damien was leaning toward the "unlucky bastards" theory for the crew of the lift shuttle at this point, but the people who'd shipped those containers...he would have *words* for them.

"Drones" was all he said aloud, watching as chunks of the wreckage began to move. "Or potentially piloted ships, but they have to know their survival chances. High-altitude interceptors hidden in the containers."

"Whatever they are, they're coming in *fast*," the pilot barked. "And apparently, my threat warnings are still working. Missiles launched."

"My lord?" Afolabi said softly.

"Hold on."

Damien studied the scans for a moment. There were at least thirty of the presumably robotic aircraft, and it must have taken them several seconds to shake whatever packaging had cocooned them in the cargo container.

This part had been well designed, he reflected absently. The container explosions and the debris were covering the interceptors from above and below—and had likely left the orbital overwatch watching the damaged shuttle, too.

Thirty-plus interceptors had sent over a hundred missiles toward the shuttle. The defensive systems had their own short-range active scanners, and they spun to life as the pilot set them loose.

They couldn't stop a hundred missiles, and he made sure he had the locations and velocity of the missiles locked in his mind...and then channeled power.

Without an amplifier matrix—or at least a window—it was more a question of math than visual targeting. The missiles were *there*, moving at *that* speed, which meant that by the time Damien's magic could act, they would be *here*.

He conjured lightning, arcing blasts of electricity that appeared from nowhere and leapt from missile to missile in a catastrophic sequence of power that vaporized hulls and warheads alike.

A third of the missiles vanished from the screen, and Damien focused on the survivors, repeating the action. Other missiles were dying to the lasers—and it looked like *Gauntlet of Honor* had finally realized what was going on, the battleship's weapons stabbing from orbit to protect the frail-seeming shuttle.

More missiles vanished as Damien sustained the lightning, arcing it back and forth across the salvo and working his way back toward the launching aircraft in a march delineated by the explosions of failing weapons.

Gauntlet of Honor beat him to the aircraft. Barely.

If nothing else, the battleship had more guns and more eyes. Once they were fully aware of the threat, hundreds of Rapid-Fire Laser Anti-Missile turrets began to fire. Damien only took out about half of the missiles in the end, and he watched as *Gauntlet's* gunners tore through the aircraft.

"We need one of them intact," he said aloud.

"We have no coms," Afolabi reminded him.

"Right."

Damien *focused*, reaching across several hundred kilometers of empty space to catch one of the handful of survivors—and they weren't even trying to evade, confirming Damien's guess of their robotic nature.

It made this task easier as he wrapped a teleport spell, something even *he* usually needed to touch the target of, around the aircraft and *moved* it.

He exhaled sharply as the expenditure hit him like a hammer to the gut.

"Afolabi, once we're down, please make sure that the Royal Guard sends a detachment to the ground a hundred and twenty-five kilometers directly north from where that drone just vanished," he said distantly. "I doubt it survived the landing, but we need to rip it apart for evid—"

He abruptly ran out of steam and collapsed back into his chair.

"I'll pass the orders on once we're down," the Guard confirmed. "Local airspace is secure. Are you all right, my lord?"

"I'm fine," Damien managed to force out past his sudden wave of exhaustion. "Teleporting something that far away is...well, jumping a starship is easier."

The Guard coughed.

"I'm not sure teleporting something two hundred and eighty kilometers away is supposed to be *possible*, sir, but I know what I guard," he concluded.

If he said anything more, Damien missed it as sleep took him.

CHAPTER 25

"WELL, ISN'T this a mess?"

Denis Romanov nodded his agreement with Samara's words as he surveyed the crash site. The drone had been moving at almost three thousand kilometers an hour, a speed easily handled in Mars's thin upper atmosphere.

It wasn't a speed that easily handled unexpected lithobraking. The Lord Regent had teleported the aircraft to a spot well away from any habitations—which had been a damn good idea, as the drone had carved an eighteen-hundred-meter-long furrow in the ground before the wreck had finally come to a halt.

"As messes Damien Montgomery makes go, I'm not sure this even makes the top ten," the Royal Guard admitted as he hopped down from the helicopter. He turned to help his charge down, but Samara was already on the ground behind him.

Two more helicopters were orbiting above the site, cameras and more esoteric sensors already at work while their cargo of Secret Service Agents and Royal Guards spread out on the ground. Another Guard and two Secret Service Agents followed Samara out of their helicopter, the Agents falling in around the Voice herself.

"The area is secure," Denis continued. "The drone appears to be disabled, but we'd have triggered any anti-intruder defenses it had already."

"Isn't that dangerous, Guard-Lieutenant?" the Voice asked.

"Yes. That's why it was tested by one of the Guard," he said grimly. "I didn't order it, if you're wondering, my lady. One of the Guard moved in to check without asking permission."

"Let's check it out," Samara ordered.

"I'm not entirely clear on why you're even here," Denis pointed out. "I know why *I'm* here—I had a Guard team ready to go in case anything came up in your investigation."

"Someone just tried to assassinate the Lord Regent," the Voice told him as she stepped around him and headed for the wreck. "I think that just might be related to my investigation."

Denis sighed. She was right.

"Check the perimeter, watch for incoming," he ordered his people over the com network after muting his external speakers. "The drone is the only evidence that hasn't been vaporized. If someone is feeling anti-loose-ends, they might try something dumb."

He almost wished their mysterious attackers would. They'd get a lot more information from a captured attacker than from a wrecked drone.

As they approached closer to the wreck, he lowered his estimate of what they would get from the aircraft even further. Even the main wreck was, well, wrecked. There was probably a bit over half of the fighter at the end of the furrow, but it was in multiple pieces.

"That's not going to be helpful," he said. "I guess we look for serial numbers and black boxes."

"Exactly," Samara told him. "If you can get the Secret Service team on that, I have a few things I want to poke at myself. Do we have an ID on the craft yet?"

Denis surveyed the fragmented and smoking crash site.

"Not this particular one, no," he admitted. "Looking at this, I'm hoping the Navy got a good eyeball on them from above, because IDing this one is going to take longer than anyone would like."

"It's one of ours."

"There is a *lot* of gradation in the concept of *ours* in this context, Agent," Romanov replied. "What am I looking at?"

"She's a Gorgon-Six high-altitude multipurpose deployment drone," the Secret Service Agent on the other end of the communicator told him. "Thirty-eight tons, ten-meter wingspan, ASI brain. Capable of deploying everything from high-altitude attack missiles to weather drones and survey probes.

"There's about fifty of them on the planet, and every damn one of them belongs to Mars Defense Command. And they mostly get used for those weather drones."

"So, is this *a* Gorgon-Six or one of MDC's Gorgon-Sixes?" Denis asked. There were too many interfacing organizations on Mars. Olympus Mons Defense Command controlled the security of the Mountain and was considered coequal to Mars Defense Command and Mars Orbital Command.

OMDC was under the authority of the Royal Guard and reported directly to the Mage-King. MDC was a Marine Corps-led organization and MOC was a Navy-led structure.

He didn't *think* the Marines would have tried to assassinate Damien Montgomery, but it had been a weird few years.

"MDC is pulling inventory now," a new voice cut into the channel. Denis felt his spine stiffen at the sound of General Spader's sharp tones. "They may or may not come up short. It's highly likely, though, that we're looking at new manufacture—given that the shuttle was leaving Avalon Automated Aircraft's primary production facility."

"Is someone checking it out?" Denis asked. He wasn't entirely sure why the General of the Royal Guard was the one updating him on this, but he'd treat it like this was normal until she told him why.

"There's an MIS*S* team on its way," she told him. The emphasis on the second S was audible—and probably critical.

MIS were the Martian Investigation Service. They were the Martian planetary police and the Protectorate's interstellar police agency.

MISS was the Martian Interstellar Security Service. *They* were spies and covert-operations specialists. An MISS team on Mars itself was a counterintelligence team with the skills, codes and authority to tear open AAA's computers and find *all* of the company's secrets.

"We'll keep investigating here," he told Spader. "We'll probably hand it over to a team of proper analysts in short order. The site seems secure and it doesn't look like anyone is sending a team of killbots to protect the wreck."

"You jest, Lieutenant, but I wouldn't have expected someone to send attack drones at the Lord Regent. We're going to get some damn answers."

And *that*, of course, was why the General of the Royal Guard was on Denis's com. Denis technically still commanded the Lord Regent's personal detail—his tasking as Samara's support was a *part* of that role because Damien Montgomery had *always* used his bodyguards as a personal strike team—but General Spader was also responsible for Montgomery's security.

This attack was a direct strike at everything she was sworn to protect.

"Agreed, sir," he told her. "We might find a black box or something here."

"Listen to Samara, Lieutenant," the General told him. "I'm not going to pretend I *don't* know she's there, after all. She's probably not *the* best investigator MIS has produced, but she's up there and she's on the site."

Denis was glad the armor concealed his momentarily distressed flush. That was the other reason why his assignment to Samara was unofficial. Montgomery hadn't briefed the Guard's commanding officer on his investigation.

"And while I'm talking to you about Samara on an encrypted black line that now only has the two of us on it," the General said with a chuckle, "you want to check out Apollo-Six Seventy-Five."

That was...an address inside the Mountain. One down near the geothermal power plants.

"Sir?" Denis asked questioningly.

"It's a secured location; as a Guard officer, you have access," she told him. "I know nothing about why Samara is in the Mountain, but I suspect what you'll find there might come in handy."

"Keep me in the loop on what you find at the wreck," she continued swiftly, as if she hadn't even mentioned the location. "I'm coordinating this whole mess and running it through the OMDC's encrypted network.

"If someone has hacked *that*, heads are going to fucking roll."

"Here, Romanov, can you lift this," Samara requested.

Denis looked at the chunk of armor that the Inspector was trying to look under and gestured slightly. It lifted smoothly into the air, and he placed it carefully to the side of the wreck.

"Well, I was thinking with the armor, but that works," the Voice told him with a smile. "Thanks."

The debris had apparently been covering what remained of the aircraft's Artificial Sequential Intelligence—an ASI or "artificial stupid." Denis couldn't make much of the collection of electronics, but he could recognize *that* much from the standardized casing.

Moving the debris had been easy—even easier than usual. Montgomery had managed to squeeze in the ten minutes necessary to "fit" a suit of Royal Guard armor to its wearer, adjusting the runic structure to fit the user.

Denis had understood that the Royal Guard exosuit armor's runes were simply an upgraded, more personally tailored version of the limited system in a Marine Combat Mage's armor that allowed him to use the projector rune on his right palm easily despite the exosuit.

He'd been wrong. From what he could tell, the rune was a simpler version of the Runes of Power born by the Hands and the Rune Wrights themselves. Without linking quite as intimately into his power as the runes carved into the Hands' flesh, it could never have been as powerful.

But it was still an augmentation of his own power. The Royal Guard were selected for powerful personal magic, and Denis was no exception. Even with the runes on their armor, a single Royal Guard was no match for a Hand...but a match for anything *weaker* than a Hand.

"Romanov, come take a look at this. How precisely can you do that?" Samara asked, gesturing at the piece of armor he'd moved.

He carefully moved down next to her. Years of practice with exosuit armor allowed him to move through the debris without damaging anything, but he had *much* less confidence in his ability to poke at the drone's electronic brain with powered gauntlets.

"Sorry, Munira, I have no idea what I'm looking at," he admitted after a moment. "I mean, this section over here is pretty standard aircraft and shuttle control systems, but once you reach this board…"

"Thank you, I was only fifty percent sure what that section was," Samara told him with a chuckle. "I know most of the key segments of an ASI, though. This one is very dead, in case you were worried."

"So long as it didn't shoot at me, I was happy either way. What did you need?" he asked.

"This section here is its active memory, its RAM," Samara told him. "We need it intact. But the black box flight recorder is *behind* it—it's designed to be accessed from the other side."

"Which is embedded in dirt that the crash has baked into ceramics," Denis guessed.

"Can you use magic to lift the RAM section without damaging it?" she asked. "It's not normally fragile, but given the impacts it's already taken…"

He studied it. That wasn't even a question of power.

"I *think* so," he admitted. "But maybe we should wait for specialists?"

"Do you trust them?" Samara asked bluntly. "I want copies of all of this before I hand it over to the rest of OMDC. Montgomery's paranoia is getting under my skin."

"He's not paranoid," Denis said. "Trust me. It's my job to be paranoid for him, and he is definitely *not* paranoid enough."

She chuckled again, then disconnected several wires she'd linked into the RAM. He hadn't noticed them before.

"I *have* a copy of the RAM data," she admitted. "There are contextual aspects I lose in copying, it's not designed to be read like this, so we're better off if we keep it intact. Plus, I don't want to admit I have it.

"But if we break it, we still have options. So, open it up, Denis."

He studied the circuit board carefully. Tendrils of his magic slid under the board, supporting it while tiny jets of force severed the remaining connections. The circuitry slowly lifted up, sliding over to the side where Samara held up a static-protected electronic evidence bag.

His magic slid the board gently into the bag and she closed it up.

"There we go," she told him as he exhaled a sigh. "One set of RAM chips, sealed up and put aside for the rest of MIS. Now the black box."

Looking past where he'd moved the circuit board, Denis could see that there was still a solid panel blocking them from anything else. Before Samara could even ask, he wove magic again. Safely opening a hole through an armor panel without damaging anything on the other side of it was *easy*, one of the first things the RMMC taught their Mages.

That panel joined the armor on the dirt outside the wrecked aircraft, and the bright orange shape of the aircraft's black box flight recorder came into view.

"All right." Samara knelt down next to it and produced wires again. "Of course, folks are going to know that *somebody* accessed the data, but that's fine. The box can't be edited; it's one-write-only storage."

She connected the box to her wrist-comp and started a program. While it ran, she looked around the wreck.

"Serial numbers were wiped," she said aloud. "I was expecting that. We'll see if they knew—or even considered—what they needed to do to the box."

A light flashed on her wrist-comp from the program, and she said something harsh in a language Denis *thought* was Arabic.

"Well, they're smarter than I hoped. The box is dead; the data connection was physically severed. Those RAM chips will tell us a lot, but with the serial numbers removed and the black box wiped, we're back to physically tracking the plane."

"Looks like it came right from the factory," Denis told her. "We're still looking into it, but the shuttle launched from the manufacturer's facility."

She nodded with a sigh.

"They missed that there was no vulnerable window in Montgomery's descent, but it looks like a lot of the work around that was clean," she admitted. "This is going to be a mess, Denis. And it ties into our investigation as well, even if no one else is looking at the Mage-King's death as an assassination yet."

"Sir!" Denis instinctively followed the indicators his suit gave him to turn to face the speaker, even as the message came by radio. "We found something weird; can you and the Inspector come take a look?"

"They found something," he told Samara. "Shall we?"

"I need to review the data from the RAM, but I can't do that here," she told him. "Lead on, Denis."

As they were picking through the wreckage to get to the Guard who'd called Denis over, he realized he'd missed when Samara had started using his first name.

"I have no idea what that is," Denis admitted as he looked at the collection of circuitry modules hanging from the Secret Service Agent's hands. The Royal Guard who'd called them over was standing back, seemingly worried their armor could break the artifact by looking at it.

"I'm not sure either, sir," the Agent admitted. "But we pulled schematics of the Gorgon-Six and it didn't belong. It's got a long-range radio, computer modules, all sorts of crap that the Gorgon already has elsewhere."

"Let me take a look," Munira ordered. The Agent happily handed the harness-like device over to her. "Where was it?"

"Attached to the main fire control data bus," the Guard behind them told her. "It looked like it had been attached but the damage to the data bus had separated it."

"I think it's a remote initiator," Samara said after several seconds' examination. "It received a radio transmission and turned the drone on, dumping a program into its computers."

"Well, that explains why something that was supposed to be turned off for shipping turned on," Denis replied. "Doesn't explain why they were fueled and *armed*, but..."

"There was probably one of these inserted in each of the planes, most likely while something was arming and fueling them. Show me *exactly* where you found it," she ordered.

The Guard paused for a moment, then turned on a targeting laser and used it to indicate the spot. Samara knelt next to it, examining it.

"The data bus didn't break in the crash," she concluded. "That was an explosion and I'm going to bet the source was jarred loose when the plane crashed. It wasn't meant to take out the data bus."

She lifted the harness and studied it again.

"It was meant to vaporize this thing and I think the reason why is *this*." She tapped a module at the center of the harness.

"There aren't many chips in the galaxy that could hold a full ASI program for a drone like this in a size that's insertable like this. This couldn't *run* the ASI, but it could hold the code and dump it into the drone when it came online."

"Useful to find, I suppose," Denis allowed.

"More than you think," Samara told him. "These kinds of chips aren't made on Mars, Denis, and the Earth-based manufacturers I know are sold out three years in advance.

"Getting your hands on chips like this is hard...unless you own the manufacturer or already have those government purchase contracts."

"Munira?" he said. "You've lost me."

"These are Legatan high-density data transfer chips, Denis," she told him. "This harness was built in the Republic. I can't be sure if it was specifically designed to override a Gorgon-Six, but its purpose was to take control of *a* drone combatant."

"And they had the coders on hand to make sure it was reset to go after Montgomery's shuttle," he concluded grimly. "That does flag a likely culprit, doesn't it?"

"They tried to bury it, but the op depended on a piece of tech they couldn't source locally," Samara agreed. "I'm not going to call it a solid case without more data, but I'd say this was the RID."

The Republic Intelligence Directorate was the intelligence and covert action arm of the Republic of Faith and Reason. Denis had known the

RID had the Protectorate badly penetrated—defectors from LMID had helped them clean up the infestation, but they still had agents seemingly everywhere.

"At least it gives us a name," he said grimly.

"For this, at least," Samara confirmed. Putting the harness down and stepping back, she nodded firmly to the Agent who'd found it.

"Well done," she told him. "There should be MIS and MISS teams landing shortly, with a Marine security detail. You'll all fall back to the Mountain at that point, but make certain the MIS and MISS teams know about the harness."

"Yes, my lady Voice."

She led Denis away with a jerk of her head.

"We need to get back to the Mountain," she told him. "This was a necessary diversion but, from the perspective of the main mission, not a wholly useful one."

"You don't think it's connected?" he asked.

"Not if this was RID," she said. "We might be seeing the same group borrowing resources—we know Nemesis had access to an LMID infiltration team when they were cleaning up the Keepers—but it doesn't smell right."

"How so?"

They were clear of the wreck now and no one else could hear them. Denis sent a signal up to call down their helicopter. Distant lights suggested more vehicles were on their way. They'd have to drive across fields, which gave them time.

"Insufficient penetration," Samara finally concluded. "Whoever went after the Mage-King had enough access in the Mountain to covertly remove their agent from the security systems. Even with a Hand's override code, that shouldn't be possible—and all I can find is that one of Hand Ndosi's codes *was* used. Whoever cleaned that up was *good*."

She gestured back at the wreck.

"These attackers didn't even know that they didn't have a vulnerability window," she told him. "They had resources and skills, but they didn't have data. They didn't have penetration of our systems or our security protocols.

"Different modes of operation, different levels of access. Different attackers." She shook her head. "And that means the RID is MISS's problem and *we*, Denis, need to keep our eyes on the main target."

"Spader gave me a place to look," he told Samara. "Just an address in the Mountain, but one apparently only officers of the Royal Guard can access."

He looked around the crash site as the helicopter touched down behind him.

"After this, I'm not going to sleep anytime soon. Want to check it out?"

"Spader isn't supposed to know about our investigation," Samara said coolly.

"Spader is supposed to know everything that happens in the Mountain, and we've been poking at her systems," Denis pointed out. "If she hasn't guessed more than she even implied to me, I'd be surprised.

"Not sure what she's directing us to, but she *is* the General of the Royal Guard. It might be useful."

"I wasn't saying we shouldn't follow up," Samara replied. "Just being twitchy about people who weren't briefed knowing about my black investigation."

CHAPTER 26

DENIS ROMANOV had spent enough time aboard ships that he had to keep himself from translating the "district" and "level" structure of addresses in Olympus Mons to "decks."

Apollo-Six Seventy-Five was Unit Seventy-Five, Level Six, of the Apollo District. The Apollo District, in turn consisted of the fifteen lowest levels in the Mountain. There were seventeen districts, with the top, Zeus, being mostly the Royal Family's section.

So, Apollo-Six was the sixth lowest level in the mountain. Apollo One through Four were entirely consumed by the geothermal power generation infrastructure that was the original purpose for the dug-out installation. The rest of Apollo—and a good chunk of Hephaestus, the next district up—was only *mostly* consumed by power-generation and -handling infrastructure. ·

The geothermal plants were still at least a third of the power produced in the mountain, but there were multiple massive fusion plants as well. If you had the open spaces, there was nowhere better to stick a power plant of any kind than inside a few kilometers of solid rock.

No one was sure now if the open spaces that made up the underground capital of the Protectorate had been blasted out by the Eugenicists or naturally occurring. None of the people who might have been able to answer that question had lived long enough to be asked questions about geology and architecture.

The door at Apollo-Six Seventy-Five looked perfectly normal, but when Denis stepped up to it and tapped his wrist-comp to the entrance panel, it took several seconds for the system to process through his security credentials.

When it finished interrogating his wrist-comp, the door slid open. It was far thicker than it looked from the outside. The regular-seeming door was heavily armored on the inside—and the space it allowed them into was empty, an antechamber with no visible exits except where they'd come in.

The door slid shut behind them, leaving Denis and Samara alone in a space that was large enough to be comfortable and small enough to be disconcerting.

A computerized voice spoke before Denis could be too bothered.

"Guard credentials verified. Voice and bio identification required."

A panel slid open in the wall, revealing an automated DNA scanner. As Denis looked at the device in apprehension, it vented a gust of steam and extended a freshly sanitized needle.

"This is weird, right?" Samara asked. "Or is this the normal process for entering a Guard facility?"

"This is weird," Denis confirmed. He put his hand in the scanner and forced himself to stoically endure the prick from the needle as it grabbed a drop of his blood.

"Voice authentication is Denis Romanov," he said aloud. He activated a program on his wrist-comp and looked at the phrase it popped up. "The sun rises over seven hills at the dawn of Rome."

Silence answered him for several seconds.

"Secondary individual identified. Bio and voice identification required."

"Munira." He gestured to her.

He heard a small clatter as the DNA scanner discarded the needle it had used for him—the machine would automatically retrieve and sanitize its needles in an internal autoclave, but it would have between two and three hundred of the things, depending on the volume of use expected.

"I am Munira Samara, Voice of the Mage-Queen of Mars," she said firmly as she put her hand in the device. She winced at the pinprick.

"Voice and bio identification recorded. Identity of Guard Lieutenant Denis Romanov verified. Identity of Voice Munira Samara provisionally accepted."

What had been seamlessly part of the wall a moment earlier slid apart, revealing a concealed exit wide enough for a Guard officer in the exosuit armor Denis had shed before heading down here.

The other side was a security surveillance room. There was nothing different or unusual about it at all, except that it wasn't on any of the maps or records Denis had seen.

"Why would General Spader send us to a random security room?" Samara asked.

"Because this one isn't on the records anywhere and is secured behind a double layer of Guard-access-only security," Denis said slowly. He took a seat at the computer and studied the screens.

There were about forty of them and they were randomly shifting every ten seconds or so, showing locations from throughout the Mountain.

"Unless I'm mistaken, this is shifting through every security camera in the Mountain," he said quietly.

The system promptly asked him for *another* layer of authentication when he tried to control the feeds, but accepted his Guard codes readily enough.

A few seconds' work locked the cameras on to the hangar bay where the Royal shuttles were maintained and prepared for duty.

"You have the time stamps for the last maintenance on the Mage-King's shuttle, I assume?" he asked.

Samara gave them to him but was looking at the screens carefully. He was setting it up so each of the screens was starting from a different point of their time window, each roughly ten minutes apart.

"The Guard is running a copy of every security feed here, aren't they?" she asked softly.

"Looks like," he agreed. "An entirely separate backup." He shivered. "At a guess, one that would refuse even Hand override codes. The security room might predate the Keepers' fake attack on the Mountain, but I suspect we blocked out any ability of the Hands to control it after—"

"Stop, there!"

Samara was pointing at one of the screens. The time stamp said it was seventy-two minutes after the maintenance staff had left...but there was a man in a set of maintenance coveralls and holding a toolbox approaching the shuttle.

"I watched the entirety of this footage from the security systems," she told him. "*Nobody* entered the hangar."

"And according to this backup, this guy did," Denis agreed. "I'll see what I can pull for visuals. How much do you need for us to ID him?"

"If he's on Mars, get me thirty seconds of footage and I'll have his address by morning."

CHAPTER 27

OLYMPUS CITY had been started under domes when the Eugenicists ruled Mars and only spread out around the domes after the Mage-King took power. At every point in its existence from the very beginning, it had been built as a capital. The centerpoint of the road structure was the massive double doors of the formal main entrance into the Mountain itself, and immense boulevards stretched out in three directions from that center.

One route went directly west from the main gate, aligned perfectly with the core tunnel the original geothermal machinery had been installed through. This was the Central Avenue—and the funeral started at the far end of it.

Damien hadn't been involved in any of the preparations for the massive public component of the funeral. He knew the final steps of the dance—they were the same for Hands who fell in the line of duty, and he'd buried Alaura Stealey, the Hand who recognized him as a Rune Wright, there.

Marines led the way, perfectly marching ranks of blue dress uniforms glittering under the weak Martian sun. A Navy contingent followed, their ranks noticeably less perfect than the Marines.

Others came after them, scattered contingents of the various branches of the Protectorate government representatives from half the worlds that paid allegiance to Mars—all who could send a formal delegation in time.

Then the traditional black cars. Damien was in the third of the armored vehicles, watching an overhead view of the entire parade on a holographic projection.

Kiera had argued to be in the same car as him, but General Spader had won. The cars were heavily armored and each was escorted by two Royal Guards walking alongside in exosuits, but they still couldn't risk having the Lord Regent and the Mage-Queen in the same vehicle.

She was in the second set of five cars, the ones following behind the two plain hearses at the heart of the parade. Those were followed by a solid block of fifty Royal Guard in the same full exosuit armor as the ones guarding the vehicles, and then more Marines.

The parade was over a kilometer long and held at least a thousand Marines—and Damien had seen the security plans. There were *ten* thousand Marines positioned through the city around Central Avenue, with aircraft orbiting above the city and shuttles and warships higher up.

They'd tried to minimize the impact the security would have on the people, but he knew it still hadn't been easy for people to gather along the route...but gather along the route they had.

Olympus City and the Mountain were home to millions of people, and he could have sworn they were all there to say goodbye to their King.

"There was a point to an open car for Kiera," he told Spader over the command net. "It would do people good to see her, I suspect."

"And how safe do you think she would be, Montgomery, exposed like that?" the Royal Guard commander asked. "Someone just threw a quarter-billion dollars of drones and missiles at you, and the only ID we'd got on them is 'probably Republican.' Our Crown Princess is now a ninety-year-old Admiral in the middle of fighting a war.

"The people need to see Kiera Alexander, yes, but she needs to survive to take the crown and the Mountain in her own right. You seem a decent-enough man, Damien Montgomery, but I have no desire to attend your coronation."

Damien shivered.

"I have even less desire to attend my coronation," he told her. "I don't disagree with you, General. I just wonder where we draw the line."

"Preferably? In pre-secured designated zones where she can give speeches but we know everyone is cleared."

"Like the one I'm speaking in shortly?" Damien asked. "Where's she supposed to be while I'm giving my remarks?"

"In one of the observation boxes set aside for VIPs," Spader told him. "Transmuted transparent titanium. It's secure and moderately visible."

"No, she needs to be with me," the Lord Regent replied. "We can't have her on the sidelines today, even if she's not speaking."

Everyone, including Kiera, he suspected, would have preferred her to speak at her father and brother's funeral. Unfortunately, even given prepared remarks, she'd simply broken into incoherent tears trying to practice.

Damien didn't blame her. *He* wanted to do the same, and the Desmonds hadn't been his blood family.

"The security is not set up for us to have the Mage-Queen on that stage," Spader objected.

"But it is set up for the Lord Regent," Damien said dryly. "I'm aware I'm more expendable than she is, but I would expect much the same security."

"I dislike changing the plan on moving the Mage-Queen of Mars," the Royal Guard's commander told him.

"I'll check with her before I make it an order," Damien told the woman, "but I suspect it's happening. As for the plan changing? General, she's sixteen. Get used to it."

That managed to get a snort of almost-humor from Spader as Damien linked to Kiera's com.

"Kiera, I want to make a last-minute change to the plans," he told her. "I know you're not feeling up to speaking, but I want you on the stage with me."

He paused, but she didn't answer immediately.

"It's your call," he reminded her. "Spader is focused on keeping you safe, but people need to see you. They need to *know* you—and we need people to remember that *I* speak for *you*, not myself."

"True," she finally answered, her voice shaky with unshed tears. "It's not easy, Damien."

"It's not supposed to be, I don't think," he told her gently. "I'm not asking you to speak, Kiera—though I'll yield the stage if you feel you can in the end—but I think you need to be there."

She exhaled a sigh that was half a sob. Even Damien was finding compartmentalizing his grief away hard today.

"I'll be there. My guards know the way?"

"They will by the time we arrive," he promised her. "I've got your back, kid. Always."

"I know. Thank you."

The stage was set up right in front of the main gates of the Mountain. The core procession would avoid those gates from there, wrapping around the side of Olympus Mons on a thirty-minute drive to a specific flank of the giant mountain.

But this was also the end of the public part of the procession and the place for the public part of the remarks.

Damien met Kiera halfway to the stage, inside a moving bubble of red-armored Guards. People were spotting the Mage-Queen, the young woman's gold circlet distinctive even in a sea of black suits like hers, and pointing as she passed.

The young Queen noticed and straightened her back. She was still crying, Damien knew, but she began to wave to the closer people on the other side of the security cordon.

As they walked, the first of the four clergy scheduled to speak began the Kel Maleh Rachamim, the Jewish prayer of mourning. The rabbi would be followed by the bishop and imam of Olympus City, and then by the senior pujari of Olympus's largest Hindu temple.

The local senior priests of no less than *seventeen* religions had offered their services for the ceremony. The Vatican had even offered the unusual concession of allowing the Pope to leave Earth to perform the ceremony—without even requiring that Her Holiness be the only speaker.

Instead, the Regency Council and Kiera had settled on the local leaders of the four largest religions. It was a simple, relatively rational selection that Damien *could* defend.

Which was good, since he'd already had to and expected to do so again. And again.

"Are you okay?" he whispered to Kiera as they walked forward together.

"No," she replied calmly, waving to a small child sitting on their parent's shoulder. "All of this...it doesn't feel like Dad. Or Des, for that matter."

"Your father understood the value of spectacle when required," Damien said gently. "Des...Des I'll give you."

Even through her barely contained tears, that got a small smile from his ward.

"There's no rush," he reminded her as the rabbi concluded his prayer. "Three more prayers and we've only got fifteen meters to go."

"Are any of them going to be in English?" she asked as the second prayer starting, the bishop of Olympus City proclaiming the funeral mass in firm and measured Latin.

"Nope," Damien told her. They were through the crowd now and the door was sliding closed behind them. Even with the cordon, that had been the most vulnerable part of the journey, and they'd made it safely.

"The imam will speak in Arabic and the pujari will speak in Hindi," he continued. "Short of including 'atheist' on the list, the top four didn't include anyone who does liturgy in English."

He'd had a moment of temptation to count all of the various non-Catholic Christian groups as one entity—that would have put them in the top four instead of the Jewish population of the city—but he'd realized that was bias from his own religious background.

And there wasn't a large-enough United Church population in Olympus City to have a United minister speaker speak for that combined group.

The imam took over from the bishop as he and Kiera finally reached the green room next to the stage. More Royal Guards were waiting for them, as were four young men from the Mountain's PR team with portable makeup trays and chairs.

"Sit down, sit down," one of them instructed. "We only have two minutes and we need to make sure you'll look right in front of the cameras."

If there was one part of ruling the Protectorate Damien had never predicted, it was the makeup.

CHAPTER 28

THE CARS came to a halt well short of the line of unmarked black basalt obelisks. The Royal Guard spread out first, securing the empty and secluded field against any potential threat.

There wasn't one. People only came there for events like this one. It wasn't a secured zone, but it was rare for someone to *want* to look at the Fields of Sorrow.

The evenly spaced black obelisks marked the edge of an immense mass grave. No one was sure how many children and youths the Eugenicists had raised, bred and murdered in their unholy quest to re-birth magic, but the Protectorate knew where their bodies were buried.

Unnamed. Uncounted. *But never forgotten.*

At the base of the fields, integrated into the obelisks that marked the lowest edge of the Fields of Sorrow, was the Black Mausoleum: a low-slung structure carved of the same basalt as the markers them-selves.

The Mausoleum held two hundred and fifty crypts. Eighty-seven held the rebels who had liberated Olympus Mons. Only nine of those had names: Eugenicist scientists and soldiers who had turned on the cult-like organization that had raised them, to fight for justice.

The others only had pictures and the six-character designation that was all the children of the Olympus Project had ever been allowed until DMA-651 had overthrown the Eugenicists and given himself the name Desmond Michael Alexander—and the title of Mage-King of Mars.

He'd buried his friends there—and then he'd buried his Hands there. Then his Queen. And then, when that incredible and broken man had finally laid down his burdens, he'd been buried there.

The Black Mausoleum held the Mage-Kings of Mars and their closest servants.

A hundred and seventy of the crypts were claimed, though seventy-two of those were empty. Hands did not often die in places or ways that let family and King inter an actual body.

Memory of Alaura Stealey's funeral shivered down Damien's spine, but even that paled to the duty laid on him today.

"With me, Kiera," he told the young Queen as he led the way to the first hearse.

A young man and woman unknown to Damien were standing by the second hearse. Des's spirit would be carried on his final journey by his friends. The empty coffin of the Mage-King of Mars would be carried by his heirs.

The coffin slid out of the hearse with ease. Nothing had been retrieved of either Desmond, their bodies vaporized by the antimatter explosion that had killed them. The weight of the coffin was purely the heavy wood it was built from.

Kiera was taller than Damien, and with him using magic instead of his hands it took them a moment to adjust the burden for both of them to carry it easily. They still had a ways to go, and this was the hardest part. Even the speech had been easier than metaphorically carrying his King.

The path to the Black Mausoleum was long and chilly, but someone had come up the previous day to make sure it was clear. Even there, even now, a security team led the way along the path. Stealey's funeral had been less secured...but the Mage-King of Mars hadn't just died then.

Two crypts stood open side by side, with the slabs to close them resting on the ground next to them, as the procession reached the end of their journey.

"Together?" he said softly to Kiera.

"Together," she agreed.

They carefully slid the empty coffin into the crypt, the stone surface angled ever so slightly to allow the weight to help them.

Des would come second, but there were two more steps. Damien exchanged a nod with Kiera, and both of them touched the basalt at the base of the crypt and reached for their magic. She started at the beginning, he started at the end, and the black basalt turned white under their power.

They met in the middle of the text. There were no dates: many of the first people buried there hadn't known when they were born, and tradition dictated silence now. That left only two lines of text on the black basalt, for all the world to see:

DESMOND MICHAEL ALEXANDER
THIRD MAGE-KING OF MARS

The wake that followed was at least partially a formal affair, but there were no more speeches for Damien or Kiera to make. Once they escaped the seemingly endless receiving line of people giving their condolences, it was *merely* a party in memory of the Mage-Queen's father and brother.

"I feel like I could probably intimidate the bartender into giving me something harder," Kiera murmured as she and Damien propped up the same wall. She was holding a glass of iced tea instead of the wine he was slowly drinking.

"Probably," he agreed. "It would be a terrible idea and might cost the poor woman her career, since she's not supposed to serve alcohol to any of the minors here."

"You'd save her. If I told you to," she replied.

"Probably," he repeated. "It's still a terrible idea."

"Fine." She took a sip of the tea and looked around. "May I ask you something, Damien?"

"I may not answer, but you can ask me anything," he told her. "There are topics you're better off finding a woman for, I'll admit."

That earned him a moment of glare.

"Not that kind of something." She glanced around the room

again. "How many people here actually care? I lost my *father*, but they just lost...a symbol. And even at that, the symbol is replaced and the Protectorate endures.

"What do any of them care?"

"There's almost certainly people here who don't," Damien agreed thoughtfully as he glanced around the room. Most of the Council was present, as were at least half the senior military officers in the systems.

"Most of the people at *this* party? They knew your father," he reminded her. "Not well, most of them. I doubt any of us knew him well except maybe you and Des, but they knew him. They mourn him.

"To answer your question, *most* of the people here care, to one degree or another. That the Protectorate endures past the death of the Mage-King is by design; it's not a flaw."

"I know. But it feels like we just...accept his death and move on. I...I don't want to move on, Damien. He was my *father*. I don't want to forget him. I don't want to forget Des!"

"Don't," Damien told her. "That's...up to you, really. I haven't forgotten my parents or my siblings, and it's been fifteen years. I haven't forgotten Alaura Stealey, Narveer Singh, Charlotte Ndosi...my list goes on for a while, Kiera.

"Friends, family, lovers...for my sins, I am the Protectorate's head of state until you turn nineteen. You will be our head of state for the rest of your life, and you *will* send people you care about to their deaths.

"Forget *none of them*," he told her fiercely. "We have to move on from those deaths; we have to live to make their sacrifices worth something. But we don't forget them, Kiera. I'll carry your father and what he taught me in my heart and my head for the rest of my life."

He smiled sadly.

"I think that might be the closest thing I know of to immortality."

Kiera was crying again and he fished a tissue out of the inside of his jacket.

"We'll remember them, Kiera," he said, blinking back hot tears of his own for a moment before giving up and grabbing more tissues to share. "We go forward, yes, but we never forget the ones we leave behind. No one's asking you to."

"Feels like it, some days," she confessed through her tears. "Like I'm only supposed to think about the next steps, what we do to replace them and move on."

"We have to think about those things," Damien agreed. "And it's hard and it *should be hard*. But we take it on together. I've got your back, Kiera."

"I know."

They were both silent then, finishing their glasses. Damien was surveying the crowd as he did and spotted people moving toward them.

That wasn't a surprise. It was a surprise they'd had the few minutes of privacy they'd had.

"Eyes up, Kiera," he instructed. "You don't have to smile and play pretty princess tonight, but we do need to talk to people."

"I know." She inhaled, sniffled, and nodded firmly. "I'll be all right, Damien. I think I can handle this. Split up, divide and conquer?"

The movement was Suresh Granger and his son, the young man who'd carried Des's coffin.

Also an ex-boyfriend of Des and someone Kiera didn't get along with as a rule. She was dodging that friction...which was fine by Damien.

"Sounds like a plan," he told her. "I'll take Granger and his kid; you go glad-hand the rest of the Council."

Several other Councilors converged on Damien and the Grangers for a conversation that managed to almost entirely stay away from business and focus on personal recollections of Desmond Michael Alexander.

"I remember the first time I was on Mars," Suresh Granger told them all. "My father was visiting as the Governor's representative for a specific matter—I was too young to remember what it was now. He'd already been King for twenty years, but he took the time to have dinner with all of us, including the kids."

The old Tau Ceti Councilor shook his head. "They even served my favorite dessert, and while I was trying not to actively dive across the table to it—I was *eleven*," he noted with a smile. "I caught him looking at me and grinning.

"He'd known and he'd made sure they served it, just to make the kid of a diplomat he'd probably never work with again happy," Granger concluded. "I still look back to that day as the moment I knew I was Desmond Alexander's man."

There were nods and chuckles around the group, and Damien looked around again, recognizing faces a bit more carefully. The Councilors surrounding him had all been in the group Desmond had called his Loyalists, the ones who'd supported his agenda in the Council.

He also realized, somewhat unexpectedly, that the group had gained a new member whose arrival he'd missed. Munira Samara winked at him when she saw he'd recognized her, then bowed.

"My Lord Regent, I can't help but note that your wine glass is empty," she told him. "May I refill it for you?"

Damien raised a questioning eyebrow, not least because he could tell Samara's own glass was full of iced tea. The Muslim detective didn't drink alcohol.

"I believe I can fill my own glass," he said slowly. "Would you care to accompany me, Lady Samara?"

Her new Warrant might not have been officially announced, but just having held the title of Voice in the past meant she was due that honorific.

"I think I spotted a dessert tray that requires further investigation," she agreed. "Lead on, my lord."

"Councilors," Damien said to his companions, nodding to them. "I look forward to speaking with you again, though we all know the next time will be less convivial."

Desmond's Loyalists in the old structure, after all, weren't entirely on the Mountain's side when it came to building a *new* structure.

"Don't worry; we'll go easy on you for at least one more meeting," Granger told him with a chuckle before bowing his farewell.

With a final nod to the rest of the crowd, Damien followed Samara off toward the banquet table.

"What do you need?" he murmured to her.

"Private appointment, off the books," she said calmly, her voice equally soft as they relied on the noise of the crowd to cover their conversation. "I didn't want a digital record of the request, either."

"I hate not trusting our systems," Damien replied. "I'm booked tomorrow, but I can drop out of this after another hour and meet with you then."

"That'll work," she confirmed. "I need to brief you."

That was...promising.

"You found something?" he asked.

"We think we've IDed the assassin, but it's not a hundred percent and the next move is pushing a Voice's authority far enough that I want backup."

"This is black-on-black, Munira," Damien reminded her. "I'll back you, within reason at least."

"We need a Hand," the Voice admitted as they reached the wine bar. "Since I haven't heard about any of those arriving in-system, I'm open to suggestions."

A Hand. The only thing a *Voice* would want a Hand for was an open assault on a fortified position.

Just what had Samara *found*?

"Give me an hour, then meet me in the Mage-King's office," Damien instructed. "There are always options."

And if they'd found Desmond the Third's assassin, the breadth of those options was *astonishing*.

CHAPTER 29

"IT WASN'T as easy as it should have been," Samara said grimly as she brought up a series of image feeds on the holoprojectors. "Even once we found unaltered footage, our target was only in the cameras for seventeen minutes."

"I didn't think we'd even get proof of alteration," Damien pointed out. "Where did you find unedited footage?"

"At some point, the Royal Guard installed a secondary feed on every security system in the Mountain, feeding to a one-write-only archive hidden near the geothermal plants. Spader gave us access," Romanov told him, the Royal Guard pacing the room behind Samara. "We confirmed our worst fears: not only were Hand codes used to allow access to rewrite the data, the software used to do so defeated our best detection tools."

"We should be able to identify something now that we have access to an unedited copy of the data, right?" Damien asked.

"We'd need to read in a more advanced programmer than me for that," Samara told him. "Once this is over, that will be necessary, but right now, I think secrecy trumps it.

"In any case, our target is *good*," she noted, drawing their attention back to the footage they had retrieved. "Good enough, in fact, that I think the couple of unforced errors I'm seeing are because they knew the footage was going to be wiped.

"They're using a digital-interface face-wrap and keeping their face away from cameras. All of that would draw attention, but as you can see in the footage, they avoid all contact with people on their way in and out."

"What are they carrying?" Damien asked, studying the imagery.

"It's a toolbox," Samara replied. "Interestingly, it's a toolbox they picked up inside the Mountain. Watching this, I don't think there was a bomb. I think they used our tools plus some additional modules to rig up a device to sever the antimatter piping."

"Is that possible?" he asked.

"We'd have to ask Chief Wattana," Romanov told him. "I think so. The tools to work with those conduits are capable of severing them, after all. They just have multi-layer safeties to make sure they don't sever an active conduit."

"I doubt the cutter they rigged would be usable afterwards, but it didn't need to be," Samara told Damien. "Assembled from what was on hand. We're looking at someone at the top of their trade, a professional determined to make it look like an accident."

"And from what you're saying, we don't have an ID?"

"I didn't say that," Samara told him. "I said it should have been easier, but the target is very good. We have only two blips of footage that got us more than just eyes. Unfortunately for our target, *my* software is better at accounting for that interference face-wrap than he thinks."

"Was it enough?" Damien asked.

She gestured. The imagery from the Mountain's security systems vanished, replaced by six faces.

"It was enough to narrow it down to these six people in the Martian civil databases," she concluded. "These two are actually sufficiently well known that I cross-verified against publicly available media records of them."

Two of the faces flashed blue. One went dull.

"Kristoff Tolwyn is a news anchor in Curiosity City," she noted. "It took me under five minutes to confirm exactly where he'd been during the time the assassin was in the Mountain: at work, prepping to go on air."

One of the faces remained lit up in blue.

"The other four I couldn't cross-verify, and as non-public figures, I have limited access to their schedules and movements," she continued. "These two I was able to sufficiently confirm locations to rule them out."

Three faces remained, one of them the one she'd lit up in blue.

"I can't confirm the location of Johnathon Brown or Caleb Wurst during the infiltration," Samara noted. "Wurst lives on the other side of the planet, so it seems likely he was at work at the time. I'm working to confirm that, but keeping this investigation under wraps slows the process.

"Brown, on the other hand, is a citizen of Olympus Mons and does not, upon investigation, appear to have been seen since Desmond's death," she concluded. "Our other remaining suspect is this man."

She gestured to the still-blue-highlighted face.

"Alexander Ryan Odysseus, stage name Xander O," she identified him. "He's a minor sports celebrity, working in several varieties of what I'd call extreme performance art more than true *sports*.

"He lives in an isolated estate paid for by a family trust fund less than one hour's flight from the Mountain." She paused. "He has multiple scheduled appearances over the next few weeks and is definitely still on Mars—he's been seen since the Mage-King's death.

"He also appears to have flown to Olympus Mons in his private shuttle for dinner and a stay at the Hotel Rhino the night of our infiltration. He was back home before the launch, but he was definitely in the City during our target time period."

"A sports celebrity acting as a hitman," Damien noted. "That seems... unlikely."

"Johnathon Brown is a hairdresser," Samara said dryly. "That seems about as likely, but they're my top two suspects."

"You can write warrants to investigate their homes and interrogate them yourself, Voice Samara," Damien pointed out. "What do you need my backup for?"

"Because the first thing I did after we IDed Odysseus as a potential suspect was call in a favor from the boys on high," Romanov said quietly. "And we found...*this*."

Damien had spent enough time aboard warships and working with Marines that he could read military iconography as easily as he could read Martian Runic or English.

The hologram now projecting in the middle of his office answered his question. It was the valley estate they'd been talking about, and it looked like a pleasant place to live. On the surface.

The icons glowing red across the display gave the lie to that surface. Several sheds, positioned to look like they held grounds maintenance equipment, concealed antiaircraft missile launchers. Several areas that appeared to be covered in grass sod had more red icons, marking concealed defensive weapons.

"Control center?" he asked calmly as he surveyed a surprisingly heavily fortified estate.

"Unclear," Romanov responded. "That alone suggests it's under the house."

"All automated or remote-controlled," Damien noted, continuing to review the data. "No personnel on the site?"

"A few life signs, nothing to suggest the kind of support I'd expect these to have."

"Would you two care to explain what you're going on about?" Samara asked. "I understand that the estate is more defended than Romanov wants to take on with just half a dozen Royal Guard, but that's about it."

"The estate is a fortified compound with *heavily* automated weapons systems covering the ground and air approaches," Damien told her. "The Royal Guard could take it, but they'd be vulnerable on approach to these antiaircraft launchers. Which, I'll note, are illegal as all hell on Mars."

"Why didn't the Navy know this was here already, then?" the detective asked.

"We don't make a policy of doing deep thermal and visual scans of civilian property," Romanov replied. "A cruiser's captain could read over the shoulder of any given individual on a bit under forty percent of Mars. We have privacy laws for a reason, Voice Samara."

"We wouldn't normally respond to the presence of illegal weapons with an assault drop, either," Damien added. "Their presence is grounds for a warrant to seize the weapons and search the property, but in the absence of an active crime, we'd deal with this slowly and peaceably."

"That's our practice for a stockpile of assault rifles in an old fortified dome," Samara countered. "I'm not sure we'd do the same thing for anti-aircraft missiles and, what, automated gun turrets?"

"All we really can say is remote-controlled pop-up turrets of some kind," Romanov said. "They could be paintball guns. In theory."

"The AA launchers and their sensors suggest differently," Damien concluded. "The threat level is enough higher than that stockpile of assault rifles that we probably would take it slowly, Voice Samara.

"But when one of our two top suspects for the assassination of the Mage-King of Mars is in an illegally fortified compound equipped with antiaircraft weaponry, I consider that a full set of strikes." He studied the map grimly.

"Denis is correct," he continued with a gesture at the Guard-Lieutenant. "The team of Guards he can pull together isn't able to assault this facility. Mostly, it's a problem of transportation: the Royal Guard has a limited air-transport pool. One of the Royal shuttles would be the best choice, but there's enough launchers in there to threaten even an assault shuttle, unless that shuttle makes a proper assault approach that will trigger every sensor on half the planet."

"And we still want to keep this secret," Samara agreed. "Damn."

"So, we have, really, three options," Damien told her. "We at least partially give up on secrecy and use the presence of an illegal set of automated weapons as grounds for a full-bore assault. Assault-drop a Marine company from orbit. They'd tear through those defenses easily enough... but they probably wouldn't succeed in taking Odysseus alive. And we'd lose Marines," he finished grimly. "Not many, most likely, but we would lose some."

"To take down the Mage-King's assassin, they'd make that trade," Romanov replied.

"I know. But I see no reason to ask it of them unless I must," Damien told his bodyguard. "Our second option is to take the Royal Guard in on one of those shuttles. Hard and fast, jump and drop. We might be able to do it without drawing attention from anyone other than the Navy, who we can order to keep things quiet."

He shook his head.

"I don't put those odds at over fifty-fifty, and there's no way to reduce the risk of the attack itself. At high-enough speed, we can *probably* avoid the AA missiles, but it's a single point of failure."

"And what's option three?" Samara asked.

"The reason you're talking to me," Damien said grimly. "The 'send in a Hand' option. A Rune of Power is used to teleport a strike team directly to the estate. I lead that team of Royal Guards directly into the main house, bypassing the entirety of the defenses while we move to secure Odysseus and the control room. Once the weapons are shut down and the target is secured, we leave the Guard to secure and clean up while Romanov and I bring Odysseus back here."

"You can't be serious," Samara snapped. "You're the Lord Regent. You can't lead an assault."

"Someone has to," Damien said quietly. "For me to elevate a new Hand and provide them with a Rune of Power will take days. Days I'm not prepared to let this problem fester.

"The simplest and cleanest way to deal with this estate is to send in a Hand. In the absence of a Hand, someone with a Rune of Power.

"Unless one of the Hands has shown up in-system in the last thirty minutes, your choices are me or Kiera—and even if I *was* prepared to let the Mage-Queen of Mars personally lead an assault team, she isn't trained for it."

He smiled thinly.

"I am."

His two subordinates looked at him in silence, then Samara turned a glare on Romanov.

"This is what you expected, isn't it?"

"It's what we needed," the Guard replied. "Is letting the Lord Regent lead an assault a good plan? No. Is it the only option to achieve this with minimal casualties and no breach of the secrecy of this investigation? Yes.

"Plus, it's his call," Romanov reminded her. "And I've learned I don't win arguments with Montgomery."

Damien snorted.

"No, you don't," he agreed. "Prep your team, Guard-Lieutenant."

"We're going now?" Romanov asked, surprised.

"I see no reason to let this wait. Do you?"

CHAPTER 30

DAMIEN GENERALLY felt small enough when surrounded by body-guards. Most of the Marines and Secret Service Agents who'd shepherded him through his career as a Hand of the Mage-King had been at least ten centimeters taller than him.

The problem was only exacerbated when everyone else was strapped into exosuits. The suits of powered battle armor were uniformly at least two meters tall, which left his guards towering fifty centimeters or more above him.

"My lord, over here," Romanov called him as he weaved his way through the team. It was only as he approached the Guard-Lieutenant that he realized there were *eleven* exosuits in the room and there were only ten Guards coming with him.

The eleventh suit was the first he'd seen under two meters tall, and it was open enough for him to see that the inner layer had been resized for a much smaller person than the average Marine. It also didn't share the red coloring of the rest of the armor. Currently, it was set into a black-and-gold livery that Damien didn't even recognize.

"I had this requisitioned before we left Mars last time," Romanov told him as he approached the suit. "His Majesty got involved while we were gone and had it built to the same standard as his own armor, so it has the same runes as the Guard armor."

Damien touched the suit hesitantly. There were two reasons he didn't generally wear armor: firstly, that he was well outside the range that the suits could adjust to fit; and secondly, because he'd lose a small but significant portion of his ability to project magic.

"Those runes have to be tailored to the individual," he said absently, but he was already probing the matrix in the suit. He could adjust it himself, given an hour, but... "Except Desmond already did that. Huh."

"I thought you needed the wearer," Romanov replied. "I was expecting to delay while you adjusted. It already works?"

"I think so. Give me a hand," Damien ordered.

Another Guard stepped over to help him and Romanov out. Despite the problems, Damien still had some practice on exosuit armor, but getting into it was a trick that would take time.

The inner layer of smart fabric wrapped around him quickly, supporting him inside a suit taller than he was. Viewscreens dropped down in front of his eyes as Romanov lowered the helmet onto his head, flickering on fast enough to prevent more than the tiniest spark of claustrophobia.

The suit closed up automatically at that point, and he could feel parts of it shifting and adjusting. It had been tailored for him and the adjustments were quick, allowing him to take a few experimental steps.

"Even for us, the suit software is primarily coded around eye and chin movement," Romanov told him, the Guard-Lieutenant's voice coming through a speaker next to his ear. "Your hands shouldn't be an obstacle, though you still can't do much with them."

"I was trained on it," Damien replied. "A while ago now, but I was trained."

He studied the screens in front of him and twitched his chin toward an icon.

"...Regent in armor is *terrifying*," an unfamiliar voice was saying.

"Montgomery on the channel!" someone barked. "Control yer bitching."

"Believe me, Guards, I've heard far worse directed at me," Damien replied. "No one is calling me 'Darth Montgomery' or 'that little fucking psychopath' or anything of the sort. I can live with *terrifying*.

"Are we ready to deploy?" he asked.

"Awaiting your order, my lord," Denis Romanov told him. "Are you ready, Lord Regent? The next step is on you."

"I'll give you all a five count," Damien replied. "Let me confirm my distances and numbers. I'd prefer not to deliver us all into a mountain."

The suit's operating system was sufficiently intuitive that he had the coordinates of his target up in moments—and, conveniently, it gave him an even better link to the Martian GPS than his wrist-comp did.

There would be no dealing with the external automated weapons. The house plans said there was a large entryway with a vaulted two-story ceiling and *plenty* of room to drop eleven exosuited troublemakers.

"Five," Damien said aloud as he completed his calculations. Even with everyone around him clad in several centimeters of metal and ceramics, he saw the postures adjust as they caught his warning.

"Four."

Guns were leveled. Most of them were carrying the heavy-penetrator rifles designed to take down similar suits to their own. There were several large-bore automatic shotguns and a magazine-fed grenade launcher, weapons less likely to over-penetrate the target. And the house behind them.

The one thing they all shared was an under-barrel SmartDart gun. The Guards were loaded for bear...but they were hoping to take that bear alive.

"Three. Two. One."

Damien's magic filled the room in a swirl of power as he took hold of his companions, locked his target in his mind and *stepped.*

He'd intentionally aimed high and the squad appeared twenty centimeters above the laminated wood floor of the house entryway. That floor shattered under the impact of twenty-two metal boots falling from the sky, the clear coating the only thing keeping splinters from flying everywhere.

"Sweep, sweep!" Romanov barked. A moment later. "Clear. All zones clear."

Damien was turning in place as the Guards spread out around him, taking in his surroundings. So far, at least, the plans appeared to match the reality.

"Everyone has the map," the Guard team commander continued. "Move by fire team. Secure the basement entrances and sweep up."

"Romanov, your team's with me," Damien said softly. The Guard worked in fire teams of two, with the most junior soldier usually paired with the squad commander.

Of course, the *most junior* Guard in this squad was actually Denis Romanov—and the newly minted Guard-Lieutenant's ten-year history in the Marines and Secret Service was on the low side for a new Royal Guard.

"Understood—Roricsen, on the Lord Regent," Romanov barked. "What's the plan, my lord?"

"Not interrupting your people, first of all," Damien told him. "But there's a *fascinating*-looking gap in the upstairs floorplan that would make for a panic room. Shall we check it out?"

Even without being able to see the Guard's face, Damien knew Romanov was resisting the urge to tell him to send another fireteam. A second passed in silence before the man finally responded.

"Yes, my lord. Lead the way."

Damien carefully paced his travel through the house to keep behind the sweeping fire teams of Guard. He was going to poke at the most dangerous zones himself, but the Guards would make sure there were no surprises.

"Anyone in the house?" Romanov asked as he and Damien reached the top of the stairs.

"Negative, we're drawing a blank on thermal and visual," one of the fire team leaders replied. "Anyone else?"

Multiple similar comments replied.

"Bedroom was occupied recently, but no one in it now," one leader replied. "Hold one." She paused. "Bed is still *warm*. Someone is *definitely* here, sirs."

"Thought so," Damien murmured. "Watch for automated defenses, people. Our target has bailed for the panic room. The million-dollar question is whether the *panic room* is the same place as the *control* room."

"Scanners aren't showing anything in the house," Romanov reported as Damien stepped past a team into the master bedroom to study the wood-paneled walls.

"They're also not showing a panic room that's definitely here," the Lord Regent replied. "Odysseus isn't registered as a Mage, and even if he's somehow secretly one, he hasn't left."

"How do you know that? He could have teleported out after we came in," Romanov replied.

"I'd have known," Damien said quietly. "There's runes in this wall," he continued, tapping on the wood paneling. The master bedroom's west wall was just over two meters away from the upstairs library's east wall. There was a big stone fireplace beneath them, but Damien doubted the chimney needed *that* much space.

"What kind of runes?" Romanov asked carefully. "I seem to recall one set we expected to take out a city block."

Damien had teleported past those. These probably wouldn't require that.

"Nothing so destructive. Just concealment; it's why your scanners aren't picking it up. Maintaining those in secret must be expensive as hell, probably why this is the only spot that's hidden."

"What do we do, my lord? I'm guessing the entrance is concealed and it's presumably not to be opened from the outside at this point, anyway."

"Get another fireteam in here," Damien ordered. "Any of us could open this up, so I'll provide the shielding instead. An extra set of guns won't go amiss."

"What are you expecting?" Romanov asked.

"Trouble," Damien said grimly. "So, let's get more Guards in here."

Another two-Guard fireteam joined them a moment later, falling into line with Romanov and his companion as they leveled weapons at the wall.

"Now," Damien said loudly as he stepped up behind them. "I'm relatively sure that the panic room has at least some cameras and that you can see me and probably hear me, Mr. Odysseus.

"From the fact that there are Royal Guards in your house, I suspect you know why we're here. Surrender remains your wisest option, Mr. Odysseus. Don't make us kill you."

Silence was his only answer and Damien shrugged.

Power audibly crackled in the room as he wove a shield in front of the four Guards, one strong enough to stop any weapon they were carrying.

"A door, if you please, my Guards," Damien ordered.

Romanov lifted his hand, took a moment to account for Damien's shield, then slashed the armored gauntlet across the air.

Blades of force ripped through the wall like tissue paper, wood paneling, supporting beams, and reinforced steel armor plating dividing with equal ease. The entire wall fell outward toward them, hitting the ground with a resounding crash as it unveiled the man behind it.

He was moving before the wall fell, faster than Damien had ever seen. Odysseus leapt the debris of the wall, his weapon firing as he came.

The discarding sabot penetrator rounds *would* have gone through the Royal Guards' armor, but they shattered against Damien's shield—and the same barrier threw Odysseus himself back. The solidified layer of air didn't leave space for the Guard to fire their own weapons, but Damien had been expecting *some* version of this.

He hadn't been expecting the man to be *quite* this fast or for the man to have a Secret Service–issue penetrator carbine. The light but magically reinforced weapon fired the same rounds with the same power as the exosuit-mounted weapon, but that made it mind-bogglingly expensive.

Odysseus tossed the gun aside and then *moved* again, a blur of motion as he dove for the wall, looking for an edge to Damien's barricade. Unfortunately for him, the Guard had adapted to his speed by now and they didn't *need* the SmartDart guns to take him alive.

A burst of lightning appeared in the man's path and he smashed into it before he could dodge. Sparks rippled across the assassin's body as he crumpled to the ground, twitching in pain.

"Bind him," Damien ordered. He could *sense* the bonds of force holding Odysseus to the ground as he dropped the barrier and crossed to the man.

"Alexander Ryan Odysseus," he told the man formally, "you are under arrest for treason and regicide. Your *only* hope, I'm afraid, is to help me find the people who hired you."

There was no response. The man was unconscious. If Damien was *lucky*, it was just the electric shock.

"Find the control room," Damien ordered. "We need to bring in med-evac immediately. We need this man alive!"

CHAPTER 31

TO DAMIEN'S RELIEF, the squad's medic quickly managed to confirm that Odysseus wasn't dead. He was apparently more vulnerable to the electroshock than anyone had expected—that was why SmartDarts were preferred. The dart would have calculated the right level of shock to apply.

Alive didn't mean *undamaged*, after all.

"I've never seen anyone move like that," Damien admitted as the medic was setting up an IV to feed medication to their captive. "The only people who came close were Augments."

"I'd guess top-tier combat cybernetics, but his scan comes up clean," Romanov replied, standing beside Damien and looking at Odysseus's unconscious form as well. "Bioaugmentation is the only thing left."

"I didn't think modified genetics could get you *that* far," Damien said quietly. He'd seen images and read reports on the small minority of the Protectorate's population that was genetically engineered. It was rarely a successful process and had yet to ever be a fully positive "upgrade" to the recipients.

Even now, human genetics wasn't fully understood. That was part of why the Mage-King's children were partial clones—to make sure the Rune Wright gift was never lost.

A lot of data had been lost when the Eugenicists had wrecked the research archives in Olympus Mons to stop the rebels taking them. Few Mages would shed tears for what had been lost there, given *how* it had been learned.

And the Eugenicists' shadow loomed large and ugly over genetic experimentation.

"Can't say for sure without dissecting him—which we're *not* doing," Romanov clarified quickly, "but there's definitely been some people working on creating and implanting super-charged versions of human organs.

"There's a lot of upgrading you can do without tripping a scanner, and I would guess our friend here has *all* of them."

Damien shivered. Now that things had calmed down, something about the house was feeling vaguely *wrong* to his Sight. There was more magic here, magic he couldn't *quite* localize, and it did not feel...right.

"How's the search of the basement going?" he asked.

"Slowly. It doesn't match the plans at all," Romanov told him. "I've ordered some special sounding gear brought in with the medevac, but we need to find the control center before they can approach. And we're still keeping this black, right?"

"Correct," Damien agreed. He studied the man and the field medicine station the medic had set up. "We need this one alive; we can't take any risks with him. The rest of us can wait until the shuttle is cleared in, but *he* needs to go back to the Mountain now. Corporal?"

That was addressed to the medic.

"Can he be moved?" Damien asked.

"Not without equipment we don't have here," the Guard replied. "A stretcher at least."

"Can he be *teleported*?" Damien countered.

The medic paused, looking down at his patient.

"I believe so, yes," he confirmed. "If you take us back to the ready room, I can get a stretcher and take him to a doctor straight away."

"He's to be taken directly to Dr. Gunther," Damien ordered. "I trust her to keep the Mountain's secrets."

He smiled thinly.

"And I'm not *taking* you, Corporal. Are you ready?"

Romanov and the other Guards in the room looked at him in confusion, but the medic clearly picked up his meaning. He crouched down next to his patient, double-checking the equipment he'd rigged up.

"I'm ready," he replied.

"Good luck," Damien told the man while running the numbers in his helmet comp. While the helmet OS wasn't designed for this, he already had the numbers from the teleport to the estate. Reversing them and adjusting for their changed location was straightforward enough.

Power *pulsed* in the room, and Odysseus and the Guard were gone.

Romanov shook his head, staring at where the unconscious man had been.

"The kind of bioaugments he has aren't legal, sir," he noted. "I doubt I even need to tell you that. Even the research should only be taking place under the most stringent of controls and ethical guidelines, let alone packing a man full of that shit."

"I'd guessed," the Lord Regent confirmed. "I trust Dr. Gunther to keep him alive, but we have work to do here still. Our answers are in that man's head, but there are answers here, too."

He shivered against the strange cold feeling in his Sight.

"I'm going to go join the team in the basement," he decided. "Something in this place is triggering my Sight without me being able to locate it. I *think* it's downstairs and I want to find it before the hairs on the back of my neck crawl out and *leave*."

Romanov snorted.

"Don't leave the house until we find the control room," he told his boss. "The situation is not secure until we do. I'm going to run oversight and check the perimeter. My neck hairs are objecting to wandering around an assassin's home base with the *Lord Regent of Mars*."

"Get used to it, Denis," Damien advised. "Once he's awake and we've torn this place apart, I'll be talking to him again."

"Are my objections to that even worth voicing?" Romanov asked.

"You can put them on the record if you'd like," the Lord Regent replied. "They're not changing anything."

The door into the basement was the same "traditional ski chalet" décor as the rest of the house. Real wood paneling and real wood doors filled the house, harkening back to an older time that the owner clearly enjoyed.

The décor didn't make it into the stairwell. The walls were bare plaster, though the lights leading down the steps were still modern and high-quality. A solid-looking security door waited at the bottom of the steps, already cut open by the Royal Guards as they came through.

One of the Guard was standing just inside the door as he came through, which was the point where Damien realized that at least one of the Guards had had eyes on him since he'd left Romanov's side.

That was probably a good thing, though he *should* have noticed before then. The Royal Guard were there to protect him, and he needed to be situationally aware enough to, if nothing else, know which way to dodge.

"The basement's a maze," the Guard told him as he looked past her. "Whatever the internal layout was, it's been gutted in favor of being confusing as hell under the cover of being sports supply storage."

He saw her point. From where he stood, there were three ways he could head deeper into the basement. Each was lined with racks holding everything from surfboards to skis. There were sensible and efficient ways to organize a space like this to be useful storage.

They hadn't been used. Instead, it looked like walls and racking had been thrown up wherever there was space whenever a new set of racks had been needed...and Damien doubted that someone with the money Odysseus seemed to have access to had been *quite* so random about their hobby and lifestyle.

"Any sign of the control center?" he asked.

"We're mapping as we go. We'll find a gap sooner or later, but it's a mess down here. Even magic isn't doing us much good."

Damien inhaled and looked around, leaning into his Sight as he tried to find any clues.

"They didn't use magic to conceal anything, at least," he told the Guard. "We're looking at a messy layout and technological stealth, not runes like upstairs."

"That means we *will* find it," the woman replied firmly. "Shouldn't take more than an hour or so."

"Send me that map," Damien ordered. He waved in a vague south-ward direction. This close, he was starting to get *some* sense of what was bothering him. "There's something *that* way that's bothering my Sight, but I don't want to start blasting holes until I have no choice."

"You start blasting holes, we'll follow suit," the Guard told him, and he could *hear* the grin in her voice. "I'm not feeling charitable about this asshole's shit. Only reason it's intact is because it might be evidence."

"And that, Guard Shaolin, is why I'm holding off on blasting holes," Damien told her. His suit's heads-up display, he'd just realized, told him the names of each of the Guards with him.

That was useful. He *liked* knowing the names of the people around him.

"There's no way you can pass off keeping eyes on me while I wander this maze," he continued as he looked around himself. "Have someone spell you on the stairs and walk with me."

"Yes, my lord," Guard Shaolin Lian replied. Another red-armored Guard appeared from the shadows a few moments later.

The armor *could* change color—Damien had an easy-access shortcut on his main screen to turn his black-and-gold royal livery red to match the Guards around him, for example—but outside of a combat environment needing camouflage, the Royal Guard would flaunt their colors.

"This way," he told her, leaving the stairs to the new Guard. "I don't know *what* is triggering my Sight...and it's not supposed to work like that."

It was reassuring, at least, to be up-front about *why* he was wandering in random directions through the basement of an assassin's house. Even his Secret Service details had only been partially briefed on the nature of his Rune Wright abilities.

The Royal Guard knew *everything*.

The house was large and the basement sprawled out even farther underground than the building above them did. Even so, with four Royal Guards and Damien scouring it, it couldn't hold its secrets for long.

The virtual map assembling in Damien's visor told him he was looking at a "missing" space of about eight square meters. There were other potential locations for the control room—most of them bigger and more likely to hold a computing center—but *this* gap held whatever was setting his skin on edge.

"Any sign of a control around here?" he asked Shaolin.

"None. If I was setting this up, it would be verbal or linked to my wrist-comp," she admitted. "A physical lever is just asking for trouble."

"So are computerized accesses," Damien replied. He ran his gaze along the rack of equipment in front of him. There was enough gear on this wall to field an entire lacrosse team...and lacrosse hadn't been on any of the lists of sports Odysseus participated in.

"Whatever," he finally said, then gestured.

The wall of equipment disappeared. If he'd done his math right, it was still intact—above them, in the middle of the empty parking pad beside the garage.

In its absence, he was looking at the back of another set of racking. He recognized the design instantly, even from this side.

The storage systems the Royal Martian Marine Corps used for weapons had a distinctive layout and structure. This was clearly two sets, designed to fold out into the space Damien was standing in at some unknown command.

"Help me," he told Shaolin. "These look like they roll outwards to you too, right?"

"I'll take the left," the Guard replied. A self-heating blade popped out of her left gauntlet and she sliced the locks holding the two panels of racking together. "Looks like the entire wall and the lacrosse display were supposed to swing open."

Exoskeletal muscles hauled the racking open against the resistance of unmoving motors, revealing one of the two things Damien had been expecting to find down there. Five meters wide and about one and a half deep, the unfolding walls eventually created a five-by-four box walled with weapon racks.

"Lacrosse is a violent sport, I'm told," Guard Shaolin noted. "But I don't recall it calling for seventeen-millimeter sniper rifles."

"Or heavy machine guns. Or lasers. Or penetrator carbines," Damien agreed, noting each item as he mentally cataloged it. There was, at least, only *one* Martian Armaments Omni-munition Heavy Support Weapon in the room.

On the other hand, the OHS was a weapon capable of firing anything from seven-millimeter anti-infantry rounds—at about thirty a *second*—to thirty-millimeter anti-armor explosive grenades—still at about six a second.

It was an exosuit-portable, barely single-person-usable-with-a-mount weapon usually installed on *armored personnel carriers*.

The armory also had two penetrator carbines, notable for individually costing more than the APC the OHS should have been mounted on, with a space for the third they'd encountered upstairs.

Six lasers from four different manufacturers. Damien had only encountered *one* functional laser weapon in his life—they were speciality weapons for specialty uses.

Covert sniper was one of those uses.

Most of the weapons in the room were long-range quiet things. One meter-wide section of racking held twenty-six varieties of suppressed pistols, at least two of which Damien could sense as being magically concealed from scanners now he was close to them.

The feeling of *wrongness* came from one of the four sections dedicated to sniper rifles. There were probably more pistols than any other weapon here, but the sniper rifles came second and definitely won out by sheer mass.

Sixteen different variants of precision long-range rifle had been mounted on the wall with care, but pride of place went to an immense weapon that looked like it was designed to shoot elephants.

From ten kilometers away.

The barrel of the seventeen-millimeter rifle looked like a gateway to hell. It was the largest weapon in the entire armory after the OHS, but Damien could see where it broke down for easy transport.

Intricately carved runes covered large chunks of the weapon, wards against detection mixed with spells to stabilize the gun against wind and vibration. If power was fed to the currently uncharged runes, the weapon wouldn't even need support. It would stay wherever it was put.

"That's a hell of a gun," Shaolin said softly. "I recognize most of the stuff in here, but that...that's custom-built."

"Probably primarily used for discarding sabot rounds," Damien replied. "Modified penetrator rounds, like...yeah, these."

He opened the highest of the drawers attached to the lower half of the racking, exposing the ammunition he expected. The rounds in the storage honeycomb were bigger than any he'd ever seen before, but the final bullet was same sharp-tipped tungsten round built to take down exosuits. Or tanks.

"I'm close," he murmured. "The gun isn't it...so..."

He touched one of the big penetrator rounds and then it finally hit him. It was in the middle. A drawer that didn't look any different from the rest of the bullet containers around the room but was radiating *something*.

Damien pulled the drawer open and stared down into it, hoping for some kind of answer. The honeycombed safety storage system was mostly empty. It was sized for the massive rounds for the big rifle, but the drawer could still hold at least twenty bullets.

This one held four and they were *definitely* the source of his itch. Shivering against the touch, he pulled one of the rounds out and put it on top of the drawer.

The tip looked plain enough. It was a big bullet, even inside a discarding-sabot launch system. Damien tried to slice the sabot off carefully...and then recoiled as the bullet sucked up the magic and tried to pull more through the spell.

"Dear God in heaven," he murmured.

"Lord Regent?" the Guard snapped, suddenly at his side with a weapon drawn.

"I'm fine, but we'll need to be very careful with these," Damien told her. "Anyone with a Rune of Power is vulnerable—and your exosuit runes are close enough."

"The hell?" Shaolin asked.

"I can't see the runes, but I can sense the matrix now I'm this close," he explained. "It's a deadly little thing, designed to force a Rune of Power into an overload feedback loop. Shoot a Hand with this, and if you're remotely lucky, well...boom."

The Guard took an unconscious step backward.

"I think I've heard of such a thing," she said slowly. "But...who would build such a thing? And why?"

"They're built to kill Hands, Guard Shaolin," Damien said calmly. "And unless I'm very mistaken, this particular set was built by the Keepers. To kill me."

His instincts had been freaking out because the last time he'd sensed this Matrix, it had been embedded in his shoulder and had nearly killed him. In a way that would have taken out the city block he was standing in.

"My questions for Mr. Odysseus just expanded significantly."

CHAPTER 32

"YOU ARE *insane."*

Damien settled down in his seat in what had been Desmond Alexander's office and let Malcolm Gregory get it out of his system.

"You can't just charge into an *assassin's* home to deliver a goddamn arrest warrant," the Chancellor continued. "You're not a Hand anymore. Not even the First bloody Hand anymore. You're the *Lord Regent of Mars.* You are *not* replaceable and you are *not* expendable."

"*Replaceable* is arguable, but I am most definitely expendable," Damien finally said, gesturing for the Chancellor to sit. "Not to play the game of who is *most* expendable, but the alternative available was Kiera."

The Mage-Queen had taken her seat at the beginning of the meeting and hadn't said a word yet. Gregory took a long look at her before taking his own seat.

"And you think this is a good example to set our Mage-Queen?" he asked.

"Not even a Jump Mage can take more than one person—at *best*— through a personal teleport with them," Damien told Gregory. "Our options were to blow the investigation completely open or to utilize a skill set unique to the Hands...and the Rune Wrights.

"Absent a Hand or the time to make one, the option was me or Kiera. And, my Queen"—he bowed slightly to Kiera—"you are neither trained nor ready for this kind of action."

"I'm still not even clear on what investigation this *is*," Gregory snapped. "What the hell is going on, Montgomery?"

"What's going on is that the Lord Regent is doing his job," Kiera said flatly. "What he was charged to do by *me*. On the other hand, Damien, perhaps *someone* should have known about this stunt before you charged into the lion's den?"

"You didn't even tell *her*?" Gregory demanded. "You. Are. Insane."

The enunciated echo brought a smile to Damien's face, one he needed after the previous night's discoveries.

"Malcolm, Alexander Odysseus is our primary suspect in the murder of my King," Damien told the Chancellor calmly. "That investigation is being kept utterly black because I have some *fascinating* questions on why certain people's expertise was neglected by the Inquiry.

"But I want the facts neatly lined up before I wreck Mylene Vemulakonda's year," he continued. "I'm reasonably sure she made a straightforward mistake, but the possibility of something darker remains."

"Murder?" Gregory's performative anger was gone now. That had been frustration of a comrade at a friend who'd unnecessarily endangered himself. What remained was the laser-sharp cold rage of the Chancellor of Mars. "You're certain."

"I'm certain," Damien confirmed. It hadn't really been a question. "We confirmed that something went wrong on the shuttle prior to the explosion in a way that was consistent with sabotage or a bomb.

"Further investigation revealed that one-time authorization codes generated from Charlotte Ndosi's Hand were used to access the security systems file before the shuttle launch. Despite our best efforts, we *still* can't find any sign that the data was edited...but thanks to General Spader's paranoia, we *do* have a copy of the original footage."

"Even with the original, we can't tell it was edited?" Gregory asked.

"We can tell it's different from the original, but even putting the two next to each other, I only know which one *is* the original because the data source for one is uneditable by hardware design instead of software design.

"Whoever covered up the presence of our saboteur in the Mountain was very, very, *very* good, with intimate familiarity with the Mountain's systems," Damien concluded. "Not our assassin. Someone else.

"I have Odysseus. He and I are going to have a conversation in a few minutes. I *want* the real murderer. I have the hand that pulled the trigger, but I want the voice that ordered it."

"Fuck me," Gregory finally concluded after a moment's thought. "What do you need, Damien?"

"For now, your confidence and your discretion," Damien told the Chancellor. "This moves in the dark for a while longer. I don't know how deep or how dirty the hole I'm digging is, and I'm worried what I'm going to find."

"Dig as far as you can as fast as you can, my lord, but there's duties you can't avoid," Gregory warned him. "You and I need to be on a ship to Council Station this evening."

"I know," Damien told him. "I'll be leaving Romanov behind to keep digging here, but I want to talk to Odysseus myself."

"Why?" Kiera demanded, the Mage-Queen inserting herself quietly into the meeting again. "The man killed my father. We strap him to a rack and pump him full of every inhibition reducer we have. I don't need his testimony to hold up in court; we already have enough to shoot him."

"Because there's a lot of moving parts here, my Queen," Damien replied. "And one of them is that the *last* time I was investigating something on Mars, I'm pretty sure Alexander Odysseus *shot me*."

To Damien's surprise, he was intercepted short of the interrogation room in the medical center. Dr. Ulrike Gunther was probably the best geneticist on Mars, if not in the Protectorate, which was part of why he'd sent the assassin to her for treatment.

She was *also* one of the people responsible for the health of the Royal Family in general—and the preservation of the Rune Wright genome specifically.

"Lord Regent, I've been trying to schedule an appointment with you for weeks," she told him swiftly as she fell in beside him. He slowed his pace to let her speak, even as he suspected he was going to regret it.

"Dr. Gunther, I *know* what my schedule is like," Damien admitted. "I can barely make appointments with myself. Plus, I haven't been back on Mars for weeks," he finished. "What's going on?"

"You and I need to sit down and talk about the continuity of the secondary Rune Wright bloodline," she told him without preamble. "The establishment of a second key family is critical to the maintenance of the Rune Wright genome, secondary only to the creation of an heir for Kiera Alexander."

Damien winced as he continued walking, realizing he'd lost track of where he was in the clinic. Fortunately, the interrogation room was supposed to be at the back of the Royal Family's private clinic, so *forward* was an option that didn't require him asking Gunther for directions.

"Right. Didn't I tell you to lay off Kiera on that one?" he told her. He vaguely recalled sending that message.

"Yes. Not exactly the response I was hoping for from my requests to speak to you, my lord," she told him. "Even disregarding the perspective of the preservation of the Royal Family in terms of continuity of government, the protection of the genome is critical."

"She's sixteen, Doctor, and she's not getting pregnant anytime soon," Damien replied flatly. "That's her call to make, not yours."

"We don't need a complete in vivo pregnancy, so long as there is an official announcement and transfer to the gestation chamber," Gunther replied. "She doesn't even need to...engage with the designated partner. We have sufficient non-Alexander material on file now to maintain the Rune Wright genome."

Damien stopped in his tracks and finally turned to look at the woman. Dr. Ulrike Gunther was a stick-thin woman in a pale blue lab coat over scrubs in the same color. Her hair was thin and frizzy, and her eyes were bright with passion.

"Dr. Gunther, who is the primary donor for your non-Alexander Rune Wright genetic material?" he said, as calmly as he could.

"You are, of course."

"Take one *goddamn second* and consider how it looks if Kiera Alexander has a child that looks remotely like me," Damien told her. "I am her Lord Regent; she is my *ward*. For the next three years, I stand in loco parentis for her. Legally, right now, *I am her father*.

"The child you are suggesting that we create for our *legal convenience* would be seen as evidence of a critical breach of trust and abuse in *every sense* by me.

"So, no, Dr. Gunther, I will not attempt to change Kiera's mind, and I *will* support her continued refusal to be used as a brood mare for the genome. Am I clear?"

Gunther was silent for several seconds.

"I had not considered that aspect," she admitted. "But if Kiera will not, then it becomes even more critical that we extend the secondary bloodline."

Damien closed his eyes and silently prayed for strength.

"You are *welcome* to make that argument to Admiral McLaughlin when she comes to visit," he told the doctor. "I'm sure as hell not broaching that with my girlfriend."

Looking around, he finally conceded he was completely lost.

"Right now, though, I need you to show me to the interrogation chamber and confirm that you have Odysseus's augments disabled."

"Of course," she said, her voice faint. "This way. Please understand, my lord, fully disabling augments of this type is impossible. We have him restrained and several chemical counteragents are being run through his saline drip, but he remains capable of extraordinary feats."

"Do I want to know what they cost him?" Damien asked.

"About a month of life expectancy every time he fires off his artificial glands," Gunther told him. "The human body simply cannot take the so-called 'upgrades' the hacks who assembled his package put together.

"Eventually, it *will* kill him."

Damien snorted.

"Right now, I'm more concerned about making sure he doesn't kill me."

CHAPTER 33

THE INTERROGATION ROOM was divided by a wall of transparent transmuted titanium. There weren't many things in the universe that could punch through that—and even fewer that could be concealed on someone undergoing medical treatment.

To Damien, the runes inlaid on his side of the transparent barrier were clear as day. They'd smother any magic used from the interrogatee side. He couldn't be more secure while still technically being in the same room as Odysseus.

That worthy was in a hospital bed that had been raised to put him in a sitting position. He was aware of Damien's presence, watching the Lord Regent frankly through the glass despite being strapped to the bed and hooked up to an IV.

The last piece, just in case the assassin had any tricks they weren't aware of, was that a Royal Guard in full armor stood in each half of the room.

"My name is Damien Montgomery," Damien introduced himself as he took a seat. "I think we need to have a conversation, Mr. Odysseus."

"Last I checked, I had the right to a lawyer," the assassin replied calmly. "I do know who you are, Lord Regent."

"I presumed. You have the right not to answer my questions until you see a lawyer, yes," Damien confirmed. "Of course, you realize we don't need you to answer them, right?"

"I'm not even sure what I've been arrested for," Odysseus replied. "I defended myself when my house was unexpectedly stormed by armored men. I have done nothing else."

"Mr. Odysseus, you are aware that on Mars, you are under the laws of the Kingdom of Mars, not the laws of the Protectorate, yes?" Damien asked. "Do you know what those laws lay out as the penalty for regicide?"

The divided room was silent, the Royal Guard looming like frozen red statues while Alexander Odysseus regarded the Lord Regent.

"Last I heard," he finally said slowly, "that *accident* was being investigated by a special prosecutor."

"Prosecutor Vemulakonda's investigation serves as a very useful smoke screen, doesn't it?" Damien asked. "We have retrieved the original security system footage from the hangar, Mr. Odysseus. Tell me, how does one destroy a shuttle with a class three arc cutter and a timer?"

"I can't say for certain," Odysseus replied. "I imagine you'd have to undo a lot of safeties on the cutter. It's really not supposed to cut an active antimatter line."

Damien smiled thinly.

"Who paid you, Alexander?" he asked. "Between the evidence on your estate and the footage we have, you're not walking out of this a free man. You *do* have the option to walk out of it a *living* man.

"I'm prepared to cut a deal. I'll even include the attempted assassination of a *Hand* in the crimes we'll take the death penalty off the table for."

Odysseus raised a hand to object, then lowered it.

"I found the bullets you shot me with in your armory, Mr. Odysseus," Damien told him. "They're functionally unique, so that makes for a rather damning piece of evidence, doesn't it? I have enough to shoot you for *two* crimes, and I'm wondering what a comparison of your travels over the last few years against unsolved murders would turn up."

He held out a hand, palm up.

"And all of those dead people deserve justice, don't you think?" he asked softly. "But at the end of the day, I need to know who tried to break the Protectorate. I need to know who hired you. Help me find that out, and you'll face a life sentence in a relatively comfortable prison.

"Refuse, and you will have a very efficient and very fair trial before you are taken out and shot."

The silence hung again for at least thirty seconds.

"Call me Xander, Lord Regent," Odysseus told him. "Then ask your questions. I know when I'm well and truly fucked."

"All right, Xander. You were hired to kill Desmond Michael Alexander the Third," Damien agreed. "Who hired you?"

"Answer is always more complicated than you want it to be," Odysseus warned. "I can tell you that. Most notably, I wasn't specifically hired to kill the Mage-King." He snorted. "I worked out what had happened afterwards."

"You knew you were sabotaging a Royal shuttle," Damien countered.

"Yes, of course. That was what I was paid to do," the assassin confirmed. "I didn't know who was going to be on it. That fleet gets used for a bunch of different people, even Hands when they're on-planet. If I'd known the target was the Mage-King, I'd have asked for a *lot* more money."

Damien managed not to do anything drastic in response to the casual tone Xander Odysseus used to admit he *would* have taken the job to kill Desmond.

"What did you know?" he asked.

"I was given a specific shuttle to sabotage, complete details on the security systems around it, and a way to confirm that the processing edit to protect me was online," Odysseus laid out. "The edit was supposed to be live in the feed, though I'm guessing it failed."

And *that* was why both sets of footage looked original, Damien suspected. The footage had already been edited by the time it hit the security systems storage databanks. Only the fact that the Royal Guards' secondary system was feeding directly from the cameras had saved the data they had used to find Odysseus.

"The money was right and the client wanted a ghost job, no sightings, no evidence." Odysseus shook his head. "I don't know how they got the network overwatch they promised, but everything I saw said it worked. I walked out of there clean. Money arrived on schedule and I had every reason to think there wasn't even grounds for suspicion. My mistress is a heavy sleeper; she'd swear up and down I spent the entire night with her."

"So who was the client?" Damien demanded.

"I don't know." The assassin shrugged. "That's how this *works*, Lord Montgomery. I never know. Dead drops and coded classified listings, cash credsticks and packages of special toys...no names, not even faces. I never know anyone."

"That's not enough, Xander," Damien warned. "If I don't have the hands that paid you, I don't have grounds not to throw you to the wolves."

"I'll tell you everything I know," Odysseus said, spreading his hands. "Get someone in here with a brain and recorder, and I'll walk you through the entire process. I can't give you a name or a face, Montgomery. But I'd hope you have enough to go one step farther than I can."

"And I'm guessing the same for the time you took a shot at me?" Damien asked coldly.

"Only difference that time was that I got the bullets as partial payment in advance. Never seen anything like them."

"Me either," the Lord Regent told him coldly. "It appears, Mr. Odysseus, that I am wasting my time here. I will be sending someone else to take down that walkthrough. Don't lie to her. The moment I think you're spinning your wheels or holding *anything* back, the deal is off."

Damien wasn't nearly as okay with cold-blooded execution as he was trying to imply, but he would be *damned* if the Mage-King's assassin walked free. Either Odysseus would give them enough to nail the people who'd hired him, or Damien would swallow his qualms.

He was *hoping* for a mastermind. He'd *settle* for the hands that pulled the trigger.

CHAPTER 34

DAMIEN DOUBLE-CHECKED his schedule as he reached his office, confirming that nothing was actively scheduled for at least a few minutes, then buried his face in his hands. He had to be on a shuttle in an hour, heading to what he was sure would be another *fascinating* conference with the Council of the Protectorate and the Constitutional Committees.

Right now, though, he could rest. Or at least bury his face in his hands and try to massage away the headache trying to dig into his skull.

"I know that posture," a familiar voice said calmly. "Ms. Waller doesn't have quite as much experience in recognizing when she shouldn't be sending people in to see you. Even old companions."

If he *hadn't* recognized Robert Christoffsen's voice, he'd probably have raised his head more quickly. As it was, he massaged his temples one more time as his old political aide took a seat across from him.

"I'm sorry I wasn't here earlier," the old man in the conservative suit told him when he finally *did* look up. "The last time you called me up, you *disappeared* before I could make contact. The Governor is far too willing to lean on me when I'm present."

He shook his head. Dr. Robert Christoffsen had multiple PhDs in law and political science; and had served two terms as Governor of Tara. He'd also spent over a year as Damien's political advisor when Damien had been a "mere" Hand.

"I can't begrudge Her Excellency my services while I'm on Tara," he admitted. "But the Lord Regent of Mars, of course, calls with a voice few will deny the priority of."

"Thank you, Professor," Damien finally said. "I've missed your sage advice for the last year. I wish I *had* waited before diving into the mission in Republic space. You'd have been valuable."

"I can't even imagine what kind of shit-show Niska dragged you into," Christoffsen replied. "Where is he, anyway?"

"On Legatus, helping keep order," the Lord Regent told him. "The discussion around his fate goes slowly, but I don't believe he's going to end up dodging the worst punishment I have available for his sins."

The older man laughed.

"You're going to make him Governor of Legatus, aren't you?" he asked.

"Most likely," Damien confirmed.

"It's a good call," the ex-Governor told him. "Military service provides a useful skill set, and he's also a man who was in the beating heart of the secession movement for a long time. Above all else, he's not seen as Mars's man. He broke with the Republic, but on ethical grounds that very few people can argue with."

"And *because* he broke with the Republic, I trust him," Damien confirmed. "He'll have a few Martian advisors around him and be ruling an occupied world, but he's one of theirs. We'll damn him with the taint of collaborator, but he's already marked with that."

"What happens to Legatus in the end?" Christoffsen asked. "And the rest of the Republic, once this is done?"

"Alexander is preparing to move on Nueva Bolivia, but that's going to take time," Damien admitted. "We have the force in place to hit and reduce their strongholds in sequence, leaving the less-critical systems to be swept later or by secondary task forces."

He shrugged.

"Or at least, so Admiral Alexander tells me, and she's been an admiral for almost as long as I've been alive."

"Naval officer," Christoffsen corrected. "Her ability to enter a career beyond *heir* was limited for most of her life. She didn't enter the Navy until she was in her fifties."

"I've read her record now," Damien replied. "There was nepotism involved, no doubt, but she made Rear Admiral in twenty-one years. So, I suppose, she's been an admiral for as long as *Kiera* has been alive."

"And a naval officer for as long as you have been alive, yes," the Professor confirmed. "I'd suggest running her plan by other officers if you can. I presume we have some kind of high command on Mars?"

"You'd be surprised," Damien muttered. "Five thousand years of recorded military history is good to have, but the Royal Martian Navy never expected to fight a war. Our High Command is brand new and still finding their feet."

"And how are you going to fix that?" the advisor asked, leaning back in his chair.

"I have notes," the Lord Regent admitted with a sigh. "Right now, it's around...fourth on my priority list? Maybe fifth."

"The Protectorate is at war and the war is fifth on your priority list?" Christoffsen asked slowly. "I did *not* make it back fast enough."

Damien shook his head and sighed again.

"Computer, seal the room," he ordered aloud. "Black Royal Protocol."

Shutters closed over the transparent titanium windows and the door. They weren't any harder to penetrate than the existing security measures...but they completed the Faraday cage. Just in case someone had bugged the office of the Lord Regent of Mars.

"This room should be secure, shouldn't it?" Christoffsen asked—as he leaned forward and steepled his hands in preparation for the conversation to come.

"It should be. But there are matters that less than a dozen people alive know about—and most of those are Royal Guard who have the minimum possible briefing," Damien told him. "But I need you fully inside."

"All right, my lord. I am yours to command," the Professor agreed.

"I know. And if you were a Mage, my friend, I'd be hanging a damn Hand around your neck right now," the Lord Regent noted. "You may still end up with a Warrant, but I've already got a Voice in the middle of this and her skill set is more immediately applicable."

"You have my attention, my lord."

"I'd hope so," Damien said with a chuckle. "Our number one priority is very, very clear: protect and train Kiera Michelle Alexander so that she is able and ready to rule as Mage-Queen of Mars on July twenty-eighth, twenty-four sixty-three.

"She is effectively my little sister and legally my daughter until that date," he continued. "Believe me, that thought terrifies me a *lot*. She got a lot of extra lessons around school, but she didn't get quite the same intensive education in leadership and governance that Des got.

"I'm going to be leaning on *you*, in particular, to fix that," he told Christoffsen. "You managed to get *me* to *useful* in eighteen months. I'm hoping you can get her to Queen in three years."

"That's a big ask, my lord," the other man said softly. "But I understand. She'll look to you for a lot of it, just from the reality that you will rule the Protectorate until her majority."

"I know," Damien agreed. "We'll work together—and she'll work with us. I have no intention of ruling the Protectorate *against* her desires, after all."

"Of course. Any way that I can assist, I will," the Professor replied.

"You'll take charge of her tutors and her education. I don't expect you to be teaching her yourself every day, but I want you to take responsibility for her education. Can you?"

Christoffsen had taught classes of ten thousand students, but even he had a moment of trepidation as Damien asked that question. After a moment, he met Damien's eyes and nodded firmly.

"I can," he confirmed. "I'm guessing that's only the beginning, though."

"Yeah. Take a look at this." Damien slid a lead-sealed box across his desk, wincing slightly as Christoffsen opened it.

Knowing what the bullet was and where it was reduced the discomfort a bit, but there was no way the matrix on those rounds would ever not feel *wrong* to his senses. The other man, of course, took the long bullet out and studied it without sensing anything.

"That's a very large bullet," the Professor said slowly. "I'm not sure I've seen one with a runic matrix carved on it before, either...wait...the one you were shot with?!"

"This is from the same set, yes," Damien told the other man. "The intact and active matrix is extraordinarily uncomfortable for a Rune Wright to be in the same room with. It wants to dismantle my magic from over there."

"Where did this come from?"

"That ties in to my second priority," Damien noted. "We took this from the assassin who rigged Desmond Michael Alexander's shuttle to explode."

Shocked silence was his only answer for at least twenty seconds.

"Desmond was assassinated," Christoffsen finally said. It wasn't even a question. "You have the assassin...and this still isn't public knowledge. You're chasing the mastermind?"

"We think it ties back to the Keepers and Nemesis," the Lord Regent told him. He gestured for his companion to put the rune-breaker back in its box and sighed in relief after Christoffsen obeyed.

"Voice Munira Samara continues her investigation with the support of Guard-Lieutenant Denis Romanov," Damien continued. "The assassin is currently in custody under medical supervision. He is heavily augmented in several unusual ways, but I believe the Mountain can contain him."

"You want me to back her up," the Professor concluded. Again, it wasn't really a question.

"Exactly. I have few people I trust who are as familiar with the Mountain's archives or the details of just who and what the Keepers were," he said. "I don't know how much Nemesis and the Keepers interfaced, but I suspect that bullet came from the Keepers.

"We might have some information on it in our archives, which could give us a line."

"And it wouldn't hurt to find out who tried to have you shot, would it?" Christoffsen murmured.

"That doesn't even register in my priority list," Damien admitted. "If it helps us trace back Nemesis, who we suspect is involved in

Desmond's assassination, it's worth following. Otherwise, it can follow usual channels."

"Someone did shoot you," the older man replied.

"And he's in a cell in the Mountain and I've already promised him his life in exchange for his full cooperation," the Lord Regent replied. "What's another death sentence I'd have to commute at that point?"

"Fair, I suppose," Christoffsen said. "I'm guessing the Constitution falls into your third or fourth priority slot?"

"Third. I'm on a shuttle within an hour now to meet up with one of the Committees, where I need to call them on their bullshit," Damien said. "I'm pretty sure I can manage that one without your help, Professor."

"Shouting down some of the most powerful people in the Protectorate? It's not like you don't have practice," his friend told him. "I am at your disposal, of course, but that's quite the priority list."

"Not to mention the other four hundred items waiting in my inbox to eat my entire day alive," Damien concluded with a chuckle. "I'm just waiting to find out Kiera has a boyfriend—or girlfriend, I suppose, given her brother's tastes—that she hadn't told anyone about prior to now."

"May I be so rude as to suggest that would potentially be for the best for the Protectorate?" Christoffsen said gently.

"You can, but it would be rude," Damien said. "I got an earful from Dr. Gunther earlier today about preserving both the Royal Genome and the 'secondary Rune Wright genome,' I believe she called it."

The Professor chuckled.

"She's not wrong, you know," he pointed out. "I fully agree with not wanting the Mage-Queen to get pregnant as a teenager, but *you* should probably be thinking about babies."

"Then you and Dr. Gunther can have that conversation with Grace when she comes to visit," Damien snapped. "I will not be treated as a stud stallion. Am I clear?"

"I understand, my friend," Christoffsen said gently. "But you need to keep that in mind. Who sits second in line for the throne right now, Damien?"

Damien was silent for several seconds, considering what the "hand-over hologram" Desmond had left him had said.

"Me, I believe," he finally sighed.

"A Rune Wright must sit the throne of Olympus Mons," the Professor said, the words a familiar lash on Damien by now. "Alexander is fighting a war. Shit happens in war. She might be at the heart of one of the most powerful warships humanity has ever built, but she is still in a war.

"Kiera is young and vulnerable. She's strong and should make a fine Queen, but if she falls, her aunt becomes Queen—and if the last Alexander is lost, well, a Rune Wright must sit the throne. What happens after that if *you* are dead?"

"The Protectorate endures," Damien said softly. "Gregory would take the throne. There would be no Rune Wrights left, not without Dr. Gunther cooking someone up in a test tube. Which, I'll note, she's entirely capable of doing.

"And has threatened to do," he admitted. "An act that brings us *far* too damned close to the Eugenicists. I am not going to father a child for no reason but the good of the Protectorate; do you understand me?"

"I do," Christoffsen told him. "And I'll back you, always. But you need to understand why everyone is starting to worry about the line of succession. Officially, it's only one name long. Even if those of us in the know presume you're on the list, that's not public information."

"Even if Grace and I were to have children, that wouldn't solve that problem," Damien replied. "It's a problem for later in any case. It will be months before Grace is on Mars."

"She is coming, though? That's good."

"To visit, not to stay," the Lord Regent said. "She is also bound by chains of duty."

"I'm familiar with the concept, Damien. You've given me a list and I'll get started immediately," Christoffsen said. "My old office is still clear?"

"Check with Ms. Waller, but I believe so," Damien told him. "Start with the bullet, if you can. Not even the man I took them from knows their source, though I know where the dead drop it was found in was."

"I've been briefed on enough investigations to know that might be enough," the ex-Governor told him. "I'll see what I can find. May I take it?"

"Please get it the hell out of my office," Damien said with a chuckle. "I had it here to go over as a Rune Wright, but it makes my skin crawl if I open the box!"

CHAPTER 35

"WE HAVE FINISHED putting together the proposal we discussed last time you and Envoy Velasquez met with us," Suresh Granger told Damien and his companions as he took his first sips of coffee.

While it was theoretically possible for someone to jump from Mars to Council Station, it would be a risky process and one stunningly uncomfortable for the Jump Mage in question. Jumping in or out of a gravity well was something reserved for emergencies, not saving a few hours—not even for the Lord Regent of Mars and the Mage-Queen of Mars.

Damien could once have jumped a ship that distance with relative ease, though it would have left him with a headache. His current lack of jump runes and the desire to keep the full extent of his and Kiera's abilities secret contraindicated that, in any case.

Which meant that it still took just over twenty-four hours to get to where *Storm of Unrelenting Fury* orbited with Council Station and he was theoretically well rested.

With everything going on, *theoretically* was a key word in that assessment.

Velasquez sat to his left hand, the poor woman tasked with dealing with the Council on a day-to-day basis and looking even less rested than Damien felt. Kiera Alexander sat to his right, and she was the only one of the three who looked like she had slept properly.

"All right," he told Granger as he let his coffee cup sink to the table. He wasn't even pretending to use his crippled hands to maneuver the cup, and he could *feel* the discomfort that was causing for the non-Mage portion of the Committee on Constitutional Balances.

Some of them were probably smart enough to know he was doing it on purpose. He doubted any of them knew him well enough to realize that it was a sign that he was very, *very* angry.

With all of the distractions, he hadn't managed to go through Desmond's notes and files on the negotiations until the flight there. In doing so, he'd confirmed his worst fears.

The Committee on Constitutional Balances and the Mage-King of Mars had already come to a verbal agreement on the *exact* structure and balances of the new government. Only parts of it were in writing—but even those parts contradicted what they'd presented to him last time.

"Why don't you lay out your current proposal," Damien told the Committee, "and then I'll let you know if I see any problems we'll need to address."

"Of course," Granger allowed with a small bow. The plushly appointed conference room's lights dimmed as he gestured toward a projected screen like a conjurer.

"We've assembled a structure based on the current Protectorate Council," he noted. A block of a hundred icons, tiny black chairs, made up the top of the image. "A seat for each system, directly appointed by the planets' Governors.

"Each world will also have a single elected junior representative," he continued, highlighting a block of gray chairs in the lower half of the image, "and both representatives will carry the title of Senator. Passage of legislation will require the entire chamber, while the senior Senate will directly approve Her Majesty's judicial appointments and have final veto on financial matters."

Locking, Damien mentally noted, both the judicial review and the power of the purse into power of the *appointed* senators. Which was not even what Granger had told *Damien* last time, let alone what they'd discussed with the Mage-Queen's father.

"That's only a high-level summary, of course," Granger concluded.

"Exact details are in the tablets in front of you and have been forwarded to you electronically."

Damien glanced at his wrist-comp, which confirmed he'd received the message. The Councilor's tech support was on the ball today.

The Lord Regent of Mars smiled, managing to project an air of calm as he slowly and intentionally floated his coffee cup up for him to take a sip.

"This does seem very heavily based on our current system," he finally said, letting that hang in the air.

"Well, what is the engineer's aphorism, my lord? 'If it isn't broken, don't fix it'?" the Senator for Eridani asked. "The Council has served the Protectorate well for two centuries."

"And yet," Damien said softly, letting the two words hang in the air for an extended pause before he repeated himself. "And yet, are we not in this room and having this discussion because we are all in agreement that the Protectorate *is* broken?"

He rose to his feet. His height didn't let him stare down at the Councilors if everyone was standing, but if he was the *only* one standing...

"Isn't the fact that the Protectorate is *literally* broken in two by secession and war proof that how we have run the Protectorate is broken? This Council served as an advisory board, and in that role, having you all be directly appointed by Governors made sense.

"But the Protectorate has *never* dictated the basis by which Governors were selected, and many of your worlds opted for implicit or even explicit constitutional monarchies," Damien continued. "Some of you represent 'democracies' that are concealed oligarchies at best. Less than a quarter of the current Council are elected directly by the people they represent... which means you represent those who *appoint* you, not the people that the Protectorate is sworn to protect."

Damien gestured to the image.

"Half of our legislature explicitly appointed? And that half to control the power of the purse and the judiciary? The Mountain will not accept this model. Not now. Not *ever*."

"My lord, we are—"

"Liars at best, traitors at worst," Damien cut Granger off flatly. "Kiera?

Would you be so kind as to project the briefing document from your father's last meeting with this Committee?"

Like the Hands she could appoint, Kiera had authorization codes to bend any governmental computer in the Protectorate to her will. Granger's presentation vanished, replaced by a distinctly more complicated map.

"I think you should all be familiar with this model," he continued. "Based on a mix of Westminster Parliamentarism and the United States Congress. One thousand elected Members of Parliament serving two-year terms, supported by an elected Senate of one Senator per world, serving a ten-year term—with both Senators and Members limited to ten years service.

"Power of the purse held explicitly by the Parliament and the power of judicial review held by the Senate; most legislation required to pass them both in joint assembly."

Damien shook his head.

"This is *your* briefing document, Councilor Granger, so I doubt any of this is news to you," he noted. "According to Desmond's notes on this meeting and the message I was sent in its wake, this Committee and Desmond had agreed on this exact model as the basis for all discussions going forward."

The Committee was silent and none of them would meet his gaze.

"There is no perfect system," Damien told them. "But I will not allow you to trap the Protectorate in a continued mess of patronage and appointment. We will not impose a standardized democracy on the Governorships—Mars will remain a monarchy itself, after all—but neither I nor Her Majesty will accept anything less than an entirely elected legislature."

"What are you accusing us of?" Granger finally managed to get out.

"I am not accusing you of anything," he replied. "I am *stating* that you have taken advantage of Desmond's death to attempt to change the entire structure of the Protectorate's future government to one that would serve you and your patrons better than the people of the Protectorate.

"I am duty-bound to see the power of the Martian monarchy reduced and limited by this document. That was Desmond Michael Alexander's choice and command," Damien reminded them. "I will *not* do so for anything less than the goals and purposes he sought.

"We are redrafting the way the vast majority of our species will be ruled for at least two centuries to come. I will not create a structure that leaves our people with an even less-balanced government. The Mountain is prepared to relinquish some level of our power, but we will not relinquish it into the hands of the clients of Core World oligarchs and MidWorld monarchs. Am I understood?"

He was being moderately unfair to the governments that the Councilors represented. Most of them were fundamentally democracies, even with their issues. Allowing those governments to continue appointing their representatives to the Protectorate would undermine the counterbalance that *kept* them democratic.

"We will go back to this document," Damien told them. "And you will draft a new proposal based on it. Once you have done so and I agree with it, we will put our agreement to it *in writing* to avoid any future confusion.

"This is your one and only warning, Councilors. Even if I have lost Desmond's notes on a matter, I fully understand his original intent—as does Her Majesty. What was agreed to with him stands.

"Am I understood?"

He waited, studying each Councilor in turn. Interestingly, the Councilors for Sherwood and Tara both met his gaze levelly, Angus Neil giving him a deep nod of respect.

"Given that understanding," Damien finally continued, "is there a point in continuing today's meeting—or was the entire planned discussion predicated on your assumption that Desmond's death allowed a complete reset of this process?"

Granger coughed.

"There are some items I think we can still discuss," he said in a shaken tone. "But I'm afraid our...misunderstanding may have underlain much of the agenda."

"Then let's get on with it," Kiera said sharply. "Before *I* start wondering what crystal ball you were looking in before my father's death."

"That was perhaps going a bit far," Damien told his ward later, as they waited for the shuttle to return from their cruiser taxi. "We can't accuse the Council of assassinating your father."

Kiera considered his words for a few seconds, then shrugged.

"Fuck. Them," she said precisely. "I don't think anyone in that room killed my father, Damien. But some of them...I think some of them might have known it was coming."

"That's a hell of an accusation, Kiera," he reminded her, glancing around. They were flanked by Royal Guards and he was *reasonably* comfortable in their privacy, but this still wasn't really a conversation to have on Council Station.

"I was watching their faces while you were steamrolling them, Damien," she told him. "I suspect we want to talk to Councilor Neil in private at some point. I got the feeling he went along with the majority and might be willing to be more frank than some of the others."

"Maybe, but we need to be careful of what we even imply here," he warned her. "Remember that your father died in an accident."

Kiera's gaze snapped back to his, her eyes flashing before she remembered where they were and got his point.

"Right," she said quietly. "But...it feels like they would never have committed to some of the things in the document we're now holding them to if they thought it was actually going to be in the final draft.

"The Councilor job has been a sinecure, a reward for loyal service, for the Governors for years. Giving up both that *and* leaving the power of the purse in a shorter-term, inherently less-controllable Parliament?"

She shook her head.

"I think they agreed to that because at least some of them knew there were currents running against Dad."

Damien shivered. This conversation was the closest Kiera was going to come, in this environment, to saying that she figured at least some of the Councilors had known there was a plot afoot. They might not have been *involved*, but they'd known the life expectancy of the Mage-King of Mars was shrinking.

"Those are troubled waters you're fishing in, my Queen," he told her. "We should continue this conversation aboard *Lioness of Justice*."

"But I'm not wrong, am I?" she asked.

"I don't know," he countered. "What I do know is that walls often have ears and *these* walls belong to the Council."

Kiera was extraordinarily intelligent—the longer he spent as her foster parent, the more Damien became convinced of that—but she hadn't been working in active politics before. His more subtle hints had been missed, but she got his message now.

"Of course, my Lord Regent," she told him. "But we *will* have that conversation."

"We will," he confirmed. He was grimly certain she was right—which meant that was something else to hand over to Samara and Christoffsen. Another loose string to yank on.

CHAPTER 36

"WELL, I NOW KNOW more about the process of hiring a professional killer on Mars than I did before," Munira Samara told the small gathering in the private dining room of the Martian Royal Family.

Christoffsen and Gregory joined the previous team now. It was still a small crowd, with Romanov joining Damien and Kiera and the rest at the table while hand-selected Royal Guard stood at the doors.

Even *with* the armored Guards, there were only nine people in the room.

"I would have expected you to know more about that topic than most," Kiera suggested. "That was your job, wasn't it?"

"I was MIS Homicide, yes," Samara told the Queen. "And while this end of it would have mostly been on MIS Organized Crime, I knew most of what MIS knew about it. And I now know things we didn't know before.

"So, one of my questions, my lords, my Queen, is when I can share that data with MIS."

"When the investigation goes public," Damien decided instantly. "We don't want to hold on to it when it might save lives, but right now, this chain of investigation is our most critical line. Until we have nailed everyone involved in Desmond's death to a wall, we keep it all under our hats."

"Understood," she told him. "The sad truth is that the whole structure is set up to protect both sides from exactly what we're doing. If we caught the contractor, as we did, they couldn't give up the employer—but the employer wouldn't be able to give up Mr. Odysseus, either.

"Odysseus has been very cooperative and I've got some teams digging into the physical and digital dead drops without knowing what they're actually looking for," she continued. "One thing I think we have confirmed is that he was hired for this mission by different people than the ones who hired him to attack Damien."

"Damn," Damien said quietly. "I was hoping the bullets would help link everything together."

"The Rune Breakers," Christoffsen said, the capitals audible. "I have good news and bad news there."

"They have a name?" Kiera asked. "That sounds ostentatious."

"Blame your great-grandfather," the Professor told her. "He designed the matrix. Designed to go on a heavy round from an anti-materiel rifle, much like the one Odysseus used."

"The Keepers had it?" Damien asked.

"Probably, but it wasn't removed from the rest of our archives," Christoffsen replied. "Once I was able to study an intact round, I was able to find the key identifiers and track it down. The design for the Rune Breaker is in the Mountain's archives...and, unless I'm severely mistaken, has never officially been stored anywhere else."

"I imagine Desmond the First thought it was wise to have a weapon he could use against his own Hands," Damien suggested, a sick feeling resting in the pit of his stomach. "That was his...style."

"By which my Lord Regent means my great-grandfather was a paranoid, broken man who only managed to do well by humanity out of pure fluke," Kiera said bluntly.

"I think he did well by us because, despite everything that made him a paranoid, broken man, he was also a fundamentally good person," Damien countered. "But, yes, him making sure that he could take out Hands with regular snipers is very in character.

"I'm guessing the bad news is that makes it hard to really source the bullets?" he asked.

"Exactly," Christoffsen confirmed. "Seventeen people have accessed that Matrix design in the last twenty years. I'm going to try and trace the manufacturer now. That, combined with the fact that we know exactly where that dead drop is, gives us a starting point."

"Unfortunately, that starting point is on the assassination attempt on me, not the *actual* assassination we're worried about," Damien noted. "So long as they weren't the same person, that doesn't really help us."

"We need to track Nemesis in any case, and everything points to Nemesis being involved in both attacks," Samara countered. "Just because different identifiers were used by the people contacting Odysseus doesn't mean the chain doesn't lead back to the same monster at the heart."

"Fair. Do we have *anything* to go on?" Damien asked.

Gregory sighed, the Chancellor leaning forward.

"I've seen your evidence," he told them. "But if we can't find the people behind Odysseus, do we have any options? Do we *want* to tell the Protectorate that the Mage-King was assassinated and we don't know who gave the order?"

"Or do we publicly proclaim it was the Republic?" Romanov suggested softly. "I don't like the idea of lying, but we need to blame somebody and a random hired assassin isn't going to put people at ease."

"Not least because we've already promised him his life," Damien noted. "He's given us a lot, even if none of it's been entirely useful yet."

"Once I can turn these interviews over to MIS, we're going to lay at least eleven murder cases to rest," Samara pointed out. "Even if we can't execute him for those, it will give the families some peace."

"That's not nothing," Damien agreed. He glanced at Kiera. "But I want to give the family in this room peace, people. And I want to give the Protectorate peace."

"I think there's one question no one has asked that might be more important than we think," Denis Romanov said into the silence that followed. "I'm new to the Royal Guard and protecting a Royal, so I've been going through Guard protocol in detail.

"I'd been wondering about it since the shuttle went down, too, but I wasn't sure if Guard protocol was the same as others in this." He shook his head. "It is," he confirmed. "The Mage-King and his heir shouldn't have been on the same shuttle. Even here, even inside the defensive perimeter of Mars Orbital Command, Des should have been riding in a different spacecraft.

"The only time we put Kiera and Damien on the same shuttle was for a five-minute transfer between ships without ever entering an atmosphere. Des and his father shouldn't have been on the same ship."

"What *happened?*"

The room was silent again and Damien turned his gaze to Gregory.

"Malcolm?" he asked softly. "You're the only one here who might have been involved in that."

"Des wasn't supposed to be on that trip at all," the Chancellor said after a few moments' thought. "The change in plans came late—very late. We could have got another shuttle online in the time we had, but it would have been a giant pain.

"I remember reviewing the documents in the morning while they were flying up and being surprised. Desmond had authorized the single shuttle flight himself. It made sense—like Guard-Lieutenant Romanov noted, we're inside the perimeter of MOC. There was no point in their flight where they weren't a hundred percent secure from external attack."

Even having *been* attacked during a similar flight, Damien wasn't sure he disagreed. Even with the massive scale of the Republican assassination attempt on him, it had failed miserably. The security around the rulers of Mars was tight.

It just hadn't been tight enough.

"Unless we want to assume this was a complicated suicide plan, that means they changed their mind at the last minute," Damien concluded. "When was Des added to the plan?"

"About ten PM the prior night, six hours before they flew out," Gregory said instantly.

"Who met with the Mage-King that night?" Samara asked.

"He didn't have any formal meetings, I don't think," the Chancellor replied. "I'd have to check his schedule records for informal meetings."

"Someone in this room needs to get on that," Damien ordered. "I want to know *everyone* His Majesty met with that evening. Someone talked him into taking Des with him...and I don't buy that whoever did that didn't know *exactly* what was going to happen.

CHAPTER 37

"GUARD-LIEUTENANT. Take a seat."

Denis Romanov obeyed the order gingerly, glancing around General Spader's utilitarian office as he perched on the edge of the chair in front of her desk.

Unlike Montgomery's office, there was no solid wood furniture here. The office of the Commandant of the Royal Guard, the woman in charge of the entire defenses of Olympus Mons, was furnished entirely with the standard prefabs of the Martian military.

The room's walls had been carefully paneled in either wood or a solid facsimile thereof, but most of that treatment was hidden by the prefabricated metal bookshelves except for one section set aside for the Commandant's "I love me" wall, though Spader's version of that was relatively understated with only copies of her original Royal Martian Marine Corps commission and her Royal Guard commission.

"You requested my presence, sir," Denis finally said after ten seconds or so of silence.

"I did," she confirmed. "I was under the impression, Guard-Lieutenant, that you were assigned to command Lord Regent Montgomery's protective detail. Am I mistaken somehow?"

"That is correct, General," he replied.

"I have reports from multiple people—who should probably know better—that suggest that you didn't even accompany Lord Montgomery off-planet on his mission to Council Station," she told him. "Others seem to think that you're almost never in His Excellency's company.

"What this suggests to me, more than anything, is a certain degree of jealousy at the fact that we brought someone in from outside to command Montgomery's detail," she admitted, "but I also cannot leave these comments unaddressed. I don't believe the Marine Corps is different on this point, but the Royal Guard especially believe that the detail commander should be part of the close-protection team a significant portion of the time they're on duty."

"That is the standard in the RMMC as well," Denis confirmed. "And my own operational preference."

"So, these are simply the murmurings of jealous officers who feel that they should command the Lord Regent's bodyguard?" she asked.

"No, sir," he told her calmly. There were limits to what he could tell Spader without orders to read her into Samara's investigation, but he also wasn't going to lie to her. "I have delegated operational command of Lord Montgomery's detail to Guard-Sergeant Afolabi as His Excellency has assigned me to another duty."

There was a long pause, followed by a sigh that was almost as long.

"Much as I presumed," she told him. "I prefer to be kept informed of assignments of my Guard personnel, Guard-Lieutenant Romanov. Did you not think this was relevant to inform me, your superior officer, of?"

"My orders came from the Lord Regent directly," Denis replied. "The situation he has engaged me in is being handled entirely from his office and under his seal. I am not authorized to discuss the matter with you."

"I rose to the rank of Colonel in the Royal Martian Marine Corps before taking a transfer to Guard-Lieutenant and rising once again to Guard-General and Commandant of the Royal Guard and the Olympus Mons Defense Command," Spader said harshly, a mostly unnecessary litany of her ranks.

"I am familiar with the concept of need to know and of confidentiality," she told him. "I am aware that you are assisting Voice Samara with the task she has been set by His Excellency. Believe me, Guard-Lieutenant, when I tell you that you have done *almost* everything correctly."

"Yes, sir. Thank you, sir."

The response was automatic. Denis *knew* there was another boot coming.

"What you did *not* do correctly was that you failed to bring the change in tasking to my attention so I could arrange reinforcement of your detail," Spader told him. "If Lord Montgomery intends to use his bodyguard as his personal trouble-shooters, that will require me to make sure he has more actual bloody *bodyguards*.

"So, the moment you were spending more of your time working for Montgomery instead of protecting Montgomery, you should have told me *that*," she said. "I don't need to know what the Lord Regent has you working on—usual protocol would have a Voice escorted and supported by a Secret Service detail, but my job is not to argue with the Lord Regent of Mars—but I need to allocate my Guards appropriately.

"Am I understood, Guard-Lieutenant?"

"Yes, General," he admitted. "I'm basically full-time supporting Voice Samara at the moment, and Lord Montgomery has requested that we have a four-Guard strike team ready to deploy at his or Voice Samara's command. That is consuming roughly half of my assigned Guards to keep ready."

"Is this at all unusual for the Lord Regent?" Spader asked.

"No," Denis replied bluntly. "His Marine details, his Secret Service details and now his Royal Guard details...he has always treated us more as a personal strike force than a protective detail. Even his injuries did not change this, so I doubt his recent elevation will."

"So, you need more Guards," the General concluded. "I perhaps grew too used to an old man who never left the Mountain and used *Hands* for those kinds of tasks."

"I don't believe Montgomery feels that the creation of new Hands is truly within his authority," Denis admitted. "That will change over time, I hope, but he is very much in the mindset of caretaker."

"Which is a good thing, if occasionally a pain in the ass," Spader replied. She shook her head with a sigh. "Pay attention, Guard-Lieutenant."

Wordlessly, she rolled up the left sleeve of her burgundy suit, revealing an extremely familiar pattern of silver whorls and knots wrapped around her left forearm.

"It is not only the Hands who the Mage-Kings have marked with Runes of Power," she murmured as she rolled the sleeve back down. "That I carry one is a closely held secret...so closely held that I think the only people who knew died on His Majesty's shuttle.

"Now you know. Both Her Majesty and His Excellency should know, but you are sufficiently in Montgomery's confidence to provide that information when he needs it."

She studied him.

"I will put an end to the whispers," she told him firmly. "We will be assigning more Guards to your detail. Is Afolabi up for the task?"

"He may need more rank," Denis admitted slowly. "He is technically an NCO, after all. Handing him ten Guards didn't cause any problems. Putting twenty or thirty under his command, well..."

"That is my concern, not yours," Spader replied. "Whatever is necessary will be done. Anyone who wishes to cause problems will be silenced.

"Understand, Denis Romanov, that the Royal Guard are a family. Like most families, we are occasionally argumentative and have our moments of internal jealousy, but every Mage under my command has proven their loyalty and fealty to the Mountain beyond question.

"I do not need to know what the Lord Regent has assigned you to assure you that you have the support of the entire Royal Guard. There are few more powerful forces on Mars...and all of *those* answer to Lord Regent Montgomery."

"We hope," Denis murmured. *Someone* had nearly managed to assassinate the Mage-King of Mars without being caught. And unless something broke unexpectedly, he was starting to suspect that the people behind Xander Odysseus might *still* go uncaught.

"That makes no sense."

Denis was reasonably sure that Munira Samara wasn't paying any attention to him. He was reasonably sure the investigator hadn't even noticed him entering the lab-slash-office she'd taken over, in fact.

A pair of armored Royal Guards stood outside the door, making sure no one entered who wasn't supposed to. One of them should have pinged Samara when he arrived, but she was clearly ignoring her messages as she stared at multiple lists on the screens in front of her.

He smiled as he crossed over to join her, noting that a long lock of black hair had escaped from the side of today's dark green headscarf. His fingers twitched to smooth it back under the garment, and he managed not to kick himself for the urge.

There was no planet and no universe in which *that* was appropriate.

"What makes no sense?" he asked, pulling a stool over to sit by the screen.

"You really want to know?" Samara replied. "I'm elbow-deep in connection maps, and I'm not liking any of my answers."

"At least you're getting answers?" Denis asked. "I'm mostly worried about us drawing giant blanks."

"Well, do you want to assume that this was Desmond the Fourth committing suicide and taking his father with him?" the Voice asked, gesturing at two of her lists. "Because he's the *only* person who has both accessed the Rune Breaker matrix schematics and met with Desmond the Third the night before their last flight."

The lists, Denis realized, were of names. He'd seen Samara do the same thing when they'd been trying to identify the Keepers, flagging connections between various people.

"While I don't want to rule anything out completely, that seems a low-order probability," Denis agreed. "What else have you got?"

"Zero overlap on the direct lists, so I'm on relationship maps," she told him, gesturing to a section of the screen where each name on a main list was connected to other lists. "Except that the list of people Desmond met with on his last night is short and insanely influential. We're talking about two Councilors, Chancellor Gregory, General Spader, and a regional infrastructure director."

"And you're trying to see if any of them know anyone who accessed the Rune Breaker matrix?" Denis asked.

"Exactly. Except, of course, they all knew Des." She stared at the map. "I really want to know what the hell the Crown Prince was doing looking at the design for a bullet intended to kill Hands."

"When did he look at it?" Denis asked. "Would it help your list if you took out everyone who looked at the design after Damien was shot with one?"

"A little," she told him, clearly having done so already. "Takes three names of seventeen out. Des is *not* one of them, though he did look at the matrix a second time after the assassination attempt."

"Checking to see if he remembered it correctly?" Denis guessed. "Strange that he didn't mention it to anyone."

"I'd guess that without an intact bullet to compare to, he wasn't sure he had the right one," Samara noted. "*I* wouldn't have wanted to suggest that the bullet came from a Martian armory."

"Wait, we've *built* some?" the Guard asked.

"The Guard has exactly one hundred Rune Breaker rounds in inventory," she told him. "They're fifty years old and I doubt anyone running the armory even knows what the armory code is for, but the Guard has them. And before you ask, yes, the Guard's rounds are all still there. The ones Odysseus had were new."

"Do we know who made them, then? That seems like another point to yank on," Denis suggested.

"Not yet. MIS is working on it, without knowing about the other half of the investigation." She shook her head. "Unless I want to accuse one of four of the most powerful people in the star system of regicide, I'm not sure I've even *got* anything to go on from the assassination side."

"What about the dead drop for Odysseus's payment?"

The assassin had been paid in transferrable credit chips, physical media payable to the bearer. With limited interstellar communications, some form of hard cash had to exist. Despite the best efforts of banks and the Protectorate, the chips remained difficult to track at the best of times and easily obfuscated by anyone wanting to transfer funds anonymously.

She snorted and tapped a command on her wrist-comp. The lists on the screen slid sideways as she brought up another saved window. This one was more names, each attached to a tiny image from a surveillance camera.

"No cameras on the dead drop itself," she told him. "Three around it. This is every person with a more than seventy-five percent likelihood of having passed the drop in the seventy-two hours. Well. The *first page* of those people."

"How many?" he asked.

"Fourteen hundred and twenty-six," Samara confirmed. "I checked, too. None of them accessed the Rune Breaker data, though just over two hundred work in the Mountain."

"What about the dead drop for the bullets?" Denis asked. "If there's a connection, it may have been the same person making the drop both times."

"Time frame is too old," she replied. "Most civilian security systems and companies hold a six-month archive, but we can't write a warrant to access data that doesn't exist."

"Makes sense," he admitted, studying the lists. "I'm guessing you already ran who among the people who accessed the data works for the people who met with Desmond?"

"At least three worked for Spader in one capacity or another," she told him. "Two worked for Gregory, including a man who was his personal secretary at the time. One worked for Councilor Granger."

"Nobody for the other Councilor?" Denis asked.

"Not directly, but there's three people linked to Councilor Coral if I dig a layer deeper." She sighed, glancing sideways at him and tugging on the loose lock of hair. "I've got lots of data, Denis, but I have no answers for you. Right now, I could connect this in a way that condemns any of those four people—but I can also connect it in a way that supports Desmond Four committing an elaborate, grandiose suicide."

"What about Nemesis?" he asked softly. "You were on that file. Does anything from that son of a bitch link to this?"

Nemesis had, after all, tried to wipe out the entire Council at one point. The man—organization? Cult? They weren't quite sure what Nemesis was—was their most likely link between the two attacks.

"I've got a bunch of gray-tier possibles on potential members or contacts of Nemesis," she admitted. "I was hoping that one of them would match up with our Rune Breaker accesses, but nada. No Nemesis possible. No Keepers either, actually. I ran that comparison, too."

"Not one?" Denis asked. "I was still operating under the assumption the attack was a Keeper operation."

"I don't have a complete list of members, but we're pretty sure we've flagged every active member who worked in the Mountain," she told him. "They're all dead, of course, but there were a lot of them."

"None of them accessed this file. There might have a been a copy in their archives, in which case all of this is *a waste of my damn time.*" Samara hissed the last few words.

"Inshallah, I'll find something sooner or later, but this feels like a brick wall."

Denis wasn't a fan of relying on God for an answer, though he knew that wasn't really what Samara meant.

"Do any of the people on the dead drop list work for anyone who met with the Mage-King?"

"A few," she told him. "Two hundred work in the Mountain, so technically all of them work for Gregory?"

A few tranches of color swept through the list of names and Samara paused.

"That's odd," she murmured. "Nobody working for Granger went near that spot. It's not *that* out of the way, or the whole point of using it as a dead drop doesn't work. It could be fluke..."

"But nobody? How many people in the Mountain work for Granger in one sense or another?" Denis asked, trying not to think too hard about what he was implying.

"Like the rest of the Councilors, he pulls double duty as ambassador to Mars," she said absently. "One hundred and fourteen people work in his embassy, ten *more* than work in Councilor Coral's...and seven of Coral's people are flagged on here."

"That's most likely coincidence, though, right?" Denis asked.

"It's *possibly* coincidence," she agreed. "Or a few senior employees were told to avoid that particular street and it's percolated through the staff. That makes no sense, though."

"Unless they knew that a dead drop for the local assassin organization, such as it is, was on that street," he said grimly. "Do we know what the person on Granger's staff who pulled the Rune Breaker schematics did with them?"

"Hard to tell. She went home to Tau Ceti over a year ago, so we can't even ask her questions in a timely fashion," Samara told him. "I can pull a profile on her relatively quickly, though. I just...can't see why Granger would be involved in this."

"Neither can I," Denis admitted. "And the problem is that I'm not seeing a link to the assassination other than his having dinner with the Mage-King, either. But several bits add up to him being linked to the attack on Montgomery.

"The bullets are the key to that link...and I think that link will give us Nemesis."

"But we have no reason to believe that Nemesis was involved in the attack on the Mage-King," she pointed out. "Following up on the attack on Montgomery is worthwhile, but I'm not sure it's going to help us."

Denis considered a conversation he'd had with Montgomery and grimaced.

"It might help us more than we think," he told her. "Montgomery suspects at least some of the Councilors knew there was a plot against the Mage-King. Not, I'm certain, in any detail—but I have to wonder.

"And since the pieces are starting to fall together, I want to see how that puzzle looks. But we must fit it into the one we *need* to solve."

CHAPTER 38

"SURESH GRANGER was one of my father's most trusted allies in the Council, a loyalist in both name and truth," Kiera Alexander told the small group read in on the secret investigation after Samara dropped her bombshell.

There weren't many people in the room. Damien himself and Kiera were in chairs leaning against the big desk, facing Samara at the other end of a rough circle containing Romanov, Gregory and Christoffsen.

"I'm not disbelieving you, Voice Samara," the Mage-Queen continued, "but this seems beyond any logical reasoning."

"I agree," Samara said calmly. "And if I could line up the pieces any other way, I would. May I walk everyone through the connections?"

"Give her a chance, Kiera," Damien told his charge. "One of the reasons Lady Samara has her Warrant is because of her ability to put together the pieces."

"I'll warn you in advance, some of the connections are tenuous and circumstantial at most," the MIS investigator told them as she took control of the screen above her and lowered it over the office's armored windows.

"One of the key assumptions we're working from here is that the organization or individual known as Nemesis was involved in both the assassination attempt on Damien Montgomery and the assassination of the Desmonds," she stated. "Even if that assumption is correct, it seems unlikely that Councilor Granger is a member of that organization.

I suspect, unfortunately, that the impetus for the first of the incidents came from Councilor Granger."

"He attacked Damien?" Kiera demanded.

"I now believe so, yes," Samara confirmed. "Even if we can't link this to His Majesty's assassination, I have sufficient evidence to lay charges of treason, attempted murder and conspiracy to commit the same against the Councilor."

The room was silent and Damien studied his companions. There was no one in the room he didn't trust completely, which meant it was a *very* small crowd. Chancellor Gregory had been silent so far, as had Denis Romanov.

Their presence brought the total number in the room to five. On the other hand, that five included the three most powerful individuals in the Protectorate. His office was more than capable of holding this crowd. He could have doubled the number of people in the meeting, and he *still* would have chairs and space for them.

"Lay it out, Samara," Damien told her.

"All right." An image of the Rune Breaker bullet appeared on the screen. "Our key point of connection is these. Desmond the First designed the Rune Breaker anti-materiel round for the sole use of the Royal Guard, as a countermeasure to his own Hands.

"While capable, as we've seen, of being fired from an anti-materiel rifle, the round is actually chambered to be fired from the standard exosuit penetrator rifle of the late twenty-third century Martian Marine Corps.

"Approximately fifty years ago, the design was accessed by a group of Royal Guard technicians during a period of suspicion around several of His Majesty's Hands. They revised the rounds to a more modern sniper caliber and manufactured one hundred units. Just in case."

"All of those rounds are still in the armory in the Mountain," Denis Romanov interjected. "I physically checked them prior to this meeting."

Damien nodded and concealed a sigh of relief.

"The rounds in Xander Odysseus's possession were manufactured in August of twenty-four fifty-eight," Samara said quietly. "They were picked up from the armorer who made them and, given the timing we now know, delivered directly to Odysseus's dead drop."

"We have that record?" Damien asked.

"We do," she confirmed. "MIS investigators executed a warrant at Chen Zhao's Custom Armaments this morning. So far, that has not leaked to the media, but we have confirmed with Mr. Chen that the rounds were made there. Mr. Chen also confirmed that he had no ability to empower the rounds and does not employ any Mages in his work."

"Who hired him?" Kiera demanded.

"According to his paperwork, no one," Samara told him. "The rounds are on the records as a personal project of Mr. Chen's. Only the legal requirements for complete records in a facility of that type allowed us to confirm they had been produced at all.

"Upon further interrogation, we discovered that Mr. Chen had just started his shop at the time and was personal friends with David Granger, the Councilor's son. The rounds were directly manufactured by the junior Granger and presumably empowered by him.

"The rounds remained in the shop for twenty-four hours before they were picked up by this gentleman."

An image of an older man in a conservative blue suit appeared on the screen. He looked vaguely familiar to Damien.

"This is Rahul Fay, a junior attaché with the Tau Ceti embassy. He picked up a sealed package from Mr. Chen's shop. We know that package was picked up from the dead drop by Mr. Odysseus six hours later, so we can only assume that Mr. Fay made the delivery."

"Is Fay still on Mars?" Gregory asked, the Chancellor's voice chilly.

"Both Fay and the younger Granger have returned to Tau Ceti," Christoffsen replied, the Professor presumably having handled that part of the investigation. "The younger Granger did so very recently, in the wake of Desmond the Fourth's death. The two were ex-lovers and still close friends. Or so I presume from David Granger being one of Des's pallbearers, anyway."

"David didn't take Des's death well," Kiera told them. "I can't see him or his father being involved in Des's assassination."

"I'll get to that connection in a moment," Samara promised. "Right now, the key remaining point is that the Rune Breaker designs were accessed by Councilor Granger's personal aide six weeks before the rounds were made. He had clearance due to a research project he was engaging in on the early history of our colonization.

"Mr. Blanchett, unfortunately, is dead," the Voice concluded. "Natural causes a year ago. Even with all of this, it's only mildly suspicious."

"So, we're looking at a chain of patsies at one or two steps removed from the Councilor," Gregory said grimly. "It's circumstantial in many ways but enough for a warrant to go through the Councilor's files."

"Attempted murder of a Hand isn't *usually* a capital crime," Samara replied. "But even the accusation would end Granger's career on Mars— and ruin any chance of his son becoming the next Prince Consort."

"The chance was already pretty damn low," Kiera noted. "David took a year to worm his way back into Des's good graces after their breakup. And, well, unlike my late brother, David is *completely* gay."

Making it less likely that Suresh would try to make him *Kiera's* Prince Consort.

"Agreed, but it was definitely a factor in Granger's thinking," the Voice told them. "I believe that the assassination attempt may have even been an attempt to *protect* the Mage-King from Damien's difficulties. Desmond would sacrifice much to protect a living Hand, but even he would smear the name of a dead man to serve the Protectorate."

Damien winced. He could see *that* chain of events all too clearly. In some ways, that assassin could have prevented the entire Secession War. Of course, Damien's death at that juncture would also have doomed the entire Council. Including Suresh Granger.

"Our evidence linking Suresh Granger to Desmond's death is slimmer," Samara noted. "But several decisions he pushed during the negotiations around the new Constitution seem to have been shaped by an expectation that Desmond would not live to see the document signed.

"Combined with the potential for someone to have blackmailed him with evidence of the assassination plot..."

"Desmond was angry," Damien murmured. "I'm not sure the fact that an attack on a Hand isn't technically a capital crime would have saved Granger if that had come out."

"He was one of the two people to join His Majesty and the Crown Prince for dinner that night. Security records Romanov accessed show he stayed to speak with them both after Councilor Coral had left," Christoffsen told them. "Monsieur Granger had potentially the only opportunity to convince His Majesty that Des needed to be present when we unveiled the Link."

The room was silent.

"Suresh Granger had the means and the opportunity to convince Desmond the Third to break protocol and fly Des up with him on the same shuttle," Samara concluded. "If our Nemesis knew about the assassination attempt on Damien Montgomery, then they had more than enough to blackmail him into making that happen, giving us motive."

"I guess there's only one way to know for sure," Damien said calmly, trying to process everything he'd just learned.

"What's that?" Kiera demanded.

"I need to talk to Councilor Granger," the Lord Regent replied.

"The Councilor is a trained Combat Mage, a veteran of Tau Ceti's defense forces," Romanov warned. "You can't confront him like—"

"If there are Guards in the room, he will sense a trap," Damien told his bodyguard. "No, Denis. Kiera and I can call him to us in terms he cannot deny, but we must meet with him and confront him alone."

"You would put both yourself and the Mage-Queen at risk?" Gregory demanded.

"There are ways we can keep Kiera safe, but yes," he confirmed. "For this task, no one else will do."

"So be it," Kiera told them, her tone decided. Damien smiled sadly to himself as he heard her father's tones in her voice. "My Lord Regent and I will meet with Councilor Granger and establish the truth of this."

Damien knew that tone. The advisors might argue, but the Mage-Queen of Mars had made up her mind—and the only person who could override her was him. And this was his idea.

CHAPTER 39

AS SURESH GRANGER stepped into Damien's office, the Lord Regent was studying him with an eye he hadn't applied to the Councilor in the past. The old Tau Cetan man *moved* like an old man, every gesture carefully calculated not to strain himself.

Damien's Sight marked other concerns as he watched Granger approach the desk. Granger was a Jump Mage, with the runes carved into his palms that would let him interface with a jump ship's runic matrix. He didn't have the projector rune of a Marine Combat Mage, but his record showed he'd been trained in combat magic for the Tau Ceti Self-Defense Force.

There were many more dangerous mages on the planet, but Suresh Granger was *quite* capable of defending himself. Nonetheless, Damien gestured for the Royal Guards to leave them and the door closed on a room that contained him, Granger, and the Mage-Queen of Mars.

"Welcome, Councilor Granger," he greeted their suspect. There was no way Kiera was talking to Granger. She was barely managing to keep a civil face and, from the way Granger was carefully eyeing his Queen, she wasn't entirely fooling him.

"We appreciate you making the time to meet with Her Majesty and myself," he continued, gesturing Granger to a seat. "I know how busy my schedule is, and I can't imagine a man wearing as many hats as you do is easily available."

"You and Her Majesty have the highest priority on my time," Granger told them. "All of the hats I wear in Sol boil down to different reasons to speak to the Mage-Queen. I am at your disposal.

"How may I serve the Mountain?"

"You can speak frankly," Kiera said, her tone iced gravel.

He blinked and bowed his head slightly.

"I do my best to speak frankly at all times," he told them. "I know the situation with the Committee's attempt to reset the negotiations after your father's death must have been upsetting. We are not entirely fans of the structure His Majesty agreed to, but that was an inappropriate way to handle matters.

"You have my deepest apologies for my own mishandling of that matter."

"That's a factor in why Kiera summoned you," Damien told the Councilor, filing away the tacit admission that most of *that* particular dance had been Granger's idea. "But it's not what we wanted to talk to you about or what we require your complete honesty on."

"I am at the Mountain's disposal," Granger replied. "What do you need, my Lord Regent?"

"I need you to explain, in detail, the events and reasoning that led to your contribution to the assassination of Desmond Michael Alexander the Third and his son."

Damien could *see* the moment that Granger realized what he was saying—about halfway through the word *assassination*. There was no surprise in the other man's face, but the blood drained from it with spectacular speed.

"I have no idea what you—"

"*Bullshit*," Kiera snapped. "*You* convinced my father to take Des up on a shuttle that shouldn't have held them both. *You* nominated the prosecutor whose blind spots allowed her to miss that an assassination even *happened*."

"And you were responsible for a negotiated agreement that was carefully not put in writing," Damien said quietly. "Like you expected Desmond to be dead before an actual document was signed.

Most of all, Councilor Granger, you aren't *surprised* to be accused of this."

Granger flung himself backward.

"I will not stand for these...these malicious accusations!" he barked.

"You can answer the questions around Desmond's assassination, Councilor, and we might come to a deal," Damien told him. "Or you could not...and we'll find a judge prepared to hang you for the attempted assassination of one of His Majesty's Hands.

"We can prove beyond any doubt that you were the man who contracted the assassin Alexander Odysseus to murder *me*. And while I will forgive many things, Suresh Granger, your list of sins grows long for even *my* mercy."

Power flashed around Granger and Damien's Sight grabbed on to it. He wasn't sure if it was a defensive spell or an attack, but he was *not* going to permit Granger to wield magic in this room.

Damien's own power slashed across the room, using the runes that filled the Mage-King's office to *smother* Granger's spell before it could take form.

The Lord Regent was not Desmond Michael Alexander—but he had learned from that worthy, the most experienced Rune Wright of their time. He'd *fought* Samuel Finley, a self-taught Rune Wright who'd mastered several tricks Damien had never learned from Alexander.

With Desmond's death, Damien might not be the most powerful Mage alive—that title rested with Admiral Jane Alexander—but he was the best-taught *Rune Wright* alive.

He was on his feet, one black-gloved hand pointed at Granger as his power wrapped around the Councilor's and squashed it. Not the spell he'd been trying to cast again—Damien now recognized the long-range personal teleport of a Jump Mage in trouble—but *every scrap* of the Mage Gift the other man possessed.

"You don't get to leave until I say you get to leave, Councilor Granger," he said softly. The Councilor was backing away, staring at him in horror.

"It's an interesting trick that Dr. Finley mastered, isn't it?" Damien continued. "The man was a psychopath, but he was extraordinarily gifted and he'd learned quite different ways of suppressing magical power than we had.

"Sit. Down," he ordered. "You *will* answer our questions or you will be tried and sentenced for regicide. There will be a list of other charges, but that one means there's no question of the penalty that will be applied, is there?"

"Please," Granger half-whispered. "I...I had no choice."

"Sit the fuck down," Kiera snarled. "Because Damien can make all the promises he wants, but *I* am the daughter of the man you killed, and *I* am the one you need to convince to spare your miserable life."

Damien waited for Granger to sit down. He was more likely to spare the man than not...but Kiera wasn't wrong in claiming the final decision on whether to send him to a trial without a deal.

He'd be tried under Protectorate Law, not the laws of the Kingdom of Mars. The Protectorate Supreme Court was *slightly* less likely to shoot him than a Martian Court, but it was still a near-certainty unless the old man made a deal.

From the way he slumped into his chair, Granger had run the same calculation. He didn't meet either Damien or Kiera's gaze, staring down at the floor beneath him.

"I truly thought you were a threat to Mountain and Protectorate," he finally said, slowly. "The rest of the Council was going to use you as a club to break the Mage-King—and I was Desmond Alexander's man, no question about it.

"So, I tried to remove a threat he was blind to." He was silent for several seconds. "If I'd succeeded, I'd be dead myself now. The irony is not lost on me. I thought I'd buried everything and was going to write it off as the worst idea I'd ever had.

"Then a man showed up in my office. I didn't know him. He introduced himself as 'Nemesis.'"

"I'm familiar with the name," Damien replied. "What did he look like?"

Damien had fought the man the Legatan spies they'd captured had IDed as "Kay," who had also seemed to operate as Nemesis.

"He was an older man, probably older than me," Granger told him. "Pure white hair. Skin like translucent parchment... That stuck in my head.

"He knew *everything* about the attempt on you. And...other things, nothing of similar weight, but let's not pretend anyone makes it to Councilor with clean hands."

"Most do, actually," Damien murmured. The description sounded *very* familiar. "They really do."

Granger seemed taken aback by that. Damien wasn't entirely surprised. Most people who were corrupt seemed to assume everyone around them was also corrupt. He'd just never taken *Suresh Granger* for that type.

"Older man, white hair, super pale skin?" he finally asked. That wasn't Kay. "You sure he called himself Nemesis? Do you have any images of him?"

"The one time I met him in person, my entire office security system was down," Granger admitted. "Everything after that was text-only communication."

"And he asked you to assassinate the Mage-King of Mars?" Damien said flatly. He heard Kiera hiss next to him and doubted the sound went unnoticed by his captive.

"I can tell you...everything," Granger said slowly. "I know more than he told me. I didn't take being blackmailed lightly, Lord Regent, but I need *something* in exchange for those truths."

Damien gestured to Kiera.

"Your call, Your Majesty," he said quietly. From the way Granger's gaze switched to the young Queen, he'd been *hoping* Damien didn't do that.

"Why should I make you *any* promises before I know the depth of your crimes?" Kiera asked coldly, anger dripping from her tones. "You murdered my father, Suresh Granger. If I even let you *live*, it will be against my better judgment."

"I did not kill your father," Granger said desperately. "Yes, I convinced him to take Des with him to the Link unveiling at the last minute, so they'd have to take one shuttle. I suspected they were going to attack him there, but I didn't *know*, I swear."

"You knew," Kiera countered. "You can argue that you only 'suspected,' Granger, but you knew there was only one reason to put my father and brother on the same shuttle. Don't pretend otherwise."

He tried to straighten in the bonds of Damien's magic but only ended up looking more pathetic.

"If you're going to kill me anyway, what reason do I have to help you?" he asked.

"Well, for one, you can help us put an end to Nemesis," Damien pointed out. "They were behind the attack on Council Station. Forced you into this position. You could blame them for your own actions, even, though my personal philosophy calls for more responsibility than that."

"I can give you Nemesis," Granger told them. "They were in intermittent contact with me for two years. I have been tracing those calls, that data, the entire time. I can give you Desmond's killers."

"I have the man who rigged the shuttle in a cell right now," Damien replied. "His aid in tracking you down earned him his life. What more do you need?"

"We both know the assassin isn't Nemesis," Granger said. "Nemesis said he'd met you. You know who you're hunting. I can give him to you."

"I have several possibilities for who I'm hunting," the Lord Regent said calmly. "One of those people is definitely you."

Granger went silent and closed his eyes.

"It's Kiera's call, not mine." Damien looked over at the Mage-Queen of Mars. "My Queen?"

"Spare him if you must," she finally snapped. "But he never sets foot in Sol again."

"Do you hear her, Suresh Granger?" Damien asked their captive.

Granger nodded.

"*If*—and *only* if—your information delivers Nemesis into the hands of the Protectorate, you will be spared," he told the older man. "In that case, you will be taken from Mars to your estate on Tau Ceti *e*, where you will be chipped like the criminal on probation you are and you will spend the *rest of your life* under house arrest.

"But you will not be executed and you will not face a public trial. *This* is your trial—and your sentence is by the will of the Mountain. Is that enough for you, Suresh, or should we give up on this conversation and proceed with chemical interrogation?"

Damien was holding the man suspended in the air, supported on the same bands of force that held him in place and blocked his magic. He'd left Granger limited mobility, but it was enough for the man to slump in defeat and nod.

CHAPTER 40

AS DAMIEN allowed Granger to sit again, he summoned Samara to join them and dug into his own files for something in particular.

"What are we waiting for?" the Councilor asked after a near minute of silence.

"Several of my best people have been on this file, and I'd prefer to only have you tell us all of this once," Damien replied. "First, though, was this the man you met?"

The picture wasn't great. It had been taken through the binoculars of a sniper's spotter, one of several teams positioned around the restaurant where Damien had met the man named Winton. The white-haired and pale-skinned old man had kidnapped Roslyn Chambers to get Damien to the meeting—the meeting where he'd offered Damien Montgomery the throne of Olympus Mons if he joined the Keepers.

Damien had nearly killed Winton for that. Letting the man go had allowed them to retrieve Chambers unharmed, though, so he couldn't quite regret letting the man live.

"That's him, yes," Granger said after a moment. "I've met a few old men of similar coloring, but that's definitely him. Who is that?"

"He introduced himself to me as Winton, back when he was trying to recruit me to join the Keepers," Damien replied. "I have reason to suspect, now, that that was part of a plan to turn me against the Keepers and weaken them. A plan, I have to admit, that worked perfectly."

"It would fit," Granger admitted, twitching slightly as the door opened behind him. Damien had let the man sit but was still holding him in place with magic and suppressing the other Mage's gift.

Romanov and Samara had been expecting the call and calmly took chairs on either side of Granger, allowing themselves to both listen to Damien and keep an eye on the Councilor.

"I believe you are familiar with Voice Munira Samara," Damien told Granger. "I don't believe you know Guard-Lieutenant Denis Romanov, the commander of my personal detail.

"Now, when did Nemesis—Winton—contact you?" he asked.

"It was less than two weeks after the attack on Council Station," the Councilor told them. "He was in my office here on Mars. The embassy security systems were down for our entire conversation, but he didn't show up on them before or afterwards, either."

"Live-edited security feeds," Romanov guessed. "They tried the trick in the Mountain, too. The Royal Guard has both more resources and more paranoia than most security teams."

"That isn't possible, is it?" Granger asked.

"It requires very good software and Hand-level overrides on government computers," Samara said grimly. "Recent evidence suggests that both Hand Ndosi and Hand Octavian left our target in possession of significant numbers of one-time codes for that purpose. Both of them are dead, but their betrayals live on."

"My research suggests that Nemesis began as a branch of the Keepers," Granger told them. "That would...line up."

"And explain why Nemesis destroyed the Keepers," Damien agreed. "Winton actively turned us on them to cover his tracks. But...a *branch* of the Keepers? You believe Nemesis to be an organization, then?"

"A powerful one, too," Granger admitted. "They had their tendrils in my own office. In the Keepers. In the Mountain itself. I don't think there's many of them, but I think they have access to a lot of reserves the Keepers had hidden away over the years."

"And with the Keepers dead and their archives destroyed, we're never going to find those," Samara concluded. "We know of Nemesis through a Mage who operated as 'Kay.' Did you ever meet anyone else?"

"Just this Winton," Granger said. "There was a limit to how much digging I could do without revealing myself. I believe my own office was compromised in advance of them making contact."

"I received several text communications over the last two years, directly to my personal inbox, bypassing the entire consular information systems architecture. Mostly requests for information, delivered to digital dead drops."

"And you obeyed, compromising yourself further," Romanov guessed. "Pretty standard asset-acquisition tactics, really."

"That wasn't lost on me, Lieutenant," Granger said dryly. "I played my own game in turn, trying to track them. I was *planning* on handing them to His Majesty on a platter, counting on that to be enough to protect me from his anger over the attempt on Montgomery."

Damien snorted. *He'd* have argued to forgive and forget in exchange for that kind of intelligence coup, even if Alexander had wanted to be stubborn.

"But they dropped the demand to get the Desmonds on the same shuttle before I had enough," he admitted. "I couldn't prove anything about them, but they had enough evidence to get me shot."

"And it didn't occur to you at *that* point that just handing over details of the assassination plot might have been enough?" Kiera demanded. "Instead, you killed my father and brother."

The office was silent.

"I was afraid," Granger said, his voice very quiet. "I had every evidence that my office was compromised, that Nemesis's reach was long. It seemed very likely that any attempt to warn His Majesty would be blocked and result in my own death."

"You were literally in a room with the Mage-King of Mars arguing to set him up for this," Damien noted. "There would have been no better time."

"I...I was not prepared to sacrifice my life for his," the Councilor admitted in a hoarse whisper. "And I *knew* that all the resources of Mars could not save me. They won't save me now, either."

"Have a little faith, Councilor," Damien told him. "You didn't have enough data to track Nemesis originally. Do you now?"

"Not enough for my resources," Granger confessed. "But..."

Carefully, straining against the bonds around him, he typed in a sequence of commands on his wrist-comp and withdrew a datachip.

"This is everything I have," he told them. "I couldn't safely store it anywhere else without fear it would be lost. I couldn't trust anyone. I don't think you realize how much two years of *that* could wear on a man."

"And I think you give yourself too much credit for your weakness," Kiera told him. "Your failures killed my family, Suresh Granger. Montgomery's mercy stands, but you will be taken from here to a cell until we know if your information helps at all.

"You have bought your life. We will see whether you have bought something as merciful as exile before We decide to grant it to you."

Everyone in the room picked up the Royal We. It wasn't often used in Martian tradition—it was, in fact, *only* used for extremely formal statements—such as when passing final judgment.

"I understand, my Queen," Granger told her. "If it eases your anger, realize that Nemesis will destroy me for this."

"You destroyed yourself a long time ago, Granger," Damien countered. "But if they kill you, it will be through no lapse of ours. Imprisonment comes hand-in-hand with protection, after all."

He nodded to Romanov.

"Have the Guard take him away," he ordered. "Let's see how long we can keep this secret. We only have so much time."

Samara had already grabbed the datachip and was looking at it greedily.

"Give me a day," she told them. "I'll find the bastards."

CHAPTER 41

DUKE OF MAGNIFICENCE hadn't left Martian orbit yet. She'd been undergoing resupply and minor maintenance, important-enough tasks that Damien hadn't interrupted them for such minor tasks as hauling him to meetings.

Now...

"Mage-Captain Denuiad, it is a pleasure to speak with you again," he greeted the woman who appeared in the hologram in front of him.

"*Duke* and her crew are at your disposal, Lord Regent," she replied. "I'm doubting this is a social call."

"Officially, it is," he said with a grin that he knew told her the truth. "I would like to join you and your senior officers for dinner this evening, in memory of old times. I'll need to bring some extra guests, of course."

The Royal Martian Navy ran on Olympus Mons Standard Time, the same time zone as the Mountain itself. Dinner, by a standard schedule, would be in under two hours.

"Should I arrange for that invitation to have been sent a day or so ago?" Denuiad asked. "We would be delighted to host you for old times' sake, Lord Montgomery. Is there anything in particular I should prepare?"

"It will be *just* like old times," Damien told her. "Just like. Prepare for that, if you would be so kind?"

Old times had been everything from covert operations to invasions to food relief to civil war. If *Duke of Magnificence* prepared for old times, she'd be ready to go to war.

"I can do that, my lord," she confirmed brightly. "We will be shipping back out for Legatus in two days, so we are well stocked for dinner."

Or war. That could come in handy.

"Thank you, Mage-Captain. My companions and I will be aboard before the regular dinner time. I look forward to discussing old times."

She chuckled.

"I'll advise my XO and my...stewards," she told him. "I look forward to seeing you again."

Her image vanished and Damien looked over his console. He had several more calls to make...and since he wasn't making them from his office, his ability to see them was promptly interrupted by Persephone's arrival on top of the touchscreen.

"No, stop," he told the cat. Somehow, she managed to dance across the active surface without actually triggering *anything* before leaping onto his shoulder as he reached for her.

She answered his aggravated sigh with a determined purr that told him he'd been working too much.

"Get used to it, cat," he warned her. "I'm glad you have Schenck. I don't think this is ever going to slow down."

He took a moment to lean into the purring kitten, letting her vibrations ease the pain in his temples. Then he gently lowered her to the ground with magic and brought his next call up.

If he was going to be on a shuttle in an hour, he had a *lot* of work to do.

Damien Montgomery was utterly unsurprised to find Kiera at the door to his quarters as he was heading to the shuttle.

"I take it the lectures on personally leading assaults didn't take?" she asked.

"They did not," he agreed.

"So, are you going to be a hypocrite?" Kiera continued.

"By which you mean, *am I going to refuse to let you come along?*" Damien said. "Yes. Violation of the two-shuttle rule *and* we have less excuse to take you up to *Duke of Magnificence* in general."

"I could teleport up there," she noted. "No one would be the wiser."

"And I'd still be taking the Mage-Queen of Mars into a probable combat zone," he countered. "It's not happening, Kiera. You're not trained for it and you're not ready for it."

"These people killed my family," Kiera told him. "I am a Rune Wright, an Alexander. I can take them."

Damien sighed, glancing around. They were still deep inside the family section of the Mountain, with Royal Guard details sweeping in front of them and following behind. No one was going to overhear this conversation.

"Potentially," he agreed. "But you don't need to and we can't risk you."

"And we can risk you?" she snapped.

"Yes," he confirmed. "If I die, it's a pain in your ass but Gregory can act as Lord Regent. *You* can use the Olympus Amplifier and are the rightful heir. I am expendable in ways that you are not."

That brought a thought, but Kiera was doubling down even as he was plotting.

"Not really," the Mage-Queen of Mars told him. "You might be expendable to you, but you are *not* expendable to me. I..." She swallowed. "I can't face this alone. These next few years? *I* need you. The Protectorate can use you, but I *need* you."

"I don't plan on dying, Kiera," he said softly. "My job is to keep you safe for the next three years, Kiera Alexander. Part of that is making sure the *people* who killed your father pay for their crimes.

"And part of it is being overprotective and keeping you on Mars while I do things that are necessary but stupid," he told her. "But, now that I'm thinking about it, I actually need you here for other reasons."

"Really," she said dryly. "And what can *I* do that no one else can?"

"You can use the Olympus Amplifier," he echoed from a few moments before. "And with the Olympus Amplifier, you can do things no one else can. Surprise is key to our operation here, Kiera. If we lose it, we will lose Winton. He will escape. My current suspicion put either him or Kay at the top of Nemesis and directly responsible for your father's death."

"And how exactly does my staying here change that?" she demanded.

"If I lock you inside a safety vault behind a hundred Royal Guards, it doesn't," Damien replied. "But if you go down to the amplifier and we work together..."

"All right, Samara, what are we looking at?"

The Voice was sitting across from Damien on the updated shuttle.

"First, has someone checked the antimatter lines on this shuttle?" she asked, glancing around nervously. "I didn't *use* to mind flying in these, but..."

"We checked," Romanov confirmed as the Royal Guard took a seat. Unlike most of the last week, he was back in his red exosuit armor. None of the Guard had their helmets up, but all of them were *in* the armor, at least.

"Oh, good."

The noises around them quieted as the shuttle slid into launch position.

"Which brings me back to my question," Damien noted. "We sent this into motion when you told me you had a target. No one—including Captain Denuiad's staff—thinks we're actually having dinner on *Duke of Magnificence*. So, where *are* we going?"

Her immediate response was cut off as the engines flared. The shuttle had been refitted to have the amenities expected for the Royal Family, but even with magic, there was only so much muffling that could be done for the engines at full power.

The thrust held them against their seats for a full minute before it cut to a quieter burn, directing them toward their battlecruiser destination.

"In answer to your question, my lord, we're going here," Samara told him, projecting a hologram in the middle of the shuttle. It was a map of the Sol System with a single flashing red dot in the asteroid belt.

"Nemesis was bouncing their messages through several automated beacons, but those were general beacons, not theirs," she noted. "Granger had traced the transmissions through those to a second set of beacons and hadn't been able to track it past there.

"*Unlike* Granger, I have full access to the military sensor networks and their archived records," Samara continued. "Combined with the location and date stamps Granger had collected, I IDed four covert beacons used over a period of two years. Each beacon was only used once and then, so far as I can tell, self-destructed.

"Neat and clean. But *not* untrackable, given the information we had. Considering orbital mechanics, the transmissions from all four intersected on this orbit in the asteroid belt, currently at its most distant from Mars."

"And?" Romanov asked.

The map zoomed in, revealing a crude-looking space station, half-built into the side of an asteroid.

"United Nations Relay Station VRF-Seven-Six-Five," she reeled off. "Built during the war, abandoned shortly afterwards. Claimed, refitted and re-abandoned at least twice after that. On a list of potential assets retrieved from the Belt Liberation Front when we broke what was left of them.

"Long-distance scans at the time showed the station as inactive, and we had the entirety of the BLF's known membership in custody, so it wasn't further investigated," she admitted. "Current scans also show it to be inactive, however, which means someone had done a *very* good job of concealing their presence."

"Is it potentially automated?" Damien asked.

"Potentially," she confirmed. "It was built for a crew of eleven under the UN. Records of the refits show that it could now hold as many as thirty people in reasonable comfort for an extended period.

"That's assuming the BLF or Nemesis haven't made further upgrades. The asteroid it's attached to could easily be hollowed out further to triple that capacity."

"We can handle that," Romanov said calmly. "There are twenty Royal Guards on this shuttle, and *Duke of Magnificence* has several hundred more Marines we can borrow if needed. A hundred Nemesis troopers don't worry me."

"The problem is that we need key components of the facility intact and we don't know if Nemesis's personnel are sufficiently fanatical as to self-destruct the facility with themselves in it," Samara said bluntly. "We know nothing about their personnel or equipment resources."

"It's entirely possible we're facing a full platoon or more of people just as capable and just as well equipped as the Royal Guard," Damien concluded. "Be prepared for anything, Romanov."

"We will be," he said grimly. "And we will have *Duke* for backup. The concern is the data, you said?"

"Yes," she confirmed. "We can get a lot of information from the BIOS on the transmitters themselves, but I doubt they actually operate from the station. It's a relay, and if we capture the computers intact, we can trace them all the way home."

"Do we know where the computers are?" Damien asked.

"Not with certainty," she admitted. "I know where they were and the most likely installation zones—but at close range, *Duke*'s sensors will be able to resolve them with relative ease."

"Getting in that close won't be easy, not if they have weapons or if we're at risk of them destroying the entire station," Romanov noted.

"That's already handled," Damien replied. "If we can locate the computer cores, then you and I can teleport straight there with the Guard. We lock down the data we need and play anvil—the Marines hit the surface and play hammer.

"Straightforward enough if you can teleport troops in."

"If *anyone* is expecting that, it's Nemesis," Samara warned. "They had to know that if anyone ever came after them, there would be Hands in the lead."

"I know. And that, my friends, is why I don't plan on giving them any warning that we're coming," Damien told them.

CHAPTER 42

AS DAMIEN and Romanov made their way back through the shuttle, they found Damien's armor waiting for them. The black-and-gold exosuit still looked undersized compared to the red armor of the Guard, but that was unavoidable.

Damien had worn full-sized exosuit armor a few times. The standard-size suits adjusted for a thirty-centimeter range of human heights, but that range started at one hundred and sixty centimeters.

Both smaller and larger suits could be made, but they were rare. The Marines tended to assign people too small for exosuit armor to shuttles and combat vehicles—and bigger Marines were usually assigned to special-purpose heavy-weapons suits.

"Armor up," Romanov told his boss. "I don't expect that you're going to stay aboard *Duke*, are you?"

"For this to be worth anything, we need to seize the data core," Damien replied. "That means I need to take you all there—and while I can *send* one or two of you away from me, if I'm teleporting a platoon, I have to come with you."

"I figured," the Royal Guard replied. "So, armor up."

Damien nodded to his bodyguard and accepted help from an already-armored Guard to get him into the suit. It closed over him and he waved the helmet over to him. He tucked it into an armored elbow to spare his hands, then glanced over at Romanov.

The Guard-Lieutenant was already fully armored up, his helmet locked on and a penetrator rifle in his hands. He was studying a black box that looked out of place in the weapons racks in the back of the shuttle.

"Are those what I think they are?" Damien asked softly. If they were, the box was lead-lined or he'd have known they were aboard the moment he'd entered the shuttle.

"Twelve Rune Breakers. Not even half a full magazine," Romanov confirmed. "Not sure if they're worth bringing. I'm *hoping* we've run out of Hands that have betrayed the Mountain."

"I'm pretty sure we have," Damien agreed. "Bring them anyway. Fire one of those into a ship's amplifier matrix anywhere near the core and, well, you'd better *hope* I'm nearby to teleport you out."

"Great. Because what I need is more ways to kill myself when I'm on a hostile warship," the Guard snapped. But he stowed the lead-lined box in one of his exosuit's compartments.

"We are touched down and the bay is cool," the pilot announced over the shuttle's intercom. "Well, cool enough to be survivable. I'm not gonna tell you you'd like it out there without armor, but you'd live."

One of the major reasons for exosuits, beyond the value of mechanical muscles increasing armor and weapon capacity, was that an exosuited warrior could cross the superheated field where a shuttle had just landed without waiting for it to cool.

Even shuttle bays could only dissipate that heat so quickly, which made for an inevitable wait after a shuttle had landed anywhere.

"Let's go," Damien ordered. "Mage-Captain Denuiad will be waiting for us."

Damien wasn't wrong. If there'd been any suspicion that Mage-Captain Denuiad had missed what he'd meant by "just like old times," it was thoroughly allayed by the presence of her Marine CO in full exosuit armor. Mage-Captain—diplomatically promoted to simply "Major" aboard ship, a rank the Royal Martian Marine Corps didn't have— Ubirajara Tupi was one of the Marines who wore oversized standard combat armor, towering over his already-tall ship CO.

The special-weapons suit he wore was designed to carry magazine-fed missile launchers, heavy portable lasers, and similar antiarmor or antiaircraft weapons. Currently, the mounts were empty and Tupi held his helmet in his hands.

"Lord Regent, welcome back aboard *Duke of Magnificence*," Denuiad greeted them. "Guard-Lieutenant Romanov, welcome as well. Will anyone else be joining us for dinner?"

"I'm afraid we're going to have to cancel dinner," Damien told her as Royal Guards continued to troop out of the shuttle behind him. "I need to commandeer your ship for the good of the Protectorate. Is *Duke of Magnificence* ready for combat, Mage-Captain?"

"We are fully fueled, fully supplied, and fully crewed, Lord Regent," she replied instantly. "Our magazines are loaded with Phoenix IXs as well. We're expected to escort a munitions convoy with the new missiles to rendezvous with Second Fleet in thirty-six hours."

"If everything goes according to plan, Mage-Captain, you'll keep that appointment," Damien told her. "But first, I need to read you in on potentially the most classified situation currently going on in the Protectorate."

"Of course, my lord. We have a secure conference room just this way," she told him.

He shook his head. There could be *no* leaks of this. Damien was certain that he'd only managed to pin down Granger because the Councilor hadn't known what was coming. Given the penetration shown by Nemesis and their organization so far, the only way he was going to catch Winton was by taking him completely by surprise.

"That's enough for our conversation, but the security of this matter requires a step beyond," he told her. "I need you to initiate covert lockdown protocols. Before we discuss this."

Denuiad blinked but slowly nodded.

"I understand," she confirmed. "Major Tupi can show you to the conference room while I speak to my XO, my lord. There will be no leaks from *Duke*. I will make certain of it."

Covert lockdown meant that the ship went onto full communications lockdown, but a series of protocols were put in place to maintain at least the appearance of communications from the outside. The deception wouldn't succeed forever, but it would buy them three or four hours before serious questions started getting asked.

Damien was going to need every one of those hours.

"The ship is now under covert lockdown protocols," Denuiad told Damien and Romanov as she entered the office. "All external communications are locked to my personal wrist-comp, and the ship's computers have initiated an ASI protocol to respond to incoming coms."

"Good," Damien said. "And this room is secure as well?" He gestured around the utilitarian secured conference room.

Denuiad tapped a command.

"We are now cut off from the universe, my lord," she said quietly. "I question the wisdom of cutting the Lord Regent off this completely, but the decision is yours."

"Communications blackouts are necessary for security, Mage-Captain," Damien told her. "I don't spend my *entire* life available to all questions, I assure you."

"Of course, my lord. What's going on?"

"The first thing you need to understand is very simple," he said quietly. "Our King was murdered."

He gave the two officers a moment to recover from that. He wasn't even sure what language Tupi's cursing was *in*, but he was quite certain what the man was saying no matter what tongue the words were from.

"We have confirmed this and have the assassin in custody," he continued. "We have made deals for information with several individuals involved, since I want to nail the people responsible for Desmond's death to a wall, not merely the hands that carried it out."

"What do you need of us?" Denuiad asked, her voice shaky for the first time since Damien had boarded her ship. "I don't... *How?*"

"Complicated," Damien said drily. "There were a lot of moving pieces and most of them were very subtle, but I am certain. What I need from your ship, Mage-Captain, is transportation and support on the next step.

"We have traced the orders to this relay station in the asteroid belt." As he spoke, Romanov was tapping commands on the armor of his arm. No one other than the Guard could see the keyboard, but the computers received the orders anyway.

The image and coordinates of the old UN relay appeared in the middle of the conference room.

"The station was built by the UN during the Eugenicist War and, despite several attempts since, has proven economically nonviable since," Damien told his people. "What information we have is in the files Denis is providing you.

"We believe the facility was occupied and expanded by the Belt Liberation Front, including the installation of crude stealth baffling to fool Protectorate scanners," he continued. "After the fall of the Belt Liberation Front, our information suggests it was reoccupied by forces of the organization we now know as Nemesis."

"That's one hell of a name, sir," Tupi told him.

"Egotistical and ostentatious, yes," Damien agreed. "In every way counter to most operations of theirs that we've encountered. We have directly linked them to the extermination campaign waged against the Keepers and the weapons provided to the BLF for their attack on Council Station."

He shrugged.

"Beyond that, we know very little about these people. That's what this is about." He gestured an armored hand at the holographic image of the relay station.

"If this station is actually under control of Nemesis, it will entail only our third confirmed direct contact with the organization," Damien told *Duke*'s officers. Their only confirmed encounters had been two very uncomfortable meetings with Winton.

"We need the station's data storage intact and we need prisoners," he continued. "That gives us two critical targets inside the station: the main data center and the reactor core. We cannot lose the information in their computers and we can't let them self-destruct the station."

"What kind of defenses are we looking at?" Denuiad asked. "Everything I'm seeing says the place is dead and abandoned."

"We're reasonably certain that *is* their main defense," Romanov replied. "To make a station like that look dead is possible but not easy. From close range, you should be able to identify both the data center and the reactor."

"Agreed, but if it's that stealthed, they'll see us coming long before I can get Marines to the data center," Tupi told them. "We couldn't resolve data-server heat signatures at more than a light-second *normally*, let alone with the kind of baffles this place must have."

"It's possible we're looking at an entirely automated relay and all we need to do is fly up to it and take what we need," Damien said. "Most likely, though, you are correct. Any conventional assault on this relay station will result in the destruction of the data long before we can retrieve it."

He smiled thinly.

"I have no intention of launching a conventional assault. Tell me, Mage-Captain, how close would you need to be to detect the data centers aboard one of our stealth ships?"

Damien *hoped* that *Rhapsody in Purple* and her sister ships were better stealthed than the installation concealed inside the asteroid they were studying. Those ships, however, had active stealth systems for when they wanted to be truly stealthy, systems they couldn't run all the time.

This station needed to be as concealed as possible always. Even with complete access, there was no way they could be certain when a random set of sensors from a random civilian ship would be pointed at them—and *complete access* in a system with Sol's interlaced jurisdictions was a myth.

"Assuming they weren't magically stealthing? Twenty thousand kilometers. Maybe even fifteen," Denuiad admitted. "I can't jump with that level of accuracy—even if jumping into the asteroid belt wasn't asking for trouble."

"I'm not expecting you to jump from Mars orbit into the asteroid belt, Mage-Captain," Damien told her. "*I* might have been able to do that when I had jump runes, but I have advantages you don't."

And even so, it probably would have been a *terrible* idea. Jumping out of a planetary gravity well was risky. Jumping *into* a planetary gravity well was risky—he'd done both with a fleet at the Battle of Ardennes, but it hadn't been *smart*. Just necessary.

None of the gravity wells in the asteroid belt were big enough to be dangerous in themselves, but the combination of hundreds of minimal gravity wells created a huge headache. There was a reason civilian ships usually jumped from at least a light-minute away from any significant masses.

"Then what are we going to do?" Denuiad asked.

"Her Majesty will use the Olympus Amplifier to deliver this ship to the relay station," Damien told them calmly. "Then you will confirm the location of the data center and I will teleport a strike team of Royal Guards to secure that location while Major Tupi launches an assault boarding of the exterior of the station.

"Depending on the location of the reactor core relative to either my insertion site or the surface, we will either detach a unit of the Guard or deploy a specific Marine strike force to secure that location.

"Once the data center and the reactor are in our possession, those units will dig in while Major Tupi's people clear the rest of the facility. If we find what we're looking for in the data center, we may need to leave Major Tupi's people to secure the facility while the rest of us move on the primary target: Nemesis's *actual* HQ in Sol."

"Which we have no intel on," Tupi guessed.

"That's why we're hitting the relay station," Damien confirmed. "Our best guess is that the relay station has less than fifty people aboard and they shouldn't be equipped to engage exosuited Marines and Guards.

"Securing the facility should be rapid, but I expect it to be ugly," he admitted. "We know very little about Nemesis—but I do know that they turned Keepers on each other. And the Keepers successfully turned at least two Hands against the Mountain.

"I don't know what motivates them, Major, Mage-Captain...but I expect them to be fanatical in its defense. We can hope for surrenders. I want prisoners.

"But at the end of the day, I *need* that data center."

"Understood," Tupi said grimly.

"The Major is understandably focused on the boarding operation," Denuiad said slowly. "But I need to go back to the beginning of this 'non-conventional' plan. *Her Majesty?*"

"At the end of the Eugenicist War, Desmond the First teleported the entire Martian battle fleet from Earth orbit to the Hellas Basin on Mars," Damien reminded her. "An Alexander sits the throne at Olympus Mons, Mage-Captain Denuiad. Transporting one ship is a tiny fraction of her abilities while she does so."

"We live in interesting times," the Mage-Captain murmured. "I have faith in you and Her Majesty, Lord Regent. I just did not expect the Mage-Queen of Mars to be involved in this operation."

"In a sane world, we wouldn't be bringing the Lord Regent," Romanov told them. "But we all know Lord Montgomery far too well to expect *that.*"

"Believe me, Captain, this is both the best use of Her Majesty's abilities and the furthest I was able to keep her from this operation," Damien pointed out. "Remember, these people killed her family.

"It was all I could do to keep her out of the assault teams!"

CHAPTER 43

DAMIEN RETURNED to his team on the main flight deck as *Duke of Magnificence* brought her engines up and headed to a quieter orbit. The Olympus Amplifier was powerful and provided Kiera with a lot of information and flexibility, but it still seemed wiser to reduce the complicating factors at the end of the teleport they could control.

They couldn't move the battlecruiser out of Martian space without drawing attention, but orbits shifted all the time—and moving the ship to reduce the people capable of taking potshots at the Lord Regent made sense to everyone.

Despite standing in the middle of the flight deck surrounded by twenty Royal Guards, most of Damien's attention was in the throne room of Olympus Mons. His view was taken up by two screens: one showed the bridge of *Duke of Magnificence* and the other showed Kiera Alexander walking up to the throne at the center of Olympus Mons.

Captain Denuiad was also on the link with Kiera, but most of the bridge crew was waiting on the Captain's orders.

"Are you ready, Your Majesty?" Damien asked as Kiera paused next to the plain stone chair.

Whatever energies his Sight picked up that allowed him to see magic, they didn't come through standard video cameras. He had no way of telling if the Mage-Queen had summoned her interface with the Olympus Amplifier or not, but he knew they were all waiting on her.

"I am."

Light sparkled on that video feed as the simulacrum of the solar system burst into existence around Kiera. Damien *heard* Captain Denuiad inhale in surprise and grinned. The Olympus Amplifier wasn't actually classified—it was hard to hide the existence of a tool that had turned the tide of a war and terraformed a planet, after all—but the people who'd seen it in action were few and far between.

The silver flickered, the camera unable to keep up with the way the molten metal changed at Kiera's command. After a moment, it settled into a clear split between two different "views" of the solar system.

One was focused on Mars, the support computers highlighting the tiny silver pyramid representing *Duke of Magnificence*. The other was focused on the relay station, and a dozen more icons were projected across the region around the station from the system.

Kiera was giving instructions to those markers as Damien watched, assessing distances and analyzing the gravity patterns around her destination.

Damien held his tongue, wishing he could have done this himself. Kiera had jumped exactly *one* starship, once—and even that was only because her training was far more advanced than most Mages' her age.

This was both more and less complicated than the regular one-light-year jump...and it was critical that it went right.

"I have you, Mage-Captain Denuiad," she said aloud in a calm voice. "Please deactivate your engines and release the simulacrum."

"Helm, cease thrust," the Mage-Captain ordered.

Damien could hear the tremor in Denuiad's voice as she released the silver model of her ship that hung directly in front of the Captain's chair. A warship's bridge was also its simulacrum chamber, the place from which a Mage could fling it between the stars.

Now, no Mage aboard *Duke of Magnificence* was touching the simulacrum or linked into the amplifier matrix—and Damien felt the tense, buzzing energy of a ship on the edge of jump anyway.

"It's all on you, Your Majesty," he told her softly. "We're ready."

"Captain Denuiad, if you could give me a five count, please," Kiera requested. "I'll be listening on the other end, but I don't plan on interrupting. You'll be busy at that point."

"That we will," Denuiad confirmed. "Crew, stand by scanners and jammers. External jump in five. Four. Three. Two. One."

"*Jump*," Kiera announced softly—and the world moved.

Damien had personally performed hundreds of jumps himself and been aboard ships being jumped by others for hundreds more jumps. He'd long ago learned that he was far more aware of the process than most people, even before he'd learned the term Rune Wright. It was that awareness that had eventually transformed into the ability to interfere with *other* people's jumps.

But everyone was aware of a jump to one degree or another. It was hard to miss...except this time, several of the people on *Duke of Magnificence*'s bridge very clearly *did* miss it for several seconds, before the change in stars and the sudden appearance of an asteroid cluster around them sank in.

The people in charge of the jamming, fortunately, were more on the ball. Icons on the displays told Damien everyone's long-range coms were now worthless.

"Get me scans of that relay station," Denuiad barked as Damien was confirming the jamming field. "Stand by boarding torpedoes and assault shuttles; I need *targets*."

Even from this close, the station looked dead at first glance. The tactical display being fed to Damien's helmet continued to update, though, and it became very clear that they'd guessed right. The station was *not* dead and there'd been a significant degree of excavation into the asteroid anchor.

"Reactor core located," someone snapped. "It's not close to *anything*."

"It's in the deep interior of the station, well away from anything except rock," Tupi replied. "I'm launching Alpha Company. Guns, *open me a hole*."

Damien saw what Tupi meant as a red line appeared on the display—Mage-Captain Tupi passing targeting data back to *Duke of Magnificence*'s tactical department. The reactor section was deep inside the station, yes, but there was only rock between one side of it and deep space.

And *Duke*'s lasers could open a tunnel for the assault shuttles to dive through.

"Holding for final thermal scans," the tactical officer replied. "We need...*got it*. Transferring data center coordinates to Lord Montgomery!"

They flashed up on his helmet and Damien had his suit computer running the numbers even as one of the battlecruiser's heavy twelve-giga-watt battle lasers spoke for a carefully calculated fraction of a second.

The icons for the first wave of assault shuttles were in the hole seconds after the laser stopped firing—and by the time they were diving in, Damien had finished his calculations.

"Royal Guard, we are jumping," he snapped. "Are you ready?"

"Sir!"

"*Now.*"

Like Kiera's power a moment before, Damien's magic swept over his strike team and the battlecruiser's flight deck was gone, replaced by bare stone walls and the blinking lights of a standard server array.

"Cut the connections to the rest of the facility and start a download," Romanov ordered after a moment's silence confirmed they were alone. "First priority: protect this site. Second priority: secure the data."

Get out alive was clearly farther down the priority list, Damien noted.

CHAPTER 44

ONE ADVANTAGE of firing a heavy battle laser into the target was that they *definitely* got everyone's attention. They were alone in the data center for at least a minute before anyone from the relay station even seemed to notice them.

By the end of that minute, Tupi's Alpha Company had touched down and the first waves of exosuited Marines were in the power center. *They* hadn't landed unopposed, and Damien's tactical display was showing red icons moving against them.

He wasn't even sure that Tupi could fit all one hundred Marines of the Alpha Company into the power core. More icons on his screen showed that *Duke* had fired the boarding torpedoes carrying Bravo Company as well. Another hundred Marines were now charging through the surface installation—and the cruiser's last company was landing on the exterior of the asteroid, moving to secure the receivers and transmitters that made the place a relay station.

"We have secured the reactor core," Tupi reported. "Defenders gave us a fight for it but withdrew before taking too many losses. I'm guessing there's an armory around here, and I'm expecting trouble shortly."

"Number estimates?" Damien snapped.

"Looked like a dozen or so," the Marine told him. "All engineers, I think, not that you could tell from the hell they gave us. Two of them are dead, but so's one of mine."

"Do I want to know how?" he asked.

"Plasma arc welder," Tupi replied. "It's not *designed* to go through exosuit armor but it will do a number regardless."

"We're in position and digging in. I expect a counterattack in the next few minutes, but I've got as many Marines in as I safely can. I'm going to hold until they've attacked to move in farther."

"Understood. Keep me inform—"

"We have incoming!" a Royal Guard snapped. Whoever was attacking them hadn't been expecting to run into magical barriers over both of the data center's entrances, which meant that the initial wave of grenades simply bounced away from the room.

"They're being careful," Romanov murmured on his private channel. "Those were gas and flashbangs. Pretty much useless against armored troops but also won't damage the server racks."

"Get at least two of your people shielding the racks and the cyber-team," Damien ordered.

"Already done, my lord," the Guard officer told him. "We've played this game before, you and I."

Gunfire now rang out, bullets ricocheting from the solidified air barriers.

"We can't hold this forever. Let them get closer, then we drop the barrier for counter-fire," Romanov continued calmly. "We have the numbers with the Marines. Sooner or later, they're going to realize their only chance of anything resembling victory is to take out this place."

"I know," Damien agreed. "We could just seal both entrances and teleport out once we have the data."

"Suit systems can't hold this much data, my lord," his subordinate told him. "We need to either bring in heavy gear or take the racks with us. I don't think either's an option without having a doorway."

Damien grunted his acknowledgement as he assessed the situation. He had twenty Combat Mages in exosuit armor. Four were working on the server racks with two more protecting them, which meant he "only" had fourteen of the most powerful individual combatants in the galaxy.

Plus him.

"I'm going to seal the inner exit," he told the Guard. "Then they can only come at us one way...and good luck to them with that."

"Let's give them one mo—"

Both barriers collapsed simultaneously, the magic of the Guards holding them overwhelmed by a simultaneous strike from multiple other Mages.

It took Damien a moment to put intent into action, his power flashing into the entrance he'd been planning to seal. Power yanked stones down from "above" the doorway—the station did have magical artificial gravity, which should have warned them there were Mages—to fill the space with debris.

Then *more* power flashed in and transmuted several thousand kilos of roughly piled stone into a meter-thick solid plug of titanium. Unless there was a Hand on the other side of the wall Damien had just created, they were secure from *that* side.

The other side was less certain. Exosuited soldiers were charging the entrance, penetrator rifles flashing in the dim lighting as they tried to target the Royal Guard. Magic flashed across the field, the Nemesis Mages trying to keep their mundane compatriots alive long enough to locate their enemies.

From what Damien could sense, there were three Mages behind the assault trying to push into the data center—but *every one* of his Royal Guard was a Mage. They were behind their own individual shields of magic that augmented their exosuit armor enough to sneer at even heavy-penetrator rounds.

The first wave of four troopers went down like tenpins, but a second wave of six more was right behind them, using exosuit muscles to leap the bodies spread across the gravity runes as they fired precisely at Damien's people.

Despite their advantages, a Royal Guard went down before that wave was gone—and a third wave was on their heels.

Damien couldn't just stand by. He reached out with his Sight, located the three Mages, and then summoned his power. He couldn't conjure electricity inside the data center without straining the people protecting the server racks.

He had no such limitations *outside* the data center. He could barely see the actinic blue-white flash of the ball lightning he summoned around the Nemesis Mages, but he knew what it looked like. He *knew* what happened when the power of a Rune Wright was unleashed in a confined space.

The magical signature of all three Mages went dark within moments of each other, and Damien stifled a moment of weary grief. Despite everything, he still didn't like killing people.

"Two more Mages coming from the other entrance," he noted as the room quieted. "Probably with another fifteen or twenty troopers. I think we underestimated how many people are on this station."

"I noticed," Romanov said grimly. "No surrenders, either. Some of these guys might only be wounded or in wrecked armor, but they put three of mine down hard. Hirschel will live, but Pavone and Bristow are gone."

"We hold," Damien told him. "I've got your back."

"I know. Tupi, report," the Guard ordered.

"They're fucking with me," the Marine replied. "No attack so far, but they've got snipers with penetrator rifles on every corridor. I can rush them, but I'll lose people."

"What about Bravo Company?" Damien asked.

"Moving towards me; we'll catch them in a vice but it will take time. Do you need us?" Tupi asked. "I can break out or direct Bravo Company units your way."

"You'll lose people," Damien said grimly. "We can hold. Unfortunately, these people are quite likely to know what it means to face a Hand, which means they have an idea of what my presence means."

"I doubt it," Romanov muttered. "They're still *here*."

"We didn't leave them an escape," he replied. "Can you link in to the station coms from here?"

"Let me check," the Guard replied. A moment later, he held up one gauntlet with a thumb up.

"We can link you in," he confirmed. "Going to tell them dark secrets and get them to break?"

Damien snorted.

"That only works when the dark secret is actually a secret," he pointed out. "Pretty sure everyone in here already knows or suspects they arranged for Desmond's death. No. Enough people are dead that I'll give them one chance to lay down their guns."

"And if they refuse, my lord?" Romanov asked.

"I may not be a Hand anymore, but I'm still familiar with the concept of Her Majesty's Sword."

"Station crew, this is Lord Regent Damien Montgomery," Damien began. "From the unhesitating violence employed to defend this station, I suspect you know why I am here and what you have done to bring me here.

"You are not soldiers in a war that requires me to treat you with grace," he reminded them. "You are not rebels in support of a cause that I would respect; you wear no uniform I recognize or am bound to respect.

"You are at best pirates and at worst terrorists. You are guilty of treason. Your lives are forfeit, but my people have already secured the critical components of this station's infrastructure. Further conflict will only result in unnecessary loss of life on both sides."

Damien figured the odds were less than twenty percent that anyone was going to listen to him, but he had to *try*.

"To avoid further bloodshed, I am prepared to treat anyone who surrenders as a civilian prisoner. You will face imprisonment for the crimes you have been involved in, but I will guarantee your lives and am prepared to negotiate further clemency in exchange for information.

"If you do not surrender, we will take this station by force and anyone who survives will be treated as a captured terrorist. The choice is yours."

He cut the channel.

"Double-check your defenses," he told Romanov.

"You're not expecting crowds of surrendering Nemesis soldiers?" the Guard officer asked drily.

"No."

The unsurprising lack of surrendering enemies was joined with a surprising few minutes of quiet. Damien had lost track of the two Mages, but his ability to locate Mages was minimal at best when they weren't actively using their Gift. He'd expected to lose them.

"I don't suppose we can get into the security system?" the Lord Regent asked Romanov.

"Technically, yes," the Guard replied. "In a very literal sense, we are in complete control of the security system of this station."

"Why does that sound less than promising?" Damien said.

"We cut off the servers to save them from being slagged," Romanov reminded him. "But they slagged just about everything *outside* this room as far as computers go. That almost certainly has doomed both the stealth systems and the life support."

"No one is planning on living here after the next few hours. Not us, not them. Anything out of the computers?"

"Not yet," the Guard commander admitted. "The encryption is solid. From what my team is saying, we may need to get all of this over to *Duke* before we can get anything reliable. Or Mars."

There was a shrug in his voice, though the armor didn't convey the gesture.

"My people would prefer Mars, but I don't think we want to spend that much time on this," he told Damien.

"We don't. Every *minute* we're spending here is a chance that our real prey escapes," Damien said. "Any sign of activity?"

"Nothing."

Damien activated his com.

"Tupi. Anything going on near you?"

"Not yet," the Marine replied. "I *think* they've pulled a few of the snipers out, but they're still taking solid potshots at anyone who sticks their head out." He paused. "I'm down two dead and half a dozen wounded. We're not going to lose any of the wounded, but they've got us bottled up with maybe four guys."

"How long until Bravo Company flanks them?" Damien asked.

"Five minutes, maybe. Then I can move to your position."

"We already know our estimates of how many people were aboard were too low," Damien replied. "But I'm guessing there's only maybe another twenty troopers to back up those two Mages. If four or five are pinning you down, it can't have taken them that long to pull everyone together."

Nemesis had had their people in exosuits within minutes of the boarding action. They were *very* ready for this.

"Any signs of problems with the core?"

"Negative," Tupi confirmed. "We cut off all data links elsewhere, but it's a standard hundred-megawatt fusion plant. Recent installation."

"Small power plants are expensive; none of the people who've moved in and out of this place would have left the cores behind," Damien replied. "*Duke* scanned for other power sources, yes?"

"Of course," the Marine confirmed. He paused. "I'd kill to talk to the Captain," he admitted.

"And the people on this station would probably kill to talk to their friends," Damien replied. "There's a reason everything is jammed."

Their gear—and presumably Nemesis's gear—could penetrate the jamming at short range. Even the big transmitters on the outside of the relay station couldn't send usable signals through *Duke*'s ECM field.

"Sensors say we have movement in the corridor," one of the Guards reported. "Twenty-plus sources, heading our way and fast."

"That's got to be everyone on their feet except the snipers poking Tupi," Romanov replied. "Where did they even *get* this many troops?"

"They're not all 'troops,'" Damien told him. "Everyone in the station was trained on and had heavy arms and an exosuit. That's not cheap...but it would allow every member of the crew to fight."

"Thirty meters and closing."

No one moved at the report. The Guards had moved their wounded behind the barrier protecting the server racks, but that still left them with nine active combatants. Twenty-plus attackers was something nine Royal Guards could handle.

Damien hoped.

Nemesis opened fire, loosing a hail of bullets through the only entrance Damien had left to the data center. The few remaining shreds of the door didn't survive the storm, but the sustained fire served the purpose of keeping the Guards out of the line of fire of the door.

"Grenades," Romanov ordered, his voice surprisingly calm.

One of the Royal Guards had a grenade launcher and the rest had secondary launchers on their heavy-penetrator rifles. A salvo of explosives answered the storm of incoming fire, rocking the station.

And then the Nemesis first wave was there, exosuited soldiers emerging from the smoke with penetrator rifles of their own. They were clearly no longer trying to save the data center, leading the way with armor-piercing grenades as well as the tungsten-cored penetrator rounds.

Damien couldn't carry a gun anymore, but he'd never been much of one for weapons. Holding a shield steady around himself, he lashed out at the attackers with beams of fire that sliced through armor like it was warm butter.

The Guards were focusing their own magic on their defenses, staying alive as double their own numbers pushed through the limited space.

It was chaotic enough that Damien missed the three soldiers not firing their guns for several critical seconds. They were through the door and charging for the data servers before anyone realized that they weren't carrying ammunition at all.

Those three suits had been fitted with special harnesses carrying black cylinders exactly one meter tall and thirty-seven centimeters in diameter.

Damien knew the dimensions the moment he saw the cylinders. His training hadn't spent much focus on the Protectorate's portable thermonuclear demolition charges, but they'd stuck in his head for some reason.

"*Nukes!*" Romanov snapped. "Take them *down.*"

And now Damien knew what the two Mages he hadn't sensed until that moment were doing. He couldn't tell if they were in the exosuits carrying the nuclear weapons, but it didn't matter. The entirety of their power was dedicated to covering the three suicide bombers as they tried to close with the server racks.

It wasn't even overkill. Anything short of a point-blank detonation might not break through the shield—especially if, say, Damien had been reinforcing it.

He was running to meet them before he even consciously had a plan, letting bullets ping off his own shields as his movement drew fire. Somewhere along the way, Romanov realized his plan.

"Cover Montgomery and keep them from the shield!" he ordered on the main channel.

A bullet sliced through Damien's shield. It was a fluke, the kind of perfectly angled round that could cut through any defense, and it slammed into his leg just above the knee. The Lord Regent went flying, hitting the ground in a heap that slid into the middle of the three suicide bombers.

All three looked down at him in surprise, and he managed to grin up at them before he teleported all four of them into deep space. They couldn't see it, but it made *him* feel better!

The silence of the void wrapped around him, only to be instantly interrupted by a warning from his suit. It was maintaining integrity, but his armor had taken serious damage—and so, incidentally, had his leg.

And then a new warning.

ACTIVE NUCLEAR CHARGE DETECTED.

Damien looked at his new companions in hell and saw one of them extend an armored middle finger his way...and then *new* deep space surrounded him as he teleported himself away in a random direction.

The fireball roughly fifty kilometers away was useful for getting his bearings and he took a deep breath as he studied the space around him. He was pretty sure *that* was the station, which meant that *Duke of Magnificence* was *that.*

Fortunately, his suit had a laser com. He wasn't going to try and teleport himself into a battlecruiser based on "pretty sure!"

CHAPTER 45

DENIS ROMANOV had just enough time to curse at the disappearance of Montgomery and the three suicide bombers before a bullet pinged off his armor, refocusing his attention.

He'd expect his idiot charge to teleport the enemy away, not *go with them.*

"Move up," he barked at his Guards in lieu of chewing out his missing boss. "They're down to the dregs now. Let anyone surrender who tries, but this ends *now.*"

He suited his actions to his words by hammering a solidified air barrier back into the entrance, sending the handful of surviving Nemesis troopers in the data center falling to the ground. One still tried to train a rifle on Denis, so the Guard officer shot them.

There was something about these troopers that was niggling at the back of his mind as his people moved up. None of them surrendered, though several of the crippled suits in the hall might have living soldiers in them.

"Black armor, no identifiers, fight like Marine spec ops...*fuck,*" he said aloud.

"Sir?" Afolabi asked, his second-in-command falling to one knee behind an impromptu barricade of several wrecked Nemesis exosuits and their occupants.

"Didn't realize I was live," Denis admitted, firing a grenade down the corridor. "Were you guys cleared for the mess at Andala?"

"It was included in the briefing when we moved to your team," the Guard confirmed, sending a five-round volley into the door. If he was aiming at anything in particular, Denis missed it.

"Someone bombed the dig site and then went in after Montgomery with ground troops. You nuked them with antimatter, right?"

"Right, but we fought a bunch of them on the ground, too," Denis replied. "Leapfrog us. Forward!"

Two Royal Guards charged past him and Afolabi, guns firing at the hip as they moved deeper into the wreckage.

"Black exosuits, all identification wiped. Special forces with self-purging armor." Holding his gun in one hand as a second pair of Guards leapfrogged his position, Denis tore the back plate off one of the fallen Nemesis suits next to him.

With the exosuit's artificial muscles backing him, he made a mess of the suit—but he still exposed the main computing harness. It was supposed to be a network of chips, circuits and wires...instead, it was a burnt-out mess, destroyed by a dozen tiny explosions and a few artificial surges.

"We won't be getting prisoners," he told his subordinate grimly. "The armor is designed to sterilize its data cores, but what they *don't* tell the troops who strap this shit on is that the process is usually fatal to anyone *in* the suit."

There was a flurry of gunshots up ahead, and then silence.

"Romanov, this is Tupi," the Marine CO's voice sounded in his head. "A platoon of Bravo Company just took a fireteam of the black-armored dudes from behind and they *think* they saw red armor.

"If they're your guys, have them say something. Or conjure purple sparks, I don't know."

"Kohls, you up front?" Denis demanded.

"Yes, sir," the Guard replied.

"Conjure up some purple sparks and play 'Amazing Grace' on your speakers, will you?" Denis told his point woman. "We might have made contact with the Marines."

"Wilco."

A moment of silence passed, then Tupi chuckled on the command net.

"My Marines confirm purple sparks and a familiar recording of 'Amazing Grace,' Guard-Lieutenant," he told Denis. "I think we might be clear."

"Let's link up and combine tac-nets," Denis ordered. They couldn't properly link their maps without having a confirmed shared location. "Then we sweep the station. I'm going to need to borrow one of your shuttles; they're the only things that can reach *Duke of Magnificence*."

"Understood. I'll have my people stand by for the Lord Regent."

Denis snorted.

"Not Montgomery. Just me. That's what I need to talk to Captain Denuiad about," he admitted. "My boss just teleported himself out of the station with three suicide bombers with nuclear charges. I'd *really* like *Duke of Magnificence* to find him for me!"

Once the tactical networks had synchronized and Denis had access to full maps of everything the Marines had seen aboard the relay station, reaching the assault shuttles Alpha Company had used to launch their assault was easy.

Their landing site left Denis with a new appreciation for the gunnery skill of the Royal Martian Navy's crews. The assault shuttles had used their own lasers and mass drivers to clear the final passageway into the station's power plant, but the smaller and rougher hole they'd blasted was only a couple of meters deep.

The hole blasted by *Duke*'s main guns was over fifty times that depth and easily thirty meters across. It wasn't necessarily clean or smooth—multi-gigawatt lasers transferred energy explosively—but it was perfectly calculated.

The method of attack also meant that there was no air in the power plant, but that didn't even qualify as an inconvenience to Tupi's people. They were starting to set up temporary airlocks since the plan called for at least some of them to remain there and secure the station while *Duke of Magnificence* went hunting.

"Any breakthrough on our prey?" the Marine Mage-Captain asked, stepping out from behind one of the shuttles as Denis approached.

"Nothing yet. We're going to need *Duke*'s computers, which means we'll be hauling things out soon."

"That'll need more shuttles," Tupi told him. "But then, pulling my people back off this rock was always going to need more shuttles. Boarding torpedoes are a one-way trip, after all."

A third of the size of an assault shuttle and carrying the same number of Marines, an RMMC boarding torpedo was politely described as "a rough ride." Accelerated while under the protection of the mothership's gravity runes, they had a far higher initial velocity than an assault shuttle.

Plus, well, the one-use magical crush compensators that assault shuttles used for emergency crashes had been designed for boarding torpedoes. They didn't slow down until they hit their target.

They were very much a one-use transport.

"Once we're in space, we'll be able to ping *Duke* and clear some channels," Denis told the Marine. "We'll probably keep the jamming up for a while, though. Even if we're in physical possession of the control rooms and transmitters, I don't trust this place not to have a sneaky way for them to call out."

"Me either," Tupi confirmed. "Get going, Lieutenant; the shuttle pilot's waiting on you. She has my update to send Denuiad too."

"Thank you, Mage-Captain," Denis told the other man. "I'm glad we had you with us."

"Your Guards took the heaviest fighting," the Marine replied. "I'm not sure I approve of the Lord Regent using himself as an insertion method, but..."

Denis laughed.

"You've served on *Duke* for a while, haven't you?" he asked. "Do the Marines on her *really* expect Montgomery to take proper care of himself?"

"Not in the slightest, Guard-Lieutenant. Go find him, please. The *Duke*'s Marines are a bit attached to the little man."

"*Duke of Magnificence*, this is Detail-Actual," Denis said into the microphone. "I say again, *Duke of Magnificence*, this is Detail-Actual. Respond if you're able."

"Detail-Actual, this is *Duke*-Actual," Denuiad's voice replied, slightly distorted from the jamming even with everything the shuttle and cruiser could do. "Care to explain just why the package is floating in deep space, calling for a rescue?"

"Because the package is the package, Captain," Denis said with a sigh. "Is the package intact?"

"Understood to be. Coms are limited, but the SAR shuttle is only a few minutes away. Package's suit is damaged, but telemetry suggests he's good for at least an hour."

Denis sighed again, in relief this time.

"Good to hear that, Captain. Station is in our hands but not entirely secure," he told the Captain. "We need new shuttles to relieve Bravo and support Alpha. Perimeter docks are in our hands. Did anyone try to run?"

"One ship. We summoned them to surrender; they refused." There was a very clear shrug in the Mage-Captain's voice. Denis had no illusions of what had happened to the ship that had tried to run.

Even if it had been a jump ship, *nobody* was going to try to jump out of the asteroid belt. Military Mages with military amplifiers *might* be able to do it. Might.

It didn't sound like they'd tried before Denuiad had burned them to ash. No one was feeling particularly charitable on this mission.

"Did you get any prisoners on the station?" the Mage-Captain asked.

"Negative," Denis told her. "They suited up in exosuits when we boarded. Black ops exosuits, with the self-sterilizing function. Supposed to trigger on a deadman switch, but I'm not expecting survivors."

"Fuckers."

That wasn't *really* appropriate for official coms, but that was life.

"Shuttles?" Denis asked. "We'll need medical support, too. Wounded and dead, unfortunately."

"Medical was planned for. Shuttles launching in sixty," the Mage-Captain replied. "Confirming pickup on the package, Detail-Actual. Do you want to rendezvous with SAR?"

"I'll meet the package on the deck," Denis replied. "We'll come in once the rest of the shuttle fleet is in motion. Target is proving difficult to crack; we'll probably move it over once there's a shuttle in place with the space."

There was a long pause.

"Understood, Detail-Actual. I have an update request from Olympus. Nothing yet?"

Denis wasn't even sure how Kiera was in communication with *Duke*. The battlecruiser's jammers should have stopped anyone from contacting her from Mars. On the other hand, Kiera was the Mage-Queen of Mars and sitting in the Olympus Amplifier.

He wasn't taking bets on what she could or couldn't do.

"I have updates aboard that we'll deliver by direct connection," he told Denuiad. "There will be people waiting to rendezvous and sync tacnets once the shuttles land. We'll want to make sure we have solid laser links at that point."

"We would have had them all along if we hadn't decided to send Marines into the *middle* of the asteroid," the Mage-Captain replied. "We'll be live all the way now. I was hoping to have some answers by the time we had the package on deck."

"I'm not in contact with my people now until you have those links up, *Duke*-Actual. But I'm not expecting miracles."

"We'll make it happen one way or another," Denuiad replied. She inhaled sharply. "Update from the SAR team, Detail-Actual. They're requesting emergency clearance through the landing process, so we may need to hold off on launching the shuttles."

That sent a chill through Denis.

"What did the little id—" He cut himself off, took a long breath. "Package's status?" he said in clipped tones.

"From what the SAR is telling me...shot."

CHAPTER 46

DUKE OF MAGNIFICENCE'S medical details were among the best the RMN had to offer. Even with half of them on their way to the Nemesis relay station, the team had Montgomery out of the SAR shuttle and into surgery before Denis's shuttle managed to touch down.

There was an observation space next to the surgery bay and Denis ended up there, watching white-scrubbed doctors poking at his charge's leg.

"What are we looking at?" he asked the nurse in the room with him.

"Penetrator round through the right leg," the nurse told him. "Dr. Kurtz says it looks clean, but the femur is fractured. She's assessing the damage before applying bone sealant."

"So it's not...bad," Denis concluded, mentally going through the assessment. "I knew his suit was damaged, but I didn't realize he'd been hit that hard."

"I can't say, sir," the nurse admitted. "That will be for Dr. Kurtz to assess once she's done surgery."

"How long?"

"I can't say, sir," the nurse repeated. "We will keep you advised as much as we can. Lord Montgomery was lucid when we brought him in and is only under anesthesia for the surgery. Once Dr. Kurtz is done with him, I suspect she'll keep him on painkillers...but I can't say for sure."

Denis chuckled lightly at the repetition and stepped back.

"I'll be remaining here," he told the nurse. "Until the rest of the Guard are back aboard, I can't leave his side."

"As you wish, Guard-Lieutenant," the nurse replied. They hadn't even objected to Denis stomping in in armor and carrying his gun. "If I may request, sir, could we run your armor through a sterilizer, at least? It's taken a few nasty knocks, and I'm concerned about what you might be tracking around sick bay."

It wasn't like Denis had a spare suit of armor kicking around. The Marines could fit him with something...except that he suspected that even the armorer was on the relay station. A Marine was a rifleman first, after all.

"There's no one else to guard the Regent," he pointed out gently. "I can't leave him."

"I suppose that's fair." The nurse shrugged. "I think I can get one of our portable units and clean the worst of it. It's not going to cause you problems, is it?"

"The armor is designed for me to walk through the steam of a shuttle having landed on water," Denis noted. "It'll survive a sterilizer unit."

"Okay. Give me a moment."

One steam sterilization and thirty minutes' wait later, Denis was able to meet with Dr. Kurtz as she exited surgery.

"Well?" he asked. "I feel like I broke my charge."

"I can't speak to how Lord Montgomery was injured," Kurtz told him as she stripped off her gloves and took a seat. "He'll be awake in about an hour. We've fitted a brace onto his thigh that he can't take off until the bone is healed. He won't be able to run or jump or wear armor until that's healed."

"As his bodyguard, it will fall on you to help make sure he listens to that restriction," she noted.

"You...haven't met Lord Montgomery, have you?" Denis asked.

"I've met him in passing, but I joined *Duke* while he was in Republic space, as I understand," the doctor replied. "I have his files from his previous injuries aboard *Duke of Magnificence*. I understand that he is a difficult patient."

The Guard snorted.

"The Lord Regent will cooperate with every instruction you give him right up to the moment they get in the way of him doing something he sees as his job," he told the doctor. "At that point, no power in the galaxy is going to stop him doing what he needs to. I don't know if that's difficult as a patient, but it's endearing in a leader and damn annoying in a man I'm supposed to keep alive.

"How bad was it?" he asked.

"Could have been much worse. Clean shot through the muscle, ricocheted off the side of the bone and kept going. The bone injury is a clean fracture and the muscle injuries are neat in-and-out holes.

"We've got everything we can in the injury for him. Give him a week and he'll be fine, so long as he doesn't aggravate it. Do you think you can sit on him for a week, Guard-Lieutenant?"

"Doctor, I don't expect to be able to sit on him for five minutes once we find what we came here for," Denis admitted. "Are you sure we can't put him in armor?"

"Even if you have his suit repaired fast enough, the brace *must* remain. For the next twenty-four hours at least, it is literally the only thing holding his femur together."

"Okay, fair enough," Denis conceded with a wince. "We'll do what we can. That's the job. Can I be in the room now? I'm feeling twitchy about being this separated from my charge."

"That armor looks like it got sterilized. You're clean?"

"As I can be without stripping out and running it through the armory system," the Guard confirmed. "And that's not happening until I have backup."

"It'll have to do. I understand that the Lord Regent needs to be watched," Dr. Kurtz told him. "Good luck, Guard-Lieutenant."

Denis reflected, as he entered Montgomery's room, that the doctor really had no idea.

"Afolabi, update me," he ordered.

"We've stripped the racks and are loading the storage units onto the shuttles," his second replied. "There's two Guards escorting our wounded; they should switch over to backing you up once they're on *Duke*—maybe five more minutes at most."

"Good to hear," Denis said. "Did we get anything useful out of the units yet?"

"The cyber-team is still working away on some tidbits they pulled out of the drives, but no luck," Afolabi told him. "I detached one of them to help the Marines tear down the on-site software for the transmitters. There might be answers in there, and tearing them down will help us make sure no one is sending messages out."

"Is the station secure?"

"So far as we can tell," the Guard-Sergeant confirmed. "We've accounted for seventy-nine people and the station looks like it had berths for eighty-five. A cutter got shot down on the way out?"

"Didn't look like a jump ship, but it could definitely have held six people, from the data *Duke* gave me," Denis replied. The long-range shuttle could easily have held three times that. "Any survivors or prisoners?"

"Negative. We've found at least two whose exosuits blew before their deadman switches triggered. Can't tell if the command source was local or remote."

"Might have been suicide, might have been murder?" Denis asked.

"Exactly. We should have all the storage units aboard *Duke* within an hour. Cybers are telling me they should have data within a couple of hours of that."

"Faster is better," the Lieutenant told his subordinate. "We don't know when Nemesis's boss was expecting to hear from this station. Every minute increases the chance the people who set the King's death in motion get away."

"They know, sir. I made sure of it."

"I know you did," Denis said with a sigh. "Just watching the clock and starting to worry."

"We've got it, sir," Afolabi reassured him. "We'll get it into your girl-friend's hands, don't worry, sir."

"My girlfriend?" Denis asked. "And just *who* are you thinking of, Sergeant?"

His tone was a bit chillier than a moment before. Last time Denis had checked, he'd been single. There was only really one person Afolabi could be referring to, but that didn't make much sense.

"Apologies, sir, I thought you and Voice Samara had been get-ting more than professionally acquainted," the Sergeant said swiftly. "Misjudgment on my part; I spoke out of turn."

"You did," Denis agreed. "Taking your misjudgment into account, though. I'm looking forward to seeing what Voice Samara and our cyber people get out of the hardware."

Now that he was thinking about it, he was looking forward to Samara's briefing for more than the chance to ID his enemies.

The Sergeant had definitely misjudged...but not as much, perhaps, as Denis had initially assumed.

Something to think about when this was over.

CHAPTER 47

DAMIEN WOKE up with a start, gathering magic to him to protect himself for a moment before he realized where he was.

Recognizing *Duke of Magnificence*'s sickbay, he took several slow breaths to calm himself and then slowly rose to a sitting position. His leg had the familiar, not-quite-numb sensation of localized painkillers and a new feeling of weight.

Feeling down his thigh, he found the locked-on pieces of a *very* secure-feeling brace. His armor must have been holding him together until he was rescued, though he vaguely recalled giving his okay for the cruiser's doctor to put him under.

"Is Romanov here?" he asked the red-armored Royal Guard standing at the door. "Or Captain Denuiad. I need to be briefed ASAP."

"I've already pinged them both," the Guard replied. "We have this part of sickbay under lockdown, but there's enough injured that there's still more traffic than we're comfortable with."

"I'm awake now; it'll be fine," Damien told her. "Anything I need to know before Romanov gets here?"

"I've been here since we brought the wounded aboard *Duke*, my lord," she admitted. "I'm a bit out of the loop."

"Understood, Corporal," he replied. He recognized her voice, though he couldn't place her name off the top of his head. "Thank you. I appreciate knowing you're all watching over me as I sleep."

He was used to it by now. It had been Marines and Secret Service before, but it had been a long time since Damien had slept without knowing there were armed officers standing by to protect him.

It no longer even felt weird.

The door slid open to reveal a tall blonde doctor whose uniform noted her name as Katherine Kurtz, followed by Denis Romanov in his burgundy uniform.

"I need to examine him before you start stressing him out," Dr. Kurtz snapped. "Get back out, Lieutenant. That's an order."

"I'm not in your chain of command, Surgeon-Commander," Romanov replied dryly. "And if I was, I count as an RMMC *Colonel*. Carry out your examination, but I need to brief the Lord Regent."

"He's not leaving this room until *I* clear him," the doctor replied. "Don't push your—"

"I'm leaving this room when I choose to, Doctor," Damien cut her off. He didn't speak with any great force. He'd never found it necessary when soft-spoken words would do. "I have no desire to impede your treatments and I intend to be a cooperative patient, Dr. Kurtz, but my duty and my authority override yours.

"The Lieutenant *will* brief me while you carry out your exams. He's seen me naked before, if it comes to that."

Romanov snorted. Kurtz death-glared at them both.

"I could refuse to treat you," she told Damien.

"Then Captain Denuiad would send me a doctor who would listen," he said gently. "I understand your concerns and would do my best to make sure that transition did not impact your career, but I have my duty, Dr. Kurtz. I will perform it."

She shook her head and threw another glare at Romanov before stepping over to the bed and starting to check the readouts.

Taking that as acquiescence, Damien turned his attention to Romanov.

"What's our status?" he asked.

"Alpha and Charlie Companies are back aboard *Duke* along with all of the Royal Guard," his subordinate told him. "We have moved all of the server racks from the Nemesis data center to a secured storage unit aboard this ship and have enlisted the ship's cyberwarfare team in cracking the encryption."

"No luck?"

"None so far. I'm told we should have something within twenty-four hours, but nothing is certain," Romanov replied. "It's been five since we left Mars orbit, since I know you haven't looked at a clock yet.

"Several of our cyber-people have ripped apart the local hardware on the transmitters, and that is looking promising, but I still don't have anything definitive," he continued. "I expect to have a list of the top ten transmission targets within the next few minutes, but without any data on what messages were sent, we can't be sure what we're looking at.

Damien winced as Kurtz poked at his leg.

"We're still jamming?" he asked.

"We are. Sooner or later, someone is going to notice, but so far, we remain covert," Denis confirmed. "I'd say our best-case scenario is twenty-four hours before we have a target."

"Should we be planning to move?" Captain Denuiad asked. Damien had missed her stepping into the room while Denis spoke. "Tupi's Bravo Company has the station secure and can maintain that until relief. We might draw less attention if we return to Mars orbit."

"If we return to Mars orbit, we are assuming the enemy has escaped us," Damien told them. "Only the fact that no one outside a very select group of allies on Mars knows where we are gives us a chance.

"As soon as we have a target, we move," he continued. "We're assuming there's a second facility or ship somewhere in the Sol System. I don't expect a covert relay station to have the kind of files necessary for us to dismantle Nemesis.

"I do suspect there is somewhere—or *someone* in the Sol System with those files."

He winced again.

"I don't know what games you're playing," Kurtz told him. "But that brace stays on for seven days at least—and doesn't come off then without a physician sign-off. Your femur is currently one wrong move away from separating into two pieces.

"And before you ask, armor won't fit over it. You can walk, but don't push that, either."

"I understand," he confirmed. "Am I allowed to leave sickbay?"

"We do have quarters set aside for you," Denuiad confirmed. "Your old space has been officially repurposed, but we can set you up somewhere."

"I was just unconscious for several hours, Captain; I don't need to rest just yet," Damien told her. "We need to be ready to move as soon as we have a target. Do we have a link to Olympus?"

"Intermittently through a laser link to a Navy sensor platform," she replied. "Not really good enough for a conversation, though."

"All right," Damien conceded. "I don't need to talk to Kiera, but we need to keep her informed. Using the Olympus Amplifier to move around is our best option."

"That's so weird," Denuiad admitted. "I'm used to jumping my own ship around, but even with a warship, moving around in-system is hard."

"Trust in the power of the Mage-Queen of Mars," he told her. "In this system? She can do many things others can not."

He and Romanov knew that *Damien* could do all of those things, but even Denuiad wasn't cleared for that. She *did* know he was a Rune Wright, but that didn't mean she knew all of the complications of that.

"You can leave," Kurtz told him. "Check in daily, either with me or with a doctor wherever you end up. That brace *should* keep you from aggravating the injury, but you'll heal better if you can rest."

"I'll try," Damien promised.

"The scary part is I believe you," she said with a sigh. "And I *still* think you're going to make it worse."

"Sir, I just got an update from the team working on the transmitters," Romanov cut in. "If you can move, I suggest you get dressed. They need to brief us, and I suspect a proper conference room will work better than a sickbay ward."

"Give me five?" Damien asked. "Previous experience tells me that dressing with a new medical accoutrement takes some learning."

Even using magic, it took him all of those five minutes to actually get dressed in the black suit with its white mock-collar dress shirt that he wore as a uniform. A golden medallion, labeling him as a member of the Mage Guild, was held at his throat by a leather collar that went over the shirt collar. Hung over that was the platinum hand of his old office and the insignia-less chain of his *current* office.

Fitting the brace into the suit pants took some doing, but he eventually managed it and limped his way through the corridors to arrive at the briefing in only twice the time he'd promised.

Romanov had a seat waiting for him and eased Damien into it as soon as he was through the door. The Lord Regent was tempted to wave off the attention, but he also realized that was dumb.

He *was* injured. He'd push through it when he needed to, but until then, he'd rest as best as he can.

Mage-Captain Denuiad had the seat to his right and Romanov took the seat to his left. Two nervous-looking junior officers, a Commander and a Lieutenant, stood in front of them, and a pair of Royal Guards flanked the door.

Neither of the presenting officers was a Mage, which was probably part of their nerves.

"Commander, Lieutenant. I think some introductions are in order," Damien suggested.

"This is Commander Chí Phan, our assistant tactical officer, and Lieutenant Blaguna Ivanov, one of our junior coms officers."

"I brought Lieutenant Ivanov in on this, as she is one of our systems specialists," Phan told them all, his tone hesitant. "She knows more about this kind of BIOS software and in-system data storage than anyone else aboard the ship. Her help was critical in establishing the data we're here to brief you on."

Nervous as Commander Phan was, his insistence on crediting the even *more* nervous-looking junior officer was a checkmark in Damien's book.

"What have we learned?" he asked gently, hoping that he could set the two officers at something resembling ease.

"The transmitters they were using were extremely modern and designed for covert operations," Phan told them. "Their on-mount storage was automatically wiping every twelve hours. We managed to pull about six hours from them, during which the relay station only made two transmissions."

"That doesn't sound helpful, Commander," Denuiad noted.

"That was where Lieutenant Ivanov came into play, sirs," Phan said. "She was the only one to realize that while the transmission dish was wiping its records every twelve hours, the systems for physically moving and targeting the array were far older.

"When the UN Expeditionary Fleet set up the initial relay station, they used a standard and cheap dish mobility system—one so reliable that versions of it are still in use today. When Nemesis set up their new systems here, there was no reason to replace it. They cleaned out the surface components and hooked up power again."

"And that hardware, sir, was *civilian*. Originally designed for American exploratory and science missions," Ivanov said quietly. "It records everything in a special black box with a twelve-month storage capacity. The data drive is old, but it was designed to endure."

"We can't confirm what power levels or anything the array was transmitting at, sirs, but we do know every position that dish has been in for most of the last year," Phan concluded. "Combined with the orbital mechanics of the station itself, we were able to identify several recurring transmission zones."

"How narrow are these zones?" Damien asked.

"They give us a starting point and not much more," Phan admitted. "One is in Saturnian orbit, but given the variances and distance...well, it could be *anything* in Saturn orbit. Another recurring location is in Mars orbit. I'd guess a station or ship positioned near Phobos."

Damien sighed. Phobos was the anchor point for significant civilian infrastructure and shipping. Presumably, the relay station had been sending very carefully targeted messages, but they couldn't identify a target just from knowing which way the dish was pointed.

"The most common target was in Earth orbit, sir," the Commander concluded. "As was the transmission we do have data on."

"That's...promising," Damien said slowly. "Do we have a recipient?"

"Not confirmed, sir," Phan admitted. "We're going through our sensor data for the time window now, but we believe we have narrowed it down to less than ten ships, sir."

Ten ships. For a moment, Damien was tempted to send the order to seize them all. If nothing else, there were still two *battleships* in orbit of Earth. No civilian ship was going to fight them.

That, of course, was assuming that Nemesis's base here was as civilian as it appeared. A military-grade amplifier could ruin even a battleship's day at that range—or allow the ship to jump away.

"How many jump-ships, Commander?" he asked. "I don't think our target is going to be a sublight clipper."

Phan paused, running through data. After a moment, he put images of the ten ships in question up on the display screen behind him—seven of them disappearing a moment later.

"Three, sir. A civilian freighter, *Runs with Dawning Light.* Two personal yachts, *Child of Voids* and *Choirgirl.*"

Damien studied the lines of the ships.

"*Dawning Light* isn't local, is she?" he asked. "When did she arrive?"

"She arrived in Earth orbit two days ago and is taking on a load of... seawater?" Phan sounded confused.

"I can think of four uses for it off the top of my head, Commander— but I don't think a ship that's just visiting Sol is our target. The yachts. What can you tell me about them?"

Denuiad was digging into the data on her own wrist-comp and answered the question first.

"*Child of Voids* is registered to Sparrowhawk Shipping but looks to be a personal vehicle for the CEO," she told him. "There's probably some tax games going on there with the expenses, but she spends seventy-five percent of her time in Earth-local space and has only left the Sol System once in the last year.

"That's her listed permanent orbit, but her *purpose* is silly tourist flights, so she's all over the place. I could see her as a covert ship for somebody, my lord," she admitted.

"Hundred thousand tons, less than eighty meters long," Damien said aloud as he looked at the data Phan had put up. "Versus *Choirgirl*, who is almost *seven* hundred thousand tons. What do we know about her?"

If he were running a covert base, he'd rather do it with a superyacht than a glorified runabout that happened to be able to jump.

"Registered to a numbered company," Phan told him. "I don't...think that's unusual?"

"Probably not. What else have we got?"

"Records show she's left Sol roughly once a month for the last year," the Commander told him. "Again, that's her permanent assigned orbit. She doesn't seem to leave it when she's in Sol, so I'd guess she's used as an interstellar transport for her owner."

"Or a movable permanent residence," Romanov snorted.

"Can you map her absences against when the relay was pointed at Earth?" Denuiad asked.

"Yes, sir."

Several different charts appeared on the screen. Neither was particularly intelligible to Damien, not least because they were moving rapidly. They lined up with each, and a large amount of green was showing up on the screen.

The room was silent for several seconds as they all looked at the screen and tried to interpret the presented information.

"Commander?" Damien finally asked.

"Sir. Every time but one that the transmitter was pointed at Earth in the last twelve months, *Choirgirl* was present in our estimate of the target zone," Phan stated firmly. "Comparing against *Child of Voids*, the ratio is actually lower despite *Child* having spent a higher portion of her time in Sol."

"People, I think that's enough," Damien concluded aloud. "I wouldn't open fire on her based on this, but I think it's enough for us to bring her in."

"Shall we prepare to move to Earth, sir?" Denuiad asked.

"No," Damien told her with a smile. "I have a far better idea, Captain. We are going to need to move away from the relay station, though. I need a direct channel to Olympus Mons."

CHAPTER 48

"WHY DO I have a report saying that you were *shot?*" Kiera demanded as the channel finally opened. There was an almost five-minute delay in the transmission going each way, and Damien was expecting the conversation to take a long time...and then realized that he'd heard the voice from *behind* him.

He turned around in the office Denuiad had lent him to see the teenage Mage-Queen standing there, her hands on her hips.

"You did *not* just teleport yourself here to scold me," he snapped. "I need you on Mars."

"And I'm on Mars," she told him, clearly intentionally putting a hand through the empty bookshelf next to her. "You were first and foremost a Jump Mage, Damien. I studied illusion and projection magic first. Combined with the Amplifier, I can put an avatar anywhere within, oh, ten light-minutes of Mars. Real time. The Amplifier is insane."

"I knew that," Damien conceded. Now that he was looking for it, he could see the signs that Kiera was just an illusion, an artificial creation of magically changed light. She wasn't *quite* on the floor, for example, and she wasn't casting a shadow on the door behind her.

"You can hear and see me in turn, I take it," he told her. With a sigh, he shut down the communicator behind him.

"It's not easy," she admitted. "Running this through the Olympus Amplifier is hard, and it's not a trick I can *normally* do at more than a few kilometers at best. Projecting is easier than receiving, but I didn't think we wanted to have this conversation with a ten-minute gap."

"Not really," Damien agreed. "There should be a data package attached to the message I sent you about a ship in Earth orbit."

The illusion closed her eyes, probably an intentional sign that Kiera's attention was on what she was doing on Mars. The illusion was not, he realized, a projection of her actual position or status. It showed what Kiera wanted it to show.

"*Choirgirl*, I see," she said. "You're sure?"

"I'm not a hundred percent, but I'm sure enough that I'd sign a warrant to detain the entire ship," Damien replied. "We'll take control of her, interview the crew, tear apart the computers. It's never true that the innocent have *nothing* to fear, but if these aren't Winton's people, they'll be fine and we'll make it up to them."

"And if they aren't Nemesis, we've hit a dead end," she assumed aloud.

"We have the relay station's computers. They're proving even harder to crack than our worst estimates," he admitted, "but we'll open them up eventually. I doubt they'll have enough for us to bring Nemesis down, but they'll give a lot more clues.

"Right now, though, *Choirgirl* is the end of where this chain leads. We can hold off until we have the station's computers...but I fear we'll lose the leadership if we do."

"That's not acceptable," Kiera told him. "I want the assholes who killed my father, Damien. Deliver them to me."

"I intend to," he promised. "But my immediate plan, my Queen, involves *you* delivering them to *me*."

From the grin that spread across the illusion's face, Kiera understood *exactly* what he meant.

"Attention, everyone!" Damien said loudly as he stepped into the briefing he'd called. "Mage-Captain Denuiad, Major Tupi, thank you for joining me. Romanov, Afolabi, I know you didn't have a choice, but thank you anyway."

"He does know *none* of us had a choice, right?" Tupi stage-whispered to one of his subordinates. Both of his company commanders that were still aboard *Duke* had joined them, as had Denuiad's executive officer.

"That's true enough, I suppose," Damien conceded. "But I appreciate everyone being here. If we've guessed right, we're about to end the little mission that we all left Mars in pursuit of.

"The bad news, for those of you who haven't been involved in this mess all along, is that success means we will be boarding a starship operated and crewed by a covert organization that has been proven to have fingers in the highest levels of the Protectorate government.

"*Choirgirl* appears to be a relatively normal large personal jump ship," he continued. "I would guess that she's set up to pass as that to even a superficial on-board inspection, but vessels of that scale in private ownership are flown by people with the money and contacts to make sure inspections are only superficial.

"That means we really have no idea what we're stepping into. Our records show she was built in Amber, which means we have zero chance of getting anything useful from her builders in a reasonable time frame," Damien told them.

The Protectorate's libertarian problem child was demonstrably *loyal*, but an Amber-based shipyard company would make even the Lord Regent jump through a near-infinite number of hoops to get the design schematics of a ship they'd built.

If they even had them. A large number of pirate and mercenary ships came out of Amber yards, and those yards had a standard price to include "we destroy all schematics after completing the ship" in the contract.

"We have to assume that we are boarding the equivalent of one of our own covert-operations ships," Romanov told the others. "We can expect a minimum of well-equipped, well-trained exosuit soldiers like we encountered here.

"Mages are almost guaranteed, as are automated defenses and magic-al security," he continued. "Nemesis has access to some of our most complex and secret magics. Even *I* don't know what kind of surprises we're going to face, but we need to expect to face surprises."

"Is Her Majesty going to deploy us on top of her again?" Denuiad asked.

"I am uninterested in starting an overt boarding action in Earth orbit," Damien admitted. "It is in the interests of avoiding that and confusing our enemies that I've had you bring *Duke* to the edge of the asteroid belt.

"In"—he checked his wrist-comp—"thirty-five minutes, Her Majesty will teleport *Choirgirl* to us. At that point, we will need to secure her as rapidly as possible. I plan on once again taking an assault team of the Royal Guard to *Choirgirl*'s data centers.

"Like the relay station, we need her computers more than anything else, but my presence is required to prevent her from jumping. I leave the rest of the boarding action to the Marines. Tupi?"

"Standard protocol is engines, life support, bridge; roughly equal priorities," the Marine CO noted. "We'll ID them while we're in flight and send two assault shuttles against each. That will be about sixty Marines on each target, leaving me a twenty-Marine reserve made up of the command teams on the final shuttle."

The Marine looked grim.

"*Choirgirl* would have a minimum crew of forty and could easily hold three hundred," he noted. "If all of them are exosuit-trained like the relay crew, we could be in trouble."

"I know," Damien conceded. "We can hold for additional support if needed, Major?"

"No, we can't," Denuiad said quietly. "Apologies, Tupi, I just got the update from coms: *Choirgirl* has requested clearance to head out-system. Her listed destination is Tau Ceti, but...I doubt its coincidence she's leaving after we captured the station.

"If we spook her, she's gone."

"I'll let Her Majesty know," Damien promised. "We'll have reinforcements arriving as quickly as humanly possible once the rocket goes up, but the first wave is just us."

The *second* wave, once he'd let Kiera know, would be the Marine contingents of at least two battleships and probably a dreadnought. This ship was *not* getting away.

"If you have any questions, raise them quickly," he noted. "Her Majesty *will* act before she'll allow *Choirgirl* to escape the system, which means our time frame just dropped drastically."

"How are you planning on staying safe aboard the enemy ship, sir?" Tupi asked. "The last report I saw said you can't run and can't wear armor."

"I didn't wear an exosuit for most of my career, Major, but that doesn't mean I'm not wearing armor," Damien pointed out. "I'll bring an oxygen system with me as well, but I'll be fine.

"We don't have much choice. We *need* to secure the data center, and that means I need to take the Guard in. No one else can."

"I understand, sir. I just don't think any of us like it," the Marine admitted, saying what Damien's Guards couldn't quite get away with.

"The alternative is unacceptable," Damien told him. "Let's go."

The *unacceptable alternative*, of course, wasn't actually to let *Choirgirl* escape—though that *was* also unacceptable.

No, the truly unacceptable alternative was that *Kiera* was just as capable of the stunt as he was.

CHAPTER 49

STANDARD TRAFFIC control would require *Choirgirl* to travel at least one light-minute away from Earth to jump. Even other ships could theoretically create enough of a gravity interaction to complicate the jump, which meant the emptier the space a Mage jumped from, the better.

If Damien's suspicions about the yacht were correct, she could leave directly from Earth orbit. One of the most closely held secrets in the Protectorate was that a civilian ship's jump matrix was a modified form of the amplifiers used by military ships.

The amplifiers could increase the power of *any* spell thousands-fold. A jump matrix could only do that to the teleport spell Mages had standardized around for interstellar travel. The restriction was tight enough that some of the spell modifications necessary for a more complex jump spell were nearly impossible with a civilian matrix.

"She's accelerating at eight gees," Denuiad told Damien over the intercom. She was back in her proper place, holding down the central seat in *Duke of Magnificence*'s bridge. "Everything I'm seeing is almost ten minutes out of date, Damien."

"And she's still over five hours from jump so long as no one spooks her," Damien replied. The Royal Guard strike team around him were ready. A graphic projected over his wrist-comp was showing him the Marines' readiness as well.

There were a lot more Marines than the sixteen Royal Guards, and they weren't *quite* all aboard their transports yet. If Kiera followed the original timeline, they had at least twenty minutes.

Kiera, however, was seeing everything in real time. If something was going to spook *Choirgirl*'s captain, she'd see it and hopefully react before the presumed Nemesis ship escaped.

"It is twenty minutes to the planned op time...now," he told Denuiad. "But if something goes wrong, our friend might just show up here anytime. Are you ready?"

"Not much of a role for *Duke* to play in this beyond covering the assault shuttles," she told him. "What's the plan for if they try to jump?"

"Me. Your job is to neutralize any weapons she demonstrates," Damien told her. "I'm expecting concealed RFLAMs at the very least."

"I'm operating on the assumption she's a concealed pirate, so I expect much the same," the Mage-Captain confirmed.

The Rapid-Fire Laser Anti-Missile turrets were designed to take down missiles, but they'd rip the assault shuttles apart all the same. They were common enough on civilian ships that Damien suspected most people didn't realize that an RFLAM was perfectly capable of *threatening* a civilian ship, too.

It was a cheap pirate who relied on those weapons for their task. If nothing else, you had to be close to threaten someone with an RFLAM as opposed to a missile or a proper battle laser.

There were always cheap pirates—but Damien doubted that Nemesis qualified.

"My fear, Captain, is that she is hiding real weapons and a real amplifier," he admitted. "Do we have a plan for that?"

"We do," Denuiad confirmed. "I'll admit our counter-amplifier doctrine is probably lacking, but it's reassuringly straightforward."

Don't get hit. Unlike with the Olympus Amplifier, someone using a regular amplifier was limited by lightspeed with their incoming data. Their attacks might be instantaneous but their sight wasn't.

Unfortunately, today's plan called for *Duke* to be *very* close to the yacht.

"Ten minutes," Damien said softly. "Hopefully *Choirgirl* is going to be very surprised by wha—"

He felt the magic tear through the space around him before *Duke*'s sensors saw anything and hoped against hope that Kiera had acted early from paranoia.

"*Jump flare!*"

The red icon flashed into existence on the display in the ready room, and the Royal Guard were on their feet, standing ready as Damien began to run the calculations for the teleport.

"Jump-ship *Choirgirl*, we have a warrant for the seizure and search of your vessel," Captain Denuiad said calmly. "You will stand down all engines and sensors and prepare to receive Marine boarders. Resistance will be met with all necessary force."

With his focus on the yacht, Damien felt a now-familiar surge of growing power. It had been in the ship-to-ship battle between Lawrence Octavian's personal warship and *Duke of Magnificence* that he'd learned he could sense amplified spells at a surprisingly large distance.

Disrupting them had been an act of panic then, but he'd practiced it since to make it a reliable skill. The attack spell someone mustered aboard *Choirgirl* died with barely a whimper, a fireball that would have devastated *Duke* dissipating back into the yacht's matrix.

"They have a full amplifier," he said calmly. "Target is hostile, I repeat, *target is hostile*."

A second spell flashed into existence. This time, the Mage was clearly aware *something* had happened to their previous spell and rushed it. Damien couldn't smother the spell fast enough, so instead, he flung it to the side.

Instead of exploding inside the battlecruiser, the fireball erupted in deep space.

At that point, the Mage tried to run. The jump spell flared out from *Choirgirl*'s core, filling every square centimeter of the yacht...and then

Damien *yanked* it out of her matrix, sending the gathered magical power scattering across the space around her in a spark of light visible to even *Duke*'s sensors.

"What was *that*?" someone demanded.

"That was their jump spell," Damien replied. "They need a new Mage in the simulacrum chamber before they can jump now. I need those data-center coordinates, Captain."

"Tactical?" Denuiad demanded.

"Got it!"

New icons appeared on the schematic of *Choirgirl* as the Marine assault shuttles blasted into space. Seven small spacecraft lunged toward their victim, and the expected RFLAM turrets lit up.

One beam hit a shuttle, leaving the ship's icon flickering with red damage codes, and then *Duke*'s own weapons spoke. At this range, her battle lasers would have gutted the ship—but *her* RFLAM turrets were gigawatt-range weapons, twice as powerful as *Choirgirl*'s civilian system.

And far more accurately targeted.

Choirgirl had six of the defensive turrets, and they vanished under *Duke*'s fire as Damien finished his calculations.

"Guards, on me," he ordered aloud. It was an unnecessary order. His bodyguard had already closed around him—and one of them handed him the oxygen mask and tank he'd promised to take.

Nodding with a smile, Damien slung the system over his shoulder and summoned his magic.

One *step* later, everything went to hell.

CHAPTER 50

DAMIEN KNEW they were in the wrong place the moment the tele-port ended, but gunfire tore through the darkness before he could say a word.

The next thing *he* knew, he was on the ground with a pair of exosuit-ed guardians kneeling over him, returning fire at unseen assailants. For a moment, he dazedly wondered why none of the Guards had created magical light—and *then* he wondered why he was so dazed.

And then he realized why *everything* about the situation felt familiar. Samuel Finley had set up the exact same trap in the Daedalus Complex, using a set of complex runes only a Rune Wright could create to draw any teleport to the same designated location.

He'd used a different set of runes to disable the Gift of any Mage in the trap. As a Rune Wright, he'd had enough understanding of his own Gift to exclude himself from the effect. Here, it seemed, someone had built the same trap and fitted it with guns.

Lots of guns.

Damien focused, pushing through the spell muffling his power, and threw a brilliant light into the air. The runes couldn't fully suppress his power, not with the Runes of Power augmenting his strength.

But it was enough to muffle the Royal Guard, and several of the exosuits had fallen to the ground with a disturbing finality. With a broad-er light than the usually unused headlamps, the remaining Guard could locate the automated weapons firing on them.

Heavy-penetrator rounds went through the computerized weapons and the walls behind them. Damien's own magic joined the fray, but the weapons weren't his target. None of the Guards could see the runes that surrounded them, certainly not with enough understanding to break the matrix and free them.

Blades of force peeled away sections of wall while penetrator rifles flayed the guns, and then, finally, there was blessed silence. The matrix broke a moment later and Damien breathed a sigh of relief as his full power returned to him.

The squad of exosuited Nemesis troopers who rounded the corner, presumably sent to finish the job the trap started, didn't share his relief. Damien's power *flared* down the corridor, ball lightning that hammered into each of the half-dozen soldiers with enough force to burn out their armor...and their nervous systems.

"We need to locate ourselves," he barked. "Romanov, report."

"We're down six," the Guard-Lieutenant said grimly—and there was pain in his voice. "That's *dead*, my lord. Most of the rest are wounded, but the suits will hold us together."

"What the *fuck* happened?"

"It seems Finley was friends with Nemesis," Damien told him. "This is the same trap he pulled on me at Daedalus...but I'm afraid I brought you all in with me. We're stuck, Denis. I can't teleport us out without ending up right back here."

He'd shredded the runes that suppressed magic, but he'd need a lot more time and access to destroy the matrix that trapped teleports.

"Coms are down," his bodyguard reported. "We need local computers. Where they were coming from?" Romanov suggested.

"Agreed. Let's move."

It was a slow procession. Damien had expected to slow the process down with his leg brace, but it looked like he was in the middle of the pack now. Damaged suits and damaged limbs held his people back, but they were moving and they had their magic back.

The first attempt at an ambush underestimated the Royal Guard and Damien. They turned a corner, searching for a computer link of any kind, and then Damien held up a hand as he sensed something.

"Wait...someone's playing clever games. Romanov—spray the corridor!"

The Guards obeyed, and the troopers concealed under the Mage's spell didn't react in time. Half of them were down before the illusion collapsed, but the survivors returned fire—only for their bullets to hammer uselessly into the Guards' defensive shields.

It was over in moments and another dozen Nemesis troopers were dead.

"Where the hell did he *get* this many fanatics?" Romanov murmured.

"A hundred billion human beings," Damien countered. "Have a cause people can believe in, and that'll produce a *lot* of people willing to die for you."

"Yeah, but what *is* their cause?"

"I don't know," the Lord Regent admitted. "And I think I need to. Console there! Someone get me a goddamn map!"

"We're nowhere bloody near the data center," the Guard who'd rigged a cable into the console reported. "They put their trap as far away from anything useful as they could. We're at the 'top' of the ship, almost the full length from the engines and life support, and the full height from the data center.

"The only thing we're remotely close to is the swimming pool they keep to distract the Inspectors."

"Show me the map," Damien ordered. The Guard tapped a few commands on her invisible keyboard, and a holographic projection of the schematics appeared in front of them.

"We're closest to the simulacrum chamber," he told them, tapping the space at the center of the ship. "Most likely the bridge and also the biggest threat to *Duke*."

He hadn't felt any attempt by the amplifier to attack his cruiser or teleport out, but that didn't mean anything. They'd only been aboard for a few minutes and they might have had to wake their other Mages up.

"With Marines on the way, they've already triggered the purge order on their data. We need to salvage this situation as best as we can," he continued. "That's prisoners and as much of the data as we can retrieve.

"The bridge is the best possible location for prisoners. I want this ship's captain and whoever's in charge of this mess, assuming they're not the same person. I'm hoping at least one is on the bridge. We also need to send people to the data center. It's the next closest."

"Fastest way is to start cutting holes in the decks," Romanov told him. "We're six decks up. Go as one until we hit the simulacrum, then send half the team onward?"

"Falling is not the best plan for my leg brace, but I can work with it," Damien replied. "Harder to ambush us if we're not taking the route they expect, and I'm not going to weep over holes in this ship."

He gestured for the Corporal to close up the data link.

"Ready?"

"We'll cut the holes, my lord," Romanov replied. "We don't know what's waiting for us. If there's a Hand-equivalent Mage on this ship, Montgomery, that's *your* job."

"Fair enough," Damien conceded. "Let's move."

He was still expecting the Guard to produce the long vibroblades his Marines would have used for the situation. Instead, they simply stood there, presumably allocating sections on a channel Damien didn't share, and then unleashed their magic.

There wasn't even a visible process of cutting. The circle of deck they were standing on just calmly sank downward, gaining speed as it did so. It didn't even slow when it hit the deck below it and the Guards cut through again.

Or the deck below that. Or the deck below that. It was only at the deck above the simulacrum chamber itself that they hit resistance, a squad of Nemesis troopers that clearly were *not* expecting this.

But they were in exosuits and carrying penetrator rifles. The assemblage of deck plating hit the ground with a *thud* as the Guards went to shielded firing positions, locking Damien inside their circle as they returned fire at the Nemesis troopers.

"No," Romanov snapped in his ear as Damien began to channel power. "We need you to conserve power."

The Guard was firing as he spoke, and the sudden encounter was over as sharply as it had begun. Another of Damien's Guards was down.

"Sandal is alive, but his leg is fucked and his suit is locked in place," Romanov reported. "I'm leaving another Guard with him and we're going down the last floor, my lord. Do we have a plan?"

"We can't wreck the computers in the bridge," Damien told him. "No penetrators. Magic first, take them alive if you can."

"Their *armor* will kill them," his bodyguard pointed out.

"Then we use our magic to get them *out* of their armor. I need answers, Denis, and corpses don't give interviews!"

"Oorah," the Royal Guard muttered. "Guards! One more floor and then we take the bridge. We need prisoners and intact systems. Magic and blades, no guns. This is why the Regent brought us. No one else could do this. Only us. Only the Royal Guard.

"Are we going to fail the Lord Regent of Mars?"

Even through the suits, Damien was pretty sure he heard the shouted answers.

"Then let's go."

This time, they tore open a hole in the plating and descended through it by careful levitation. The Guards landed first, forming a circular shield around Damien as he landed even more carefully amidst them.

The simulacrum chamber, the beating heart of any starship, would have been on even the most superficial of inspection tours. This corridor, unlike most of the ones they'd just cut their way through, actually looked like a luxury yacht instead of a warship.

Each wall was covered in a continuously painted mural of a woodland setting, leading up to the very *non*-luxury-yacht-like security hatch covering the entrance to the simulacrum chamber. That had probably been concealed during those inspection but formed a massive barrier now.

"We can—"

"No time," Damien interrupted Romanov, gesturing his gloved and crippled hand toward the door. "Send a team on to the data center; I'll deal with the door."

There was a moment of silent discussion. There were only eight Guards left, which clearly meant that Romanov wasn't going to have as many people watching Damien as he'd like. After a moment, a new hole appeared in the floor, and four of the Royal Guard dropped toward their target.

"Are we ready?" Damien asked.

"Always, my lord."

The heavy security door vanished. If Damien had done his math right, it was only about a kilometer outside the ship's hull...but it definitely wasn't blocking the way anymore.

The door behind it was open and a tired voice shouted out from behind it.

"I surrender. You may as well come in, Lord Montgomery. It's well past time you and I had another chat, isn't it?"

Two of the Guards went first, but Damien was right behind them. He recognized the voice, which meant he wasn't entirely surprised to find the simulacrum chamber empty other than the pale-skinned form of the man who'd been introduced to him as Winton.

"Order your people to surrender," Damien snapped.

"I can't," Winton told him. "My internal coms are fucked. The jammers can only be turned off manually, and they're not controlled from here. Last report I had was that my people were blocking your Marines. A battle, I suspect, that they cannot win."

Winton was sitting in the chair next to the simulacrum, but he was ignoring the liquid silver model. So far as Damien could tell, the other man wasn't a Mage at all. Despite the incongruous nature of the moment, it made near-perfect sense when the old man gestured Damien to a seat.

"I do believe this mess is over," he admitted. "So, why don't you have a seat, Lord Montgomery? I'm too old to run anymore. I won't promise to answer all of your questions, but you may as well ask them."

CHAPTER 51

"WHY DID you kill Desmond Alexander?" Damien snapped. He did not take the indicated seat.

"I would have thought that was obvious the moment you put on that chain, Lord Montgomery," Winton said dryly. "I had no faith in the strength of the Mountain under Desmond the Third. He was an old man who'd never left Mars. He had no concept of war or of what the Republic had unleashed.

"For the Protectorate to be strong, Desmond Alexander had to die. For the Protectorate to be strong, its ruler could not be an old man or a child who'd never left Mars. It needed a ruler who'd seen the worst and best of humanity, who'd walked the ruins of Andala IV and the murderous labs of the Daedalus Complex.

"The Protectorate needed a ruler who'd *lived*, not one who'd merely been protected," Winton told them. "It needed you, Damien Montgomery, and I knew there was no power in the universe that would convince you to betray the Alexanders. I did what I had to do."

"Fancy words and bullshit from a regicide," Damien snapped.

"You don't understand what's coming," the old man replied. "Even the Keepers, who had *everything*, did not truly grasp the warning they were meant to give. They did not understand their duty, and so the Protectorate's sword had rusted into nothingness.

"How many ships, Lord Montgomery, would the RMN muster today if Legatus had not set their feet on the path to where we stand? Do you even know?"

"No. And I don't need to," Damien replied. "Nothing could justify all that you have done. The murder, the death. Even laying aside the regicide that I will by *God* hang you for, your hands are running in blood."

"You know, I really didn't want this ship in Protectorate hands," Winton replied, ignoring Damien's words. "My intention, once I realized how perfectly trapped I was, was to self-destruct her...and then suddenly *you* were aboard. I can't kill you, Damien Montgomery. The Protectorate needs you. *Humanity* needs you; they just don't know how badly yet.

"Everything I have done has been in the service of mankind. I understand the price of my cause, Damien Montgomery. Today, that price is my life." He shrugged. "I wasn't ready, but who ever is?"

"Not quite yet, I don't think," Damien told him. "This is hardly the last conversation we're going to have."

"Perhaps," Winton said. "You're asking the wrong questions, you know."

"And what questions should I be asking?" Damien replied. "You're a psychopath who has left a trail of death across the Protectorate. Why would I care what you know?"

"I am not alone," the old man said. "Nemesis is an understanding, not an organization. A realization, not a cause. I can help you realize what you have missed, Damien. Help you understand why I had to act."

"Why, then?" Damien demanded. "You destroyed the Keepers; you killed my King, I don't even know what else to hang on you, but evidence suggests that Samuel Finley knew you."

Winton was silent for a moment, like he was in pain, then sighed.

"I knew Samuel Finley, yes. I can't imagine it *helps* my cause to admit I helped him create the Promethean Interface, does it?"

Damien swallowed a snarl.

"What kind of monster are you?"

"The kind that accepts that someone like him was needed," Winton told him, his voice suddenly hoarse. "You know, this was supposed to be painless. I think you're out of time, Damien Montgomery, so I'll ask the question you didn't ask.

"Who built the Olympus Amplifier?" he coughed out.

Damien realized what was going on now.

"Romanov, medpack," he snapped.

"No, you need the answer," Winton told them. "They're called the Reejit. Their existence is what the Keepers guarded. They created human mages for a reason and they will be coming to harvest their cro..."

He faded out into a fit of coughing in mid-word, falling sideways off the chair as it grew more violent. Romanov tried to approach him with a syringe, but the flailing old man knocked it away—and was suddenly still.

Damien looked at the body in silence.

"Guard-Lieutenant?"

"He's gone," Romanov confirmed. "Pulse is zero, brain activity fading. I don't know what the poison was, but I doubt defib and an anti-venin are going to cut it."

"No," Damien agreed. "He was buying time for something. Can we link with your team in the data center yet?"

"No, everything's still jammed," his bodyguard replied. "Your orders?"

"See what you can shut down from here," Damien ordered. "Otherwise, we dig in and wait for the Marines."

He grimaced.

"I don't think we're going to get many prisoners, so I hope you got his confession on recording," he told Romanov. "Explaining this is going to be a nightmare."

CHAPTER 52

"WHAT DO YOU make of it, Munira?"

There were no words for how grateful Denis Romanov was to be back on Mars. He'd left the red planet with twenty Royal Guards, each of them a combat veteran and a powerful Combat Mage.

He'd returned with thirteen, only three of them unwounded. He wasn't part of the unwounded list, as the cast around his right arm reminded him as he tried to look over Munira Samara's shoulder at the data she was manipulating.

"What I make of it, Denis," the MIS Inspector replied, "was that we put a lot of effort into retrieving some seriously screwed-up data. One set is encrypted to hell and back again and has frustrated our best efforts for four days.

"The other set appears to be just as heavily encrypted but has been partially deleted, shredded and hashed," she concluded. "I have only the most basic of even file structures out of either set, but..."

"But?" Denis prompted.

"It's promising," she told him. "The bad news is that it looks like the most promising data is in the archives from *Choirgirl*. Unless I'm misreading this, I'd say she had a complete copy of the *Keeper* Archive aboard."

"Damn. Is it intact?" Denis asked.

They'd known Nemesis had seemed to have it in for the Keepers, but they'd never been sure *why*. Damien had suggested that Winton was an ex-Keeper, but there was no real information there.

"I don't know yet," Samara replied. "I'm going to guess not. With everything Nemesis did to keep this data under wraps, I suspect it was the first target of their purge protocols. We'll see what I can extract, but we lost a lot of data."

"Be glad we got any," he told her. "If Montgomery hadn't insisted on sending a team to the data center, we wouldn't have retrieved anything. Winton was playing for time with us, and the Marines would never have reached it in time. The one thing we did get out of Winton, though, is a keyword to search for. One that doesn't leave this room, Samara: Reejit."

He looked down.

"I hope that finds us something useful," he growled. "My people died to get this data."

"And we appreciate what your people did," she said softly, looking up from her work to touch his uninjured arm gently. "Have the funerals been scheduled yet?"

"Next week. I can give you the schedule, if you'd like."

"I'll see if I can attend them," she promised. "You look like you could use the support."

"The Mountain trusted me with twenty of the best Mages we had, and from the sounds of it, we sacrificed a third of them for nothing."

"*Not* for nothing," she told him firmly. "The data will be valuable. It's going to take us a lot longer to crack than we'd like. We might need to talk to Obscura. See what it wants this week."

Denis chuckled.

"What does a complex quantum intelligence charge for its services?" he asked. Obscura was one of only four true AIs humanity had ever created. None of the four were particularly hostile to humanity...but none of the four *were* human, either. They were difficult to motivate out of their usual philosophical musings on the nature of the universe.

"Obscura answers about two questions a month in exchange for its power grid," Samara told him. "MIS uses it a few times a year for pattern-seeking where we can't find anything, but to crack this encryption, it'll ask something extra."

"Like what?"

"Last time I was involved? Three teddy bears and physical copies of several original twentieth-century pinup posters." She shrugged. "I heard rumors of a case it helped crack in exchange for detailed three-dimensional scans of the investigative team nude. Obscura is..."

"A horny teenager the size of a battleship with a brain that can solve math problems we haven't invented the language for yet?" Denis suggested. "That's...not a point of view I'm enthused with."

"It's closer than the people who regard it as a digital god," Samara told him. "Inshallah, Obscura can crack this. I think it has some interest in the continuation of the Martian power grid, if not necessarily the Protectorate or humanity."

And at that, Denis understood Obscura to be the most cooperative of the complex quantum intelligences. There was a reason the Protectorate hadn't built more of them.

"And if it helps, that'll make this worth it?" he asked.

"No, it was already worth it, Denis," Samara told him. "*Choirgirl* was a hostile military headquarters in our own home space. The data we already have suggests that 'Winton' was running covert operations across the entire Protectorate from that ship.

"We'll learn what he was doing, who was doing it for him and why. I promise you, Denis. But even without that, you *stopped* him. That's worth something."

"I suppose," he admitted. "Hard, though. We were hoping for more."

"Well, there's one thing I can give you," she said with a sad smile as an icon popped up on her screen and she opened a message. "MISS identified him."

"Seriously?" Denis asked.

"Take a look."

The man on the screen was very clearly *much* younger, but it was also recognizably Winton. In the photo, he was about fifty, clad in a plain suit, and shaking hands...with Desmond the Third?

"Who is he?"

"Roger Bradley Clinton," Samara told him, reading from the screen. "Retired as senior regional diplomatic attaché to four systems in the

Fringe." She shook her head. "One of them was Chrysanthemum, and he retired right before the civil war there."

"Resigned in protest over the fact we weren't paying any damn attention?" Denis suggested. Chrysanthemum was a Fringe UnArcana World that had revolted against an oppressive corporate owner. Mars had badly misread the situation until it was far too late to salvage their reputation with the planet, though they held the distinction of being one of exactly two UnArcana Worlds to remain in the Protectorate after the Secession.

"That's not in the file, but it seems likely," she admitted. "Interesting point, though: take a look at the bottom."

DATE OF DEATH: DECEMBER 11, 2422

"He *died?*" Denis asked.

"Over thirty years ago," Samara agreed, digging deeper into the data. "Five years after he retired, he was reported dead in a shuttle accident. No survivors. Legally dead, our friend Winton proceeded to cause a *lot* of trouble."

"We'll need to brief Montgomery on this, but he's swamped," Denis said. "Any idea how quickly we'll have anything more to tell him?"

"No. The system is running; I need to take a break," she admitted.

"Would you like to go grab dinner?" Denis asked before his brain caught up with his mouth.

She laughed, turning to face him fully and meeting his gaze. She studied him for a long moment as the laugh faded, then smiled softly and nodded.

"Yes, Denis, I would like that."

CHAPTER 53

GENERALS, ADMIRALS, Chancellors, Councilors...the meetings of the Regency Council were a crowd of people who were hard to get into one room. This was only the second time that Damien had managed to get them all on a call and the first time he'd put them in the same room.

It had been only three weeks since he'd returned to Mars. Only a month since the Mage-King had died, but he was starting to feel like he had a grip on what was going on.

"We will, of course, present all of the information acquired under the black investigation to the Protectorate Supreme Court to validate the plea bargain made with Odysseus," he concluded the briefing he'd given them on the last few weeks' chaos.

"Councilor Granger's fate will *not* be presented to the Court," he continued. "His deal was with the Mountain and was validated by myself and Her Majesty. As part of that deal, the exact reasons for his resignation and exile will remain classified for as long as Suresh Granger remains alive.

"I will leave the investigation of Prosecutor Vemulakonda in the hands of more qualified individuals," he noted. "I personally do not believe that the misdirection of her Inquiry was intentional, but that misdirection *did* take place. Madame Vemulakonda has already agreed to be placed under house arrest in the Mountain until that investigation is complete."

Her willingness to accept that investigation and confinement certainly didn't hurt the presumption of innocence.

"Our largest outstanding concern from the investigation of His Majesty's murder is that the individual classified in our files as 'Nemesis-K' remains at large," Damien noted. "All evidence suggests that he wasn't aboard *Choirgirl* when we boarded her. It is unclear if he left as *Choirgirl* was leaving Earth orbit or if he was entirely absent from the Sol System.

"The data extracted from *Choirgirl* and Relay Station VRF-Seven-Six-Five will allow us to neutralize much of what remains of the organization, but Nemesis-K is a critical threat that I do wish we'd captured."

Damien glanced around the room. He was *reasonably* sure, at this point, that the taint of treason had been removed from the highest levels of his government. Most of that seemed to have hung on Granger—and the Hands that had been corrupted by the Keepers.

He was still going to be watching his back for knives.

"The weeks since His Majesty's death have been a struggle for us all, but I believe Councilor Ayodele has an announcement to make as well," Damien continued, gesturing to the shaven-headed black man who spoke for Terra at the Council.

"Everyone, it is my pleasure to report that we have achieved a complete first draft of the new Constitution," Ayodele told them. "There are still aspects to be established and some months of work left, but we and Her Majesty have reached agreements on much of the fundamental structures that will guide the Protectorate in the future.

"Our expectation is that we will be able to present a final document for Her Majesty to sign on January first, a bit less than four months from now."

That earned a smattering of applause and Damien smiled. He'd been the club, but it had been Envoy Velasquez who'd done the lion's share of the lifting. It was a bigger victory than it felt, too, for all that it was a win of papers and agreements.

He gave Christoffsen an arched eyebrow in question, and the Professor nodded confirmation.

"A full briefing will be forwarded electronically to you all," Damien told the Council, "but we have settled on a structure that we believe will make certain the voice of the people is heard at the highest levels of our government."

Not governors and their clients. That was the big victory from his point of view.

"That leaves us, people, with one big, ugly item hanging on everyone's plates," he said grimly. "There will be small business to suck up the rest of this meeting, but I wanted Admiral Caliver to brief us on the status of the war."

Amanda Caliver stood as Damien tapped a release of the conference room's display functions to her.

"Our victory at Legatus clears the way for further campaigns against the Republic but has also exposed some critical weaknesses," she said calmly. "From a naval perspective, we have stretched our resources to the limit.

"It took longer for us to rearm Second Fleet than any of us would have preferred. Protectorate High Command is still coming up to speed in many ways and we bear some responsibility for that, but the truth is that our munitions production was never designed to stand up to the demands of a full-scale war."

The Protectorate High Command was less than six months old. It had been created after the war had begun, when Desmond had realized that the Martian military didn't *have* a formal structure that could handle fighting a war.

"We need to get started on changing that, don't we?" Kiera said dryly. "We may have taken the Republic's shipyards, but so long as they can build gunships and missiles, they're going to stay in this war."

"Agreed," Caliver confirmed with a small bow to where the Mage-Queen sat opposite Damien. "We did have new production centers brought online over the last few months, but with the need to replace the missile stockpiles of the entire fleet with the new Phoenix IXs, we appear to have drastically underestimated the need.

"New factories have been ordered and old facilities are being restored or retooled, but we do not currently have the manufacturing capacity to support the level of active operations that Admiral Alexander wants."

And there, Damien realized, was the kicker. He knew that Alexander had wanted to already be in Nueva Bolivia by now. A lack of modern missiles had held her back.

"Why don't we simply use the old missiles?" the Mage-Queen asked.

"We could, but the Republic's current weapons significantly outrange the Phoenix VIII," Caliver told her after a moment's pause. "Until those facilities are online, we cannot provide Admiral Alexander with the munitions for more than one major fleet action every three months at best."

"Fighting a war on those terms requires far more cooperation than the Republic is likely to give us," Damien said grimly. "How fast can we fix that?"

"Our best estimate is that we should have production up to speed in another four months. Including transportation timelines, it will be closer to six months before we will be able to support a sustained offensive against the Republic."

"Damn." Damien let the curse hang in the air. "Expedite that if you can, Admiral. Money is no object, but money can't allow us to conjure missiles from thin air."

There were a lot of things Mages *could* conjure—or at least, transmute other objects into—but missiles were a bit beyond human magic.

If the Reejit were the threat Winton had believed them to be, then humanity would need those missile factories. Hopefully later rather than sooner, but they'd need to keep them open after the war ended.

That would take some selling but was a future-proofing problem.

"We will do all we can," Caliver promised. "A delay in the offensives might be necessary anyway. General McConnell?"

The second representative from the High Command was the second-in-command of the Royal Martian Marine Corps. General Nevan McConnell's boss had been smart enough to avoid the job, leaving the pudgy redheaded man to face Damien with bad news.

"The occupation of Legatus has consumed any slack the Marine Corps can be considered to have ever possessed," McConnell said flatly. "We have eight hundred thousand Marines. Just over four hundred thousand of those are assigned to the ships of Her Majesty's Navy, leaving us with approximately eighty RMMC strike brigades.

"The strike brigade is traditionally the largest deployable force the RMMC organizes, as it rarely takes more than five thousand exosuited troopers to secure a planetary capital, and we have never expected to need to impose more than regime change on any given world.

"Currently, seventeen brigades' worth of troops are tied up in various missions around the Protectorate. Eight are providing security in the Sol System. The other fifty-five brigades are on Legatus, attempting to impose order on a local populace that is barely reconciled to our presence at best.

"Three hundred thousand soldiers, even Marines, are a drop in the bucket against a planetary population of billions. There is no way the RMMC can take on responsibility for further occupied planets without a major expansion."

"So, we do what we did at Ardennes with the fleets," Kiera told him. "Make arrangements with the system governments to draw units of volunteers from the planetary armies. Most of the MidWorlds have as many people under arms as the RMMC does. Most of the Core Worlds have more."

"That won't work," McConnell said flatly. "We need soldiers directly answerable to the Protectorate, which means we need to train new Marines."

Damien started to lean forward, but Kiera was already asking the critical question.

"Why?"

The word hung in the air, and McConnell turned to Damien in frustration.

"My lord, I do not have time to explain the nuances of the relationship between the Protectorate and our member systems to a teenager," he said flatly. "May I suggest that Her Majesty allow us to discuss these matters in closed council and be briefed later?"

"You may suggest that, yes," Damien said calmly. "*I* suggest you answer her question."

"Everyone here knows damn well why we can't 'borrow' armies from the member systems," he snapped. "Why waste time explaining what her tutors should have already covered?"

"Very well," Damien told General McConnell. "You may leave, General."

"What?" the redheaded man stared at him.

"You will leave, General McConnell," Damien repeated. "I expect your resignation on my desk by this evening. I will ask General Tunison to recommend your replacement as her second and the ground forces representative to the High Command."

"I don't—"

"There is only one person in this room whose presence is beyond question," Damien said, speaking quietly enough that he knew everyone in the room would struggle to hear him.

"Her name is Kiera Michelle Alexander and she is the Mage-Queen of Mars. You all serve at her will—as do I.

"You are dismissed, General McConnell."

The room was completely still as every eye focused on McConnell. He opened his mouth to protest again, then looked over at Kiera Alexander.

The Mage-Queen of Mars's face was iron. She'd learned enough self-control not to have yelled at the man when he was dismissing her, but Damien could still read her.

That was a good thing. It would fall to him to make sure she learned what she needed to—including when she did and didn't have to suffer fools.

He was, after all, her Lord Regent.

ABOUT THE AUTHOR

GLYNN STEWART is the author of Starship's Mage, a bestselling science fiction and fantasy series where faster-than-light travel is possible–but only because of magic. His other works include science fiction series Duchy of Terra, Castle Federation and Vigilante, as well as the urban fantasy series ONSET and Changeling Blood.

Writing managed to liberate Glynn from a bleak future as an accountant. With his personality and hope for a high-tech future intact, he lives in Kitchener, Ontario with his partner, their cats, and an unstoppable writing habit.

OTHER BOOKS
BY GLYNN STEWART

For release announcements join the
mailing list or visit **GlynnStewart.com**

STARSHIP'S MAGE
Starship's Mage
Hand of Mars
Voice of Mars
Alien Arcana
Judgment of Mars
UnArcana Stars
Sword of Mars
Mountain of Mars
The Service of Mars
A Darker Magic
Mage-Commander
Beyond the Eyes of Mars (upcoming)

Starship's Mage: Red Falcon
Interstellar Mage
Mage-Provocateur
Agents of Mars

Pulsar Race: A Starship's Mage Universe Novella

DUCHY OF TERRA
The Terran Privateer
Duchess of Terra
Terra and Imperium
Darkness Beyond
Shield of Terra
Imperium Defiant
Relics of Eternity
Shadows of the Fall
Eyes of Tomorrow

Made in the USA
Las Vegas, NV
30 July 2024

93103737R00204